MORNING WALK

MORNING WALK

A Journey of Discovery

To Rita,
Best wishes for
your continued journey
Hope you enjoy this one
Lona Smith
Lona 2004

LONA SMITH

To order additional copies of this book, contact:
Xlibris Corporation
1-888-795-4274
www.Xlibris.com
Orders@Xlibris.com
24563

To Ronnie Hart
who rekindled the flame,
and provided the creative atmosphere.

ACKNOWLEDGEMENTS

In addition to expressing my deepest gratitude to my family and friends for their support and encouragement, I would personally like to thank the following people.

To my writing partners, Ronnie, Bob, Pat and Sue, I treasure our hours of silence and our times of sharing. Thanks to Terri for so generously sharing her experiences, and to Elise Dallemagne and Alexandria Rudenko for their good advice.

Special thanks to Kathryn for reading my manuscript, and to Cal for keeping my computer operating at top performance.

It was a pleasure to work with the Lee County Extension staff at Terry Park in Fort Myers Florida as I researched the flora, fauna, and the history of citrus growing in south Florida.

I am always grateful to my husband George, who allows me to be who I am. Finally, to the staff at Xlibris, it is a pleasure working with you.

CHAPTER ONE

It was barely light. I could just make out the shapes of the pool furniture as I pulled the door quietly shut behind me and skirted the picnic table with its umbrella pulled and tied tight against possible gusts of wind. We'd had a cold snap swooping down from the north and west. I pulled up the hood of my windbreaker and shoved my hands into my pockets. However, the cold felt good against my eyes, raw from tears, and my aching head.

The bedside clock read 6:30 as I'd quietly slipped out of bed, splashed cold water on my face, pulled on my jacket, and let myself out the door. Mal—Malcolm—was still asleep and I hoped he would be when I got back, if I came back. At the moment I felt like I just wanted to keep on walking.

It had been one of those senseless arguments that seemed to be happening more frequently since we'd arrived at his house in Lee County two weeks ago. At nearly one o'clock this morning Malcolm, his face set in stone, had finally risen from his chair, pulled himself to his full six-foot-two-inch height, and had announced, "I'm going to bed. Are you coming?"

I nodded. "Yes, in a few minutes." In the twenty minutes it took me to wash my throbbing face and brush my teeth, he was sound asleep. His back was turned to me, his parted lips making soft purring snores. *Nothing will disturb your sleep*, I thought as I slipped in beside him, curling my knees to my chest, my arms clutching an extra pillow.

When Malcolm had suggested a few weeks ago, on a frigid New York day that we come to his first wife's family home in southwest Florida instead of going to his home in Spain, I was excited. I seized on the idea that just maybe I could find out something of my birth and early childhood years. I had been raised by my mother and knew nothing about my father, not even his name. I knew only that I had been born in this part of the country.

Huntington House was one of the many houses my husband owned. Carol, the first Mrs. Steele, had grown up here, an orange grower's daughter. Her father, Richard Huntington, one of the legendary citrus growers of this area, had been master of rows and rows of orange and grapefruit trees as far as the eye could see. And Carol's face, smiling from the framed photograph on the mantle, had been the cause of last night's senseless argument. It was one more of the growing number of disagreements we seemed to be having.

"Malcolm," I'd asked, coming into the great room where he sat reading, "would you mind if I put this picture in your office?" I reached up and lifted it down.

"Leave it there!" His words shot across the room.

I looked at him, stunned at the anger in his tone. His heavy white brows formed a V above his icy blue eyes. Light from the lamp beside him cast a partial shadow across his face, making his look fiercer. "What's wrong with you? Is that such a terrible request?"

"Jessica, you're just being sensitive," he said in a dismissive manner.

"And you're being insensitive. I've felt like I'm intruding ever since I walked in the door." I pleaded for understanding, but I got none.

"I thought you were more adaptable. You know this was Carol's home. Things like that shouldn't bother you," he said with a tight smile. "Just put the picture back."

My throat constricted against the pain of tears. I should have swallowed my hurt and allowed the conversation to end there, but I didn't. I couldn't, anymore than I could stop the tears that coursed uninvited down my cheeks. "Carol is dead," I hissed through clenched teeth as I marched into his office and stood the photograph in the middle of his desk. That was a mistake.

I couldn't really say why it bothered me so much, I thought as

I headed down the drive beneath the canopy of live oaks, hung with the gray beards of Spanish moss.

Slivers of dawn penetrated openings in the dense trees as so many pewter-colored spears. An arch, a paler shade of gray at the end of the drive, and bird song in the branches above me, held the promise of morning.

When we'd first met I'd certainly had no problem listening to Malcolm when he told me about Carol's death and his guilt at being away when it happened. I had been a sympathetic listener, as he had for me as I described in detail my mother's painful final weeks before her death. Here though I felt I was being tolerated as a guest. Conversations, now less frequent and less comfortable, were punctuated with comparisons and criticisms of my behavior and me. Perhaps I was being sensitive.

The street that passed in front of Huntington House, aptly named Blossom Lane, ended at the Caloosahatchee River. Only one other house sat across the road. It was an, unpainted, dilapidated square old structure. Even now, at this early hour a dim lamp burned in a front window.

As I reached the street leading out to the highway, the awakening day presented itself in the shapes of mailboxes and garbage cans set out last night for early morning collection. At this time of the morning there was little traffic—the occasional four-wheel drive pickup truck, its diesel engine heard in the darkness before its lights came into view; contractors, plumbers, men of trade going to work. There were smaller, older, compact cars—a red Escort, black Neon—their drivers, waitresses, nurses, and line workers racing against a 7 A.M. time clock.

Where citrus groves once thrived, a collage of homes had sprung up along the old highway that once was the main artery connecting towns to the east. For the most part they were small, low ranch styles of the 1960s on oversize lots overgrown with whatever foliage was hearty enough to survive.

In pockets of development, newer, larger homes in stuccoed shades of pinks and tans posed on manicured lawns. They sported screened-in appendages known as Florida rooms. Palladium doors and windows seemed to be the current trend, as incongruent as jeweled brooches on a bag lady's shabby coat.

By the time I walked nearly a mile, my face was chilled, the throbbing behind my eyes had subsided and my mind more or less had sorted itself into rational thoughts. What was happening to the life I thought had so much promise? Certainly at age forty-five I had not expected the "happily ever after" fairy tale marriage of a twenty-year-old. I'd witnessed relationships among my contemporaries, and had even had one of them myself, that played havoc with rationale and left stability and sensibility on shaky ground. As the only child of a single parent, I understood that there was sometimes more unhappiness than happiness in life. I did, however, expect in this late marriage some understanding and compromise in working out the meshing of two strong personalities. A cold shiver crept up my spine like an electric current, as I realized the man I was legally bound to was not the man I thought I had married, and I was not behaving as the person I knew myself to be.

An hour later I quietly let myself into the still dark house, quickly put the coffee on to brew and jumped into the shower. In just three hours I would have my first golf lesson. I was not looking forward to it. When I walked into the kitchen a few minutes later Malcolm greeted me as though nothing had happened.

The next day I woke slowly to early dawn. Even though my complaining muscles reminded me of the torture of yesterday's golf session, I knew that I would creep out of bed and walk again in the freshness of the day. Quickly I scrawled Malcolm a note. "Good morning. Gone for a walk." As I skirted through the great room, the lady of the house smiled knowingly at me from her frame on the mantle.

"You don't play golf?" Malcolm exclaimed soon after we'd first met. It was our third or fourth evening together and we were seated at a white-linen-draped table at Aerole, wine glasses in our hands as we waited for dinner.

"I never wanted to learn," I stated. "I could never get up the enthusiasm some people have for chasing a little white ball. Besides, I don't think I would be very good at it. I probably wouldn't have many partners," I laughed.

"Of course you must learn, Jessica," Malcolm insisted, "then we can play together. Once you have a few lessons, you'll like it."

Yesterday had been quite another story. "No, not like that. Place your hands just so." The golf pro demonstrated. "Look at me. See how my knees are bent? Yes, just a little more. Relieve the tension here." He placed his hand on my back.

In the eighty-degree weather, perspiration rolled down my face and stung my eyes under the new golf hat Malcolm had presented to me yesterday afternoon. The hat was accompanied by a matching golf costume as though being properly dressed would transform me into a player. At least I must have looked the part to casual passersby as twosomes and foursomes, scooting past in their "state of the art" golf carts, turned their heads in our direction. My five-foot-seven-inch frame was athletic looking. Exercise and care of my body had always been part of my life, not for vanity's sake, but because it made me feel and function better. In the two weeks we'd been here my skin had turned a shade of gold. Malcolm watched with amused delight. I gave him a strained smile as I tried to focus on the instructions of my teacher.

Now, as I struck a brisk pace, a breeze caught my hair and lifted it from my neck. I was later than I had been yesterday and I saw details I hadn't noticed before. At one house, a Harlequin Great Dane sat motionless in the corner of a screened porch. I observed, too, that many of the palm trees and banana plants had suffered from a recent freeze. Fronds and leaves were left limp, brown, and lifeless. Bird choruses increased, as did the traffic along the road. More than once I found myself heading for the grassy shoulder as heavy four-wheel drive diesel trucks rumbled too close for comfort. Small creatures scurried in the underbrush and the sound of snorting and ripping grass, coming from the fenced pasture, turned out to be cattle grazing on sparse fare.

Back on Blossom Lane I slowed down to study the old house across the road. Even though I had seen a light in the window, it looked abandoned. How sad. It once had been a beautiful home in what must have been a thriving, productive orange grove.

Across the driveway a loading dock, its platform now rough and sprung, supported a growth of vines that had worked their way through planks and up an electric pole which stood beside it. Overgrown brown grass indicated that it hadn't been used for a long time. To the back and left of the house, an extended shed housed outdated equipment: an ancient tractor, some kind of spraying machine, a stack of picking baskets. I made a mental note to ask Malcolm about the place.

The house itself was a square two-storied structure of cypress wood. Cypress, I'm told, didn't need painting and would last forever. Three tall brick chimneys rose several feet above a rusted tin roof. There was one on either side, exteriorly, and a third in the back that penetrated the brown metal at what must be the kitchen area. Across the front was a wide, sagging porch, one corner held up by concrete blocks. A dirty brown lounge chair, which has seemingly survived whatever weather was sent in its direction, sat to the side of the front door.

Pairs of windows framed the central door. On the second story, above the door and beneath a dormer, there was a tall window surrounded by small panes of colored glass. Several panes were missing. To either side of it there were paired windows identical to those below.

A mailbox with an address lettered on the side, an emptied and upturned garbage can and a cat sitting immobile in the chair on the porch, indicated that the house wasn't abandoned. Someone indeed lived there. The cat was gray and white with long hair matted beyond grooming, yet it seemed to be well fed. It sat watching, its eyes never leaving me.

As soon as I opened the door of Huntington House I smelled the aroma of bacon and saw that the table was set with juice glasses, pleasant place mats, and napkins. However, when I saw Malcolm's hooded look, any questions about the Cypress House died on my lips. What's wrong with this picture, I thought, as I attempted a smile and headed to the bathroom to wash my hands. "That smells good. I'll be just a minute."

Malcolm set our plates of bacon, eggs, slices of tomato and avocado on the table. He fetched a basket of croissants, warm from the oven. "Why morning walks all of a sudden?" he asked.

I tried to make my voice light and my tone casual. "The other morning," I began as I buttered a roll, "after our argument I woke early and thought a walk and some fresh air would do me good."

When I looked up and saw his raise eyebrows, his fork halfway to his mouth, I remembered that he had not known about that walk.

"And did it?" he asked in a cool tone of voice. I knew by the challenging look in his eyes that this was not a question for conversation but for explanation. "I don't like the idea of you out walking alone, particularly when it's still dark," he continued.

"It was light enough," I defended, "and it's certainly safe *here*. For heaven's sake, I used to jog in Central Park all the time."

"That, my dear, was before you were my wife and I was responsible for you."

"But Mal—Malcolm, I'm responsible for myself. I have been for a long time." I knew I was pleading. *I don't have to defend my actions*, I scolded myself silently. *Why am I doing this?*

"Besides," my husband continued as though I'd said nothing, "You have the pool. You can get plenty of exercise there. Your tan is coming along nicely." He smiled as though praising a first-grader. "You have another golf lesson coming up and you'll find that as you improve, *that* is good exercise too."

I felt my throat close and the tasty eggs, so carefully seasoned with fresh herbs, congealed in my stomach. I pushed my plate away. It would be so easy to aggravate this conversation into an argument. Instead, I picked up my plate and took it to the sink.

"What do you know about the old house across the road?" I asked when I could speak again. "It once was beautiful, I think. Does anybody live there?"

It took Malcolm a moment to realize our conversation was not going where he thought it was. "No . . . no," he stammered. "I mean I don't know if anybody lives there."

"Do you know who used to live there?"

"Well, yes, I did at one time. I believe his name was Jack. I don't remember his last name. When I first met Carol he and Richard sometimes shared pickers and haulers. His groves used to be well tended, and yes, the house used to be quite nice—never as nice as this one, of course." Malcolm paused. "Jack did have a family a long time ago I think, but I don't know what happened."

Malcolm pushed his chair back from the table. "I've got to get ready for my ten o'clock tee off." He came and put his arm around me. "Do you want to come along and hit some golf balls?"

"*No*! Ah, no, I think I'll do a few laps in the pool, then I've some sketches I have to finish."

He tilted my chin. "No more walks in the dark, okay?"

"No, Malcolm," I said as I pulled away. "I won't promise that."

CHAPTER TWO

Malcolm and I met just over three years ago, a few months after my mother died. My friend Christine cornered me at work. "I have an extra ticket to see La Boehme Lincoln Center tomorrow night. Come with me."

The word "no" was already forming on my lips when she said, "You don't have any reason to say 'no' now. It'll do you good. We can grab a late supper afterward."

For the past several months my world had been to rush home from work to relieve the day-care nurse and spend as much time as I could with my mother. It was a painful time for both of us, but it was also a time we cherished. Watching her pitiful decline was agony. She struggled so to keep me from seeing her pain. Still I'd treasured our hurried mornings, making breakfast for her and the sharing my day's activities with her each evening before I tucked her in for the night. When I could, I brought assignments home to work on. There had always been just the two of us, Mari Parker and me. I spent my early years on my grandparents' sheep ranch in Colorado, but Mari and I had lived in New York for the past twenty-five years. Even in those last few weeks when I'd pressed her for information about my father she wouldn't talk about it. Finally, I didn't ask anymore. Now that she was gone, I guess there would forever be that question mark in my life.

"Sure, Chris, I'd like to go—it's just that I haven't gotten used to the idea that I don't have to rush home every night."

"I know." Christine's blue eyes smiled behind her copper-rimmed "granny" glasses. "But this will be fun."

"Oh geez, Jessica, I'm so sorry," Christine said the following evening as we sat across the table from one another at Un Deux Trois, a restaurant near Broadway that catered to the after-theater crowd. The corners of her mouth turned down and her springy red curls bounced as she shook her head back and forth. "I can't believe I was so thoughtless." She looked as if she were about to cry. For three hours we had listened as starving, struggling artists sang of their woes, of their futile efforts to support themselves and of their attempts to find money for medicine for their dying friend, Mimi.

"How could you sit through that?" Christine asked as she pressed her lips together and looked away.

"It's all right, Chris. I'm okay." I reached across the table and put my hand over hers. "My mother is not the only person to ever die you know. Besides, we had time to say our good-byes and to get everything in order—almost."

Christine was a jolly, upbeat person, the kind I'd often needed during the last months of my mother's illness. She was plump and constantly fought the warm Danish and butter battle, which she never seemed to come close to winning. She had excellent taste in clothes she bought at size-plus stores, flowing skirts and tops in bright colors that accented her coppery curly hair and her rusty freckles. I had no idea where all her interesting jewelry came from.

Christine and I met at the Pratt Institute and reconnected a few years ago when we ended up working on a project together. She is good company and her natural exuberance draws people to her, but I've never known her to have a serious relationship.

It was late so we'd ordered only light pasta and a salad, and of course, we shared a bottle of wine. "This evening is my treat," Christine said as she whipped out her credit card. "Besides the tickets didn't cost anything. A guy I know in the chorus gave them to me."

"Christine!" a baritone voice exclaimed. I looked up to see a tall, good-looking man approaching our table.

"Malcolm!" Christine cried as she jumped up to hug him. I caught her wine glass before it toppled. "What are you doing here? I didn't know you were in New York."

"Just got here. Came to check on my show. It's been running

for two weeks and I wanted to find out if it's going to survive or if I'm going to have a tax loss," he laughed.

"What show? I didn't know you were producing a show," Christine accused as though she hadn't received her memo.

"Sticks and Stones."

"That's yours? I . . . I've read some reviews," Chris hesitated.

"Not the best." He shook his head then looked at me.

"Oh, forgive me," Chris said as she followed his gaze. "This is my friend Jessica Parker. Jessica, meet Malcolm—Malcolm Steele, a sometimes client."

"Please don't get up," he said as I started to rise. "Christine, sit too, please." He pushed her gently into her seat and extended his hand to me. He looked at me with deep blue eyes, set under heavy silvery white brows. His face was tanned as though he spent considerable time outdoors. His white hair, which fell back on his head in waves, was still plentiful. I guessed his age to be around sixty.

"Let me buy you ladies a nightcap," he said with a charming one-sided smile as he signaled a waiter, pulled up a chair, and sat down.

I started to protest but Christine was already ordering. Later when the cab dropped me off at my apartment Christine gave me a quick hug. "Oh, Jessica, maybe the night wasn't so bad after all."

The swim did little to lift my mood. I felt distracted and anxious as I sat at my drawing board, picking up first one pencil then another. No lines seemed to transfer themselves to the blank paper in front of me. For the past two winters, we had spent some months in Spain at a house he owned there. This year for business reasons he said he needed to be nearer New York. I had not, however, counted on finding the presence of his long-dead wife still here. By the time Malcolm returned from golf for a late lunch, I knew that in spite of his displeasure, I would walk again in the morning.

That evening we took our drinks and walked down to the river as we sometimes did, while we waited for the grill to heat. We watched the sunset and waved at the fishing boats and small pleasure craft that cruised the river. If we were lucky we would see manatees feeding their way down the river. The first time I'd seen one of these rare, ancient endangered mammals that looked like overstuffed seals, I thought it was a brown plastic bag of garbage floating beneath the surface of the water.

We sat on a glider at the water's edge. "Malcolm, I'm going for a walk in the morning. Would you like to come with me?"

His drink was at his mouth and he held it there several moments before he took a sip and lowered his glass. "I've told you I don't like the idea of you walking before daylight on a heavily traveled road, but as you said, you *are* an adult. And no, I don't want to go."

As it turns out I didn't go the next morning either. At six o'clock when I started to ease out of bed, I felt Malcolm's hand on my shoulder. "Come, give me a kiss before you go," he said in a sleepy voice. He pulled me to his bare chest and gently began rubbing my back, then more firmly moving his long fingers to my buttocks and legs.

Malcolm is an experienced lover. So, almost an hour later, I gave him one last kiss and headed for the shower. I was satiated but angry—very angry, because I knew his plea for passion was designed to keep me from going for my morning walk.

My morning walk was not discussed again in the days that followed. Cold air gave way to milder temperatures. Shorts and a tee shirt replaced my jogging suit, and new scents freshened each day. When I passed the house with the screened-in porch I saw that the Great Dane was sitting in the same place. I laughed out loud when, on closer look, I realized the sentinel was a life-sized, very-real-looking dog, cast of concrete.

I didn't laugh further on my journey when a snarling, drooling Doberman charged a chain-linked enclosure. The fence shook as he threw his weight against it. On the gate was a yellow-and-black metal sign with his silhouette and a caption that read, "I can make it to the gate in three seconds. Can you?"

I never told Malcolm about vicious dogs behind chain-link

fences or tethered in yards. I never told him about the massive king-of-the-road pickup trucks with their powerful engines that came roaring past, not giving an inch. I never told Malcolm any of these things. He didn't ask.

The overgrown underbrush along the road was littered with all sorts of debris, soft-drink bottles, the proverbial beer can, and remains of somebody's fast-food meal. There was even a pair of brown socks laid carefully side by side as though someone was going to come back and put them on. I made a mental note to bring a garbage bag and some plastic gloves.

At one corner a concrete culvert ran underneath the road. Each morning I noticed there were a half dozen or so empty cat food cans and a couple of empty metal plates. They were not always the same cans and they were never quite in the same place. I realized with a certain good feeling that someone was feeding stray cats although I never saw any of them.

The smell of overripe oranges greeted me as I passed the weathered old house that I now called "The Cypress House." While some trees in the grove still bore abundant fruit, others struggled valiantly to survive under aggressive vines and against whatever blights or viruses attacked them. Still others, already dead, stood on as skeletons. A rusted sign warned trespassers of fine or imprisonment should they help themselves to fruit.

A towering Norfolk pine grew beside the house, and in the front yard was a huge live oak tree. Spanish moss like the scraggly gray beard of an old man hung from its ancient branches and dipped almost to the ground. Sansevieria, or Mother-in-law's Tongue, so named because of its long, sharp-pointed leaves, grew around its trunk to a width of several feet. Usually the cat was not around when I first passed the house, but on my return trip it often lay on the seat of the old chair, feet tucked under its chest, eying my progress. Since cats are curious creatures, it probably wondered what was in the plastic bags I lugged home with me every day. One day I even toted home an old battery.

Our days grew into a cautiously compatible routine. If Malcolm wasn't playing golf, he was in his office on the telephone or at his computer. In addition to my two times a week golf—lesson-from-hell, I sketched and painted in that corner in the sunroom that had been assigned to me, mailing off assignments as they were completed.

Little else required our attention. I was expected to provide a shopping list for the housekeeper who had been with the family for years. Louisa came in most days, prepared meals, and did the cleaning. A crew of gardeners maintained the grounds and attended the pool. We often swam late in the late morning, later having an easy lunch by the pool. Once we took a day trip to Key West in the four-passenger Piper Cub the family kept at a nearby airport. The family did not lack for toys of pleasure. Occasionally we took the family yacht up the river to Port Charlotte or down the gulf to Marco Island for dinner. I had, for my use, a bright red Mercedes sports car.

I was careful not to disturb anything in the house. Malcolm made sure I understood that I was not part of this place that these groves had been in Carol's family for generations. He pointed out that her ancestry was traceable to the Spaniards who first brought seeds of citrus trees with them to this continent.

I avoided the great room when I could. It was not one of my favorite places. Here the framed lady with a smile that didn't quite reach her blue eyes followed me with her gaze. In her photograph, Carol's blond shoulder-length hair fell straight and loose around her face. She wore an open-necked blouse. A free-form-shaped, open-heart gold pendant on a gold chain nestled at her throat. The picture appeared to be an enlargement of a snapshot and the woman in it looked to be in her forties, about the age I am now. She had a finishing-school look and a certain poise and assurance that spoke of culture.

Physically there are few similarities between us. My complexion is, while not dark, certainly not fair. My hair, which is so dark it is almost black, now shows threads of white. It is naturally wavy and I wear it short. My brows and lashes are dark as well, but my eyes are a smoky gray. My high cheekbones give me a wide-eyed expression. I can tell that I am taller than she by several inches but I don't have her cheerleader curves.

Carol died at age fifty-two from a massive cranial aneurysm. She had just gotten home from several sets of tennis with friends and was on her way from the kitchen counter to the table to feed hungry grandchildren who were visiting her when a massive explosion occurred in her arterial wall. Peanut butter and jelly sandwiches on Pooh Bear plates and a pitcher of milk flew from her hands and were sent flying across the kitchen. Screams of the terrified children brought their mother from another room. Malcolm was not at home. He was not even in the country and it took two days to find him in a hotel in Zurich.

My road looks good, I thought, as I set out at a brisk pace. Welcomed morning showers a couple of days ago brought new green color to the roadside in this parched area of Florida that badly needed a good drenching. As I neared the Cypress House the remains of someone's fast-food dinner that had been tossed into the struggling grove caught my eye. I stepped across the ditch, heedless of the warning on the rusty sign, and bent over to retrieve the trash.

"What do you think you're doing?" a deep voice cracked behind me.

I jumped up, my free hand pressing my chest. "Oh! Oh my, you frightened me." I turned to face the voice. "Good morning. I was just picking up this trash. I . . . I hope you don't mind."

"Can't you read? The sign says, 'no trespassing.'"

I faced a formidable-looking man who glared at me fiercely. Though stooped, he was still tall and remnants of a once-robust figure remained in the bent form. A rounded pouch of a belly hung over baggy, rumpled khaki pants. A dingy tee shirt of telltale gray peeked through the open front of a dirty blue work shirt. Below a thatch of spiky gray hair, his red-rimmed eyes, the color of brooding storm clouds, bore into mine. They looked out from a weathered face, now gone bulbous with traces of broken veins from what I guessed to be years of drinking.

"I didn't think anyone would mind if I picked up this stuff that had been thrown here," I stammered.

"It doesn't bother me. Why should it bother you?" he asked in a voice hoarse with disuse.

"Well, it doesn't belong here and I'm not going to put it back," I said suddenly defiant. An ever-so-slight twitch of a muscle at the corner of his mouth seemed to crack stern expression and prompted me to continue. "I admire your house. I walk by here almost every day."

"I know that," he barked.

My look of surprise was not lost on him. "Are you Jack?" I asked. Now it was his turn to raise his eyebrows, but when he didn't answer, I continued, "This house must have once been beautiful."

"Everything was," he muttered as he turned and walked back to his house, leaning heavily on a rough-hewn walking stick. As I watched his retreating back and saw him crab his way up the steps, I had a strange empathy for this bitter old man who now knew only how to bark at the world.

Heavy rains kept us inside for the next several days. When Malcolm was not on the phone he was pacing and cursing the weather for keeping him off the golf course. I, in turn, blessed the elements for canceling *the golf lesson*.

Finally, a morning dawned bright and clear. I was greeted with crisp air as I pulled down my hat, hugged my windbreaker about me, and headed down the drive. Today I carried no plastic bag. I was not on garbage detail. I just wanted to stretch my legs, breath in the refreshing air, and be grateful for the beautiful day. I slowed down as I passed the Cypress House.

The cat was not on the porch—too cold, I thought. I peered at the soiled paned windows and, with a big smile on my face, waved at the eyes I supposed were watching me.

Malcolm met me as I walked into the kitchen. "You need to get packed," he said. "I have to go to Italy to take care of a problem at one of the plants. Steve is flying the Gulfstream down from New York to get us there in time for the five o'clock flight to Milan. When I finish we can go to Spain for a while."

I didn't answer as I peeled off my gloves and jacket. Early in our relationship I'd gone with Malcolm on many of his business trips. I enjoyed it at first since I'd never traveled much. During the day, when he was in meetings, I took in the sights, spent hours in the museums, and shopped. Malcolm devoted at least one day during each of our trips to go shopping with me. In spite of the fact that I had grown up in the fashion world, it had all become repetitious and routine.

Malcolm's house in Madrid was near Calla Serrano in the exclusive Salamanaca area. Not only was it close to his offices but was adjacent to the highest fashion and the best restaurants Spain had to offer. Madrid is a city of elegantly dressed women, strolling on the arms of their men in their Burberry and dark stockings. And, Malcolm liked having his elegantly dressed woman on his arm as we spent evenings entertaining clients or having dinner with his senior employees. He also kept an apartment in Malaga on the Costa del Sol. Having logged miles in the museums of Madrid, as wonderful as they were, I much preferred the casual feeling of the coast and escaped to the apartment as often as I could. The prospect of packing and tagging along now seemed hopelessly boring to me. I stood there staring at him. Impatiently, he turned and walked back to the bedroom.

"I'm not going," I said to his retreating back.

He stopped as though he'd been turned to stone. It was several seconds before he turned to me, a look of total disbelief on his face. "What did you say?"

"I don't want to go. I want to stay here," were the words that formed in my mind, but it sounded like begging and I was not going to do that. "I'm not going this time. I'll stay here," I added a little more gently.

"I don't want you here." He spoke through clinched jaws. "Get packed." His emphatic tone left no invitation for discussion.

My throat tightened against tears that threatened to form, but I held my jaws together and took a deep breath. "No," I repeated. "If you don't want me to stay in this house I'll go to a hotel."

"Jessica, you know I don't have time to discuss this now." He bit the words. "You're being childish. Besides, I thought you didn't like this house."

"I don't want to discuss it either," I replied, willing my gaze to hold his. "When you're ready I'll drive you to the airport then I'll come back and get my things."

"That won't be necessary," Malcolm said as he left the room to finish packing.

CHAPTER THREE

My phone rang one evening nearly a month after Christine and I had gone to the opera. "You'll never guess who just called me." No introduction, no words of greeting, just Chris's ever-bubbly voice on the line.

"I couldn't," I replied.

"Malcolm Steele!" Her voice was practically a screech. "He wanted your phone number."

I hadn't thought about the man since that night but the image of the distinguished man associated with that name immediately formed in my mind. "Did you hear what I said?" Christine asked when I didn't respond. "You impressed him. He thought you were *bea-u-ti-ful*." She pronounced each syllable distinctly.

"Oh, Chris, I'm not interested."

"Why ever not?" she fairly shouted. "He's certainly attractive. He's so-oo rich *and* he's available. What more does the man need? I mean he's not like one of those rich, married men who keep their left hand in their pocket all evening. He's good company, too. Didn't you think so when we met him?"

"I did," I admitted, "but he's so-oo old too."

"Not *that* old."

"Why aren't *you* interested in him then?"

"Well, he had *my* phone number. Besides I'm just a pal. Haven't you noticed I'm just everybody's pal?" I heard a certain longing in her usually bright voice. "So just go and have a good time. You don't have to fall in love with him, you know."

"I'll think about it. Thanks, Chris," I said as we hung up. "But, I'm not going," I announced to the empty apartment.

However, a half hour later, when I heard the smooth-textured voice on the phone, I agreed to meet Mr. Steele the following evening at an opening reception for an artist friend of his and for dinner afterward.

It wasn't as though being alone and being lonely hadn't been part of my life. It's easy to pretend you're not alone in New York; it's easy to obsess about your work or go out with a crowd. In the Big Apple it's even okay to go out alone, but suddenly the apartment I'd shared with my mother seemed bleak and empty. The hospital bed had been taken away and Mari's clothes had been distributed to clothing banks and resale shops, and the few precious things she owned—and precious few they were—had been packed and stored. The space within these walls suddenly became claustrophobic.

For as long as I could remember, it had been just the two of us, Mari Parker and me, her daughter Jessica. She was born Maria Sanchez but she didn't like that classification so she legally changed her name to Parker, and a Parker I was. It was not even my father's name.

"I just liked the name 'Parker,'" she'd said when I'd questioned her.

I grew up in a self-contained community of Basque sheepherders in the high mountain meadows on the western slope of the Colorado Rockies. My grandparents were Pyrenees mountain people who had come to America in the 1920s with several other Basque families after yet another internal conflict. They were content to live in a new country with their old traditions. It had not been a bad life.

As we sat over a dinner of delicious pasta and exquisite Chianti at Anthony's in Little Italy we laughed and shared our real thoughts about the artist's work. Without knowing how the conversation got there I found that I was telling a man I'd just met the story of my life. I stopped in midsentence.

"What's wrong?" Malcolm asked. A furrow of concern brought his thick brows together until they were almost touching.

"I've . . . I've never talked about myself so much to anyone. I don't even know you."

"I'm hoping we can change that."

"I think it's your turn," I said as I rolled the pasta around my fork. "I'll eat and you talk."

"You're funny," he laughed.

My dinner partner, the perfectly dressed, self-assured, attractive man sitting across from me, was a man of many talents and interests. He was born in the Midwest in 1923, the eldest son of a small-town physician. "I hated being 'the doctor's son,'" he said, shaking his head. "And I had no intention of following in his footsteps despite of all his pressure and the promises," he emphasized with a certain bitterness in his voice. That lot, he explained, had fallen to his younger brother.

Malcolm, I learned, preferred physical activity and being outdoors. He liked solving problems. He liked fixing things that wouldn't work, whether it was an old car or his mother's can opener. He weighed enough to qualify for the high school, then the college football team. He was tall enough to be a "starter" on the basketball team and he could hit a ball hard enough to even play baseball one summer for a farm team. I had no idea what a farm team was, but I didn't interrupt as this bionic man told me about himself.

Malcolm Steele graduated from the University of Nebraska with a degree in civil engineering, followed a year later by a master's degree in business. After his first year of college he never spent a summer at home. Toward the end of his freshman year he formed a construction crew, hiring several of his classmates to clean up, repair and, in some cases, renovate houses near the campus that were "used and abused" by college students. His company, newly formed and never proven, had more than enough work. The need was there.

By the time he entered his second year of college, he'd made enough money to pay his tuition. From that time on he never accepted another penny from his father. That same year he took a course in horticulture and expanded his business to include landscaping and yard maintenance. "My dad never acknowledged my accomplishments," he added quietly as the waiter offered us dessert menus.

How many countless dates or casual meetings over cocktails, I thought, had I listened to men wearing their egos as epaulets on their shoulders go for hours about themselves. "What does he say now?" I asked.

"I don't know," he replied quietly. "I haven't seen him in thirty-five years. My mother is in a nursing home, but when she was able to travel I often brought her to visit us. When Carol and I married, my father didn't even come to the wedding, and if he knows any of his grandchildren it's because they go to visit him. I think they may have," he added with such sadness that I felt my chest tighten.

Five years after he'd entered college, at the age of twenty-three, Malcolm rented office space, hired fifteen full-time employees and numerous subcontractors. He went from remodeling old houses to building new ones. He progressed from constructing houses to designing and building shopping centers.

His passion though, he explained, was building bridges. His design of a cable system for suspension bridges took him to Florida in the 1960s. So while other young men and women his age were springing up as "flower children" on the coasts of the nation and the American flag was being burned across the country, Mal Steele was connecting waterways in a state with lots of water that wished to be connected.

"Enough," Malcolm said finally, holding up his hands in surrender. "I've managed to talk through dessert. You are so easy to talk to. Do you feel like walking?"

In the late New York evening we walked and we talked until we were tired. When it grew late and my shoes that were not made for walking started arguing with my feet, Malcolm's limousine magically appeared.

It seemed good, back in the beginning, I thought, as I set my brisk pace down the shrouded driveway to the approaching dawn. Yesterday I had ended up driving Malcolm to the airport to meet Steve and his plane. Sitting beside me he reached for my hand on the steering wheel. "I'm sorry you're not going with me, Jess," he said as he brought my fingers to his lips. "I'll call you."

As I neared what I had now called the Cat Corner, I heard the low rumble of an idling diesel engine and saw that a truck was sitting at the corner—the driver's door open. When I saw that someone was standing behind the truck, I ducked behind a saw palmetto tree. The man who turned toward me was holding something in his hands. He walked down into the ditch and placed several objects just outside the culvert.

From what I could see in the gray grid of morning he appeared to be a man in his late thirties or early forties, at least six feet tall. He wore a white tight-fitting tee shirt that outlined his broad shoulders and a muscular torso, dark pants, and heavy work boots. He was dark skinned and wore his thick, long hair in a ponytail.

For some moments he stood looking around and I realized he'd discovered that there were no empty cans to be picked up from the day before. I held my breath, my arms pressed against my sides as he scanned the trees and the road as though he sensed my presence. He got back in his truck and, casting one last glance behind him, drove away.

I released a deep sigh and realized that I'd been holding my breath. Then I saw them, pairs of glowing eyes from within the culvert and among the surrounding bushes. As I retreated to my hiding place I watched as one by one, in twos and threes, cats of various sizes and colors darted from cover to devour their meal. A calico mother with three spindly kittens charged one of the plates. She hissed and swatted at an old tiger who slunk away to let her precious progeny have their fill. It crossed my mind that I might be here all morning.

As the occasional vehicle sped by, the animals flattened themselves into motionless crouches. However, when the road was silent and the food was gone, they sat, paw upon tongue, paw upon ear, and paw upon face, contentedly washing themselves. My morning walk was becoming an adventure.

The message light on the phone was flashing when I got back to the house. "Hello, Jess dear." Malcolm's oiled and velvet voice slid through the earpiece. "Sorry I missed you. I'm on my way to a meeting with the managers at the plant. I'm staying at the Principe Di Savoia tonight, but tomorrow I'm flying to Madrid. You know how to reach me there." There was a pause then he added, "I wish our parting had been happier. We'll make up for it when I get home. Ciao."

CHAPTER FOUR

On our second or third date when I addressed him as "Mal," he took my arm and turned me to face him. "Jessica," he said, "I would prefer that you call me Malcolm."

"But," I stammered, "I've heard you refer to yourself as Mal, particularly when you talk about growing up. And, isn't that what your friends call you?"

"Yes. I grew up as Mal Steele and Carol called me Mal, but *that* is the past. This is now," he replied with firmness and a look in his eyes that emphasized his seriousness.

"Sure," I replied, "if that's what you want."

"Then it's settled." His tone was severe, but he smiled his disarming smile as if to soften his words.

Malcolm it was! Sometimes, however, in excitement or frustration "Mal" would slip from my lips, but he always corrected me.

I replayed the message on the machine as though listening to it again would give me some clue to understanding the man I'd married. He was a virile, good-looking man who took great care with his person and his dress. He was perpetually tanned because he spent so much time outdoors—with his jobs, on his boat, on the golf course. He seemed equally comfortable in an open-necked shirt, shorts, and docksiders as he did in expensive formalwear so expertly tailored that one sleeve and one shirt cuff was a half-inch shorter than the other to compensate for the fact that his arms were not the same length. Malcolm demanded perfection of himself and, as I was beginning to understand, expected it in others. If charm and persuasiveness couldn't accomplish his objectives, his money usually did.

I wandered through the house feeling restless. It was still early and the sun had burned off the early morning mist, exhibiting a lovely March day. I decided to take the small outboard motor boat up the river to see if I could spot any manatees. I put a big shirt on over my bathing suit, made a sandwich, put a book, a bottle of water, and a pair of binoculars in a bag. I donned a big straw hat and set off for the dock. I am less-than-an-expert navigator so I carefully steered the boat around the point in the river that took me to the locks.

While Malcolm's house and the Cypress House were across the road from each other, both properties backed up to the river, for here the Caloosahatchee took a sharp turn. Huntington grounds were carefully landscaped and immaculately tended, offering a picturesque view from the river. The other, I noted, was overgrown with weeds and tangled foliage, forbidding entry. An ancient aluminum fishing boat was tied to the piling at a rickety dock. Jack was sitting there in a rusty, sprung lawn chair. I waved but he didn't acknowledge my presence.

I don't know what made me do it, but I turned the small craft and headed toward him. I cut the engine, but not soon enough, and the boat slammed into the shaky piling with a sharp thud.

"Sorry," I said, peering up at him from beneath the brim of my hat.

"I could get you an axe and you could do a better job of knocking it down," he barked as fierce, smoky eyes glared at me. The stormy colors of his irises were tempered by the opaqueness of cataracts.

"I'm sorry, Mr. Jack," I repeated.

"What da you want?"

"I was heading up the river to the locks hoping to see some manatees. I understand that you've lived here a long time. If you're not too busy, I was wondering if you would come along and explain some of the things I see." I waved my arms to either side of me. "I don't know the names of any of these trees and plants or what lives here in the river.

"Busy," he snorted. "You're damned right I'm busy." His laugh was raspy as he grabbed hold of an iron ring bolted into the heavy post and laboriously pulled himself to his feet.

I didn't know if that was a "yes" or a "no." Using his cane he brought the bow of the boat closer to the dock and awkwardly lowered himself into the vessel. I grabbed a rope hanging from the piling and held on for a dear life, as he landed with a thud onto the seat across from me.

"Are you all right?" I asked as a grimace shot across his face and I heard a deep intake of breath. He didn't answer but pushed his lips together and refused to look at me.

"I'm Jessica Steele," I said, extending my hand.

"I know who you are." He made no move to take the offered hand. Meekly I started the engine and backed away from the dock. Behind dark glasses, I studied the old man as we headed up the river. He seemed to be wearing the same soiled work shirt over the same dingy undershirt I'd seen before. Today his work pants were dark gray. Across the outer sides of worn work shoes the leather was slashed away, exposing sock-covered, misshapen toes. Strands of his shock of iron gray hair escaped from the misshapen hat he had jammed on his head.

I wrinkled my nose at the smell of day-old, rebreathed booze and sour sweat. What had I gotten myself into? I smiled to think of what Malcolm's reaction would be. I certainly couldn't explain the impulse of inviting this crotchety, smelly old man to come along on my outing. I was challenged to get to know him.

I kept the small boat close to shore, out of the path of larger pleasure yachts. I strained to hear his low answers as Jack gave names to moss-laden trees and weaving vines. Behind fences cattle and a few horses grazed on sparse fare on land that had been cleared. Most houses possessed docks and occasionally there were small, improvised, sandy beaches. We passed a campground where residents from colder parts of the country parked their homes on wheels to wait out the winter season in this much kinder climate.

Near the locks, Jack pointed to a dock jutting out into the river alongside a man-made beach. "You can tie up there," he said.

Children splashed in murky river water, heedless of slimy, growing things under the surface. Passengers, heady with the excitement of being on vacation, waved to us from a crowded sightseeing paddleboat as it waited to pass through the locks. I waved back.

Noon high sun beat down on us as I guided the boat alongside the dock. Jack threw a rope over an iron spike driven into the wooden platform and secured it. I was glad when the boat drifted into the shade of the structure. Jack pulled off his oily crowned hat and wiped perspiration from his face with the corner of his shirt. He looked dangerously flushed.

"Would you like part of a sandwich?" I asked, pulling my plastic-wrapped lunch out of the bag beside me. "We'll share it. I only brought one bottle of water though." I must have been right on cue because he reached in his back pocket and pulled out a brown paper bag. It was molded to the size and shape of a pint whiskey bottle.

"I brought my own refreshments," he said as he unscrewed the cap, tipped the lip to his mouth, and took a long drink. I stared at him. When he saw my expression he threw back his head and gave a loud cackle of a laugh that caused nearby picnickers to look in our direction.

"Mr. Jack," I began, glaring at the disgusting old codger across from me.

"Webster." The word was spoken so low I didn't quite catch it.

"I beg your pardon?"

"It's John Arnold Webster," he repeated, separating each word. "That's my name. I don't like being called *Mister* Jack."

I felt myself getting angry. What a terrible idea this had been. Why couldn't I have just kept going up the river as I had planned? "Well, Mr. John Arnold Webster, if this is your idea of a good time, it isn't mine. You remind me of a junkyard dog that's been chained to a rusty bumper too long." I'd had enough of this. I reached up to unfasten the rope.

"There!" I turned to look where he was pointing into the murky water about ten feet away from us. A bulbous brown object was floating just under the surface. Moments later, a flat, whiskered snout broke through the surface. The creature snorted to clear its nostrils and breathed in a supply of air before submerging to feed on the marine plants growing along the bottom of the river. Just behind the large aquatic mammal I saw a smaller one repeat the same action.

"A manatee!" I whispered.

"That's Bella. She's a cow and that's her calf."

"How do you know its Bella?"

"See those two marks on her back near her flippers? They're scars. I did that to her."

"How?"

"Blades of my boat motor." Jack lowered his eyes. "I didn't see her."

"I wonder why," I muttered unkindly under my breath.

After Bella and her calf passed, we headed back down the river, keeping the pair in sight. I handed Mr. Webster half of my sandwich, which he took without saying anything, but he didn't take the bottle from his pocket again.

The phone was ringing when I went into the house. I was hot and sweaty and out of sorts with the way the day had turned out. I just wanted to get in the shower and cool off. It was two o'clock in the afternoon according to the kitchen clock when I picked up the receiver and eight o'clock in the evening in Madrid when I heard Malcolm's voice on the other end of the connection. He told me he was flying back to New York the next morning. "I can only be there a few days before I have to come back here. I don't have time to come down. Why don't you fly up and meet me?" His voice was warm and inviting.

The idea of digging out coat and gloves and slugging through dirty March snow did not appeal to me. Twenty-three years, I thought. I had lived in the Big Apple for almost a quarter of a century and had given little thought to bundling up against freezing winds, blowing on frosted fingers, and entering crowded subways, where the smell of damp wool, too long in mothballs and too infrequently sent to the dry cleaners, accosted my senses.

His voice grew cool when I told him I didn't want to come

back to that cold place. "I understand," he said in the same impersonal tone he used with a potential client who'd just informed him he'd accepted a bid from another company. "It's your decision." I knew that he didn't understand. And neither do I, I thought, as I hung up the phone. The fragrance of orange blossoms greeted me through the open door and the shimmering pool beckoned as I suppressed my guilty feelings.

For the next several days I rose early. I made a point of being in place in time to witness the lean, coffee-skinned, ponytailed man feed the feral cats. He was punctual, six-thirty on the dot. So were the cats. I kept sentry under the protection of the palmetto tree until the containers were licked clean and a certain amount of preening was done.

I spent afternoons in the public library and at my computer learning the history of the area and reading about the citrus industry. Mr. Webster's struggling, uncared-for groves bothered me. Surely, I thought, with some care, pruning and fertilizing those trees could be reclaimed.

One afternoon I went to the Lee County Court House and poured through birth records for the spring of 1952. Then I drove home with the lead of disappointment sitting in my chest—there had been no baby girl with the name of Parker or Sanchez born there during that time.

CHAPTER FIVE

My mother and I moved to New York in 1974 when I was twenty-two years old. I remember, just after I'd graduated from college, sitting on my grandparent's rustic porch looking down a long gravel road that led from the ranch house to the main highway through a wrought iron gate. The curved sign across the top announced the Sanchez Sheep Ranch. There was an argument going on in the house behind me. It was about me.

"Mama, of course we have to go." My mother's insistent voice came through the screen door.

Mama had just broken the news that we were moving to New York so that I could attend the Pratt Institute. Yaya's voice wailed. "You don't know anything about living in a big city like New York. It's too dangerous for a woman alone with her young daughter. There're many evils there. I was there. I know!" My grandmother's experience in New York had been fifty years ago when she immigrated to the United States—but that's all she ever needed to know about that city.

"What's wrong with Colorado?" Yaya continued in her accented English. "Are there no art schools in Colorado? Besides, look what happened when you ran away before."

"I am not running away, Mama."

I strained to hear. *What happened when she ran away before?* I wanted to run inside and ask. I sat still.

"Would you deprive your granddaughter, your *only* granddaughter, of the best opportunities?" my mother argued. "Jessica has talent that shouldn't be wasted."

"You would take her away from us too," my grandmother wailed. "Where is the thanks?"

"Mama, you know I'm grateful for everything." Mother's tone softened and I knew she would soon win her argument.

got up and walked away. It was feeding time so I walked down to the sheep barns. Most of the flocks were out in the meadows. Only the mothers with very young lambs were still inside.

Even though it was my life they were discussing I didn't want to hear any more. I loved my yaya dearly. There was no place more comforting than the warmth of her abundant bosom with her callused hands caressing my hair or my back, but she was a woman of strong opinions and strict rules that caused frequent arguments with her oldest daughter, also a woman of strong opinions.

I was excited about the idea of going to New York. As a new graduate of Colorado Women's College with a major in art, with Mother's prodding, I had applied for and been accepted to the Pratt Institute. I felt sad about leaving this place that had been my home for almost twenty years, but the joy at being able to study at the institute, and the excitement of living in New York was more than I could keep inside me. I threw up my arms and twirled around.

Among my earliest memories were that of a long, uncomfortable train ride that brought us into Denver early on a morning when I was not quite three years old. I remember being roused from sleep and having to go to the bathroom as the train huffed into the station.

"Oh, Jessica," Mother sighed. Strain from the long trip was evident in her voice. "We won't have time to get our things and get off before the train pulls out. And, I've been on this train long enough." Tears of fatigue and frustration spilled down her pretty face.

"I'm sorry, Mommy," I said. I clung to her hand, running to keep up with her as she dragged me down the narrow corridor to the lavatory. She strode with her halting gait that favored her left leg.

"What happened to your leg, Mommy?" I'd asked not long before we got on the train to take this big trip.

"Mommy fell," she replied. "I need to be more careful. You need to be careful too," she said, pulling me into a tight hug.

"Mommy fell," I announced to the two old people who rushed toward us as we stumbled off the train, "bag and baggage" as they say.

As a child I had pressed my ear against closed doors, listening to excited conversations and not understanding their meanings. I knew that my mother brought me here to get away from my father. I begged, threatened, and gave her the silent treatment during different periods in my life to try to get her to tell me about him, but she never would. I knew that I was born in south Florida and I have my father's eyes and height, but these things I learned by accident.

We had a good life, both on the sheep ranch and in the Big Apple. Mother devoted her life to me. Almost as soon as we were settled in the spare bedrooms in the north wing of the rambling ranch house, Mother drove Yaya and Yayo's good car down to Denver to look for a job.

What a remarkable woman she was, I thought, as I towel-dried my hair and slipped into a soft terry robe. She was barely twenty years old when I was born, yet, except for occasional dates and a host of casual friends, there were never any serious relationships in her life. She made it clear to any would-be suitors that I was her first priority, yet she never stifled me. We each had our own circle of friends and she encouraged me to be independent. I never stopped to consider how she came to know the virtue of self-worth, which she so diligently instilled in me.

From the time I could hold a crayon I drew pictures; first, oddly shaped sheep or horses and stick figures of the ranch hands, then later, I would spend hours trying to capture with paper and paint, vistas of the beauty of nature that surrounded my life.

Yaya and Aunt Jean congratulated my efforts, but Mother prodded me and bought my supplies. Twice a week every summer from the time I started high school, someone from the ranch drove me to Meeker to take lessons from a well-known artist who had retreated there to live and paint.

I slipped into a comfortable cotton dress and sandals, poured myself a glass of chilled white wine and, as the sun dipped closer to the Caloosahatchee, walked down to the river to watch it set. Even this peaceful scene did little to ease the confusion of my feelings; the sadness for a bitter old man who anesthetized his thoughts and memories with alcohol; my guilt at refusing my husband's invitation to join him for the few days he was going to be in the country.

I was married to a man, not with millions, but billions of dollars, who saw that I wanted for nothing. The first of each month five thousand dollars was deposited into my personal account for spending money. I had a deck of charge cards in my wallet thick enough to shuffle, and Malcolm loved to take me on shopping trips, filling my closets with clothes I wore only to please him. I had my own income from the sale of Mari's shop, from her sizable insurance, and from fashions I still designed.

The sun was gone now, bleeding blood-orange red, into the river. In the dusk details were diminished into shapes and the mosquitoes started to bite. Feeling melancholy, I picked up my empty glass and headed into the house.

I picked up the phone. "Aunt Jean, it's Jessica," I said. I heard surprise and pleasure in her voice that reached across the miles that separated southwest Florida from the western slope of the Colorado Rockies. "I'm fine. Yes . . . really I'm fine . . . no, I'm in Florida. Yes, Florida," I repeated and then was forced into an explanation. "I just got to thinking about you."

Aunt Jean, her husband, their two sons, my younger cousins and their families were all the relatives I had. A sense of void flooded me from time to time when I thought that maybe I had other family somewhere that I didn't know. Perhaps my father, whoever he was, had another whole family and I would have half brothers or sisters. I envied people who did.

Aunt Jean, seven years younger than my mother, was like an older sister to me. She was the one who took me by the hand and led me onto that frightening, rumbling yellow school bus for my first day at school. She was the one who herded me into Miss Springer's classroom where some twenty other five-year-olds sat pale faced and sniffling, or outright bawling.

She was my overseer during those early years while Mother commuted to Denver to work. Aunt Jean was the one who reported my achievements and the one who helped me fight my battles.

My yaya, with her old country ways, did not have the social confidence or the knowledge to do what Aunt Jean did for me.

Mother spent as much time with me as she could. She came home late on the evenings before her day off, at first on the nine o'clock bus that arrived in Grand Junction, and then in the second-hand car she bought. Yayo, or one of the ranch hands, would drive the two-hour trip down to meet her. Sometimes, when winter storms clogged Douglas Pass, she never made it at all.

By the time I was ready to go to college, Mari had worked her way from stockroom girl to sales clerk, to department manager, to buyer for Neusteadters'a privately owned department store in Cherry Creek. She found a comfortable apartment in Denver and brought me to live with her.

By the time Mother and I moved to New York in 1974 Aunt Jean was married to a man she'd met in her first year of college— a real cowboy. He rode the rodeo circuit, broke horses for a living, and was saving all his prize money for a ranch of his own. Within a year she had given birth to the first of my cousins, Darryl, and two years later, Walker. On rare occasions when we saw each other we had little to talk about.

Aunt Jean came to New York for Mother's memorial service and together we flew back to Colorado to bury her in the little cemetery next to my grandparents. The last time I had seen her two years before when she came to New York one more time—for my wedding. She was the only family there. None of Malcolm's children came. When she showed me pictures of my uncle and cousins, I didn't recognize them.

"Are you sure everything is all right?" she asked once more.

"Aunt Jean," I began hesitantly, "do you know anything about my father you haven't told me?"

"Oh, honey," she answered in her quiet, flat mountain voice, "you've asked me that so many times. I wish I could tell you but my answer is still the same. Mari and I never talked sister talk, and to Mama and Papa it never even happened."

"But that's to say I was never born," I protested. I looked around the perfectly appointed room, silent except for the subtle clicking of the clock, and empty, except for me. A light flashed on the phone indicating that I had an incoming call, but I chose to ignore the signal.

"Jessica?" My aunt's voice broke through my thoughts.

"I'm here, Aunt Jean." I took a deep breath. "I am standing in a beautiful home but I feel like an intruder. I have everything I could ever need or want. I have a doting husband but I can't seem to please him. He wants me to meet him in New York before he goes back to Spain for God knows how long. I told him no and I'm not sure why. I guess I'm just feeling sorry for myself," I sighed.

"Oh, Jess," she whispered, "I know how much you've wanted answers, and I don't have any to give. I wish I were there to give you a hug." Then she added, "I'll go through the boxes in the attic that we moved from the ranch when it was sold to see if there's anything I missed."

"Thanks, Aunt Jean. I love you," I added before I hung up.

I punched the button on the answering machine to listen to the message that had been left. "Hi, Jess, it's me, Christine. I was just wondering how things were going—I mean, is everything okay? I . . . uh, thought maybe you were in New York . . . I . . . well, if you were I'm sure you'd call me. Talk to you later."

Why was Christine stuttering? This hesitancy was not like her. I dialed her number and she answered on the first ring. I pictured her in her apartment, relaxing in some kind of exotic at-home caftan.

"Chris, it's Jessica, is something wrong?"

"Oh, Jess, it's so good to hear your voice. I really miss you." Her voice fell like a welcomed caress on my ear.

"Well, come down to visit then," I said, my heart lightening. "Why did you think I was in New York?"

"I . . . well, I just thought you might be," she stammered.

I frowned at the vagueness in her voice. "You don't sound like yourself. Are you sure everything is all right?" A little pocket of worry took up space in my mind as I waited in several seconds before she answered.

"Oh," Christine wailed. "Oh, I don't know why I have to do things like this. Why can't I just let things alone?"

"What are you talking about? What's wrong?" I insisted.

"It's just . . . just that I saw Malcolm getting into a limo this evening. There was someone with him. I . . . I thought it was you."

I visualized the creases in her forehead as she wrinkled her face in distress. "It's all right, Chris. I'm sure everything is fine."

"But friends don't do what I just did to you. I'm so sorry. I . . . I guess I'm just naïve."

"I'm sure there's an explanation," I said making my voice sound light, but I felt another rock drop in my chest.

When I went to bed, sleep would not come. Fingers of suspicion wove their way through my thoughts. I looked at the bedside clock at 2 a.m., then 3 a.m., and then I started comparing Malcolm to the one other man to whom I'd given my heart. I remembered what hurt felt like.

CHAPTER SIX

B right warmth of sunshine layered over me like a blanket when I finally forced my eyes open a few hours later. As I squinted at the clock beside the bed, a feeling of dread forced its way into my conscious. It was that feeling one has knowing something is wrong without remembering what it was. Then I remembered Chris' phone call—poor innocent Chris.

I splashed cold water on my face, pulled on shorts, an athletic bra, and a tee shirt. Even though I was tired I was determined to walk. I wanted, needed, to get out of this house where, even in his absence, I felt Malcolm's presence. Maybe I'm just not cut out to be a rich man's wife, I thought, as I poured a cup of strong coffee.

It was Saturday and traffic today was different, not so many commercial trucks, or cars with single occupants scurrying to work, but vans and sedans with families heading to the mall or to the beach. There were conservative vehicles—sedans, Buicks, Lincolns—with white haired occupants going grocery shopping or to the Flea Market. As I passed the Cypress House, I looked for the old man or his cat. I saw neither but I called out, "Good morning, Mr. Webster. How are you today?" I smiled and waved toward the opaque windows in need of a good washing. There, I thought, I feel better.

I paused at a side street I'd never followed before. The marker identified it as Manatee Lane and it led toward the river. A hand-lettered sign announced that this was also the way to the community church. "Non-denominational," it read. "All Are Welcome." Printed times indicated that services were at 11 a.m. on Sunday and 7 p.m. each Wednesday.

Along the street there were more of the typical stucco houses with barking dogs behind chain-link fences. Campers or boats perched beside houses under makeshift carports. Young children played in some yards; in others, teenage boys worked on their cars.

As I neared the river, cracked blacktopped pavement gave way to a sandy road. There, on my left, with a wide expanse of neat green lawn, sat the prettiest little church I'd ever seen. It absolutely sparkled in its whiteness of clean fresh paint. Black shutters glistened in contrast, shiny as polished ebony. I stopped at the end of a paved path leading to the front door and stood gaping at its beauty. The door, arched and ornately carved, was not painted but protected only by a coating of clear varnish that allowed the details of the grain of its wood to be seen.

Small panes of beveled glass in an intricate design adorned the upper portion. Large cement urns filled to overflowing with red geraniums dressed either side of the entry. Wet puddles around them indicated that they had just been watered. I heard a lawnmower running somewhere behind the church.

To the left of the building was a small—no, not small, tiny— bungalow almost hidden by the moss-laden branches of a large live oak tree. A familiar-looking pickup truck was parked near the dollhouse building. I recognized it as the one belonging to the "Cat Man." I was sure of it. Just then the sound of the mower grew louder, and the man I'd witnessed feeding homeless cats came around the corner pushing the machine. He waved to me. He kept going, but my open-jawed expression must have stopped him because he turned off the machine and walked toward me.

"Good morning," he said, "may I help you?"

I just stared. A narrow leather thong tied his long black hair into its ponytail. He wore faded Levi's, work boots, and a white tee shirt with a sunburst of color and sky painted in vivid shades of the rainbow. The words "Christ Is Risen" were printed across the front.

His arms were brown and muscled, and tattooed. He had a high forehead and prominent cheekbones. While his lashes and brows were as black as his hair, his penetrating eyes were the color of topaz. His face, I thought, would have been perfect except for a long ragged scar, which began at the upper corner of his lip and ran across his left cheek to the top of his ear. When he spoke, the scar pulled up the edge of his mouth and formed wrinkles at the corner of his eye.

You must be the rudest person in the world, I scolded myself. "You're the Cat Man, I finally stammered.

He laughed, not a loud laugh, but a soft chuckle that seemed to pass his pleasure to me. His smile showed even white teeth. "And you must be the presence I felt the last few times I've stopped there." He walked forward and extended his hand. "I'm Benjamin Rodriguez."

"Jess . . . Jessica Steele," I managed to utter as I wiped sweating palms down the side of my shorts before I reached my hand out to take his. "Why do you do that?" I asked.

"Do what? Feed the cats?"

I nodded.

"Because they're hungry."

I laughed out loud. "I'm sorry," I said, regaining my composure, "you don't look like a person who would take his time to feed stray cats. Do you work here to—take care of the grounds?"

Again he laughed that easy laugh. "I work here. I live there." He pointed toward the small cottage, and then extending his arm toward the church, he continued, "I preach here."

"You're a priest!"

"No, not a priest. I'm the pastor of this little congregation. I'm an ordained minister." He smiled, "it doesn't figure, does it?"

I shook my head. Then I remembered also seeing on the church sign the name Pastor Ben Rodriguez. "Well, maybe it does."

"It's getting hot. Could I offer you a glass of cold tea, Ms. Steele? I always keep some made."

"Thanks, but I'm just out for a walk. I'm keeping you from your work. You must be getting ready for tomorrow's services," I rushed on.

"I'm almost finished and I need a drink myself." He motioned that I should come with him. I followed but I felt uncomfortable and, I had to admit, a little awed. I'd never been in the presence of a preacher—a man of God. In my grandparents' home I had grown up with a crucifix on the wall and my yaya's rosary always on her bedside table, except when it was in her fingers.

We attended mass every Saturday or Sunday in the little church tucked in the Rockies. The Hail Marys and the Our Fathers were then as familiar to me as the singsong cadence of Father McMahon as he read the scriptures in Latin. I even went through Catechism to please Yaya, who on our departure to New York pleaded, "Please go to church. Find yourselves a nice church." We never did.

The memorial service I planned for Mari was more of a holistic celebration of her life than anything religious. We did have a "lukewarm" reading of Psalm 23—just in case. Although I told myself I didn't believe it, in a small corner of my mind there was a tiny hope that I would see my mother again in another life.

He ushered me to one of two metal lawn chairs under the canopy of the live oak. The chairs were the kind that had been around forty years ago—metal, with curved backs and seats. The legs were a length of chrome tubing that ran from the back on one side, along the seat to the ground, then curved around to form support for the opposite side. They always bounce when you sat down. This pair of chairs was meticulously restored and freshly painted. Everything about the place was so neat and clean that I was sure there was a woman's touch. "What do people call you?" I asked when he returned with two tall plastic glasses filled with ice and tea. A slice of lemon was perched on the rim.

"Most people call me Ben, or Pastor Ben," he replied as he handed me a glass and seated himself. An old collie with only three legs hobbled around the corner of the house. She positioned herself near his feet with one paw resting on his boot. "This is Ginger. A 'gator' took off her leg when she was a puppy. She manages quite well."

At the sound of his voice, a plaintive meow came from the edge of the porch where a tiger cat peered out from a wire cage I hadn't noticed. "She doesn't have a name yet," Ben said as he nodded toward the cry. "I found her last week on the road. She'd been hit by a car but she's going to be all right."

"Maybe your name should be Francis," I said. When his brow furrowed into a question, I explained, "Saint Francis of Assisi—the priest who was friend to animals."

"I'm not too familiar with saints," he smiled.

As the sun reached its zenith, we shifted our chairs to follow the shade. I learned about Benjamin Rodriguez. He was forty-two years old and had grown up in Immokalee, a community east of Fort Myers that was largely Hispanic and home to a population of migrant workers who worked the groves and vegetable farms. His mother was Latina, born in Florida. Ben's father, from Central America, was a man who came and went in his early life—mostly went because he hadn't seen him in twenty years.

The police picked up Ben Rodriguez for the first time when he was ten years old. Since that time he'd been in and out of juvenile detention, foster homes, and finally, prison.

"I was mean, really mean," he said. "I made it a game to see how many times I could break the law and get away with it. I was married at seventeen and twice a father by the time I was twenty-one years old. I beat my wife, but only when I was drunk or angry." He shrugged his shoulder and gave a wry grimace. "My two daughters, who are now young women, have only recently become part of my life. Well, I didn't always get away," he continued. "After several armed robberies, the last one with injuries, I was arrested, tried, and sent to the state penitentiary. Did you ever hear of the Prison Fellowship Ministry?" he asked, looking at me.

I shook my head. "I never have."

"Prison wasn't all bad." When I looked surprised he continued, "I was able to get my high school diploma and even a two-year college degree. I started going to the church services the prison ministry held. The idea of a way out becomes very appealing when you have four concrete walls and bars to look at day in and day out. Some days you got an hour in the exercise yard. 'Course, if you really like the outdoors, there's always the chain gang.

"So you start thinking about things, like maybe you don't have to hate all the time. Maybe it would feel good to have someone who cared about you, put an arm around you, and talk to you about love. You see, I never understood the word 'love,' I thought it meant sex."

Just then his cell phone rang. I hadn't even noticed it clipped to his belt. He listened intently for a moment then said, "I'll be there as soon as I can."

"I'm sorry, Ms. Steele," he said, standing up. "The daughter of one of the families in my congregation tried to kill herself with an overdose. She's in intensive care and I need to be with them."

"Of course," I said as I stood. "But," I hesitated, "it's Mrs. Steele, but please call me Jessica."

"Forgive me." His amber eyes pleaded with mine. "Your husband must be wondering what happened to you. I had no idea it was so late. Perhaps you and he could come to our church sometime. I would like to meet him."

"My husband is away on business," I muttered as he jumped in his truck and started the engine.

He leaned out the window and said, "If you pray, pray for Ashley." With that he backed out to the road and was gone.

When I looked at my watch I saw that it was one o'clock in the afternoon. My stomach began to scold me as I hurried home. I hadn't had breakfast and it was past lunchtime. As I neared the Cypress House I saw a brown paper bag sitting on the ground next to the rusted mailbox. In shaky letters, written in pencil and barely legible was the word "Jessica." Inside there were oranges and grapefruit. *Was this a peace offering?* I wondered. I turned to the blank windows and waved. "Thank you, Mr. Webster," I shouted.

I didn't have any intention of going to church when I woke Sunday morning, but curiosity won out and at ten o'clock I was standing in front of my closet deciding what to wear. It was March. Although mornings began cool, by midday the temperatures were into the eighties. I chose a navy cotton skirt, a white blouse, and threw a navy plaid blazer over my shoulders.

I had hoped to slip quietly into the back of the church but as I neared the building several cars that had passed me on the road pulled on to the shoulder to park. People spilled out of them and hurried toward the open church door. They waved and smiled and greeted me. A bell began to peal from the tower as I stepped into the entrance. The crowd grew quiet, and a crowd it was. I didn't readily see an empty seat. A woman near the back motioned as she nudged her husband to move over and make room for me.

As the bell finished its eleventh stroke, two Latina girls, about eight or nine years old, in frilly dresses, walked carefully down the aisle toward the altar with lighted tapers. One was chubby and round faced with dancing eyes that darted around the room, while the other was slender, her dark eyes intent on watching the flame of the torch she was bearing. As the candles were lit, Pastor Ben Rodriguez stepped to the center of the raised platform at the front of the sanctuary. He wore no robe. He had on a white high-collared shirt and black Levi's. His hair looked freshly washed and its blackness shone like a satin cap. Around his neck, on a heavy chain was a hammered silver cross.

He raised his hands in greeting as his eyes scanned the congregation. When his look rested on me, a smile pulled at the corner of his damaged mouth. He made me feel welcomed and blessed at the same time. The hour passed quickly, from the first hymn of praise that not only filled the room but, I was sure, could be heard blocks away through the open windows, to the uplifting words he spoke, to the final prayer. To others he was Ben or Pastor Ben, but I thought of him as the beautiful man who fed stray cats under the misty blanket of dawn.

After the service, Ben stood on the front steps in the noon heat and spoke with everyone, bending down to listen to a child or raising his voice when he addressed an ancient man wearing hearing aids in both ears. I held back until all the others had filed past, finally stepping forward to take his stretched hand. "Thank you for accepting my invitation," he smiled.

"I'm impressed. I wanted to ask you," I continued, "how is Ashley?"

"She's going to be all right. They'll keep her in the hospital a few days to monitor her organ functions and then she'll have the benefit of counseling for as long as she needs it."

I hesitated still. "I was wondering too, if sometime you would tell me the rest of your story?"

"I'm always glad to share my story." Again there was that turned-up smile. "I'm here on Saturdays and most evenings unless I visit some of my families or have a meeting. And, I always have a supply of ice tea."

After the service, instead of heading back to the house, I turned toward the river. There was a wooden barricade across the end of the road with a red reflecting sign that shouted the warnings, Danger, Dead End. Someone had cleared an area underneath the overhanging branches of a tree that was laden with a tangle of vines. A park bench, one of those you can buy almost anywhere, sat beneath, obscured from the road.

It was surprisingly cool in this little sanctuary. A slight breeze came off the river. The lapping of the water against the rocks below had a hypnotic effect. Water birds skimmed the surface of the river and I watched pleasure crafts on Sunday outings as they sailed up and down the river.

Anxieties of the previous days were replaced with a feeling of contentment I had not experienced in a long time. Surely everything would be all right.

CHAPTER SEVEN

Any plans I had to hear the rest of Ben Rodriguez story were put on hold when the phone rang at six-thirty the following morning. "Malcolm!"

"You sound surprised," he said, "Thought I would catch you before you went out on your daily walk. You're still doing that, aren't you?" Was the hint of sarcasm in his voice only my imagination? Without waiting for my reply he informed me that he'd had a change of plans and would be flying down that day. There was no need for me to meet him, he said. Steve, his pilot would drive him out from the airport.

"So you won't be going back to Spain?" I asked.

"No, something else has come up. I tried to get you yesterday, about noon," he said.

"I went to church."

"To church?"

I heard the surprise linger in his question. "I'll tell you about it when I see you," I said.

"Yes, we have lots to talk about."

Malcolm greeted me with a curious expression when he arrived the next day. He had lost some of his tan and his face seemed drawn, but his body felt good to me when he drew me to him that night.

Our conversation over the dinner Louisa left for us was casual. He told me about people in Spain that I knew and the weather in New York. I tried to put the nagging thoughts of his being with another woman out of my mind.

Malcolm listened with his forehead creased and his lips pushed together when I related the story of the man who fed cats and how I found him at his little church. I told him about the grapefruit

and oranges Mr. Webster left for me. I sensed his disapproval so I
chose not to tell him of my trip up the river with the old man.
Perhaps this is how couples begin to become dishonest with each
other, I thought.

For the next several days we returned to our, if somewhat uneasy,
at least normal routine. I continued my walks, and Malcolm had
his morning golf. I even had another "lesson from hell," and seemed
to be getting the knack of swinging the clubs. I might even be a
reasonable golfer—if I wanted to be. My husband seemed more
tense than usual. Each time the phone rang he rushed to take the
call behind the closed door of his office.

Friday evening, as was our habit, we took a bottle of wine down
to the dock to watch the sunset over the river. After a few minutes of
compatible silence, Malcolm set his glass on the table beside him
then took my drink from my hand. He turned me to face him then
took my hands in his. "Your hands are cold," he said.

My mind raced ahead, grabbing at random thoughts. A feeling
of dread twisted my stomach as I waited for Malcolm's words. I
clenched my teeth together to control the tremor that started in
my jaw.

"I told you when I called you from New York," he began,
"that my plans had changed. I didn't want to mention anything
until things were definite. The phone call that came today finalized
everything. For several months I've been negotiating with the
Chinese government and our state department for a contract to
build bridges in China. With their new government a lot of progress
is being made over there. I have been asked to come over this week
and look over the projects. It is huge. It's not just a network of
bridges but they want me to build factories too, the kind I have in
Europe, so that supplies can be produced there and don't have to
be shipped. It seems pretty certain." His voice grew excited, the
way it did when he talked about his work. "I'll have to be there
most of the time for the next two years, until things were up and
running . . ."

I pulled my hands away and stood up. "And what is supposed
to happen to us?" I asked, hating the quiver in my voice.

"Well, of course I'd love to have you with me, but I think you'd be happier in New York. Once things get ironed out you could come spend some time. I plan to keep an apartment in Beijing. I would love to show you the Orient."

A knot of fear formed between my breasts and I felt like I couldn't breathe. Then suddenly that feeling gave way to a different emotion. Heat rose in my body and blood rushed to my cheeks. I faced him. I was angry. "If this has been under discussion for months why am I just finding out about it? I *am* your wife. Or doesn't that count for anything?" I challenged.

"Carol was never interested in the details. She just went along with my decision."

I managed to get control of my voice. "Malcolm," I said quietly, "I would like to finish this discussion in the house. It's getting dark and I want to be able to look at you when we talk." I picked up the wine bottle, filled my glass and, taking it in hand, marched up the path.

In the house I went into the great room and turned on lights. When Malcolm entered the room I was standing by the mantle.

"Jessica, I'm sorry." he started toward me. I stopped him with my outstretched palm.

"Look at me, Malcolm," I said, willing my voice to be steady. "*I am Jessica. I-am-not-Carol*," I bit off each word. I waved toward the photograph. "Do I look like Carol? Do I sound like Carol? Did you think when I came here I would be cloned into another Carol? What did you think, Malcolm?"

He stood a few feet from me. His hands were clenched into fists at his sides. His jaws tightened as they did when he was angry, but in his face was a look of something else—uncertainty. "I'm sorry," he repeated. "It was a mistake not to tell you, but we can talk about it now. Let's be calm." He went over and sat on the arm of a chair across from me, assuming a relaxed pose.

"I am calm." To convince myself I drew a deep breath. "What else haven't you told me?" I asked.

"I suppose there are a lot of details. What is it you want to know?" A note of impatience crept into his voice.

"Christine called last week. She thought I was in New York and wondered why I didn't let her know."

"I asked you to meet me there," Malcolm reminded me.

"She saw you helping someone—some woman into your limousine. Naturally she thought it was me. You didn't mention that when you were telling me what you did in New York." I didn't care that I sounded accusatory.

He didn't answer right away. He rubbed the bridge of his nose with his fingers. "That," he said in measured tones, "was Daisy Chang. She is a civil engineer with whom I'm working, and yes, she will be going to China. She lives there." He raised an eyebrow. "If you had been there you could have met her. Christine should mind her own business."

"She was minding her business," I said pointedly. "She introduced us."

"Touché," Malcolm laughed and came and took my hands. "Jess, we can talk about this all you want to but I'm hungry. Let's do something ordinary and sinful like going down to Rib City and eat 'baby backs,' baked beans, and coleslaw."

"All right," I agreed and gave him a tentative smile. A momentary truce was made even as feelings of rejection formed inside my chest. What I really wanted was to run to that beautiful little church, slip into a pew, and quietly figure out what I was supposed to do now. Our uneasy truce ended when Malcolm insisted that I go back to New York and I refused.

"This is not your house," he began, when I told him I planned to stay in Florida. My look stopped him. "But why?" he asked instead. "You don't know anybody here. What if you need help?"

"Louisa comes in every day," I replied. "The yard men come twice a week and I can always call 911."

"You're being flippant, Jessica."

"We both had lives before we met. We knew we would have to make adjustments, and if not adjustments, allowances. I admit I was—am—truly hurt by the fact that you never told me anything about this. Did you think I would try to stop you? Did you think I would tell somebody, perhaps the old man across the road?" I heard my voice start to rise and took a deep breath.

"Your decision's been made," I continued. "And, you're right. I would not want to spend several months in a hotel room or an apartment." But, I thought meanly, Miss Chang will be there if you need anything. "Besides," I said, as I spread my hands in a casual gesture of acceptance, "I'm not even fond of Chinese food."

"I don't understand your fascination with this place," he said. "Carol loved it of course, but I never really cared much about coming here."

"I don't understand it either," I said simply.

The morning Malcolm left, several days later, he called a taxi to take him to the plane. Steve, who often came to pick him up, waited for him at the airport. Malcolm explained that he would be in New York several days getting documents in order. This time he didn't invite me to come with him. Neither of us said much while his luggage was being loaded into the trunk of the cab.

With the taxi waiting, he took me in his arms. "Look, maybe you want to fly over in a month or so. I could meet you in Hong Kong for a few days." As I started to shake my head, he continued, "I'm sorry. I did this all wrong. It's just that . . ." and then he stopped.

"Just what, Malcolm?"

He gave a twisted smile. "Just nothing."

"Just what?" I repeated.

He stepped away and held me at arm's length. "Carol never paid much attention when I came and went. She had the children. She had her friends and her organizations."

And, she knew she didn't have you, I thought. "Go," I said, "the taxi's waiting. That's a cliché," I laughed. "I wish you well with your mammoth undertaking. It involves two powerful governments and that is awesome. Godspeed."

Malcolm's look was indiscernible. He bent his lips to mine and gave me a lingering kiss. "I love you, Jessica." He didn't look back as he strode to the taxi, slid into the seat, and closed the door.

I sank into a chair in the sunroom as tears spilled down my face. Of course I didn't want to go with him. Of course I didn't want to go back to New York. I wanted to be here. So why did I have this empty feeling inside me?

I hadn't walked for several days. I wondered if Old Man Webster or Ben noticed my absence. Even though it was late, I did a few stretches and put on my walking shoes. When I passed through the great room, I went to the mantel and took down Carol's picture. "Well, Carol," I said, as I slipped the framed photograph into a nearby drawer, "it's just you and me. If I need you, I know where to find you." I grabbed my visor off a hook on the wall and as I passed the refrigerator I impulsively took out the remains of last night's jambalaya and set off down the road.

Today I purposefully turned up the drive to the Cypress House. The gray-and-white cat eyed me from the recliner on the porch. Tentatively I stepped up the wobbly stairs that led to the back door. "Mr. Webster," I called. "Mr. Webster, its Jessica."

After what must have been a minute, but seemed longer, I heard footsteps and the knocking sound of his cane on the wooden floor. He appeared at a screen door that separated us. Black suspenders, over a soiled undershirt, held up the usual work pants. When he didn't say anything, I opened the door. I thought I was going to lose the breakfast I hadn't eaten when stench of decaying garbage reached my nose.

"I want to thank you for the oranges and the grapefruit. That was very kind of you." When he didn't answer, I stepped forward and held out the dish. "I brought you some jambalaya for your supper." I waited, standing there stupidly with my arm extended, holding the dish toward him. His eyes were bloodshot and his stock of unruly gray hair stood at various angles. Had I just wakened him? The sour smell of stale whiskey and the unbathed body made me wish my arms were longer.

I became annoyed. "Where would you like me to put it?" I asked as I started to move past him.

He reached out and took the container. "Much obliged," he muttered, as he turned and put it on the table. When he moved, I saw dirt and clutter, not of months, but years. Countertops were piled with empty cereal boxes and tin cans. Near the sink, a dingy plastic drainer held dishes that looked as if they had not even been washed. I hurried down the steps. The air, even the sultry air, helped quiet the churning inside me.

I turned to see Mr. Webster watching me. "How do you get your groceries?" I asked. "I don't see a car."

He considered me for a moment then said, "That preacher—over at the church—he brings me stuff."

I stared at him. "You mean Pastor Ben?"

Now it was his turn to stare. "You know him?"

"I met him. I went to church there. Do you go there too—I mean, to church?"

He snorted. "Lightning would strike it if I did."

I laughed, "I don't think so. I was there and it's still standing." He chuckled. I actually had made him laugh.

That evening, after an early supper, I headed for Manatee Lane. Ben's truck was parked where it had been before. He was under a magnolia tree beside his house, painting a small wooden chair, a child's chair. Others, already painted in bright colors, sat nearby. He was stripped to the waist and barefoot. His jeans were streaked with spatters of the bright colors he'd used. So intent was he on his work that he didn't hear me. Ginger, who was lying nearby, raised up her head.

"Hello," I called as I walked toward him.

His face broke into a wide, lip-lifting smile. "Mrs. Steele! I was thinking about you and wondering if you're all right."

"Yes, I'm fine," I lied. "But please call me Jessica. Are you always working?" I spread my hand to indicate the painted chairs.

"It's one of the things I learned to do after I got my act together. I found that I like it." He carefully placed his brush in a can of water.

"Please, finish what you're doing," I said. "I took you at your work and stopped by."

"All through," he said as he wiped his hands down the sides of his pants, adding yet another color to the rainbow of paint that was already there.

"What are the chairs for?"

"One of the downtown churches gave them to us. We use them in Sunday school."

"They're great. Children love bright colors. So do you, I think."

He laughed and spread his hands. "Of course, I'm Mexican." I laughed with him.

"I understand you take groceries to Mr. Webster, that old man who lives in the Cypress House on Blossom Lane," I said.

"You know *him*?" His eyes widened in question, the scar on his cheek stretching to make creases near his left eye.

"Not really. I've met him and I'm curious about him. It makes me sad to see his groves overgrown and dying. They must have been productive at one time," I said as I sat in one of the metal chairs. I declined this offer of ice tea. "I took some food to him today. The inside of his house is *filthy*!"

Ben listened quietly, his topaz eyes trained on my face, as I told him about the trip up the river, the grapefruit and today's visit. "What do you know about him?" I asked.

He shook his head. "Not much except that he's an angry old man. When we first started this church I went to every house for miles around inviting people to come worship with us. I stopped at his house. He, of course, did not let me in. One evening I drove over there and saw him sitting on the porch. He looked so lonely. Did you ever hear of the Apostle Paul?" Ben asked abruptly.

"You mean the one in the Bible?"

"Yes, that's the one," he laughed. "In my other life—the one I'm ashamed of now—I was a daredevil. There was nothing I admitted to being afraid of and I'd go to any lengths to prove it.

"Well, now, I'm just as daring about approaching people in the name of Christ. 'I am bold for the Gospel,' the Apostle Paul said. So, I sat down on his porch and began talking to him. The only way he ended the conversation was to get up and walk in the house."

"He's done that with me too."

"I found out," Ben continued, "that he has no family. I think he did once. He's lived here longer than anybody else around, so there are not many people who know anything of his past.

"His license had been taken away for driving while intoxicated so he takes his boat up the river to Jack's Marina to buy a few groceries and his liquor. The first time I brought food he refused it, saying he didn't accept charity. I put it on the steps and left. A few days later when I stopped again, he handed me some money and a grocery list." We laughed.

"My husband knew him, or about him. Malcolm's first wife's father and Mr. Webster were large citrus growers in the area. Now everything is falling down around him and he doesn't seem to care."

As darkness settled in streetlights came on, and a chorus of night critters raised their evening voices. Somewhere a dog barked. In a moment of quiet we heard a boat go down the river. "Well, he's not going to get rid of me." I rose to leave. "Would you mind if I buy the groceries for him?" "No," Ben replied, "this way he'll have two people in his life."

"You're such a good man. It's no wonder your church is full on Sunday morning. Do that many people always come?"

"Now they do. I'm hoping it gets so crowded that we'll have to have two services." Ben rose to stand in front of me. "By the way, I'm glad you stopped by. Is your husband still away?"

"Yes, I . . . I mean no," I stammered. I willed my voice not to betray me. "He came back. He's gone again—to China."

"Is everything really all right?" When I didn't answer, he took my elbow and steered me back to the chair. "Tell me," he said quietly, "If you want to. I have the time."

For the next hour I outlined my life for him and he listened, just as Malcolm Steele once had done. Ben insisted on driving me home and waited until I was inside the house before he headed out the drive. I promised to keep him posted about Mr. Webster, and I promised I would come to church the following Sunday.

CHAPTER EIGHT

The sun was higher when I walked out from under the shroud of the live oaks onto the street Monday morning. Tomorrow would be April 1. Malcolm was in Beijing. He'd called twice and I'd had one E-mail from him. He expected to be there for several months and wanted to know when I thought I would go back to New York. "Isn't it getting hot there?" he asked.

I'd said "no" to both questions. I didn't know when I'd be going north, and no, it wasn't too hot. I'd also said "no" to three or four jobs I'd been offered. Sooner or later the offers would stop coming. Is that what I wanted? I didn't know.

As I neared the Cypress House I saw the gray-and-white cat sitting on the back step looking up at the closed door. I heard its insistent *meow* from the street. The cat was usually not outside when I first went by. The morning paper was still in the driveway, but it often was. Mr. Webster did not seem to be an early riser. I noticed that the light over the back door was on.

I walked up the drive toward the house. "Is something wrong, kitty?" I asked. He looked at me and meowed, but didn't move away from the door. I tried the screen. It was unlatched so I walked on to the enclosed porch. The cat darted in front of me. When I tried the door it wouldn't open. "Something's wrong," I muttered.

Through the dingy pane I saw the same cluttered counter, the red Formica-topped table with its chrome legs. There were two matching chairs with stuffing spilling out of ripped seats. The table was covered with everything the counter wouldn't hold. Piles of yellowing newspapers were stacked around the room.

Cupping my hands against my eyes, I peered further into the room. Two doors led from the kitchen, one to the right, probably to a dining room. The one across from me opened into a hall.

Across the hall there was a third door, and through that door, I saw a man's legs stretched across the floor.

"Mr. Webster," I yelled, pounding on the doorframe. "Mr. Webster, it's Jessica." The cat stood on its hind legs and stretched its forepaws up the side of the door. I screamed his name again then ran around to the front of the house and tried that door. It wouldn't budge. At the back of the house I found the door that Mr. Webster had come out when I was picking up litter. No luck there either. The cat trotted after me, crying plaintively. I reached down and patted its head. "I know," I said. "I'll be right back."

I sprinted back down the road to Huntington House, grabbed the kitchen phone, and punched in 911. *Yes, Malcolm, I can dial 911 if I have to.* Convincing the emergency crew to come was more difficult.

"*No,*" I fairly shouted into the phone, "I told you, *I am not a relative.* I'm a neighbor. I can't get into the house. And, *no, I don't know if he's alive.*" When I was sure they knew where to come I hung up the phone and then called the nearest police station. If I couldn't break down the door, surely they could.

I stopped long enough to splash cold water on my face. I grabbed my wallet and car keys and was standing in Mr. Webster's driveway, the cat beside me, when the emergency vehicle and the police cruiser arrived at the same time. They wheeled into the driveway from opposite directions, their lights flashing. As the First Responders pulled their equipment from the van I led the policemen to the door and stood back while the officers mounted the steps. One man was older, probably in his fifties, and beefy. The other was young and pale with sandy hair and brows. He seemed unsure of himself. After peering through the door, knocking and shouting as I'd done, they broke the lock.

I stepped aside as the paramedics, a stout Caucasian woman and a slender black man, rushed past the officers.

I waited just inside the kitchen. Four people blocked my view, but I wasn't sure I wanted to see what they found anyway.

"He's breathing," I heard someone say. "He's unconscious," another voice added. "Looks like he banged his head on the lavatory here."

"Hello, sir? Hello, can you hear me?" I recognized the voice of the female responder. "We've got to get him in a better position. Uh-oh, wait a minute. Stop! Looks like his leg is broken."

The policemen backed out of the way as the young paramedic ran out the door, returning momentarily with a leg board. I could see a mask on Mr. Webster's face and watched his breathing as the attendant monitored his vital signs. With awesome efficiency his broken leg was secured to the rigid support and, with the help of the policemen he was lifted on to a gurney in the hall. An intravenous was started, and I saw Mr. Webster's eyes flutter.

"His name is John Arnold Webster," I said to the senior officer who questioned me, pen and pad in hand. "He lives here alone, and as far as I know he hasn't any family." The cat rubbed against my legs, alternately purring and meowing. I found a bag of dry cat food and poured some in his dish.

"Mr. Webster, it's Jessica," I said as his gurney was wheeled past me. His defiant eyes fixed on mine. "You're going to be all right. I'll come with you to the hospital."

"Why?"

Damned if I know, I thought. I didn't answer him.

As the female medic climbed in the back of the van with the patient, the young man turned to me. "You'll be there to take care of the paperwork?" he asked.

"What paperwork?"

"Insurance, admission papers—that kind of thing. Someone needs to fill that out if he can't."

"Look," I said exasperated, "I hardly know the man. I'll ask the officers to stay with me while I see if I can find that information in the house."

In the front of the house there were identical-sized rooms on either side of the central front door. The one on left was a parlor, its furniture covered in a knobby brown plaid fabric of the sixties. A teakwood and brass coffee table sat on matted gold shag carpet. It had that "retro" look that was becoming popular. Shades and heavy drapes covered the windows and defied entry of any sunlight. The room smelled moldy and surfaces were layered with dust.

Across the hall in a room that seemed to serve Mr. Webster's living and sleeping area, we found his wallet containing a Medicare card and an expired driver's license. An unmade bed sat in one corner. It was anybody's guess as to how long it had been since the bedding had seen a washing machine. There was a dresser, the surface of which was filled with empty Jim Beam whiskey bottles. In an opposite corner was an antique rolltop desk. Every one of its many cubbyholes was jammed full of scraps of paper. The drawers were so full they wouldn't close. Crumpled clothes were thrown over the backs of chairs and piled in smelly heaps on the floor. Near the front window, looking out onto the street sat a recliner covered with nubby olive green fabric. Here was where Old Man Webster watched the world—and me—pass by. The only thing of a recent date was a color television, which sat on a wobbly table. The remote control rested on the arm of the chair.

A hall led from the front entry to a set of stairs rising to the second floor, then continued on to the back of the house. We passed the bathroom where Mr. Webster had been found. I noticed that a towel rack was pulled loose from the wall. The basin of the washbowl, the toilet, and the ancient tub all bore stains of permanent rust and pits from endless dripping faucets.

"I'll see that the door is repaired," I told the officers. I put a bowl of food out for the cat who now watched apprehensively from underneath the steps. "You'll be okay," I said as I patted its matted fur.

How had I gotten myself into this? I wondered as I drove down Palm Beach Boulevard toward Lee County Memorial Hospital. I could imagine Malcolm's reaction and blessed the fact that he wasn't here. No doubt he would have offered monetary assistance and insisted that I distance myself of the affair. How could anybody live like that? I thought as I mentally reviewed the disgustingly unsanitary rooms.

After I parked the car I went in search of the patient. He was still in the emergency room having his leg set and cast.

Yes, I was told, he had lain there for several hours, but except for a mild concussion, the broken leg and a few bruises, he was all right.

I gave the girl at the admitting desk his Medicare card. "We'll keep him here for a few days," she said, "but you know he won't be able to be by himself, and he will need therapy."

"I know," I replied. *What am I supposed to do about it?* I thought.

The housekeeper was just leaving when I got home at two o'clock. There was food in the refrigerator she told me in her accented English. Louisa was in her fifties and had worked for the Huntington family soon after she arrived in the states from her native country of Honduras, almost thirty years ago. She was now a grandmother several times over. Her husband, Carlos, a gardener and landscaper, took care of the grounds. She was a squat, sturdy figure who quietly went about her duties, smiling her crinkly smile that all but hid her eyes behinds folds of flesh and answering simply, "*Si, Señora,*" when addressed. She listened attentively with a look of warm compassion on her face as I explained the morning's events.

After a quick lunch and a refreshing shower, I fell asleep on a lounge chair in the shade of the cabana beside the pool. However, when Pastor Ben arrived home at six o'clock that evening, I was waiting in his driveway. He looked tired as he climbed out of his truck, but broke into his uneven smile when he saw me.

"This isn't fair," I said as I approached him. "You've been working hard all day and I'm sure you're looking forward to the refuge of your home and not one more problem."

"Don't apologize," he told me.

I suspect he thought I was there to cry on his shoulder about another marital crisis in the life of a middle-aged woman. He looked surprised when I told him about Mr. Webster.

"Why don't I get cleaned up and we'll go see our crotchety old friend." He reached down and scratched Ginger, who waited patiently for his attention.

"I've got another idea. While you shower I'll go to the supermarket deli and get something for us to eat. You're probably starved." When he hesitated, I continued, "I'll bet the next thing you were going to do after you cleaned up was to have supper, right?"

"Yeah," he grinned, "right."

By the time I returned with roasted chicken, cold potato salad, and baked beans, two places were set on a cloth-covered table in his tiny kitchen. Tall refreshing-looking glasses of ice tea from his eternal ice tea "well" sat at either place.

He'd put on clean Levi's and a blue denim shirt. His long black hair, loose and damp, hung down to his shoulders. "You look like a rock star," I said. He mimicked a typical disjointed stance as though he was playing an electric guitar. We both laughed but the image of another guitar player with dark hair flashed through my mind.

When we sat down at the table he reached for my hand. "Let's pray for Mr. Webster," he said as he folded my hand in his. I felt raised calluses across his palm. His quiet voice filled the room, not as though he was talking to someone far away, but to a friend about another friend. I didn't feel uncomfortable, but strange, as though I'd been pulled on to another plane with him.

While we ate I completed the details of that morning's events. "He can't go back to that house," I exclaimed. "That place is—is sickening," I said finally, not being able to come up with a more appropriate word.

"We can take my car," I offered as we headed out of the house. "Let's take my truck," he said. He eyed the red Mercedes pulled to the side of the drive. "I wouldn't be comfortable in a car like that unless I'd stolen it, and since I don't do that anymore, let's go in the truck."

We were directed to the second floor, Room 204B, where a nurse, who looked to be a veteran, was seated at the nurse's station. "Family?" she inquired.

"Friends," we replied.

"Well, that's a relief," she snorted. "That's one mean old man in there. I didn't think he'd have any friends."

We entered the room and pulled aside the curtain that partitioned off his bed. "Mr. Webster, I see they've got you all fixed up," Ben said. For a moment he didn't respond but finally he turned toward us and looked at us with bleary eyes. They indeed did have him fixed up. He was bathed and shaven, although not too neatly. No doubt the orderly assigned to the job had his work cut out for him. He wore a greenish-colored hospital gown with little blue flowers on it. His right leg was elevated and a bluish toe protruded from a cast.

He gave muttered responses to the questions we asked. Yes, he knew what happened. No, he wasn't in pain and yes, he'd been told he couldn't go home until he could take care of himself. A look of sadness came over his face when he nodded the answer to that question.

The only real response came when I said, "I'll take care of your cat." His eyes softened and I think he mumbled the words "thank you." It was enough.

CHAPTER NINE

As it turned out Mr. Webster did come home a week later. "Good morning, Mr. Webster," I said when I entered his hospital room the next day. He lay there staring at the ceiling. I knew he heard me but he didn't answer. "How are you feeling?"

"Jack," he muttered.

"I beg your pardon?"

"*Jack*. Don't call me Mr. Webster," he replied, giving a prissy intonation to the "mister." Don't call me Mr. Jack either. Jack, that's my name."

"Suits me, Jack," I replied. "We need to talk. Would you like to sit up?"

I took the grunt to be an affirmative and raised the head of the bed, propping a pillow behind his shoulders. I moved a chair close to the bed and turned it so that I faced him. "I've spoken to your doctors. They tell me you will be here about a week. After that you'll go to an extended care facility until you are able to get around with a walker. How long that takes depends on you."

I looked him in the eye. He stared me down. "What business is this of yours?" His usual bark came through stronger today.

"It seems to me that I'm the only one who cares what happens to you, except for Pastor Ben who is a busy man. I've got more time than he does. The way I see it," I went on, "is that you have two choices. You can either go to rehab, and when they say you can go home, you can get yourself there and go on as you've been. Do you have anybody—any family who would come take care of you? I imagine Pastor Ben will still buy your groceries," I went on when he didn't respond, "but I don't think you'll be able to get in your boat to go buy your whiskey. If you fall in the Caloosahatchee, where would you be?" I knew I was being unfair, but he had to think about it.

"With the manatees," he said quietly.

"Or," I continued as though I hadn't heard him. "I could get your house cleaned up and find people to help take care of you."

"Is this some kind of service you rich women do—to make yourselves feel good?" He stared at me with hostility.

I returned his look. "No," I replied softly, "it's not. I don't even think of myself as a rich woman, but if you want to look at it that way, you can." For several moments there was silence in the room and then he looked away.

"I have some money," he said.

"We'll get to that." I stood up. "Have you been out of bed today? Has the nurse made you walk?" When he didn't answer I headed for the door. "I can find out."

"No."

"No what?" I challenged.

"*No,* I haven't."

"Well, you're going to have that big bundle on your leg for a while and the sooner you learn how to handle it, the better. Let me see if it's all right."

With the help of an aide we walked from the nurse's station to the end of the hall and back. By the time Jack got in bed he was panting and sweating profusely. He looked at me curiously as I helped him settle in. "I know how to do this," I said. "My mother was sick for several months before she died. I come with experience."

"Oh, by the way," I said as I got ready to leave, "what's your cat's name?"

"Cat."

My lips twitched in amusement. "Why does that not surprise me?"

When Louisa arrived Wednesday morning, I was waiting for her with my proposal. "Do you know anybody who can help me with the cleaning and with taking care of Mr. Webster?"

Louisa's smile broke into a wide grin. "Oh, *si, Señora, muy personas.*" She clapped her hands together.

"What's so funny? Why so happy?"

"Nothing like this ever happened in this house before—*nada*." I realized how boring it must be for her to keep cleaning a house in which there were no people. She must have enjoyed it more when Carol was here and the children were young. At seven o'clock on Saturday morning Louisa, two of her daughters, Carlos, and one of his helpers met me at the Cypress House. Carlos had his gardening tools and I had purchased a large supply of cleaning materials and rolls of plastic garbage bags. "We probably won't get it all done today," I explained, not wanting them to be discouraged when they saw what waited for us. Cat waited for us by the door. Just as I was unlocking the simple padlock I'd bought, Ben's pickup truck turned into the driveway. There were three men in the back of the truck and two women sat beside Ben in the cab.

"We've come to help," he said as he hopped out. The others, grinning broadly climbed out too. I stood there with my hand over my mouth.

"Thank you," I said when I trusted myself to speak. We introduced ourselves all around. The two couples were from Ben's church. The other young man, named Scott, who looked to be about sixteen, was certainly distinctive with his orange-spiked hair, pants that barely clung to his hips, and jewelry that pierced his body in odd and multiple places.

"We'll forget about the upstairs," I said, assuming the role of chief. "We'll concentrate on the kitchen, the bathroom, and the room Jack uses in the front of the house. I think we should begin by throwing away as much garbage as we can. If there's anything in question, just put it aside."

Ben set a large orange cooler on the tailgate of his truck, along with a sleeve of paper cups. It was, of course, the eternal iced tea. It was as if someone pointed a finger at us and divided us into teams. Louisa and I started in the kitchen, her two daughters headed for the bathroom, but since they were as round and short as their mother, there wasn't room for both of them. Their giggles sent the rest of us into fits of laughter as their bottoms collided when they tried to scrub the tub and the toilet at the same time. One of them went to clean a second small bedroom we'd discovered. If someone were to stay here, there would have to be another place to sleep. The two women who came with Ben tackled the bed-sitting room. One woman began stripping dirty linens off the bed and stuffing soiled clothes into plastic bags.

The mattress, stained beyond redemption, was pulled out onto the grass. After a quick consultation with Ben, we determined he should go to the Salvation Army store and buy a renovated one. We also decided he should drop Shirley at the Laundromat. I seriously doubted the ancient Maytag in the back room even worked. A ramp would have to be built to the back door so Jack would be able to negotiate his walker. Ben made a list of building materials he would need. I peeled off several bills from the pile of cash I'd gotten the day before.

Carlos and his helper immediately began trimming back the undergrowth around the house. Frank, Shirley's husband was a carpenter who worked with Ben. He began ripping away rotted boards to make room for the ramp. The other man went through the house freeing and opening windows that had been closed for years. Any breath of air was welcome inside the smelly, stuffy house. There was no air conditioner—not even the sign of a fan.

Perspiration ran into our eyes and dripped off our noses as we emptied pail after pail of murky water behind the house. Louisa was up to her elbows in hot soapy water, rewashing every dish I pulled from the cupboards. Moisture lay in the creases of her ever-present smile. She seemed unmindful of the heat.

Scott, I learned, was a juvenile offender entrusted to Ben's custody for the weekend. He didn't seem to mind that it fell his lot to cart the filled bags of trash outside to be taken away. An hour later Ben returned with lumber, and a clean mattress and box springs. He would go back later to pick up Shirley, he said. The Laundromat was busy, and she could only use a few machines.

Although nobody had uttered a word of complaint, at eleven o'clock I announced it was time for a break. The heat was tiring. While Ben went to pick up Shirley, I raced down the street to

Winn Dixie and bought cold cuts, rolls, potato salad, and coleslaw. I picked up an assortment of cookies from the bakery, paper plates, and plastic forks. We gathered under the shade of one of the big trees, sitting on whatever we could find and waited while Ben offered the blessing.

It took the carpenters no time to construct the new ramp. By midafternoon even the handrail was in place and we'd made up fresh beds and put our cleaning supplies away. I pulled Ben aside and pressed some bills into his had. When he started to refuse, I pleaded. "Please, Louisa and her family were hired to help me. If they see you refusing money they would feel bad. Your friends can put it in the collection plate tomorrow if they want to." He nodded in understanding.

"I can't tell you how grateful I am to all of you," I said as they climbed, weary but smiling, into their vehicles. I waved good-bye to them as Cat, who'd escaped the commotion by hiding under the porch all day, came out to rub against my leg. I looked down at his matted hair. "You're on my list too," I said.

Later that afternoon, after a rest and a swim, I walked back over to the Cypress House. Its newly washed windows gleamed at me. If a house can look happy, it looks happy, I thought. I let myself in the back door, gave Cat some food, and walked through the rooms turning on lamps. The freshness of the evening air drifted through the windows adding its soft fragrance to the clean smell. We weren't finished by any means. We had done little with the parlor and hadn't tackled the back room that held the washing machine and served as a pantry. Then, there was the upstairs. I heard the rumble of a diesel engine and the crunch of tires on the driveway. I knew who it was.

"I thought you would be here," Ben said as he got out of the truck.

"Do you want to see how good it looks?" I asked as I held open the door. "Try out the new ramp."

"This is amazing," Ben exclaimed as he walked through the tidy, and if not sparkling, at least reasonably clean house.

"Do you think he'll be pleased or furious?" I asked.

Ben chuckled, "I think he'll be pleased while pretending to be furious."

"I called him a junkyard dog once," I said. I turned to face him. "This has taken up so much of your day, I thought you'd be working on your sermon, or doing whatever it is you do for tomorrow."

"I know what I'm going to say tomorrow. I was wondering," Ben hesitated, "if you're not too tired, is this the time for me to tell you the rest of my story? I have another reason too," he went on before I could answer. "I want Scott to hear it." He motioned toward the truck.

I leaned over to look out the window. I hadn't noticed the boy slumped down in the passenger seat. "No, no I'm not tired," I said, suddenly realizing that it was true. Even if I had been, I owed the Cat Man one. "The view of the sunset is better from my side of the river. Let's go over there. I can provide cheese and crackers and lemonade.

"But, are you sure it's all right?"

"Of course," I said hastily, but stopped when I saw him looking at me. "Why not?" It was the first time I had seen Ben look uncomfortable. He nodded toward the truck. "Scott is doing time for robbery." His voice trailed off.

"Oh," I said as the words sunk in. Kids like Scott only came to houses like mine to rob them. Ben's Abyssinian eyes were fixed on my face as I stood there weighing the possibilities. It certainly wouldn't be happening if Malcolm were here. Rich people only sent their wealth into the ghettos or the barrios, they didn't invite them into their homes. I had not thought about that huge barrier— I'd never had to. Even though Malcolm is a snob, I told myself, but it is his property. "Yes, it's fine. Let's go."

Ben put a hand on my arm. I felt the calluses of a worker's hand, saw the strength of a carpenter's hand, and responded to the warmth of a friend's hand. "Thank you."

I smiled and shook my head. "You're there for everybody, aren't you? Is there enough of you to go around?"

"I hope so."

We took a plate of cheese and crackers, some soft drinks and a thermos of tea down the path to the riverbank. Scott took his hands out of his baggy pants pockets only when I shoved a plate of cheese into his hands for him to carry. On the walk down to the river I talked nervously about what we might see, and thanked him again for his help this morning.

Ben and I sat on the swing and Scott dropped, cross-legged onto the wooden deck. We sipped our drinks and munched our cheese and let the feeling and the sounds of the evening absorb us. The teenager, who'd first sat with his eyes on the glass in his hand, soon focused on mullets leaping from the water and splashing ahead on their way down stream.

"What are those?"

"Mullets," I said.

"I never knew fish could do that," Scott said, amazement in his voice.

"Scott?" Ben waited until Scott looked up at him. "We came over to see Mrs. Steele tonight so she and I could finish a conversation we started a few weeks ago. I thought it might be good for you to hear it too.

"I could wait in the truck."

"I don't think so," Ben said firmly. I'd never heard him use that tone of voice. He placed his elbows on his knees and leaned over to look Scott in the eye. "You know don't you, that I've been in trouble before—lots of trouble?" He waited until Scott nodded.

"In 1983 I went to prison—big time. I was twenty-five years old. By the time I was your age I had already been in and out of Juvie several times. I had even done a couple of stints in the county jail for probation violation. And, there were lots of things I never got caught for." Ben's voice grew husky. "I became a member of a gang. It was easier to be a member than not, the pressure was so great." Ben chuckled, "It was the safest thing to do." Ben pushed up the sleeve of his tee shirt, exposing the triceps of his left arm. Carved into his flesh were two, two-inch high letters *LS* "Los Satanos—The Satans," he said in a quiet voice.

I winced at the ugly raised scars that looked like angry engorged worms against the smooth milk chocolate of his skin. Although Scott sat looking toward the river, Ben waited until Scott raised his eyes to look at the scars. The boy's face was eerily pale in the evening light as his gaze riveted on the disfigurement.

"The gashes took a year to heal," Ben went on, "they were that deep. They were always getting infected, but I never let on how much they bothered me—none of us did—we were too tough."

Ben sat quietly for a few moments. "One night," he went on, "we picked on the wrong man. He fought back. One of my amigos was shot and killed. The rest of us were arrested. Then," Ben emphasized the words carefully, "I repaid society in the way the law extracts payment, behind bars, in prison." He turned to me. "Have you ever been inside a prison?"

"No," I whispered.

"Prisons are awful places. There is so much hate and anger that it's visible. It's visible in thoughts and stares, in words and actions. There's always somebody bigger and tougher and meaner than you. The COs, correction officers, and the guards wait for you to mess up. Well, I was there and I deserved to be—I had put myself there—for eight years with a chance of parole in five. I was determined I was not going to stay there any longer than I had to. So, I learned to keep my mouth shut." Ben snorted, "That was hard because I'd always spouted off. I'd always been a wise ass about everything."

I could not even picture that behavior in the man sitting beside me.

"But," Ben continued, "sometimes good things can happen in prison. There are groups that come into those places to try to help people turn their lives around. That's how I learned about the prison ministry. That's how I got my high school diploma. That's how I found out that God loved me no matter what." The emotion in his voice sent a shiver through me.

"I became a trustee," Ben went on. "That meant I could go out and mow the grass without chains, mop halls, and work in the cafeteria. It also meant I could attend church services and classes.

When I came up for parole at four years and eight months, my heart was in my throat. Cons count their time in digits—days, but nobody counts until you're down to double digits—until the end is in sight. I was convinced I could do all right on the outside. I thought that perhaps with some power helping me, I could stay clean. So, I prayed. There are lots of prayers and promises behind bars, most of which are meaningless, and almost all are selfish. Mine were too.

"The day I learned my parole was granted was one of the happiest days of my life—double digits and counting. None of my friends who were sent up with me made parole. My brother came to pick me up. I had a job waiting, arranged by a group associated with the ministry who help inmates adjust being back on the outside. On my thirtieth birthday I started my new job as a carpenter's helper."

The sun was now just a red disc lying on the river. It colored Ben's face a deep bronze and made Scott's hair look like leaping orange flames. Ben took a deep breath. "Not more than a couple weeks passes before members of my old gang started showing at the little apartment I'd rented. The apartment was really just a pathetic motel room to which a minirefrigerator, a two-burner stove, and a sink had been added, but it was home to me."

Ben shook his head. "They didn't believe me when I told them I was through with that life. They thought they could change my mind. *"Cobarde,"* they called me—coward—but it didn't bother me. At least my insides weren't churning anymore and I wasn't always looking over my shoulder. It felt good.

"One evening two of my friends, Juan and Raul, showed up at my work site. 'Come on Ben, we'll give you a ride home,' they said. 'We never see you anymore.'"

Ben buried his head in his hands. "I don't know why I agreed, except that maybe that was the way it had to be. Juan was driving his souped-up Mustang. I was in the passenger seat and Raul was in the back. However, when we pulled on to the street we did not head toward my place. 'Hey man,' I said. 'Where're you going? You're not taking me home.'"

"'Look, we got this one little thing going—it's a piece of cake.' Out of the corner of my eye I saw that Raul had a gun in his hand. 'We just need someone to stay with the car—that's all you have to do,' he said.

"We were coming up to Route 80. 'Just let me out at the corner,' I said. 'I don't want any part of this.'

"'Hey man,' Juan said, 'it'll be over before you know it. Nobody will ever know you were there.' He reached the corner and looked to the left for oncoming traffic as I reached for the door handle. As he gunned the car onto the highway he grabbed for me. He never saw the tractor trailer that had moved into our lane to pass until it was right in front of us."

I gasped. Scott's eyes were riveted on him as Ben drew a ragged breath and buried his face in his hands. It was silent, except for the night sounds.

After a few moments Ben continued, "Five days later I woke up in the hospital. I couldn't move. I was in traction. I had a broken back, crushed ribs, a punctured lung and this." Ben pointed to the scar across his face. "I floated in and out of this world. From time to time I was aware of what went on around me. A priest came and gave me last rites. Someone told me that my mother brought my daughters to see me. Both of my friends had been killed instantly.

"During one of my lucid moments I remember screaming inside my head, '*God, why did this happen? Just when I was getting my life together, why did this have to happen?*' Then, later I made that promise a lot of dying people make, 'God, if you will just let me live, my life is yours.'"

Tears coursed down Ben's cheeks, and sprang up in mine. My throat seemed to close around a rock. Scott was looking toward the river but I saw his Adam's apple working as he swallowed.

Ben spoke quietly. "That was the most wonderful promise I ever made. I shouldn't have lived. Three men who were involved with the prison ministry came regularly to visit me. They sat, they waited, they prayed. A few weeks later, after it was determined that I was going to live, they, and others, were there for me. For the next year and a half people helped me with my therapy, took care of my needs, and encouraged me." Ben looked at me. Even though it was almost dark, I could feel the heat of his look. "That is why there's enough of me to go around."

We sat for two or three minutes without moving, dealing with the impact of Ben's story. He reached over and put a hand on Scott's shoulder. "Well, my man, we'd better be going. Thanks for listening." Then he reached out and offered a hand to help me to my feet. Silently we gathered up our things and walked to the house.

CHAPTER TEN

As tired as I was, I should have gone to sleep quickly, but my arms and legs ached and my mind would not shut down. There were few days in my life that had been as full of emotion as this one had been. The day Mother and I moved to New York was one of them, when we learned of her cancer and the limited time she had left was another, and the day Philip left me was another.

I remember how excited I was the day Aunt Jean drove Mother and me into Denver to catch the plane that would take us to our new lives in the big city. Yaya, who would not be left behind, sobbed all the long way—four hours—from the ranch to Stapleton Airport. Consoling her only made it worse so we finally stopped talking to her. I did feel sorry for her and was already homesick for the place that had been so familiar to me for twenty years. At the same time, my stomach was fluttering with anticipation for what lay ahead.

The take-off was thrilling, but after that the ride grew monotonous. We saw nothing but murky clouds around us, or the tapestry of the landscape far below us. We settled into several uneventful hours of sitting in cramped seats. I sketched, read a book I'd brought along, and then finally fell asleep. Mother chatted with the stewardess and the passenger across the aisle. From time to time she studied her small notebook with all the information she'd gathered about what we were to do and how we needed to do it. Mari Parker left little to chance.

The descent, the announcements of the stewardess, and the motion of passengers brought me suddenly awake. I strained to catch a glimpse of the Manhattan skyline and the Statue of Liberty. The man across the aisle, who had been charmed by Mother's bright conversation, invited us to share his taxi. We were dropped off at the YWCA where Mari had made reservations for a week. That would give us time to find an apartment and get settled before she reported to her new job at Bloomingdale's, she said. The owners of Neusteadters, where she worked for twenty years, had arranged for the job that awaited her. I never knew how she accomplished that.

A week later, when it was time for me to head off to my first day at the Pratt, Mother gave me an approving look, a big hug, and sent me on my way. "You'll be all right, dear Jess. You know what to do."

The city was so exciting those first few weeks that I still tremble when I think of it. It was during this time that my relationship with my mother irrevocably changed. It was about that time that I started calling her Mari. It wasn't that I didn't think of her as my mother—she would always be my mother but she was more. When our schedules permitted we explored the city by subway, often getting on and riding until we felt like getting off. We got to know many of the ethnic communities, listening to their fascinating languages, learning their ways, and sampling their exotic smelling foods. If it was dangerous, Mari didn't think so. She was surprised at how much Spanish she understood, from the Basque that Yaya and Yayo sometimes spoke.

One day, in a little Irish pub, she was telling me she'd just been offered a promotion at Bloomingdale's and she wasn't sure she was ready for it. I locked my eyes on hers and said, "Dear Mari, you'll be all right. You know what to do." We burst into peals of laughter and everybody turned to look at us. "I've just been promoted," Mari announced to the dozens of pairs of eyes trained on us. Everyone cheered and raised their glasses in our direction.

When our finances permitted we went to museums and exhibits, stood in line for half-price theater tickets, and occasionally ate at expensive well-known restaurants. Our sojourns were sometimes limited by Mari's endurance. To those who didn't know, her limp was barely noticeable. She spent hours on her feet and, although she never told me, I knew she took far too many pain pills. It was denial on my part to pretend not to notice. On our outings she would simply say, "Don't you think it's time to go home?" and I would agree.

After I graduated from the Pratt Institute and had pounded the streets with my portfolio, I finally got a job with an advertising firm. Among their clients were several mail-order catalogues. It was my job to set up pages that went to print. It didn't bother me that I was at the bottom of the pay scale. I was, after all, only twenty-four years old. I was prepared to work hard and work my way up. I'd had a good teacher; I had seen Mari do it often. We began talking of moving into a nicer apartment, in a better neighborhood.

One day I came home from work and found her sitting at the kitchen table with sheets of paper spread before her. Figures were scribbled all over them. "Oh, Jess honey, you're just the person I wanted to see," she exclaimed.

"Just who else do you want to see that would be unlocking this door and walking in?" I teased as I walked over and gave her a hug. "What's this?"

"Oh, there's nothing wrong," she assured me. "There's something we need to discuss." She handed me several photographs. One of them was a shot of a storefront. The sign on the awning over the door read, "Bonnie's Boutique." Other photographs showed interior views of women's clothing and accessories. The business was for sale. Bonnie, it seems, had married and become pregnant. Now her interests lay elsewhere.

"This opportunity just fell into my lap," Mari exclaimed, her rich brown eyes dancing with excitement. "The location is great, just a half block off of Fifth Avenue, and the rent is not out of this world. If we use ten thousand dollars of our savings, we would still have several thousand left for emergencies. With the business as collateral, I'm sure I can get a loan. Bonnie is willing to work out a payment scale. What do you think?" She grabbed my hands. "Can we do it?"

There was only one answer. "Of course," I said.

Mari jumped up, kicked off her shoes, and grabbed my hands. "Let's go see it, shall we? There's a wonderful little restaurant around the corner. We can grab dinner there."

My mother was a small woman—five feet and a couple of inches. I was several inches taller, but she always wore the highest of heels so as we stood in front of the green-canopied store, we were almost the same height. We had some of the same features, the same dark hair and large expressive eyes, but her eyes were a warm milk chocolate brown and mine were smoky gray. While my frame was slender and athletic, Mari's, though small, was curvy. She was not afraid to dress innovatively, or put together the same kind of wardrobe for her customers.

"It means," Mari said over dinner, "that we won't be able to move for a while. Of course we'll have to change the name and the look of the shop."

"And what will that be?" I asked, knowing she already had something in mind.

"Classy Lady," she announced. "We'll move to more upscale styles. You can even design for us." Sure, I thought.

I kept my job, added my paycheck to our mutual account, and helped out at the shop when I had time. Within a couple of years Classy Lady was the chic boutique Mari had envisioned: new storefront, new logo, new interior, and new fashions. It was after Philip came into and went out of my life that Mari encouraged— no—prodded me into designing clothes for the shop. I enrolled for a year's study at the Institute of Fashion and Design.

The only time I remember Mari becoming really upset with me was about Philip. The only time she tried to give me advice was about Philip. I didn't listen. There were never a lot of rules; I was after all, an adult. There was never "I told you so." There was only "You know what to do," except I didn't do it.

Friday night after work, several of my friends and I decided to go over to a club in SoHo to listen to a new group we'd heard about. It was called The Eye of the Hurricane. There were five guys and a girl singer and they were good. They had played together in college, someplace in upstate New York, and had worked their way to the Big Apple. The name of the band reflected their music, from soft rock of the "eye" with a lot of mood, to a beat that gained hurricane force in its intensity.

After the first set, I excused my self to go to the ladies' room. As I was coming down the hall, Philip, the lead guitarist literally materialized in front of me. "Hi there," he said.

"Hello," I stammered. "I like your music."

"Do you?" He actually sounded surprised. He was maybe four or five inches taller with a muscular torso that tapered to a narrow waist and even narrower hips and long legs. His hair, thick and dark, was cut evenly just below his ears. He wore bangs and could easily have passed for Robin Hood. I envisioned him in a plumed hat, vest, and breeches with a quiver of arrows on his back. "I've been watching you," he said.

"I don't believe it."

"Why not?" His question seemed serious and not flirtatious, as though he really wanted to know.

"Because I don't think you can see past those lights," I said.

"Well, you're wrong. After a while you learn to look through the lights. And yes, I think you like our music."

As I started to move past him, he put a hand on my arm. There was heat I'd never felt from another touch. The tremor I felt was not unlike the shock I used to receive from electric fences on the ranch. "Some of us usually get together after hours to unwind. Would you join us? I'll see that you get home."

The rational portion of my brain kicked in. Tomorrow was Saturday; I didn't have anything special planned, but I said, "No, I'm with a group. They'll expect me to go with them."

"Do you always do what people expect?"

"It works for me," I replied.

We heard the other band members back on stage, tuning their instruments. "Uh-oh," he said as he looked over his shoulder.

"I've still got to go to the little boy's room. Do me a favor, would you? Come back tomorrow night. I need to find out how to get in touch with you, and I know you're not going to tell me now."

"We'll see."

"One more thing. What kind of white wine are you drinking?" he asked.

I gaped at him. Either he could really see past the lights, or he was a good guesser. As the band went into the bars of their first song, a cocktail waitress set a glass of Sauvignon Blanc in front of me.

The following evening Mari and I paid our cover and were ushered to a table near the stage. Sitting in the center of the white linen-covered table was a silver wine cooler and a chilling bottle of the same wine I'd had the night before. Propped against the cooler was an envelope and inside was a card that read simply, "Thanks for coming."

Mari's eyebrows rose in question. "He seems very sure of himself," she commented.

Now, with only the sounds of night creatures and an occasional automobile in the distance, I remembered the beauty of that evening. In my twenty-eight years I'd never felt the way Philip made me feel. Any crush I may have had was a mere tickle compared to the feeling that flooded me when he smiled at me or touched me. The pain and hurt came later.

Mari thoroughly enjoyed the evening, but during the cab ride home she was quiet. As I undressed for bed I heard her in the kitchen. Minutes later she stood at my bedroom door with two mugs of hot chocolate in her hands. "I think you fell in love tonight," she said quietly. Catching my eye as she handed me the mug, she gave a crooked little smile. "Thank you for sharing this evening with me."

"Is this what it feels like?" I whispered.

"I imagine if the look on your face is any indication."

"Did you ever feel this way?"

"Yes," she murmured, looking down at her hands cupped around the cocoa.

"About my father?"

Her eyes rose to mine; eyes so inexpressibly sad. "Yes, about your father—only ever about your father." Before I could pose another question she rushed on. "Jess darling, you have a life to live. Your happiness means everything to me, but as you follow your heart, don't think you have to do anything because of me. But please," she pleaded, "if Philip—or anyone—ever hurts you, *please* come to me." She held my gaze until I nodded. Her concern frightened me.

"Did my father hurt you?"

"Well," Mari said as she reached for my empty mug, "it's time we got some sleep." It was as though a book slammed shut.

"Mother, why won't you ever talk about my father?" Tears of frustration made my voice raspy.

"I can't."

For the first year I was sensible. Philip's schedule was so much different from mine. He went to bed at five in the morning and slept until noon. He and the other Hurricanes rehearsed for two or three hours most afternoons. Then they took care of necessary errands like normal people: banking, doing their laundry, shopping. Toni, the singer was married to Carl, the drummer. I was never sure that was her real name, because her husband called her Gert. I was convinced Carl was his real name; he looked like a Carl. Two of the other members had wives who showed up occasionally. One, the steel guitar player, had three small children. The sixth member, Ward, was Philip's cousin. They were from Rochester, New York, and had roomed together at Syracuse University where they'd met the others.

When the Hurricanes weren't performing, Philip spent his time with me. He'd meet me after work then we usually stop by the Classy Lady where he and my mother charmed the customers. The Robin Hood in my life would steal a brooch from one mannequin or a scarf from another display and convince some "poor" client it was just what she needed to make her outfit complete. After the shop closed, the three of us would often go out for dinner or pick up something to eat in our apartment.

Philip was thirty-two years old, and his band was taking the city by storm. He had an apartment in SoHo, a nice third-floor walk-up with large floor-to-ceiling windows and skylights. There was even a little balcony garden where we could sit and watch the pulse of the vibrant city below us. The apartment was actually one huge room with a kitchen in one corner. In another, there was an elevated platform that served as a stage where the Hurricanes sometimes practiced. A comfortable suede sofa and chairs, clustered around a huge wooden door, turned coffee table sat in the middle of the room facing the windows. The bathroom was the only part of the apartment that was fully enclosed. Philip's bedroom was against another wall and was separated by a series of curtains. It was here that Philip first made love to me. I was not a virgin, but I certainly was not accomplished in the art of making love. Being handled by boys with "high school hormones" does not list well on a résumé of sexual experiences. Most of my men friends at Pratt were only just that—friends. Philip was a good teacher.

At first I lived with Mari, concentrated on my work and only went to Philip's gigs on Friday and Saturday nights. I usually spent the weekends with him. He'd wanted me to move in, but I hadn't been ready for that.

Several months later the Hurricanes went on the road. I was miserable. One weekend I even traveled to Philadelphia to be with him. I performed my work with little interest, refused invitations for get-togethers with friends, and when I wasn't helping out at Classy Lady, I stayed in the apartment. As enthusiastic as Mari was about her success, I often caught a wisp of sadness in her smile.

When Philip called me to tell me they were heading back to New York, my world came together again. I was waiting for him, bag and baggage, in his apartment when he arrived early on a Monday morning. As different as our schedules were, we made them work the best we could. I was dragging myself through my workdays because, when I didn't go with him, I waited up for him to come home. I was getting only a few hours sleep. Makeup couldn't cover the circles under my eyes, and every time I stepped on the scales there was another pound gone. Mari was always cordial toward Philip but I sensed coolness in her attitude toward him. She never said anything to me.

When the band went on the road again, I quit my job and went with them. I couldn't stand to be separated from Philip. To me he was excitement, he was tenderness, he made me laugh, and I loved him. I waited for him to mention a more permanent relationship. After all, four of the band members were married. When we'd been together almost two years, I finally brought up what I learned was that dreaded "M" word.

Philip began treating me differently. I was being introduced to his mood swings, but at the time I didn't know it. I took the blame for them. One night he told me he didn't want me to go to the club with him. I couldn't believe it. "Why not," I demanded. "What have I done?"

"Don't you understand? I need space. Every time I turn around you're there. I haven't been able to write any new songs, and I need to work the crowd so the bookings keep coming." He looked at me with total disgust, grabbed his guitar, and made a point of slamming the door behind him. When he came home at 4 a.m., I was not asleep but I lay hugging my side of the bed, my back to him. He threw down his instrument, shed his clothes, and when he crawled into bed, he didn't touch me. In two minutes he was sound asleep. Four hours later, exhausted, I tiptoed into the kitchen to make coffee.

By one-thirty that afternoon Philip had not wakened. I knew a rehearsal had been scheduled for one o'clock. The sound of the intercom startled me.

"Yes," I whispered into the speaker.

"It's Ward, buzz me in."

I opened the door just as Ward reached our floor. He gave me a penetrating stare, then looked at the bed. "Oh, shit!"

"What's wrong? What's happening?" I heard my voice rising.

Ward ignored me and went straight to the bed. He threw the covers back, exposing Philip's nude body. "Man," he said, "what have you done?" He grabbed Philip by the arm and hoisted him up, threw an arm over his shoulder and half drug him to the bathroom. Moments later I heard the shower and Philip's mumbled protests.

"Jessica," Ward called. I rushed to the bathroom. "Keep an eye on him," he ordered as he took a vial out of his pocket and headed for the kitchen. "Don't let him fall and hit his head." I wondered just how I could keep this one hundred and eighty pounds of dead weight from falling, if he decided to. Steam seeped over the shower door, fogging the window and mirror. I was grateful for the moans and few unrepeatable words I heard.

Ward came back into the room, shoved a glass of water and two pills into my hands. "Hold these." He reached in and turned off the water. "Maybe you should stand over there," he pointed, looking at me for the first time. "There isn't much room in here." I nodded and backed out of the way.

Phil fell against his cousin when he pulled the shower door open. Ward, the bigger man, held on, bracing himself against Philip's weight. He pivoted him around and sat him on the toilet seat. Then, he pulled a towel from the rack and roughly began drying his face, his hair and his shoulders, all the while swearing, "Damn it, man. Damn it."

Ward held his hand out to me. "Pills," he ordered as though speaking to an operating room nurse. He pulled Philip's head back by his hair and threw the pills in his open mouth. "Water." I shoved the glass at him. He poured water into Philip's open mouth, slammed the glass into my hand, and then forced the protesting mouth closed. "Swallow," he commanded. It reminded me of when my grandfather and the ranch hands would force medications down the throats of stubborn sheep.

"Come on, Bud," Ward said in a now-calmer tone as he helped Philip to his feet and awkwardly tucked the towel around his waist as though, crisis passed, modesty somehow mattered.

Wanting to help, I placed Philip's other arm over my shoulder. "Where are we going?"

"Back to bed for now. He'll be better in half an hour. Guess our rehearsal is shot for the afternoon, but he'll be okay for tonight's gig." We steered Philip toward the bed, lay him down and covered

him with a sheet. Ward collapsed into the overstuffed chair. "Got
a beer?" he asked as he ran his hand through his wet hair. The
entire front of his shirt and pants were soaked.

I fetched a bottle from the fridge and handed it to him. "What
happened?" I whimpered. "What's wrong with him?"

Ward stared at me. "He hasn't been taking his meds, has he?"
When he saw my blank look he shook his head and swore. "You
don't know? He hasn't told you that he has to take medication—
he hasn't told you about his problem?"

I shook my head. "What kind of medication?" I felt both stupid
and hurt.

"Antidepressants—Lithium, Effexor, Neurontin—depending
on which way he's going; it's a fine line, really." Ward set his beer
on the floor and put his head in his hands.

"Why didn't somebody tell me?" I asked.

"He told me he had." He nodded toward the motionless figure
on the bed. "His mother and my father are sister and brother. I'm
two years older than he, and I guess I've been taking care of him all
his life. When he has someone in his life—like you," he hesitated,
"I try to stay out of it. *I* should have told you."

I'd never been around anybody with problems like this. I tried
to take it all in. "What's wrong with him? What's it called?"

"Bipolar personality. He's manic depressive. He's hypomanic
most of the time, meaning he's not off-the-wall manic. His behavior
is controlled by his medications, but from time to time he goes
into depression—a really dark funk that can last for weeks—
especially when he doesn't do his meds. Fooled you." He curled
his fingers and pointed his forefinger at me, firing an imaginary
shot, and then he grinned a sad little smile. "I would suggest," he
said as he grew serious, "that you leave for a while." When I started
to protest, he held up his hand.

"You're a wonderful person and I know he cares for you, but
until he's stabilized, it might be better."

"How could it be better?" I protested. "He'll think I've
abandoned him."

"He'll be embarrassed—especially knowing that you've seen

him this way. I'd move in with him. I've done it before." Ward furrowed his eyebrows together and stared. "Watch him like a hawk." I laughed at his funny, burley face with teenage acne scars.

"You could tell me what to do," I persisted.

"It's your call."

"What happens to the band when he's like this?"

"Mostly we cover for him—make him look good. A few times we've had to cancel an engagement."

So, I stayed. That was the beginning of the end, although I didn't know it. At Classy Lady, Mari's concerned look followed me. For the first time, I didn't confide in her. I should have. It was the only time I ever knew her to be really angry with me. "Why can't you tell me what's wrong?" she yelled, her small fists balled up at her side. You know you don't have to be in this by yourself."

Some days seemed to be the way they had been. However, there were many that were not. I insisted that we talk about this illness. He became furious at that identification and insisted that it was not an illness, but a problem. I learned to call it a "problem." I began to dread those erratic highs. Sometimes he apologized for his behavior. Other times he didn't even seem to be aware of it. My relationship with Mari was strained.

I soon learned the warning signs that indicated his mood changes and reacted accordingly. I wonder now, if he enjoyed, or even knew, the power he had over me.

Several weeks later the band had an engagement in Trenton, New Jersey. They were going to be gone for four nights, Thursday through Sunday. Philip didn't invite me to go along, so I stayed behind. I moved like an automaton through my duties at Classy Lady, which was now the only job I had.

I didn't hear Philip's key in the door until five o'clock Monday morning. I pretended to be asleep as he fell into bed beside me. When he woke just after noon I made sandwiches that we ate on the balcony. It was mid-May and New York was dressed in her finest spring garments of bight green leaves, adorned with blossoms of various colors and scents—from the bright yellow of forsythia to the deep pink of crab apple, to the yet more vibrant redbud trees.

The air was fresh, not yet tainted with the heat of summer, and the sun was warm. Irritations of winter passed. We heard people call to one another or laugh in friendly conversation.

Philip seemed relaxed as he sat with his long legs crossed on the balcony railing. "That was good," he said of the sandwich as he picked the remaining crumbs off his plate. As I got up to take his plate he reached for my arm, pulling me around behind him and lacing my arms across his bare chest. "You're so good to me," he murmured into my hair, and then he patted my arm and let me go.

The following Friday the group headed out to Elizabeth for a three-day gig. Although I expected him, he didn't come home that night either. I spent most of Saturday looking out the long windows of the apartment. As dusk settled I couldn't stand it any longer. I showered and dressed in one of the outfits Philip liked and headed for the subway. Although it was several train changes, at least I could be there for the second set.

At the door I paid my cover and was looking for an empty place when the band went into their break vamp. Philip announced that they would be back in fifteen minutes.

He laid down his instrument and bounced off the stage. I waited to see where he was going. Then I saw. He headed for a table near the front of the room. Placed in the center was a napkin-draped bottle of wine in a cooler. He bent over, resting his palms on the table. The girl sitting there looked up and smiled. Although I was clear across a noisy, crowded room, I could hear as plain as if she'd whispered in my ear, "How did you know what kind of wine I was drinking?"

Humiliation flooded me in a wave of heat. I forced back a knot of bile in my throat as I rushed out the door. I struggled to catch my breath as I waited for the train. I felt that my chest was being crushed. The ride back to the city in the nearly empty train was a blur. In the apartment I crawled into bed, hugging my knees with my arms, and allowed the desolate feeling of emptiness to pull me into its void.

Philip did not come back that day or the next. Is this the way sick people treat people, I wondered as I roamed around the apartment, tidying up the room for lack of something better to do. Occasionally I looked in the fridge for something to eat, but closed the door each time a queasy feeling rose in my stomach. Most of the time I kept vigil at the window. The phone rang twice, but I didn't answer. The machine picked up one call from the Hurricane's agent about a booking and the other call left only silence and a click.

Late Tuesday afternoon the door buzzer sounded. Philip had a key. Ward had a key, and I didn't want to talk to anybody else, so I didn't answer it. Suddenly there was a strong knock of the door. "Manager," a voice called. "Manager. Are you there?" I heard a key turn in the lock. A sandy-haired non-descript man I'd seen around the building was standing there. Beside him was the lovely, petite woman I called Mari, my mother. My tears began to fall.

Mari, ever gracious turned to him. "Thank you so very much, Mr. Carson. It's all right." *Mr. Carson? Mr. Carson,* I thought, *I've been in this building over a year and I never bothered to learn his name. Leave it to Mari.*

As he closed the door Mari came to me with outstretched arms, and I fell into them. She led me to the sofa and simply held me and stroked my hair until I'd cried myself empty.

"Do you want to tell me?" she asked. I told her. "Do you want to go home?" I nodded. Together we packed up my belongings, which really weren't all that much. Mari called a taxi, and then prevailed on the driver to help us carry my things down several flights of stairs.

Philip began calling Mari's apartment on Thursday. I didn't answer the phone. He left messages, "Jess, I need to talk to you. I need to explain." Friday morning he showed up at Classy Lady. They had an engagement upstate that weekend, he explained to Mari. Could she persuade me to talk with him?

"I don't think so," Mari answered. "It's not the right time. Maybe when you get back."

For several days I did little but stay in bed. I tossed and turned all night, falling asleep near daylight, then not wake up until afternoon. When Mari got home she would either bring food with her or make us something light and insist that I eat. Other than that she left me alone. She seemed to know that when I was through licking my wounds, I would allow them to begin healing. And that's what I did.

One afternoon when I woke up and looked in the mirror, I saw a woman who looked as old as my mother. My complexion was the shade of coal dust, my eyes were sunken, and my usually thick and buoyant hair was oily and limp. I glared at the image in the mirror, daring her to speak. She didn't. After a moment I saluted her and said, "Welcome to the world, Baby Girl." I had supper ready when Mari got home that night. She took one look and me, threw out her arms and said, "You're back!"

I never saw Philip again. He called the following week. I squeezed the pain in my heart so tight, it dared not speak as I thanked him for a lovely interlude and wished him well. A couple of years later I read in one of the theatrical rag sheets that the group called the Eye of the Hurricane had broken up, and yet later I saw an obituary in the *Village Voice* that Philip Marlett had died at age thirty-seven. I never learned from what.

Red streaks were already appearing in the morning sky and birds began their preludes for the day before I fell asleep. I thought I heard my mother's voice saying, "You did what you had to do." I didn't wake up until afternoon.

CHAPTER ELEVEN

W hat I had to do, or thought I had to do Tuesday, was to bring a cantankerous old man home from the hospital and get him settled in his now-neater-and-cleaner home. Monday, Louisa and I finished cleaning the downstairs as the May temperatures climbed toward ninety degrees. Droplets of salty perspiration ran down my forehead and stung my eyes. I glimpsed my image in the mottled silver mirror in the parlor. A tall forty-something-year-old woman in stained clothes looked back at me. Her dark, wavy hair separated itself into damp ringlets around tired, haunted eyes. No hint of a breeze stirred curtains at the open windows and there wasn't an air conditioner—not even the sign of a fan.

How could someone exist, I wondered, summer after summer in the stifling enclosure of this ancient house full of foul odors? Carlos stopped by late in the afternoon to install a waist-high railing that ran down the hall from the bedroom to the bathroom. A few minutes later I was tearing down Palm Beach Boulevard toward Cleveland Avenue to buy window fans. Even though the top was down on my little red convertible I cranked up the air-conditioning. A woman possessed, though I was, I couldn't bring myself to buy an air conditioner. That was too foreign to Mr. Webster's nature.

The following afternoon a medical transport brought him home. I was waiting at the back door when the van pulled into the driveway. Jack's face was stoic as the attendant pushed the wheelchair up the newly installed ramp, but I could see his eyes absorbing the changes. His gnarled, age-spotted hands gripped the arms of his chair. Just as he was rolled into the kitchen, Cat appeared, gave a low meow and jumped into his lap. Jack's hand automatically reached for the scruffy neck. He quickly lowered his head but not before I saw wetness rim his eyes and the movement of his throat as he swallowed. Cat pressed himself against his master's chest and rode with him into his newly cleaned quarters. It was a poignant homecoming.

Kirk, the attendant who'd accompanied his patient in the ambulance, gave me explicit instructions for Jack's daily exercises. Then, as a final act, he insisted that he escort Mr. Webster to the bathroom. Jack protested loudly that he didn't have to "pee." What have I gotten myself into? I wondered. It wasn't that I couldn't help Jack with his personal needs—bathe him, clean up after him— I had done it all for my mother. But, here I was, a woman at loose ends with nothing better to do than take over an old man's life against his wishes.

When we were alone I quietly peeked into his room. He sat in his old easy chair with his casted leg elevated on a padded stool. The new floor fan circulated warm air around the room. Cat was curled up in his lap and I could hear a contented purr. I expected him to be dozing, but the old man sat staring out the window at the rows of long neglected trees, seeing what, I couldn't guess.

"Would you like some ice tea?" I asked. When I didn't get a response I went into kitchen and poured a glass for myself. "Would you like a shot of Jim Beam?" I asked as I walked back into his room. His head jerked in my direction as his eyes focused on my hands. "That was mean," I laughed, as I pulled a chair across the room and sat in front of him. "There's no bourbon in the house. I just wanted to get your attention. Sooner or later we have to talk."

"I don't."

"Well, I'll talk then. There are some things that need to be said." I sat my glass of tea on the floor and clasped my hands together as I took a deep breath. "I know I haven't any right to do the things I've done. I've interfered in your life, trespassed on your property, and made decisions that weren't mine to make.

"That morning when I saw Cat yowling at the door, I knew something was wrong. I could have kept on walking. Even when I looked through the door and saw you on the floor I could have just gone and reported it to the authorities and let them take care of it.

You probably would be in some rehab facility, and maybe that's how it will end up anyway—if not this time—some time."

I stood up and walked to the window. "I couldn't understand how anyone could live this way," I said as I faced him. "I can't believe there is no one who cares about the way you live. Oh, I know Pastor Ben and the people at his church have tried to help you—they're the ones who helped Carlos and Louisa and me clean up this place. You must know Louisa and Carlos," I continued, "they've been with the Huntington family for years." There was ever the slightest nod.

"When I first started walking past here several months ago, I was attracted to this house. It must have been lovely at one time," I said softly, "the groves too. My husband tells me that your groves and the Huntington groves covered this whole area. And, I believe, too, that underneath that leathery crust of hostility you've created to keep people away from you, there is a real person." When there was no response I kept talking. "I don't know what happened to you, but I do know that life isn't always fair."

"What do you know about life, girlie?" The hard, guttural words startled me as I stared at angry, red-rimed eyes under bushy brows.

I drew in my breath. "Maybe more than you know. I think," I said hesitantly, "that you've spent much of your life avoiding life." Our eyes locked before Jack lowered his. I no longer heard Cat's contented purr.

I dropped into the chair. "I'm sorry. I'm so sorry. This is no way to help you recover. I don't even know what I'm doing here, or why I care. You have every right to order me out of your house. But," I hesitated, "I don't know how you would manage." I waited, but he sat there looking perplexed.

"I have arranged," I said finally, "for Carlos to spend the nights with you. We've cleaned up the bedroom on the other side of the bathroom. He can sleep there. A home health care nurse will come each morning to do your breakfast and lunch and help you bathe. I will come in the afternoon. I'll be here in the afternoon to help you with your walking and your exercises and make your supper. I can cook a little," I finished with a half smile.

Suddenly the frown on his forehead grew slack and Jack's face seemed defeated and sad. He took a deep breath that spoke of resignation. I too, suddenly felt exhausted. "Maybe you'd like to rest now. Do you need anything? Pain medication?" I stood up. "Would you like to get in bed?" He lifted one hand and waved me away. His fingers trembled as he lowered them to his lap.

Pastor Ben's truck pulled into the driveway just as I lifted the chicken off the grill. I hadn't seen or spoken with him since last Saturday evening when Scott and I listened to his story. Emotions from that night flooded through me again. I felt a discomfort I couldn't explain. He walked up the new ramp in his sweaty work clothes, grinning his reassuring one-sided grin. "How's the patient?"

"I'm not sure," I replied, lifting my eyebrows. "He's resting— I think. He won't talk to me."

"Is it all right if I look in on him?"

"Of course. Maybe it'll help. Will you stay for dinner?"

"I didn't plan it, but I was hoping you would ask."

At my insistence Jack agreed to take a pain pill. While I served up our plates, Ben found two old TV trays for us, and positioned the rented hospital table in front of Jack's chair. Over plates of grilled chicken, potato salad, coleslaw, and warm rolls, Ben, in his quiet voice, blessed our food and thanked God for Mr. Webster's recovery. Not for the first time, on hearing the converted Ben converse with his God, I felt a soft covering of peace, like a gauzy mantle of protection descend upon me. I hoped the old man, into whose house we'd intruded could feel it too.

When Carlos arrived, Ben insisted that he would share the night shift, explaining that Carlos had a family. After a lively discussion, some of which was in Spanish, they agreed that Ben would stay Monday through Thursday and Carlos come on weekends so the pastor could tend to his flock. That evening we established a schedule that lasted through the month of May and into June. The nurse I'd hired came at six o'clock to give Ben time to go home and feed his dog and cat and get ready for work.

Bea was a no-nonsense person of hefty size and muscular arms, and a veteran at caring for patients. By the time I arrived in the afternoon, Jack had been bathed for the day, an occurrence of which, I'm sure he had no recent acquaintance. Laundry was done, clothes and linens coaxed clean in the ancient Maytag, and the kitchen cleaned and tidy after the noon meal.

While natives and transplanted Floridians took the heat in stride, ordering their lives around air-conditioned houses and cars, swimming pools, and screen-enclosed Florida rooms, I struggled. I vowed I would get used to it but I was reluctant to leave Malcolm's air-conditioned house at midday. I still coveted my morning walk and had taken over the job of feeding the feral cats. The tiny dependent kittens of a few months ago were now self-reliant, lanky felines, aggressively establishing their order of dominance.

I made it a game to seek out different routes and had grown familiar with all the surrounding areas. I knew which house had schoolchildren and what time the bus stopped at their front door. I made acquaintance with resident pets, and lean cows grazing in the brush. I petted the saddle horses that trotted to the fence to observe me. Even the guard dogs, protectors of their property, who initially, with ferocious, salivating barks, skidded against their chain-link fences, now paid me little attention.

The following week I went to the hospital with Jack for his checkup. His cast was replaced with a lighter, more manageable "air cast," which he would probably wear through the summer. Without his daily supply of bourbon his color improved. His disposition didn't. I imagined withdrawal from what I supposed to be many years of drinking must be painful.

Following our visit to the hospital the doctor called me aside and informed me that Jack had an elevated blood sugar, enormously high cholesterol, and that he really should have his right hip replaced. "I'm not his keeper," I wanted to shout, but I knew that I had forced myself into that role. So, in spite of his angry outbursts and reluctant cooperation, Ben, Bea, Carlos, and I became the team that was going to make Jack Webster a healthier man by controlling his diet, his exercise, and his hygiene. He threatened us but stopped just short of ordering us off his property. When I suggested that Louisa and I clean the upstairs he absolutely exploded. "*You will not go upstairs,*" he thundered. "*Leave my house alone.*"

One afternoon, following a sudden summer rain shower, which cooled the air, I walked around the periphery of the property. There seemed to be areas of healthy trees and on others leaves were sparse and a pale green wrinkled scab covered much of their trunks and limbs. Isolated trees totally choked by vines, were void of leaves and fruit. Ripe oranges and grapefruit hung heavy on limbs, and other fruit in varying stages of decay, lay rotting underneath the trees.

At the back of the property, I cut through the grove, following a well-worn path. Droplets of water that had collected on the waxy leaves cooled my arms as I brushed against them. Something could be done with this grove, I thought. What a waste! The path broke through near the tool shed behind the house and I looked up to see Jack standing in the driveway. "Well, I guess it takes me trespassing again to bring you outside," I said before he could scold me. "I'm going to get a glass of tea and sit out here. Will you join me?" I indicated some plastic lawn chairs Ben had found in the shed and placed under the tree near the back door. We sometimes sat and talked there in the evenings after supper. Jack always refused to join us.

By the time I returned with two frosty glasses of tea, Mr. Webster had lowered himself into one of the chairs. Cat was perched on the other. When I laughed and shooed the cat away, I saw the faintest of smiles at the corners of Jack's lips.

"When was the last time you harvested your fruit?" I asked.

To my surprise, he answered. "About fifteen years ago."

"Why did you stop?"

"Why do you think, girlie?' It dawned on me that he had never called me by my name.

"My name is Jessica," I said. "I don't like being called 'Girlie' any more than you liked being called 'Mr. Jack.' I don't mind even being called Jess—it's what I was called when I was growing up— but I really don't like to be called Jessie, okay?" He sensed my anger. His eyes were trained on me, and what I thought I saw, was a look of approval.

"Why did you stop?" I asked quietly.

"Couldn't do it anymore. Didn't have any help."

"And nothing's been done since then?"

"Oh, there's a crew that'll come in and cart away the good juice oranges in March."

"That didn't happen this year. I didn't see anybody here," I persisted.

"I didn't call them."

Mentally I calculated that Jack would have been fifty-seven years old when he stopped working the groves. Not old, but old enough to have the body reject daylong labor, if nights, and perhaps days, were spent drinking.

"Could this grove be reclaimed?" I asked after a while. When Jack frowned in my direction I repeated, "Could they?"

"Most of them."

"What would you have to do?"

"Now wait a minute, gir—Je-ssi-ca," he formed the word slowly. "Don't go getting any ideas." He shook his finger at me just as Ben's truck pulled into the driveway. Ginger sat on the seat beside him. Now, when Ben came for the evening he brought her with him. Cat, seeming to recognize her limitations, tolerated the three-legged dog. They touched noses.

"Hey," I said, jumping up. "I haven't done anything about supper."

"No hurry," Ben replied. "I could go get Chinese."

"I was going to grill hamburgers," I said. "It won't take long. Maybe Jack could walk with you out to the shed and show you what equipment he has for farming his groves."

I laughed as Ben looked at me in surprise, his black brows forming question marks. Jack shrugged his shoulders and struggled to his feet. There was a trace of a smile at the corners of his mouth. The lowering sun bathed the groves in a golden glow, and the scent of citrus was euphoric as my heart sang an anthem of joy.

CHAPTER TWELVE

I f anyone had told me six months ago, or even two months ago, that I would still be here in southern Florida, in the heat of summer, spending much of my time taking care of a contentious old man, and obsessed with neglected and diseased orange groves, I could not have even imagined it. I stopped trying to explain it to Malcolm during his weekly phone calls. "I don't understand you, Jessica. You don't have to do that. Hire someone if you want to do a good deed." His icy words, even nine thousand miles away, let me know that he expected the wife of Malcolm Steele to behave in a certain way.

"If you insist on staying there," he said, "I can arrange for you to join one of the country clubs. You could meet people with whom you'd have more in common." I bit my tongue to keep from calling him a snob. Truth be known, I didn't understand my behavior either.

Even my light-hearted conversations with Christine lacked their old ease. "Why are you still there?" she would shout into the earpiece. "How can you stand the heat? Are you still sketching? Why not? What about your clients?" I could visualize her running her fingers through her unruly, rust-colored hair in frustration.

"I am sketching," I told her the last time we talked.

"Oh. Jess, that's wonderful!" she exclaimed. "I was worried about you."

I hadn't told her my sketches were of a ninety-year-old house, of misshapen orange trees, strangled by Virginia Creeper, or of fat, sassy, horned Florida cattle grazing among palmettos. I didn't describe the sketches tucked in the back of my pad of an old man with a craggy profile, prominent chin, and startling coal gray eyes beneath bushy brows. And, I certainly didn't describe the man I really wanted to draw, who was sitting across from me now in the deepening twilight of the evening of our longest day. I wanted to commit to paper his distinctive profile, his high cheekbones, and angular nose that must have come from some Aztec ancestor several generations ago.

Most of the other Hispanic men I'd seen in this part of the country were short and slight with deep brown skin and either flat or hawklike faces. Ben's features and height held him apart. I wanted to capture the intensity of his expression when he preached on a Sunday morning, and the softness of his look when he petted Ginger who now lay beside his chair. I wanted to secure on paper the way he looked with his tool belt strapped around his hips, sweaty and dirty after a day's work.

"What did you find in the shed?" I whispered. I had barely been able to wait until we finished dinner and Jack was settled in for the evening. Today had been a milestone. I had seen the first spark of interest in an otherwise hostile face.

Ben chuckled. I don't really know. Jack pointed out a spraying device, a stack of crates, and an old tractor with a flat tire. "I don't think there's much there but I don't know, I never worked in the groves." He looked at me curiously. "What's happening, Jessica?"

"I want to reclaim this grove," I said with passion rising in my voice.

"Why?"

Words I could never say to Malcolm or to Christine tumbled out. "Because this is all such a waste—this house, these trees." I spread my hand to encompass my surroundings. "The fruit's just been left to rot. Even the old man inside has been neglected for so long. What if I hadn't found him?" Ginger raised her head at the intensity of my voice.

"But you did," he said quietly.

"I did," I declared emphatically. "I did, and I've forced my way into his life. Isn't there some culture that believes that when you save a person's life you become responsible for him? Lately I've been thinking about my life too. I can't find any real purpose there either. I guess," I continued, shaking my head. "When I married

Malcolm I didn't think that far into the future. Oh, I can use the excuse that I was lonely after my mother died. I have only casual friends, and an aunt who is two thousand miles away. I guess I wanted to be important to somebody. Malcolm treated me special at first." I leaned forward, clasping my hands between my knees and staring at the cone of light at my feet, cast by light coming through the kitchen door. "I don't think I was cut out to be a rich man's wife. I don't know how to play the role."

I raised my eyes to meet Ben's gaze. I saw his jaw working, but he didn't say anything. "I hate dressing up—hard to believe isn't it—someone who designs clothes for a living. Malcolm loves buying me expensive clothes. I wear them to please him. I don't even wear the elaborate fashions I design. I guess I played the role for Mari, too. *She* loved fashion and was always aware of how she looked— even when she was sick. I guess the clothes I designed were for her, or someone like her—not for me.

"I'm more comfortable like this." I spread my hands to indicate my wrinkled blouse, dirty shorts, and scruffy sneakers.

He smiled, "This is the way I know you."

"Mari devoted her whole life to my well-being, but she's gone and I don't want to play role any more."

"You can use your talents in other ways," Ben encouraged.

"Tonight for the first time there was a hint of interest in Jack's eyes. It's so sad to think that his whole life's been wasted. I know he loves this place," I declared emphatically, "yet he seems intent on destroying it. I think I can change that."

"That's the way the Savior feels about us. He patiently looks for that spark in us and waits to ignite it," Ben said quietly. Recognition dawned in those words but I wasn't ready to go there.

"I need to find out what has to be done," I continued. "I know there are dead and diseased trees that have to be removed. I could start with just cleaning up. I'm sure I could find people to help me if Jack will just go along with it."

"I can help you," Ben said as he stood up.

"But you already have so much to do. You take care of so many people."

"No, I mean I could help you line up people. I know lots of people who have spent their lives working the groves. Immokalee is full of them."

"Would you?" I jumped up and grabbed him by the shoulders. Through the thin texture of his tee shirt I felt the engorged scar of his brand, L.S. My fingers recoiled as if they'd been burned.

In a flash Ben grabbed my wrist and held it tightly. I felt the strength in his hands—carpenter's hands that used a hammer and held a saw, day in and day out. He waited until I looked at him. "Don't be afraid of that," he said with more ferocity in his voice than I'd ever heard. "And don't ignore it. It's part of who I am. It's my reminder—my testimony. If I am to be your friend, Jessicacita, you have to accept that." With his other hand he pushed up the sleeve of his shirt, exposing the raised angry scar in the scant light from the house. Ever so gently, with the hand that petted disabled dogs and fed stray cats, he took my fingers and lightly traced the outline of the hard flesh. The *L* and the *S*. The *L* and the *S*.

Tears sprang into my eyes and began coursing down my cheeks. "I'm sorry," I whispered. "I'm so sorry. You are my friend. I so need you to be my friend—and I admire you so much. I can't think of anybody I admire and respect more than you."

Gently he pulled me toward him and put his arms around me. I felt the firm muscled plane of his chest and smelled his essence, a scent of masculinity mixed with the fragrance of soap. "I think we are going to have a wonderful adventure together," he said. I heard his voice change to an intimacy I had come to recognize as he continued, "My Dear Father, I stand here tonight under the vast skies of your universe with your child, my friend Jessica. Your love for us frightens us because we don't understand a love such as yours. You have created us to be strong, independent, intelligent beings who must choose our way in life. Sometimes we struggle with our choices and sometimes we get lost. Tonight, just for tonight, I ask you to give Jessica peace in her heart, a sound and restful sleep, and tomorrow, plant her feet in the direction she should go."

He did not utter the "Amen" I expected. He simply pushed

me away, held my shoulders for a moment and looked into my eyes. *"Hasta luego, mi amiga."*

I lifted my finger and traced the *L* and the *S* and recognized them for the badge of courage they were. "Amen," I whispered before I turned and went to my car.

The next afternoon when I walked to Jack's back door, my arms cradling a stack of books and pamphlets I'd gotten at the extension center, Bea stood in the door, her hands on her ample hips. I imagined I could see smoke bellowing from her nostrils.

"What is it? What's wrong, Bea?"

"It's a waste of my time and your good money to make a nice lunch for *that man*," she fumed.

"Where is he?" I eased past her and dumped the books on the kitchen counter. A bountiful sandwich and a cup of soup on a plate sat on an attractive placemat on the table. I had no idea where the placemat had come from. A glass of iced tea, with melting ice cubes made a wet circle on the mat. A crust had already formed on a cup of pudding beside the plate.

Bea gestured toward the shed as she slung her handbag over her shoulder and stomped down the ramp. "He's been out there all morning," she complained. "I didn't even get a chance to give him his bath."

"Don't worry. The lunch looks lovely. I'll see that he eats it," I said to her retreating back.

"Just what do you think you're doing?" I asked as my eyes adjusted from the bright sunlight to the dimness of the shed. Using his walker for support, Jack leaned into the forepart of the old tractor. Bits and pieces, spark plugs, an air filter, and other parts I couldn't identify lay on the fender. The smell of gasoline permeated the air. Typically he ignored me. When he finally looked at me I burst out laughing. A wide black smudge was smeared across his nose and down his cheek. His hands were black and oily. His shirt looked as though he'd used it for a cleaning rag. "Bea said she couldn't give you a bath, and you wouldn't come in for lunch. Wait until she sees your clothes."

"If I don't get this back together some of the parts will get lost or I'll forget how they fit," he said with just a hint of amusement in his voice.

"How long since it's been started?" I asked.

"Two years or better."

"Is there anything I can do to help?"

"Not unless you're a mechanic," he grumbled.

"I'm no mechanic," I replied with a grin, "but I do know that even if you get it started, it's not going very far with that flat tire. I'll be in the house."

A half hour later as I was at the dining room table pouring over the information I'd brought home, I heard the grinding noise of a starter. Once, twice, three times it labored before the rough sound of a motor vibrated for just a moment before it stalled. After two or three more tries, the engine stayed running, albeit missing a few strokes. Shortly I heard the gait of the walker and Jack's dragging step up the ramp. Perspiration glistened on his forehead and his shirt was soaked through. I recognized from the clench of his jaw that he was in pain, but there was also a look of satisfied pride on his face.

At the table he pushed away his sandwich, but he ate his soup and the pudding, film and all. He did not refuse the pain pill I offered.

"What's that?" he demanded when he saw the stack of books.

"Some information I picked up about growing citrus."

"You don't need those," he blustered. "I know as much as what's in those books—and then some. Those experts don't half know what they're writing about." He snorted with derision. "They've never been out in freezing temperatures spraying down trees so they won't freeze or worked from daylight to dark to get in on the prime market."

"But would *you* teach *me* what you know?" I pointed to my chest. It seemed like forever before his eyes locked mine. He simply nodded. "Thank you," I exclaimed, smiling at him. I grabbed his hands in mine. For a moment his arms tensed as though he was going to pull away, but he didn't.

Within a half hour Jack was snoring in his old chair, the fan rotating back and forth, back and forth. Soon afternoon clouds moved in and the rain began. We were in the rainy season, and there were few days without rain and more often than not, the rain came noisily as thunderstorms. I ran outside and lifted my arms and face to the drops. "Oh thank you, thank you," I said over and over as I allowed the warm shower to rinse away the dust and sweat from my body.

That evening I phoned Louisa to ask if she would relieve me the following afternoon. I had some errands to run, I told her. The next afternoon I followed a big flatbed truck that rumbled into Jack's driveway. By the time the driver had backed a new four-wheeled all-terrain vehicle off the bed, Jack and Louisa were standing in the yard. I hopped on to the seat beside the driver as he instructed me in starting the engine, shifting gears, and applying the brakes. After stalling only once, with a few jerks, I cautiously made a tour around the yard. I shook hands with my instructor as he got off the machine and returned to his truck. Then, I revved up the engine and with increasing speed made several sweeping circles around the driveway, coming to a stop in front of Jack and Louisa.

"Come for a ride," I motioned to Jack. It had not been easy to find what I wanted. My first idea had been a golf cart, but immediately dismissed those tiny tires as unsuitable for rough, sandy grounds. Some four-wheelers had only one motorcycle-type seat, but I needed one that would accommodate two people. Finally I found what I wanted—two seats, hand throttle, and hand brakes. It was perfect!

"Where would you like to go?" I asked after Louisa and I helped him onto the seat. He didn't answer, but I knew that it wasn't out of rudeness. I saw his lips tremble and heard his throat work on a noisy swallow. "Hold on," I cautioned as I engaged the gears.

Slowly I circled the property then began driving up and down the rows. Some trees had faithfully bloomed through the months of March and April and sported small green promising knobs of fruit. In one section many of the vine-covered trees were already dead. Others, with pale leaves and dwarfed fruit fought to survive.

"These will have to go," Jack said above the sound of the machine.

A surge of excitement raced through me. "I suppose so," I answered mildly.

"Valencias," Jack shouted as we approached an area in which trees were covered with both ripe and green fruit. Piles of rotting oranges lay beneath. "Some are still good." I idled the engine and went to pick several pieces of fruit that fell easily into my hands. Jack pulled out a battered pocketknife. With the sharp blade he cut the fruit into sections. He handed me a piece then, with his thumb, peeled back the skin and with his teeth, pulled the flesh into his mouth. I did the same. The taste was sweeter and the flesh juicer than any overpriced, highly polished fruit I had ever bought in any gourmet market in Manhattan. We wiped the juice from our chins, and with sticky hands I revved up the engine and continued up the backside of the property. Here numerous white cratelike boxes were stacked side by side. Beehives. I remembered those from the Alpine meadows on my grandfather's ranch. *Orange Blossom Honey!* Of course, everybody knows about "orange blossom honey" yet I'd never considered the source. Jack chuckled, actually chuckled, when I explained my amazement.

He grimaced as we bounced along the uneven terrain, yet I felt he was enjoying this. His eyes were never still, scanning the trees, the ground, and occasionally the sky. The boiling clouds passed over us today. It was getting late as I headed back through the center of the grove. A butterscotch sun hung just above the trees as I entered the clearing I'd discovered in the middle of the property. I stopped the vehicle and shut off the engine. "I walked through here the other day," I said. "Why aren't there any trees?"

Jack's eyes focused, not on the acre of overgrown grass in front of us, but as some distant sight only he could see. Then he looked at me acutely. "You don't miss anything do you, gir—?" his voice trailed off. I waited. "Was going to build a house here." He spoke in a rough voice that sounded as though his throat was recovering from a wound. "Had planned to build a house for my family."

"You have a family?" I exclaimed.

"Had."

I felt a rush of excitement, like a current of electricity pass through me. I drew a breath. "Where is your family? What happened to them?"

Seconds passed but he didn't answer. The seconds seemed like forever but I waited. I had learned to wait for his responses.

"That was my folks' house," he said finally, gesturing toward the old house barely visible through the trees. My sister and I were born here—grew up here. I was young when I got married—too young. We moved in with my folks. We had planned to build a house here."

"You were married?" He nodded and swallowed, not looking at me. Jack's memories had dwelt so long inside him that it was like forcing open a rusty door to bring them out. I could almost hear the shattering of corroded metal and the abrasive screech of hinges as he struggled to force thoughts to the surface of his mind. I was the hand tugging at that door. "What happened to your wife?"

"She left." He cast wounded eyes toward me. "I worked with my dad here in the groves. I'd graduated from Florida State a couple of years before and it was his plan that I take over the groves. I was the son. My sister had already married and moved away. That was *his* plan." Jack spoke bitterly. "I hated it. I hated the long, dirty, regimented days he planned for me. We fought a lot. We fought over anything new I wanted to try—things I'd learned in school. 'Why did you send me to college,' I used to yell at him. Mom, who was afraid of Dad's temper always tried to smooth things over. So did my wife."

Suddenly laughter rose from my throat, quieting even the birds in their evening song. Jack looked at me, startled at my outburst. "I'm sorry," I said, my hand against my mouth. "Are you very much like your father?" A hint of a smile twitched at the corners of his mouth as he looked at me knowingly.

"Did you have any children?" I asked. He nodded and I waited in the long silence until he decided to answer.

"We had a little girl and when we found out we were going to have another baby, Dad decided we should have a place of our own. He and I were getting along better then. He was fond of my wife and adored his granddaughter. This was where the house was going to be." He surveyed the open area around us, visioning things I could not see.

"What happened?" I asked again.

He looked at me a moment. "Can't," he whispered hoarsely, straightened in his seat and stared ahead.

If regret was measured on a scale of one to ten, the look on his face was off the top of the meter. I knew I'd overstepped my bounds, but I also knew there was a person inside that leathery old shell. I started the engine and headed toward the house.

CHAPTER THIRTEEN

"Damn," I muttered as I struggled to lift Jack's leg into the cab of Ben's truck. I pushed my lips together. "Won't I be glad when you get this thing off next week."

"Quit your bitchin', girlie," Jack grumbled. "You aren't the one who's had to lug this thing around for three months."

"You're right," I conceded, "I'll try to be as patient as you are." Ben smiled his benevolent smile on both of us as we scooted Jack into the passenger seat.

When he found out Ben and I were going to Immokalee to line up help, he insisted on coming along. "If wet backs're going to come here and chop away at my trees I ought to have something to say about it."

"Didn't you have migrants—uh, 'wet backs' work for you before?"

"Sure, but I knew 'em."

"Well, I know *these* men," Ben replied. He didn't take offense at my swearing or Jack's ethnic slang. I marveled at his understanding. What a big heart he has. *What makes a big heart? I* wondered. *One that accepts and cares and loves without condition,* my same mind answered.

It was ten o'clock by the time we headed down Route Twenty-Nine to the principally Hispanic community some thirty miles away. I sat in the middle with my feet propped on the rise in the floor in front of me. Gospel music played on the radio and frigid air blasted from the air conditioner. We didn't speak. Jack wore a clean blue work shirt and pants with the right leg split at the seam and pinned up above his cast. He'd taken care to shave, I noticed, but his hair was badly in need of a trim. Ben's hair was pulled back in his customary ponytail. His tee shirt stated another of his affirmations: "O Sing to the Lord a New Song."

We rushed by levees filled with water and tall grasses where white, long-legged egrets stood statuelike. Miles of citrus groves gave way to broad fields from which vegetables were being harvested.

Ben broke the silence. "What were their names, the men who used to work for you?"

Jack, as usual, took his time in answering. "Well," he began, "there was Miguel Ruiz his two sons. I don't remember their names. Juan Herrera and then there was Salvador—Salvador Dali."

"Salvador Dali?" I screamed.

"Salvador Dali," Ben laughed.

"That's what we called him. I don't remember his last name. He only had one arm—lost the other in a tractor accident. It was his own damn fault," Jack sputtered. "Got off the tractor with the power take-off running. He knew better. Mangled his arm. Had to be taken off above the elbow. He came back to work though after he recovered. Could still outwork most men. One of the toughest men I ever knew," he muttered admiringly. "It was while he was getting well that he started painting. That's why we called him Dali."

Immokalee was a mixture of processing plants, large warehouses, and pockets of Mexican communities in which names of businesses were written in Spanish. Women with shapeless dresses hugging their rotund figures hurried through their Saturday morning activities of shopping, gossiping, and herding children. Dark-eyed, raven-haired teenage girls, wearing suggestive midriffs and molded jeans, headed for the Dollar Store. Groups of men of indeterminate ages stood in clusters, talking.

Ben pulled his truck into a dusty parking lot beside an open-air pavilion. Signs above stores along a littered strip mall read, "Cantina," "Mercado," "Comercial," "Lavenderia." A hand-lettered sign in one plate glass storefront, "Emparisaro," announced that it served as an employment agency.

Groups of men sat in the open-sided cantina at oilcloth-covered tables, drinking cerveza from amber long-necked bottles and eating rolled-up, filled tortillas while juices ran down their fingers.

"Wait here," Ben said as he moved the gearshift into park and left the engine running to keep the air conditioner going. I wanted desperately to follow him but I held on to Jack's arm as he made a move to open the door.

Hands rose in greeting, and broad smiles broke across the tan faces of men as Ben approached. He talked and pointed toward the truck. Other men joined the group and there was much-animated conversation. Digging into my memory, I struggled to reclaim words from my grandparents' vocabulary that would enable me to communicate with these people. Today there was nothing stoic about Jack's manner. He kept his eyes riveted on the parking lot activity, searching for what—a familiar face—positive signs of agreement?

A few men walked with Ben as he entered the cantina. Others went back to their conversations. Several minutes went by. I could feel my heart pounding in my chest and I knew that Jack, who sat twisting his hands together, was as nervous as I. Then we saw Ben coming out of the building. His arm was draped around the shoulders of a smaller, older man. He wore black Levi's and a white shirt that gleamed almost iridescent against his leathery brown skin. His wide-brimmed straw hat, rolled up on the sides was worn low over his forehead. As they got closer to the truck I saw that the left sleeve of his shirt was folded and pinned up. I knew I was looking at Salvador Dali.

"Help me get out!" Jack commanded with such urgency that I jumped. As he fumbled for the door handle I slid across the driver's seat and raced around to his side of the car. It never occurred to me not to obey his order. He had the door open and was handing me his walker by the time I reached him. I unfolded the collapsible medical aid and held it in place as Jack slid off the high seat and landed the foot of his good leg on the ground.

"So much easier than getting you in," I muttered. But, his broad smile was not for me. His eyes glistened as the two men rounded the truck.

"Senior Webster!"

"Dali."

Jack held on to his walker with one hand and both men embraced, one arm each. Ben caught my eye and gave me a wink and his crooked smile. I couldn't return it because my lips were trembling, tears prickled my eyes, and my throat felt like I'd swallowed ice cubes. But, joy rose inside me at the spark of life I saw in the soul of this old man beside me. It was like watching a shoot of green grass force its way through the brown earth of a parched desert after a rain.

"I have another surprise," Ben announced proudly after several minutes of handshakes, shoulder clasps and repeated, "it's been a long time." "Salvador has invited us to lunch. Of course," he said as he took Jack's arm, "that means getting you back into the truck."

We drove several blocks to yet another Mexican neighborhood with well-tended houses and gardens. There was a mixture of shops and private residences. We stopped in front of an ochre-colored stucco building with blue trim and a red tiled roof. "Dos Arbolitos," read a sign across the front. Two small lime trees, one on either side of the front door graced the front entrance—"two little trees." The restaurant stood charmingly fresh and neat, dispelling the feel and look of poverty of the surrounding area. Inviting odors of cooking meats and Mexican spices allured us as we helped Jack out of the truck. I noted that it was already one o'clock. No wonder my stomach propelled me toward those tantalizing smells.

Salvador, who'd driven his own vehicle, rushed over to escort his old employer and friend into his establishment. His wife, Ella, hurried from the kitchen to be introduced and to greet us. An apron, no longer clean, was tied around her waist and her sleek black hair was pulled to a knot at the back of her neck. She pulled up a corner of her apron and wiped her perspiration-soaked face before extending her hand to me. Ben explained that she was responsible for the platters of tempting food being carried to tables. The brightly colored interior with its fiestalike atmosphere was Salvador's work. Through a door at one side of the room was another room. It was identified as "Galleria," and it was here that Salvador exhibited and sold his paintings.

In spite of a seemingly full restaurant with its Saturday noontime crowd, we were ushered to a quiet table in a corner. After we'd eaten until we couldn't swallow another bite, Salvador gave us a tour of his studio. Paintings depicting Latin scenes were bold and vibrant and energetic. They seemed to pulsate and I sensed the enthusiasm with which he painted each stroke. Here was a man who indeed had turned a lemon into lemonade. As we toured the gallery, I noticed that Jack lingered particularly long in front of a painting of an orange grove in which dark-skinned men in sombreros on ladders were harvesting fruit. The title of the work was *The Pickers.*

"You knew we would find him here," I said to Ben when he came to stand beside me. He nodded, his amber eyes dancing. I smiled at him with gratitude. "You go ahead," I told him. "I want to buy a painting."

As the men walked toward the truck, Ella's bright-eyed daughter wrapped up *The Pickers* for me. I had remembered from Jack's Medicare card that on August 15, he would be seventy-three years old.

We drove home in a celebratory mood. On Monday morning workers would come to begin cleaning the groves. There would be eight or ten men—nobody was sure how many. They would come with dump trucks to haul away the diseased trees, a small bulldozer, and a brush hog for mowing between the rows. By this time next week the place would look different, and by this time next week, God willing, the cast on Jack's leg would be gone too. "When you get the cast off," I told him, "we will go to church."

Monday proved to be a day like none other I had ever experienced. It arrived with the intensity of heat and humidity for which these late July days are noted. In spite of the air-conditioning I woke drenched with perspiration. At seven o'clock the thermometer read seventy-two degrees. When I got to Jack's place a cadre of workers and equipment was already in motion. The bulldozer uprooted lifeless tress, and two men, with chainsaws promptly reduced the limbs and trunks to manageable sizes while others piled them on waiting trucks. I was told that if this were not a populated area the trees would simply be piled up and burned. Here they had to be hauled away. A man on a tractor with whirling blades attached to a machine behind it moved slowly up and down the rows of trees, mowing overgrown grass and weeds. To the man, everyone wore white shirts, dark pants, and wide-brimmed straw hats. How do they know what to do, I thought? Someone must be in charge.

There was. He was standing near the shed at the edge of the trees, walker and all. Before I reached him I heard the back door slam and saw Bea marching toward me.

"What am I supposed to do about this?" she demanded, waving her jellylike arm in the direction of the activity.

"Nothing, Bea. It's not your responsibility."

"He," she slung her head in Jack's direction, "was already out here when I arrived a six o'clock. Told me he didn't have time for breakfast. Said he's had a bowl of cereal."

I touched her arm. "He gets his cast off Thursday. Your job is almost over. You've done a remarkable job of taking care of him, but I think he'll soon be able to be on his own."

"And what will happen to him then?"

In spite of her histrionics I knew she truly cared about her patient. "I think he'll be all right. There are several of us to keep an eye on him. He won't be completely alone. In fact, why don't you take the rest of the day off—with pay," I added when I saw her hesitate.

"Jess," Jack called to me.

"Gotta go." I patted her shoulder and gave her my brightest smile.

"Where you been, girlie?" Jack demanded.

"Jessica," I corrected firmly.

"Whose idea was this anyway?" he scolded, but he couldn't hide the excitement in his voice.

"Mine!"

"Well, the day's wasting, and we've got work to do. Go get your toy." It was the name he'd given the all-terrain vehicle.

In his hand he held multiple strips of colored cloth. For the next three hours we worked our way up and down the rows of trees. I drove slowly as Jack studied each tree. When he motioned, I stopped and tied a colored strip of cloth on a branch. A red strip meant that the tree was diseased and was to be removed. A blue strip indicated the tree could be treated and saved.

Each time we came in view of where the men were working, I could see that they were making progress. They worked with slow deliberation. From time to time one or two men went to the large thermos of water on the back of an old pickup truck to take a drink or splash water on their faces. At eleven o'clock all activity ceased as though someone had pulled a plug. Engines were shut off. Chainsaws stilled. Amidst much conversation the men piled into the back of one of the trucks and they drove off down the road. "Over to Ortiz to eat," Jack replied to my questioning look.

We found the chicken salad sandwiches Bea had left for us in the fridge. When we finished eating, Jack handed me a fifty-dollar bill. "Go buy a case of cold beer," he instructed. "It's not for me," he added when he saw my raised eyebrows.

Two hours later the men returned, but instead of going back to work they sought the shade of various trees. Some walked down to the river's edge. It was siesta time. Even Jack had made his way to his easy chair and was snoring loudly, a whistling sound escaping his teeth.

I sat motionless at the kitchen table in front of a circulating fan, willing its movement to dry my skin. In spite of the long sleeves I'd worn there were scratches on my arms and hands. My sneakers were dusty and my legs were covered with brown streaks where dirt had dried and more scratches. I was tempted to go home for a dip in the pool, but I was afraid I would miss something. A while later I heard voices outside. *"Vamanos! Vamanos!"* And the work resumed.

Just before six o'clock that evening Jack instructed me to load the cold beer on the back of the ATV. "Three more days," I told him as I watched him maneuver himself into the seat. He'd even learned to bring his mending leg in by lifting on his pant leg.

When we reached the section of the grove where the men were, they began stowing their equipment. One by one, they approached Jack with broad grins as he handed each of them a *cerveza fria. "Por*

favor, gracias," each responded as tops could be heard popping all
around.

Lastly, Jack handed a can of icy beer to me. *"Gracias,"* I replied
and was rewarded by a smile that even reached those smoky gray
eyes. I took a swallow of the cold, bitter, malty liquid. No two-
hundred-dollar bottle of wine, no twenty-dollar glass of champagne
in the Rainbow Room ever tasted as good as this, I thought.

The men finished their beer and deposited the empty cans in
a paper bag that miraculously appeared. Jack reached into his pants
pocket and pulled out a roll of bills as one by one each man stepped
forwarded and accepted the twenty-dollar bills he counted out to
them. Again, *"Gracias."*

When the last man approached Jack, he said, "This is Roberto,
Salvador's son." Roberto looked to be about fifty years old and had
the leathery, wiry features of his father. I soon learned that *he* was
the man in charge—the crew leader. With dignity, Jack shook his
hand as he handed him his pay. The junkyard dog has cleaned up
his manners, I thought.

"Was that a good idea to pay them?" I asked, after the truck
was out of sight. "Maybe they won't be back."

He looked at me as if I'd just asked him if the world was flat.
"You don't know much about business, do you, gir—ah, Jess?"

"No, I don't," I admitted. "My mother did though. She had her
own business. She was good at business. I was the artist. But what
about records, social security, unemployment," I continued. "Mari
had to file regularly and make payments, and, from time to time,
produce her books for auditors." It wasn't so much a movement, but
a current I felt from Jack's body as he trained his eyes on me.

"Mari?" he asked.

"My mother. I called her Mari."

For a moment he was absolutely still. "Mari? Well," he said,
returning to his gruff manner, "that may be the way you did things
in New York, but this is the way we do things down here in Florida.
You don't ask for their Social Security numbers or their work cards,
or if they have liability insurance. You pay them in cash, every day.

They'll be back." He swept his arm around us. "They left their equipment, didn't they?" It was a rhetorical question.

Maybe this is the way you do it, I thought, *but you can bet corporations and the large producers do those things. They have to. But, this is your show. This is the way you know to do it.* "About the cash," I said out loud, "this was my idea. I started all this and I want to help pay for it. I want to be a part of it."

"I don't need your money. What you see doesn't tell the whole story. Besides, you are a part of it." He fixed me with a fierce stare. "Tomorrow, first thing, you are going to buy fertilizer and insecticide." We burst out laughing.

When Ben arrived a little later I pleaded exhaustion and left them eating their supper. At home, after a shower and a few laps in the pool, I fell into a lounge chair with a glass of cold white wine beside me. An insistent, piercing ringing brought me out of a deep sleep. I realized it was the telephone. As I stumbled to reach for the cordless on the table beside me, the wine glass tumbled and shattered on the floor. It was ten o'clock. I'd been asleep for two hours.

"Jessica?" the voice on the line questioned my groggy "Hello."

"Mal—Malcolm?"

"Jessica, are you all right? Is something wrong?'

"No, nothing's wrong. I fell asleep." I rubbed my forehead in an effort to clear my mind.

"I'm sorry, baby," he said in his familiar, well-modulated voice. "I'm flying to New York on Thursday. The trip just came up. I wanted to let you know so you can meet me. I'm so anxious to see you," he added.

"Thur . . . Thursday," I stammered. I must have sounded like a dullard. *Thursday,* a voice inside my head shouted. *Not Thursday— Jack's getting his cast off on Thursday.* "That's wonderful," I whispered.

"I'll send Steve down for you in the lear."

"No. No, that's not necessary. I'll fly commercially. You'll be jet-lagged and besides, I have an appointment on Thursday. I'll come Friday."

"What kind of appointment?"

My mind fought to make up an acceptable excuse, but I stopped that thought. I would not lie and I would *not* apologize. "I'm taking Mr. Webster to the hospital to get his cast off. You remember, I told you about his accident?"

"For God's sake, Jessica," he exploded. "Someone else can do that. I haven't seen you in four months."

"I know." I willed myself to suppress the anger I felt physically rising inside me. "So one more day won't make a difference. I'll be there Friday." And, I sure as hell wasn't going to let AT&T or Sprint, or whomever, benefit from a ten-thousand-mile argument that would only get worse. I made my voice light. "How long will you be here?"

"Two weeks." I heard the frost in his voice.

"See you Friday, then."

"Damn!" I muttered as I threw the phone on the lounge. "Damn!" I shouted as I went into the empty house. "Damn! Damn! Damn!" I shook my closed fists in the air as I walked into the great room and took Carol's picture out of the drawer. I looked at her smiling face with the sad eyes and tears began to fall. "Did he do this to you too—just come in and out of your life when he wanted, demanding that you put everything else on hold?" I whispered.

I was still crying when I brushed my teeth and when I crawled into bed and pulled up the sheet. I wished desperately for Mari. *I wanted my mommy.* Part of it was the exhaustion of the exciting day and part of it was the frustration of not knowing what to do about the situation I was in.

"What's wrong?" Jack asked the following morning. He sat in a straight back chair behind a card table that had been set up in the shade of the shed. He was busily scribbling on a pad of paper, but had his eye on the men who were already at work.

"Your new office?" I tried to smile.

"What's wrong?" he repeated, his sober gaze locked on mine.

I pulled up an overturned crate and sat down. "Malcolm is coming to New York this week. He wants me to meet him. He'll be here for two weeks."

"So?"

"So, I told him I would come up Friday. But, there's so much to do. I hadn't planned on this."

"Don't think I can handle it without you?" He cocked a bushy eyebrow at me.

"Of course—it's just that I want to be here. Besides, with your cast off someone has to make sure you don't do anything foolish."

"Don't you want to go?" he asked quietly.

"I . . . I don't know. We weren't getting along before he left." I hesitated and wondered why I was sharing this personal information with an old man. "It's been easier, just not thinking about it. Besides, I've been happy doing this." I smiled, waving my hand toward the activity in the grove.

"You have to go," he said emphatically. "You have to work it out."

"Yes," I replied. And this is from someone who didn't, I thought, as I took the list he handed me and listened to his instructions.

Driving toward La Belle to an agricultural supply co-op, I vowed that upon my return I would garage my useless little sports car, and find a second-hand van, something I could carry things in.

Late in the afternoon heavy black clouds rolled in, bringing with them the smell of rain. Long rumbles, growing louder, were heard in the distance. The crew hurriedly put their equipment under cover and rushed to their truck as great drops rain began to pelt them. "*Hasta luego,*" they called. "*Mañana.*" They were already rolling a canvas tarp over the bed of the truck to cover themselves. I put the "toy" in high gear and headed for the house just as rain began coming in sheets.

Inside the kitchen it sounded deafening on the tin roof. Moments later Ben's truck came splashing in the driveway. He pulled as close as possible to the back steps as he and Ginger made a dash for the door. The dog rushed passed us and wedged herself under the bed where Ben usually slept. "Ginger doesn't like thunderstorms very much," Ben said.

Louisa had left chili and cornbread for our supper. We ate in relative silence because conversation was difficult amidst the cracking lightening, booming thunder and pounding rain on the roof. Occasionally lights flickered.

Jack pushed himself back from the table declaring that he was going to turn in early. "Can't turn on the TV," he complained. While Ben settled him in, I stacked the dishes in the sink.

"You can't go home in this," Ben said when he came back into the kitchen. "Are you afraid to sit on the porch? We're used to this. Did you know that Florida has more thunderstorms than any other state?"

"I'd love to sit on the porch," I replied. "I used to do that when I was growing up at my grandfather's house. Florida may have more thunderstorms, but I bet the ones in the Rockies were more dramatic," I teased.

We carried kitchen chairs and quietly pried open the little-used front door. Inside the house was still close and hot, so the cooled air from the rain felt refreshingly good. "My God is an awesome God!" Ben exclaimed as he stood at the edge of the porch and held his hands up to the sky. In a flash of lightening I saw a look of rapture on his face. Then he came and sat beside me. "What's wrong, *mi amiga?*"

"Why?" I asked. "Did Jack say something to you?" Ben shook his head. I drew in a deep breath. "Malcolm's coming back to the states. He'll be in New York Thursday and wants me to meet him there."

"You'll go, of course?"

"Yes, yes, I'll go," but I said it without enthusiasm. "I won't go until Friday. Jack's getting his cast off, remember?"

"Someone else can take care of that—Carlos, a home health service, even me, if necessary."

"But I want to do it," I insisted. "I think I'm as excited about it as he is."

"You should be. You've invested time and care in his recovery, and, I think he wants you to be there. You've made a difference in his life whether he admits it or not. We can take care of him for a few days." Ben smiled, "Trust me."

I laughed. "That's what the IRS always says. But I do, I do trust you," I said with emphasis. "You can't know how much I rely on your friendship."

We were quiet for several moments as the storm moved away. Thunder rolls grew more distant and the rain diminished. "What about your marriage?" he asked. I heard a sigh in his voice. In spite of his sensitivity to issues, Ben never avoided them. Avoiding problems doesn't make them go away, he'd once told me. How we deal with them is what mattered to the man of God sitting beside me.

"What about it?" I asked, with an edge to my voice. "That's what I have to find out. I don't know how marriages are supposed to work. I didn't have an example."

"You made a commitment," he reminded me.

"Yes," I whispered. Suddenly I was very tired. I stood up. "I have to go home," I said. Ben walked me to my car. Ginger crept out from under the bed to join us. Tonight there was no prayer, no comforting arms. It would have been too unacceptable for either of us.

The next morning I reserved a first-class ticket on the Friday morning flight to New York. I was more comfortable with public travel than I was in the luxury of the private plane with a pilot at my disposal. Malcolm never understood that, but I realized, we understood little about each other. I did however request that his limousine meet me at LaGuardia.

Other than debris and some twigs and leaves on the ground and the ditches beside the road full of water, there was little evidence of yesterday's storm. The soil, which was mostly sand absorbed the moisture like a sponge. Humidity had fallen and the day was more pleasant. The crew continued their methodical clearing and trimming. Ten acres had not seemed large at first, but I began to appreciate the effort it must take to maintain top-producing groves. I wondered if any of us who bought an orange at a fruit stand or drank a glass of juice for breakfast, ever realized the work involved in getting that fresh citrus to us.

Over Jack's objections, Roberto insisted on bringing a mechanic who, when I arrived, was working on the sprayer with Jack looking over his shoulder. I put things in the fridge that I had brought for lunch and sent Bea on her way. "One more day," I told her. Alone in the house I looked at the forbidden stairs that led to the second story, and wondered if there had been any leaks from last night's downpour. I ignored Jack's fierce order not to go upstairs and decided to take a look.

There was barely room to place my feet as I made my way between stacks of papers, magazines and boxes. Several boxes contained farming periodicals and citrus-growing journals. Among the stacks of books were classic fiction but nothing of any recent publication. I moved carefully, fearful of knocking something over or ending up back down the stairs myself. I gingerly held on to an ineffective handrail that had pulled loose from the plaster at the top of the stairs and probably would not have supported me if I'd needed it.

At the top of the stairs I stood in an open area facing the tall, oval, etched glass window that could be seen from the street. Part of the sill had rotted away. Beneath the tall window was what appeared to be a hinged window seat. I couldn't tell for sure because it too was piled high with books and boxes. A hallway ran around either side of the open stairs, which was cordoned off by a banister supported by turned spindles. I ran a finger through the layer of dust, exposing darkened varnish. There were two doors on either side, separated by walls covered with floral-patterned wallpaper, yellowed and peeling. The two front doors exposed bedrooms, identical in size to the two rooms below them. The windows were large and would have let in light and air, had they not been hung with heavy drapes. On the north side there was a second bedroom and a bathroom, again replicas of the rooms below. A claw-footed tub, a cast iron sink, and an ancient toilet had all been disconnected. Across the hall, the area above the dining room and kitchen were two other doors. Both were locked. Strange, I thought, every other room simply seemed to be in a time warp of a half a century ago. At the back of the house a piece of plywood was nailed over the door that led to the exterior, rotting stairs I'd seen from outside. I suppose it had been easier to board up the door than to repair the steps.

I had been right. On the floor in front of the boarded-up door there was a puddle of water. The wallpaper around it was damp and water stained where wind-driven rain had found its way through. I looked at my watch. The men would be quitting soon. I hurried downstairs, taking care to smudge away footprints.

By seven o'clock I had supper ready. When Ben had not arrived by eight o'clock, I suggested that we go ahead and eat. During the meal Jack responded halfheartedly to my questions. Yes, they had gotten the sprayer working. No, he would not plant any new trees in the newly cleared and treated plot until I got back from New York. That was my project. It was a promise of the future. We both kept glancing at the clock.

An hour later Jack went to watch television. I wrapped a plate of food in foil and placed it in the oven. I tried not to worry. Of course Ben had other things to do. Of course he had another life. And yes, of course he had his cell phone. He would have called if something were wrong. At five minutes to nine I heard his truck turn into the driveway. I rushed to the door like—like what—a worried wife—a worried mother?

Ginger, who always rode beside him in the cab, was sitting in the back of the truck. By the time I was outside Ben had the passenger door open and was talking to someone. Two little girls sat on the seat. I could see little of their features in the now, almost dark evening. They looked to be five to seven years old. When Ben looked at me I noticed the stretched lines that formed along his scar when he was tired or worried.

"I told them I knew a nice lady who would give them something to eat," he said, his voice full of reassurance.

Oh dear God! I thought of the grilled fish inside, enough food for one hungry man, but what do little girls eat? As if reading my mind he said, "They're hungry. They haven't had anything to eat today. Whatever you have will be fine."

"Of course," I said brightly. *Wing it*, I coached myself silently. I was totally in a foreign country here, having never dealt with children in my life. None of my friends had children and my younger cousins in Colorado were a hazy memory to me.

Ben reached for the girl nearest the door. "I'll carry Allie," he said, gently pulling her away from the fierce hold she had on the younger child. He lifted her to the ground and put her hand in mine. "This is Peggy," he said.

"*Peggy Sue*," she corrected.

Peggy Sue looked to be about six or seven years old. She had brown hair, and had it not been so tangled and matted, would, I thought, be curly. Somber, dark eyes, void of all expression stared at me. Her knobby knees protruded from tattered shorts. A knitted top, too small and too tight, hugged her upper body.

Ben lifted the other child from the truck. She had her thumb in her mouth and was sniffling the way one does when they are trying not to cry. She was fairer and chubby. Her blond hair was equally as curly, gnarled and dirty. When she looked up, her wide, blue eyes held a look of fear. Tears filled her lower lids and ran down her cheeks. Peggy Sue pulled away from me and reached for her hand. "Don't cry, Allie," she said. "I'm gonna take care of you."

"This is Alicia," Ben introduced as he cradled her in his arms.

"She likes to be called Allie," the older child announced.

"And this lady is Jessica," Ben said with a twitch of a smile at the corners of his mouth. "*She does not like to be called Jessie.*" Peggy Sue looked at me with what I felt was a bit of connection.

We sat each child in a chair at the table but Allie immediately scooted out of hers and climbed into her sister's lap. *Oh God,* I thought once again, but it must have been a prayer because, somewhere from within, my maternal soul kicked in. When I opened the cupboard I stared at a package of macaroni and cheese just waiting to be cooked. I quickly put water on to boil, then took a banana from a fruit bowl, peeled it, and handed half to each girl.

Dirty hands reached out and grabbed my offering. An instant before the bite that would quell gnawing hunger, Peggy Sue looked at me and murmured, "Thank you."

"Tank yu," Allie added. Manners, I thought. Someone has taught them manners.

When the macaroni and cheese was ready, I portioned out three plates, dividing up the fish and vegetables I'd saved for Ben.

Allie stared at her plate for a second, then tugged at her older sister. "She has to pee," Peggy Sue informed us.

Ben looked at me. "Of course. Maybe you'd like to wash your hands too." I led them to the bathroom. I heard Ben go into Jack's room. If he'd heard us, he for once, was being discrete.

The little girls held their hands under running water while I sponged their faces with a warm washcloth. There were scratches and scrapes on their dirty arms and legs.

By the time all three plates were scraped down to the yellow buttercups in the pattern, I'd found ice cream in the freezer. While the girls, with tentative smiles on their faces, dug into theirs, Ben declined. He cleared the plates from the table and brought them to the sink where I was standing. "They need a place to stay tonight," he said quietly. I wanted to asked questions but when I realized there was no sound of scraping spoons behind me, I turned to see Peggy Sue watching me with the eyes of a deer caught in headlights. Allie had nodded off to sleep, her head all but in her ice cream bowl.

"*Oh, bende a tu corazon,*" I exclaimed as I went around to scoop up the sleeping child.

"What did you say?" Ben asked in a strange voice.

"It's something my grandmother used to say to me when I was little. 'Bless your heart.'"

"I know," he said, a curious look on his face. "It's Spanish."

"Yes," I smiled. "I guess it is."

Peggy Sue grabbed her sister by her arm as I started to pick her up. Her sleepy eyes briefly flew open. "Let's put her on the bed," I coaxed.

"It's right in there." Ben pointed through the open doorway. "You can even lie down beside her to make sure she's all right," he added.

Open windows and a circulating fan on the old dresser made the room somewhat comfortable. I laid Allie down as her fierce protector climbed up beside her. I spread a clean sheet over them. We'd hardly left the room before sleep also claimed Peggy Sue.

"They need a bath," I said.

"They need food and rest more," Ben replied.

"Jess?" Jack called from his room. He was sitting on the edge of his bed. "I was just going to make some coffee," I said. "Will java jangle your nerves this time of the night?"

"Who can sleep?" he retorted.

When the coffee was ready, I carried three mugs into his room.

"Their mother is in the psyche unit at Lee County," Ben explained. Maggie, their mother, had a history of substance abuse. She was found in an ally, beaten and incoherent. It was not the first time it happened. "She's a good mother," Ben said with conviction, "and one of these days she'll make it. However, Social Services won't give her many more chances before they take her children away from her.

"When a neighbor realized she hadn't seen Maggie coming and going for the past couple of days, and hadn't seen the girls, she called the authorities. Peggy Sue tried to take care of her sister so nobody would find out. There was evidence that she had heated some soup, and there was milk and cereal in the house. When she saw the Black and White stop in front of their house she knew they would be taken away, so she grabbed her sister and ran out the back door. They were found hiding in a vacant overgrown field behind the mobile home park where they lived."

They, whoever *they* were, were trying to find an emergency foster family, even as we waited. *They* would phone Ben soon as someone was located.

"How did you get involved?" I asked.

"Can't keep out of other people's affairs," Jack scoffed. We laughed.

"My name is registered with the police, Social Services and the Crisis Center—you name it. I've worked with Maggie before. I'm often called in situations like this."

"How can you do it?" I demanded. I spread my hands in frustration. "You've been here many nights for the past three months, you have your physical job, you have your church and you," I concluded pointedly, "have no time for yourself." Suddenly I was angry. I stood up and ran my hands through my hair, which, when I had time to think about it, needed shampooing, not to mention cutting. The clock on Jack's bedside table read ten-thirty.

We had all been up and working for more than sixteen hours. Tomorrow Jack would have his cast off and, the following day I was flying to New York to meet my estranged husband. And— there were two precious little girls down the hall, who didn't know what their life would be like when they woke up.

Ben's cell phone rang. He stood up. It seems people can only talk on cell phones standing up or in their cars, I thought. I wanted to laugh, but I knew if I did, I would become hysterical.

"Yes? Yes, I see. That will be fine," he said as he disconnected. "They can't find anybody tonight," he told us.

"What will we do?" I looked at Ben.

"I," he nodded toward the parlor, "will sleep in there, and you," he said, "will go home and get some rest."

"I could take them to my place," I offered.

"Better let them sleep here," Jack cautioned. "They don't need another strange place tonight." He was right, of course.

"I remember seeing some clothes that belong to Malcolm's grandchildren in one of the dressers. I'll see what I can find." I hesitated. "Maybe I could take them over in the morning and give them baths. Louisa can make breakfast for them. It would be more than Bea could handle."

Jack chuckled and Ben smiled as I went out the door.

CHAPTER FOURTEEN

Was it only yesterday, I thought, as I eased myself into the first-class seat for my flight to New York, that so much had happened? I waved away the flight attendant who offered me a drink. In the short two-hour journey to the city, I planned to put my head back, close my eyes, and not think about anything. Fat chance! My mind raced from the thoughts of two little girls, of the expression on the wasted face of their once-beautiful mother, to Jack who felt his new freedom, restricted though it was, to the diary I'd found when I searched for little girl clothing at Malcolm's house. However, the elephant sitting on my chest was my anxiety at seeing Malcolm.

I'd been looking through dresser drawers in the children's bedroom when the phone rang. It was Ben.

"I didn't think you would be in bed yet," he said.

"Why aren't *you* in bed?" I asked. "Is everybody else asleep?"

"Jack's snoring and the little girls haven't moved. Ginger's ready for bed but she's waiting for me."

"I found some things I think will fit, more or less."

"That's just their size," he replied. "Jess, I'm taking off a couple hours tomorrow afternoon. While Jack's with the doctor, would you go with me to visit Maggie? She's just upstairs from where he'll be."

His question caught me by surprise. "Ben," I pleaded, "That's so out of my territory. What good would I do?"

"You could reassure her that her children are all right."

When I didn't respond right away he waited. Most people would have jumped in with convincing arguments, not Ben. He waited out the silence of my decision. Yes, I thought, I could do that—hadn't I lived with Phil? "Yes," I said, "I can do that."

"*Gracias.* Thank you. Sleep well, Jessicacita, I'll see you tomorrow."

Oh, I want to sleep, I'm so tired, I thought. As I began lifting piles of clothes back into the bureau I felt something hard among the folds. Tucked inside a pair of toddler-sized pants was a small book—a diary—a journal? It seemed to have been Carol's. Some of the sentences I scanned were disturbing but I didn't want to read it now. I dropped it into my flight bag.

By the time I'd gotten to Jack's yesterday morning, the little girls were standing on the back steps, looking much as they had the night before.

"I offered them some orange juice," Bea announced, "But they wouldn't take any. Reverend Ben said to tell you a Mrs. Gomez would be picking them up about ten o'clock."

"Thanks, Bea. Louisa is making breakfast as we speak."

I reached to pick up Allie. "Come on, sweetie. I have a surprise for you, and a good breakfast."

"We don't like surprises," Peggy Sue stated, her face drawn and her eyes wary. I realized she had not shed a tear, and I'd seen neither girl smile.

"No," I said as I reached for her hand. "I bet you don't."

The little girls sat in the tub together while Louisa and I soaped them and shampooed their hair. Thank goodness for Louisa who had soaped and shampooed children and grandchildren. "You're both look beautiful," I said when they were dressed. Clean hair bounced in soft curls around their scrubbed faces. They looked just like any seven and five-year-old in the shorts and tops I'd found. I put extra clothes in a bag for them.

When we sat down to a breakfast of scrambled eggs with ketchup and toast with grape jelly I said, "I have another surprise. It's a good surprise and a not-so-good surprise," I added quickly. "I'm going to see your mother this afternoon."

Both girls stopped eating. "Can we go?" Allie asked. Peggy Sue just looked at me waiting for my answer.

"No, that's the not-so-good part, but you already knew the answer to that didn't you, Peggy Sue?" She nodded. "She had an accident and she's in a hospital, but she's going to be all right. I'll be able to tell her," I went on, "that you are okay, and what we had for breakfast, and about your new clothes.

"The other news is that—"

"I know," Peggy Sue interrupted, "we're going to have to go live with some other people who don't want us."

The wise seven-year-old had been down this road before and there was no use building castles, or even dollhouses for her. "I hope these people want you and will take good care of you until your mom can come home," I said.

Allie's lower lip began to tremble. "Wh . . . what about Soot?" Suddenly Peggy Sue looked frantic.

"What is Soot?" I asked.

"Soot is our kitty. He's at home. He has to be fed. He hasn't had anything to eat since yesterday," Peggy Sue added accusingly.

Right, I thought. I'll add "pick up kitten" to the list of things I have to do today.

Seeing Maggie was equally as heartbreaking. She was in a room with three other women. One was in restraints and talking to herself, another was crying, and the third, like Maggie, was curled in a fetal position facing the wall.

"Hi, Maggie. It's Pastor Ben." There was no response. "I just wanted you to know that Peggy Sue and Allie are all right." When the only movement was a shudder, he continued, "I brought someone to meet you. She's been helping take care of your girls. This is Jessica."

When she rolled over, I was staring at the face of a woman who was probably in her late twenties, but looked forty. She was, or could have been beautiful, but one side of her faces looked like it was made of purple and blue marshmallows. Her left eye was swollen shut. My stomach did a flip, not at the disfigurement, but at the defeated look I saw in her eyes.

"Hello, Maggie." I smiled and took a step toward her. She drew back, a frightened animal, pulling her knees and the sheet up to her chin. I kept talking. "Your daughters are fine." I hoped I sounded convincing. "Peggy Sue takes such good care of Allie. She'll see that nothing happens to her." Tears leaked from beneath closed lids. "They had baths this morning and I found some clothes that belong to my husband's grandchildren that fit them. And, oh yes, I'm picking up Soot this afternoon."

Maggie lifted her head and looked at Ben. "One of these times they won't let me have them back." Russet hair was a frame of curls around her face. I could see where the girls got their ringlets.

"One of these times will be the last time this happens—maybe this is it," he stated with calm authority. "God doesn't give up on his creation."

Maggie put her face in her hands and when I heard muffled sobs, I left the room. Ben knew the words to say, I didn't. I was embarrassed to hear words so personal, confessions so deep.

You'll have to get used to that, a voice said beside me. I looked around but there was no one there.

The bright spot of the day was when Jack walked out of the examining room using only his cane. Of course he wouldn't do anything foolish, he promised the doctor. Of course he'd do his exercises, and of course he'd be in twice a week for therapy.

"You bet he will," I declared.

"And of course he still needs that hip replacement," the doctor added as a parting shot.

One thing was certain, I assured myself, as the plane touched down and began its taxi to the gate, I would not stay in New York for two weeks. I was planning a party for Jack's seventy-third birthday the following Saturday.

"Good afternoon, Mrs. Steele. It's so good to see you." The doorman at the apartment building greeted me enthusiastically as I climbed out of the limo.

"Good afternoon, Curtis. Thank you, I can manage this," I said as he reached for my bag. "I only brought this." The heat from the sidewalk rose up to blast my face. August heat in New York was not only steamy it was smelly. No wonder people escaped to the country when they could.

Malcolm's apartment occupied the entire twelfth floor of the building and overlooked the East River. It was beautifully appointed and as immaculate as I'd remembered. Perpetual care. All of his houses are routinely and religiously made ready for occupants, staffed by who knows how many people, on call and on payroll.

A huge bouquet of wine-red roses sat on a living room table. There was note in Malcolm's bold script was propped against the vase.

Welcome home, dearest Jessica. Sorry I wasn't here when you arrived, but had a meeting I couldn't skip. Dinner reservations at eight tonight. There's a box on the bed—something for you to wear this evening. Should be home by five. Love, Malcolm.

A beautifully wrapped box from Saks was propped against the mound of pillows on the king-sized bed. I lifted out a summer dress of light flowing fabric in shades of deep blues and purples, the color of the sky at dusk. There was also a long jacket in yet a deeper tone, the shade of woods iris. These were colors Malcolm liked and looked good on me. Tucked inside the box was a smaller, elegantly wrapped package containing a single amethyst drop of several carats on a silver rope. There were matching earrings. A second note read *if you need shoes for this, you have time to buy some.* What I really need, I thought is a shower and a nap.

After I showered, I slipped on the dress and burst out laughing when I looked in the mirror. I hadn't realized I'd lost so much weight and couldn't remember when I'd last stepped on a scale. The dress hung unappealingly loose. My tan line formed a bronze circle above the white "V" between my breasts. I noticed too that my hair had grown long in my neglect. My initial reaction was to rush over to Saks to see if I could exchange the outfit for a smaller size, and to get a haircut. My second thought was that I would just wear something else. But, it was the third thought that won. I pulled on a light robe from the closet and crawled between the smooth silk sheets.

"Jessica? Jessica?" A voice called from the tunnel of my mind as I struggled from sleep. The setting sun dipped into the west behind the building, casting shadows across the room, but the trees across the river were bright in the late afternoon light. The clock read 6 p.m. I sat up just as Malcolm came through the door. "There you are. I wasn't sure you got here." He took off his jacket and hung it on the polished wooden clothes caddy.

"Hello, Malcolm," I whispered as he lifted me up and kissed me. The back of his shirt was moist with perspiration, but he smelled the familiar fragrance of sandalwood that was his favorite soap. He reached over and turned on the lamp.

"Let me look at you." He undid the sash of the robe and pushed it off my shoulders. His eyes grew wide in surprise as he stared at me. The look turned into a frown. "What have you done to yourself? You've lost so much weight. And, what kind of tan is this?" he questioned, tracing the dark outline across my front. The tone I heard in his voice was criticism and not concern.

I stepped away, feeling timid under his scrutiny. "You've lost weight too," I countered. His face *was* thin, without the healthy outdoor look he usually had. I attributed the circles under his eyes to jet lag. He looked old.

"I had one of those Asian bugs a few weeks ago."

"You didn't tell me."

"There wasn't anything you could do."

"I guess I would have liked to know if you weren't well." I felt myself getting upset. "Don't husbands and wives tell each other that sort of thing? Wouldn't you want to know if something was wrong with me?"

"Is something wrong with you?" He peered at me, the furrow between his brows deepening.

""No, I—"

"Well, what are we talking about then?" A derisive smile lifted the corners of his mouth. "Look, this is getting off to a poor start. I've missed you. Did you see the roses?"

I nodded. "They're beautiful. Thank you. And," I added, "the dress and the jewelry are exquisite."

"I have champagne. Let me get out of these clothes and jump in the shower. We can have champagne in our robes." He smiled his charming smile. Malcolm Steele, I recalled, has a whole inventory of smiles.

We sat on the bed, our backs against the headboard, and sipped champagne that had cost two hundred dollars from Tiffany glasses that had cost even more and all I could think about was the cold beer Roberto and his crew was having about now.

Malcolm told me about the fever and dysentery that had disabled him and many of his employees. When he began talking about the details of his project, my mind drifted. I wondered how Jack was getting around. I was curious how Cat was tolerating Soot, whom I had deposited there before I left, and I said a prayer for Allie and Peggy Sue.

"But," he said, taking my glass from me, "enough of that." He slipped his hands beneath my robe and pulled me to him. "I *have* missed you. You feel so good to me." I've missed this too, I thought as my body responded to his touch.

"Oh damn!" he exclaimed.

"What's wrong?"

"Look at the time," he said jumping up. "It's after seven. I told Edward to have the car here at seven-thirty. It will take us a while to get across town."

"Where are we going?"

"Windows on the World. Not my choice but—"

"Then why are we going there?" I queried as I slid into my underclothes and walked to the closet to get my dress.

"Dai, ah, Miss Chang thought it would impress Dr. Woo," he stammered. Our contracts for bridges in Nanjing rest on him."

I gripped the doorjamb as something as hot and heavy as a burning coal fell into the pit of my stomach. The taste of nausea rose in my throat. "*The Miss Chang?* I hadn't realized anyone else was joining us," I said.

"Oh, I thought I mentioned it in my note. I haven't met Dr. Woo," he said as casually as if he was talking about a next-door neighbor. He adjusted his bow tie and began inserting his gold cuff links. He either didn't hear, or chose to ignore my comment.

What the hell, I thought as I dropped the new dress over my head and found some black medium-heel sandals that seemed to look right. The jacket disguised the loose dress beneath. Fortunately I didn't require a lot of makeup—a little eye color, a sweep of blush on my cheeks. I lifted my hair and secured it with silver combs I'd found. I noticed more streaks of gray, but I really didn't mind. In fact I rather liked it. The new earrings were lovely and the pendant hung just in the cleavage of my breasts. So, when Malcolm called, "Are you ready?" I was.

"You're beautiful!" he exclaimed when I walked into the living room. He planted a quick kiss on my lips. "I wish this evening were already over." He offered me his arm and we walked to the elevator.

The evening was over, finally. I forced myself to eat some of the elegantly prepared food set before me and drank too much of the excellent wine that was offered with each course. I smiled and hopefully made intelligent comments when the conversation included me, however much of the table discussion was business oriented. While Dr. Woo spoke and understood English he obviously had limited practice in using it. So, Miss Chang spent considerable time translating. I wondered why I was even here.

Daisy Chang was as tall as I. She wore her ebony hair in a straight cut that fell just above her shoulders. She had a habit of tucking it behind her ear as she talked. She wore a black silk, tailored dinner suit with a white satin blouse. Her only jewelry was a jade brooch and small jade earrings. She had the appearance of being both strong and fragile. From time to time I caught her elliptical-shaped eyes looking at me curiously and perhaps cautiously.

It was late when we got home. The bed was turned down and a low lamp beside it cast an inviting glow. Some mysterious service genie had been there to remove any trace of humans. Even the champagne glasses had been washed and put away. When we slid into bed Malcolm reached for me. I fitted myself into the circle of his arms, but moments later I heard his steady breathing and knew he was already asleep.

"I didn't hear you get up," I said the next morning when I went into the kitchen to pour myself a cup of coffee.

"You were sleeping so soundly I didn't want to wake you. The day woman, I can't remember her name, left some breakfast for you."

"No thanks, just this. Join me?" I asked, holding up another mug.

"I've got one in the office," he said. "Bring yours and come in. I have a surprise."

I followed him into the office and placed my mug on the table between us as I eased in to the soft leather chair.

"I should have things tied up here in the next few days so I've phoned up to Timber Ridge and asked them to get the lodge ready," Malcolm said, stretching his body out in the chair and crossing his long legs in front of him. "A few days in the mountains away from this heat will be good. I can't remember when I've been cool. It will be good to be together—just the two of us," he added.

"Timber Ridge?" I repeated like an echo. Timber Ridge was another of Malcolm's homes, a spacious house of natural cedar with lots of glass on Lost Lake in the Adirondacks. It had a captivating view of the lake, the woods, and the surrounding mountains. The evenings would already be crisp there, I knew, and I could almost smell the scents of pine and wood smoke. Usually I enjoyed the time we spent there, but not now. *I don't like surprises,* my mind screamed in Peggy Sue's words.

"I don't fly back to Beijing until the twentieth," he continued. "We could have a week there if we drive up on Wednesday. I have tickets for a play tonight. We can have dinner in, or catch something after the performance." He spouted the itinerary as though listing his schedule for a secretary. "Tomorrow there's a new art show opening and I imagine you'll want to see Christine."

"Wait a minute, Malcolm," I said standing up. "This is too much for me to think about right now. I'll get dressed, and then we can discuss it."

"We are discussing it," he countered.

"No." I turned at the door to look at him. "You are telling me what we're going to do. Theater tonight is a wonderful idea and the art show sounds fine, but I won't be able to go to Timber Ridge with you." For a moment, his expression looked as if he'd been slapped. Then he closed his mouth and his face became the all-too-familiar stone mask.

"You didn't let me know until Tuesday night that you were coming," I said. "Surely you must have known before that. I have to be back in Florida by Friday. I've already made other plans." The only difference in the rigidity of his expression was the fury that blazed in his eyes.

When I emerged from the bedroom a few minutes later, Malcolm was nowhere to be found. Although the apartment was more than twenty-five hundred square feet, there weren't many rooms. In addition to the entry and the large living room with a dining area at one end, there was the master suite, a guest bedroom and bath, the kitchen and a room that served as a library and Malcolm's office. He wasn't there. Behind the kitchen was a smaller bedroom and bath for the convenience of live-in staff. Sliding glass doors opened off the dining area onto a rooftop garden that now shimmered in the late morning sun.

I walked to the phone in the kitchen and dialed Ben's cell phone. "Hi! It's Jessica."

"Jessica, how are you?" I felt the pleasure in his voice.

"*I miss you,*" I wanted to say. "*I would rather be there,*" I wanted to say. "Fine," I said. "I want to know how Jack is getting along and how the work is going. How are the little girls, and Maggie and Soot?" I had only been away one day, but I realized too how important these things were to me.

"Jack is reconciling himself to the fact that just having his cast off does not make him a new man. The men are getting ready to leave." It was Saturday and they only worked half a day. "I went to see the foster parents yesterday to tell the girls that we got Soot and that he's okay. They seem like kind people. They are caring for two other foster children. Allie, of course is bewildered, and Peggy Sue is just plain angry.

"Cat," he continued, "is hiding on a ledge in the shed to keep the little black kitten from pouncing on him, and Soot, on the other hand, can't understand a playmate who doesn't want to play."

"Wow," I exclaimed. "That's a pretty comprehensive summary."

"Did I leave anything out?" he laughed.

"You. How are you? What are you doing?"

There was a pause. "Me? I'm fighting the devil today."

"What does that mean?"

"Nothing, never mind. I'm working on my sermon for tomorrow. How are things there?"

It was my turn to pause. "Okay," I replied. "Just okay. I'll be back Thursday night," I added quickly.

When Malcolm hadn't returned by noon I made a sandwich from deli food I found in the fridge and called Christine.

"Why didn't you let me know you were coming?" she cried into the phone. We agreed to have lunch on Monday. "I'll rearrange my schedule and we can have a long three-wine lunch. I can't wait to see you," she bubbled.

I thought about dropping into Classy Lady to see how things were going, but when I thought of the ninety-degree temperature and the closeness of so many bodies rushing around, I opted to stay in the cool apartment.

With a casualness I didn't feel, I went into the bedroom and took Carol's journal out of my flight bag and settled myself into a chair by the window. The book itself was hardbound with a paisley cover in shades of muted blues and rose, outlined in gold leaf. The edges of the pages were metallic gold and a creamy satin ribbon marked a page near the back of the book. Behind that marker there, a dozen or so blank pages were waiting for the entries that never were recorded. The few pages in front of the marker appeared to be her last entry. It was dated April 22, 1992. I remembered that she had died a short time later.

"Mal was angrier than ever when he left this morning. I stayed out of his way while he packed. I hadn't meant to upset him when he told me a few days ago that he was going to Europe and I asked if I could come with him. 'Why Carol?' he asked. 'You were the one who wanted to come down here. Your friends are here, you told me. Well, this place is too damn hot for me. You stay here and enjoy your friends. I have work to do.'

"I should have left it alone but no, I had to ask if Valerie was going too. 'What if she is?' he asked. 'She's part of the company. We'll be working, and what would you do?' His tone was sarcastic.

"'Look,' he went on, 'you have everything you need. If there's anything else you want, just let me know. I'll get it.'

"'You're right, Mal,' I said. 'I have everything I need.'

"Thank goodness Marcy is coming with the children this week. They'll keep me busy. I so look forward to having them here to fill up this empty space. And Mitchell will be here in a couple of weeks before he starts his summer job. It's hard to believe that my baby boy is already through with his first year of college. So unlike his father, he hasn't a clue about what he wants to do. But he's having a good time and I'm glad. Of course, I can't expect Malcolm to understand that.

"It still would have been all right if I hadn't tried to explain this morning as Malcolm was leaving. 'I'm sorry, Mal,' I said as he walked over, luggage in hand to give me a parting kiss. 'I didn't mean to upset you. I just wish—'

"'Forget it, Carol, the car is waiting.'

"'Please, Mal!' I called after him. 'Please don't leave like this.'"

I felt heavy with sadness. I shivered and felt connected to the woman I'd looked at as my competition—the wife who was held up to me as perfection—the wife who'd died wanting only the love and companionship of her husband. That husband, I now realized, was now my husband. She was no longer my enemy. We, it seems, were on the same team.

I flipped to the beginning. The first entry was made in 1980 and while so many pages expressed her unhappiness, she was also able to record the happy times.

"June 1, 1981. Rebecca's sixteenth birthday party was lovely and she behaved beautifully. None of the guests knew her disappointment that her father hadn't made it home for the occasion. No one but me noticed her glances toward the door each time someone entered the room. The club was beautifully decorated filled with spring flowers of every color, for a child so filled with spring. Her little brother, bless him, asked her for the first dance—the one her father should have had. At twelve, Mitchell is not that much shorter than she, and in a few years will, no doubt, look down on her when they dance. Becca beamed at him. I am so wonderfully proud of my children.

"Mal, the absentee father, will no doubt be home tomorrow, or the *next day, or the next, bringing expensive, inappropriate gifts, along with his apologies, for which Becca will throw her arms around him and say, 'Thank you, Daddy. It's just what I wanted,' and, 'That's all right.'"*

I flipped through other entries. The one dated September 12, 1986, caught my eye.

"Marcy and Steve left on their honeymoon this morning. They have a wonderful trip planned to the south of France. Her choice because of the special memories she had of her time there as an exchange student. She declined her father's offer of the use of one of his planes.

"I'm exhausted. Everybody's nerves have been raw with anxiety, wondering if the father of the bride would make it home in time for the wedding.

"I will not forget, nor perhaps, will I ever forgive the phone call that came the morning before, telling me he would not be here in time for the rehearsal dinner. His plane landed only hours before the ceremony and he didn't reach the apartment until two hours before we were to be at the church. But, when the music began, he looked so poised and handsome as he took his daughter's gloved hand and placed it on his arm. Puffiness around Tracy's eyes from angry sobs the night before were miraculously gone, and she looked radiant as only a bride can look.

"Malcolm was the perfect host at the reception, sparing no expense with food and drink. He made it a point to visit each table and in his charming manner welcomed each guest. I even felt special when we danced. He told me I looked lovely and thanked me for giving him a beautiful daughter. This morning, that feeling disappeared when he flew into a rage when I mentioned the empty chair beside me at the rehearsal dinner. I should not have brought it up. I'm so tired. I'm going to take a nap."

The journal contained a hundred pages, so it stated on the flyleaf. There were gaps of weeks, and sometimes months during which nothing was written. Other times there were daily entries, most of which were personal and emotional. A few were a single sentence.

"January 12, 1992. Came to Huntington House by myself. It's no lonelier than being by myself in New York and I feel more peaceful here."

"*February 1, 1992. Just got back from the doctor. Blood pressure was frighteningly high. He increased my medications. I'm to go back in two weeks. 'Try not to get excited,' he cautioned.*"

The most terrifying entry of all was written early in 1990.

"*My bruises are beginning to turn from blue and purple to yellow. Fortunately they don't show. A short-sleeved shirt covers the one on my arm and of course, nobody sees the one on my thigh but it is really sore. I don't think Malcolm knew he was holding my arm so tight, nor did he intend for me to hit the corner of the dresser when he pushed me away.*

"*I'm sure I'd cleared the dinner date with him. And, I'm equally sure he agreed when I told him my college friends were in town and I wanted to invite them and their husbands to dinner.*

"'*What's this?' he demanded when he saw the dining table set for six, complete with flowers, candles, and crystal. 'The Carlsons and Littles are coming for dinner, remember?'*

"'*Well, I have an important meeting,' he said as he headed for the bedroom, throwing off his coat and loosening his tie. I followed him and grabbed his arm. 'Mal, what am I supposed to do?' He shoved me away. That's when I hit the corner of the dresser. 'I don't care what you do,' he stormed. 'Call them and cancel, or have dinner without me. I have nothing in common with those people anyway.'*

"*I was proud of myself for not crying, not begging. 'Very well,' I said, 'I'll give them your regrets.' When I turned to leave the room he grabbed my arm. 'For God's sake, Carol, don't be a martyr. Just how do you think you're able to live like this?' He waved his arms around the room. Like this! I'd give anything not to live like this.*"

I laid the book aside and went to stand by the window. So that's what's expected of me: the tennis group, club luncheons, charity balls. The laughing woman in the photograph was only playing a role.

It was nearly four o'clock when I heard Malcolm's key in the door. I quickly slid the journal into my satchel and went into the bathroom. I wasn't quite ready to face him. I found him in the courtyard looking out over the city. He had a drink in his hand— two fingers of single malt scotch with two ice cubes—his only drink except for good wines. "Would you like something?" he asked.

"No thanks. What have you decided about dinner?"

"If you're hungry we can have something sent in now, or we could go to *Un Deux Trois* for old times' sake." He smiled at me above his glass. I knew he was not ready to pick up this morning's conversation.

"Oh, let's go to the restaurant," I said, suddenly preferring noise and crowds and activity.

The play was *Mama Mia*. Thankfully it was not something dark and brooding. During intermission we engaged in innocent chatter and I could almost forget the past four months. I could almost forget the words I'd read that afternoon—almost.

The restaurant was jammed with after-theater crowds, both performers and patrons. Groups were clustered around the bar, drinks in hand, waiting for seating. We were ushered through the crowded room, dodging rushing waiters, miraculously to a table for two in a corner near a window. Just across the room was where I first met Malcolm Steele. I wondered where my life would be now if I had not had that encounter.

When we were seated, the wine steward magically appeared with a crisply chilled bottle of Fume Blanc, which he poured into Malcolm's waiting glass. My husband nodded his acceptance. The server finished filling the glasses and retreated. "Here's to us," he said and raised his glass to me. I clinked my glass and smiled.

"I will wager," he said as he took my hand across the table, "that you have not had one golf lesson since I left."

"No, I haven't. I haven't joined a country club or gone to lunch with any women I've met." I gave a quiet laugh.

"What's so funny?"

"But, I have had breakfast with two little girls whose mother is in the hospital and I sometimes have lunch with Roberto and his men. I'm getting plenty of exercise too, working in Mr. Webster's grove. I really haven't had time for golf."

His scowl quickly turned into a smile as the waiter came to take our order. I suddenly realized it had been almost twelve hours since I'd eaten.

"Are you as famished as I am?" I asked, breaking open a roll and reaching for the butter. "Did you have any lunch?"

"I had lunch at the club."

Naturally, I thought, *lunch at the club.*

"Why are you doing this to me?" he said in a low voice that had the overtone of anger.

"Malcolm, I'm not doing anything to you," I replied as calmly as I could. Over our dinners of blackened fish for me and a rare steak for him, I explained my activities. I told him how excited I was about reclaiming the neglected citrus trees. I told him about Peggy Sue and Allie. When I described how Louisa and I had given them baths he looked at me in disbelief.

"At Huntington House?"

"Yes, of course at Huntington House. Malcolm, children have been bathed in that house before—even your grandchildren."

When I told him about going to Immokalee with Mr. Webster and Pastor Ben he held up his hand. "That's enough, Jessica! What's gotten into you?" he hissed through clenched teeth. "I've told you that if you want to help these unfortunates I'll provide any amount of money you want to give them."

"But this makes me feel good," I defended.

"*This is inappropriate!*"

"Why?"

"Because—you—are—Mrs. Malcolm Steele." He spoke each word as though he was striking a blow.

I did not look away. In equally measures words I said, "and you, Malcolm Steele, are—a—snob."

His hand gripped the wine glass so hard I expected to hear it snap. His face was red with anger. He asked for the check in a voice so icy that you could have skated on his words.

We left the restaurant in silence, and rode home in silence. He went immediately to the bar and poured himself a drink. I went into the bedroom and closed the door. It was after one o'clock in the morning.

A few minutes later the door opened. "Will you go to Timber Ridge with me?"

"No, I told you that."

"Why not?"

"I already made other plans. I told you that too."

"What other plans?"

"I'm giving a birthday party for Jack, ah—Mr. Webster. He'll be seventy-three."

"What do you see in that old man?"

It seemed like a genuine question. "I don't know," I admitted. "He's not very lovable. But, it's such a waste, his life, and his grove. Maybe I see it as a challenge. I really have no part in your life," I continued, "but it's obvious you don't approve of the things I do."

Malcolm didn't answer right away. "China is really no place for you. I am out at the project sites much of the time."

"Nor do I want to be there," I agreed. "I think too, that I'll find another place to live."

"Why?"

"You keep reminding me that it's Carol's house. I really don't feel comfortable there." I went into the bathroom and closed the door.

Sometime later I felt him slip in bed beside me. He reached over and touched my shoulder. "Jessica?" he said. When I didn't respond he sighed and turned away from me.

Malcolm and I managed to get through the art exhibit, moving from painting to painting, politely commenting. If anybody watched us they would think we were enjoying ourselves. When we came out of the show, a late-evening shower had cooled the air. Wet streets glistened in the lights. We walked the short distance to Union Street Station for dinner, and when we had nothing more to say about the paintings, the artist or her style, we fell to eating in silence. "Are we going to make it?" Malcolm asked. "Is there any hope for us?"

Sitting across from him in the cross hairs of his penetrating look, I was totally unprepared for the question. My throat closed up when I tried to swallow. My eyes stung, and my vision blurred with tears that I refused to let fall.

"I don't know." Last night I would have said "no." Last night I had just wanted to be away from his anger and his displeasure. "I can't mold myself into something I'm not." When he didn't answer

I continued, "When you went to China you told me you were going to be gone for a couple of months. It's already been four, and if these new jobs come through . . ." My voice trailed off. "This is not a marriage. I can't fill my days with luncheons and swimming and golf. In fact, I *hate* golf." There. I'd said it. "I seem to have found a place for my heart. I'm happy," I said with a shrug and a smile. "If you can't accept that, then what is there for us?"

I expected anger. I expected arguments. I got neither. He looked at me with a certain sadness and I wondered if he too had a pain in his chest.

"I've booked a flight back tomorrow afternoon," I told him when we got back to the apartment, "after I have lunch with Christine."

Malcolm did not come to bed that night.

Christine swept into the restaurant like a minitornado, her floral summer skirt swirling around her legs and her bright hair lighting up the aisle as she made her way toward the table. Her smile of welcome disappeared as a look of utter shock froze on her face when she reached me.

"Jess! Jessica, is it you? What happened?"

"Nothing," I said as I stood up to give her a hug.

"You look so different. Your face is brown. You've hair is long and you've lost weight," she enumerated as she slid into the booth. "Look at your hands," she screamed. "You look like you're wearing brown gloves. You . . . you don't look like a New Yorker any more," she stammered.

"And I know a sixteen-year-old boy who would steal to have hair the color of yours. He has to get his out of a bottle," I told her.

"So what does Malcolm say about all this?" Chris asked.

"He doesn't like it," I admitted with a sigh.

"Did we make a mistake?" she asked quietly, searching my face for a clue. I'd forgotten how intuitive Christine was.

"I don't know."

CHAPTER FIFTEEN

"What's wrong with Jack?" I asked. Ben sat at the table while I put away the supper dishes. "He's back to being the old grump he used to be. I'd have thought with work going so well and having his cast off he'd be in a better mood. All he said when I got here today was 'Couldn't stay away, could you, girlie?' Did something happen while I was gone?"

Cat had stalked off to bed with his master, but Soot scampered around the floor at Ben's feet, playing with a toy Peggy Sue and Allie had sent him. When Ben didn't answer right away I took my glass of tea and sat across from him. He too had been quiet during supper. "No," he replied. "Nothing happened."

"Then why does it seem like it has?" I asked.

Ben, cradling his glass in his hands, raised his eyes to mine. "I guess he doesn't know how to express happiness. He was afraid you wouldn't come back. Because he wasn't able to let you know how glad he was to see you I guess he just reverted to his old ways."

My heart gave a little flip. "How nice," I smiled. "And you, Ben? You've been quiet tonight too?"

He set down his glass and, placing his elbows on the table, buried his face in his hands.

"Ben, what's the matter?" I asked, alarmed.

When he looked up his eyes were moist. "Oh, Jessica, God forgive me, I was afraid of that too," he said with a rush of breath. "Neither one of us voiced our thoughts but we both seemed to know what the other was thinking—and fearing. You've become so much a part of our lives that we tiptoed around our feelings all the time you were gone, afraid that you might stay there—or even go to China. Even the little girls wanted to know when they would see you again. Oh, Jess, I missed you so much."

My nose began to sting as tears flooded my eyes. My heart felt so full I thought it would rise out of my chest. So this is what it's like to be loved and wanted, I thought. I was filled with happiness but I felt sad at the same time.

"Oh, Ben," I said as I reached across the table and took his hands. His grip was warm and firm. "It is so important to me to have your friendship. It is probably the most important thing to me right now. My thoughts are so mixed up." My voice became thick with tears. I put one hand to my mouth to stifle a sob and tugged on Ben's arm to follow me. We stood outside at the bottom of the ramp while I pressed my hand to my mouth and took deep breaths to stop the sobs that were about to erupt. I fought to control the emotions I'd suppressed for days.

The sun was just dipping into the river. "Let's walk down to the dock," I said. We took off our shoes, and settling ourselves on the edge of the dock, dangled our feet in the water. The peace that comes with dusk of the evening here in this soft time of the day, enfolded me. Or, maybe it was Ben's peace that calmed me.

"I cannot be the kind of wife Malcolm wants me to be," I said after a few moments. "He'd planned for me to go with him to his mountain lodge for a week, I didn't—I couldn't. When I put on the new dress he'd bought me that must have cost a fortune, all I wanted was to be here in shorts, swatting insects and smelling citrus. When we went out to dinner with people to impress them," I continued, "all I wanted was to be having a glass of tea with *mis amigos* out here under the trees. I've discovered my heart is here. Malcolm doesn't approve of what I do, but I cannot be a Stepford wife."

Ben listened quietly. Tears flowed when I told him about Daisy Chang. "I don't know yet what I'm going to do, but I have to do something," I declared.

"I'll be here, Jessicacita."

The first thing I decided to do was to find a house. There were a number of "For Sale" or "For Rent" signs in front of the pleasant houses along the streets where I drove or walked. I looked around the great room of Huntington House. While charming, luxuriously furnished, and immaculately maintained it wasn't mine. Nor, did I want it to be. "It's all yours," I announced to the rightful mistress as I put Carol's photograph back in its place back on the mantle. "On the one hand, I admire the strength you had to stay with Malcolm Steele. On the other, I wonder why?"

"*Señora* Steele?" a voice said behind me.

My hand flew to my chest. "Oh, Louisa, I didn't hear you come in. Here I am talking to myself."

"Is something wrong?" A look of concern registered in her chestnut-colored eyes. "I didn't expect you until tomorrow,"

"Well, I guess there is something wrong," I said as I walked over and took her arm. "Come, sit and have a cup of coffee with me."

I wondered how to begin as I poured mugs of coffee for each of us and brought milk from the fridge for her to add. She didn't look at me as she stirred the liquid in her cup.

"Louisa, Mr. Steele is in China. He has business there that is going to keep him away for an indefinite period of time. I want to thank you for taking such good care of me, but I can't stay here. I'm going to find another place to live." Her concerned eyes captured mine. "I don't feel as though I should stay in this house that is really a family home. And to tell the truth," I drew a deep breath, "I'm having trouble being the kind of wife Mr. Steele wants me to be." There! I'd said it. "I *am* going to stay here in Florida—I'm happy here."

"*Sí,*" she smiled as the apprehensive look disappeared from her face.

"You knew Mrs. Steele—a-Carol?" I asked.

"Oh, *sí*. I worked for Mr. and Mrs. Huntington and for Mrs. Steele for many, many years. Our children were babies together." Her face softened in the pleasure of remembering. "Sometimes I would bring my children with me and they would play together when she was here by herself."

"Were you here the day she died?"

"*Dios Mio!*" she exclaimed, crossing herself. "Yes. *Sí*, right here."

She pointed to a place on the floor near us. "It wasn't right, his leaving her all the time. She was a nice lady. She deserved to be treated better, and so do you," she added with a tone in her voice I'd never heard before. Her determined eyes held my gaze as though challenging me to disagree.

"It's very sad for all of us," I said. "But," I added brightly, "I'm counting on you to help me get ready for Jack's party Saturday night. We'll go ahead as we planned."

A guest list had not been difficult, given Jack's vast circle of friends. There was Ben of course, Louisa and Carlos, Salvador and Ella. Roberto, who was more reticent than his mother and father, had declined my invitation. I hadn't insisted. Ella was catering the meal and I was already looking forward to her wonderful food. Scott, who had been helping out on Saturdays at his mentor's insistence, was coming—also at Ben's insistence—orange-spiked hair, baggy pants and all.

Jack sputtered and protested when Ben instructed him to be ready to be picked up at six o'clock Saturday evening. "Clean clothes," Ben warned with a smile.

I set the glass-topped table in the screen-enclosed patio with bright-colored place mats and napkins. Then, I filled a large low bowl with melon-colored hibiscus and floating candles for the centerpiece. A sideboard held a stack of equally vivid plates and serving dishes ready to be filled with food. Louisa hummed in the kitchen as she put together a wonderful punch of citrus juices and seltzer. It was her own special recipe. I bought chilled sparkling grape juice for a toast.

Sal and Ella arrived at five-thirty with the food, bringing in far too many foil-covered containers for our small number. Tantalizing smells followed them into the room as they placed them in the oven or the refrigerator. Louisa ran to hold open the door as Carlos, with his broad smile of gleaming gold-capped teeth, carried in the birthday cake she had made at home. It was fittingly called "Orange Surprise Cake." There was orange juice in the batter and orange and lemon zest in the fluffy frosting that was piled high on top and sides. The surprise was a mixture of finely crushed pecans, brown sugar and butter pasted between the layers. We surrounded the platter with green baby oranges with a few leaves attached that I had surreptitiously snipped from Jack's trees. Laughter and happy chatter filled the room as we fussed with the final preparations.

Ben dropped Scott off on his way to fetch Jack. "How are things going?" I asked him. He gave me a thumbs-up and a quirky smile. I handed him an igniter. "Your job is to light the tiki lights around the pool when it starts to get dark. No mosquitoes invited to this party."

Several minutes after we heard Ben's truck pull into the driveway he pushed Jack through the door. "Happy Birthday!" we shouted. His eyes scanned the room as the look on his face went from shock to recognition. The corners of his mouth quivered and I saw his Adam's apple move as he swallowed. "Happy Birthday, Jack," I said as I stepped forward and planted a kiss on his cheek.

"You can't ever mind your own business," he scolded. At least he didn't add "girlie." He reached up and gripped my shoulder, a gesture that, I'm sure, caused him great effort.

Scott dutifully remembered his assignment and went around the pool lighting the torches. Thunder rumbled in the distance but tonight we were spared our daily rain shower. While Louisa and Ella filled the serving dishes, I lit the candles on the table and put on some music. There were tacos and enchiladas, homemade tamales, chili rellenos, and refried beans. Bowls of Pico De Gallo, pungent with the smell of fresh cilantro, were passed. The evening became magical. None of the people, I thought, were educated in the "social graces," yet grace was among us.

Jack's prickly attitude was swept away as stories from the past were told. Jack and Salvador relived the day of his accident while the rest of us listened with horror at the vivid description. They talked of growing citrus and the way it "used to be done." Scott, who I thought would be bored, was fascinated.

When we'd eaten more than we should and plates were cleared, I decided to present the painting before Louisa brought out the birthday cake. Scott helped me carry out the gift, wrapped in bright birthday paper. Jack muttered something about this being kid stuff as he was encouraged to unwrap his present. We all stood silently as he tugged at the ribbon and paper crackled under his trembling hands.

Jack's face was impassive as we held *The Pickers* up for him to see. A muscle twitched above his jaw, and I saw tears in his eyes before he buried his face in his blue-veined hands. We propped the painting on a chair and quickly busied ourselves with clearing the table and the food to give him a chance to recover his composure.

"Where are you going to hang it?" Ben asked as slices of moist, delicious-looking cake were passed.

"In my bedroom," Jack stated, as though it should have been obvious to us.

Louisa was the one who first heard a sound. She seemed to be sensitive to the noises and groans of the house in which she had worked for so long. Her hand stopped with a forkful of cake halfway to her mouth as her eyes shot toward the front of the house. Momentarily the rest of us heard a door slam. Suddenly Malcolm was standing in the door that led from the kitchen to the patio. He held a small leather bag in his hand. Once I'd registered the expression of shock on his face I saw that his face looked tired and drawn. My heart slammed against my chest so hard I could hear it in my ears. Then I felt as though someone had dropped a handful of ice cubes in the pit of my stomach. In slow motion, it seemed, everyone put down their forks and turned to face the doorway.

"Malcolm!" I jumped up, willing my heart to calm. "What a surprise. I didn't know you were coming." I forced a deep breath that I hoped would stop my rushing words. "We're celebrating Mr. Webster's birthday. You're just in time for some cake."

"I changed my plans," he said as he lowered his case to the floor.

"Come and meet my friends." I walked over and took his arm. His self-image would not allow him to make a scene in front of strangers, especially *these* strangers. I led him to the table. Louisa jumped up and offered him her chair. "This is Mr. Webster," I said, pausing in front of the guest of honor. "Do you remember Jack?"

While Ben, Carlos, and Sal rose to their feet, Jack remained seated. I saw Ben nod his head toward Scott who quickly pushed back his chair and stood up. "I haven't had the pleasure," Malcolm said with satin-coated words as he reached out and shook Jack's hand.

I made introductions around the table and when I got to Ben, I said, "This is Pastor Ben Rodriguez."

"My wife has mentioned you," Malcolm said with a tight smile.

"I'm pleased to meet you," Ben said warmly as he grasped Malcolm's hand between his two, the way he greeted parishioners every Sunday. Malcolm all but jerked his hand away from the too-familiar gesture.

"Here is some cake, *Señor* Steele," Louisa said, standing at his elbow.

"No thanks, Louisa." He turned and gave her a conciliatory pat on the shoulder. "Save it for me. I've had a long day." To the rest of us he said, "Go on with your party." He picked up his bag and went into his office, closing the door a little harder than necessary, I thought.

It didn't take long for the party to come to an end. I understood fully the meaning of the cliché "wet blanket," and I thought I would suffocate from it as we cleared the table and I said good-bye to my guests.

It was still early, only nine-thirty. I wasn't ready for bed, nor was I ready to face Malcolm in a conversation I knew was waiting. Why did he come? I wondered. I felt embarrassed as though I'd been caught doing something wrong. I was humiliated by his icy treatment of my guests and I was angry. Maybe I would go for a swim.

He was not in the bedroom but his suitcase lay open on the luggage rack and his blazer was hung neatly on the clothes caddy. Even his pocket change was carefully ordered in the mahogany depression there. He must have heard me because as I pulled my swimsuit out of the drawer, the door opened. He wore only his lightweight robe but his whole body seemed engulfed in a purple radiance of rage. His jaws were set and skin around his eyes pinched into tight wrinkles. I almost laughed when another trite saying "shooting daggers" came to mind. If his eyes had the power to throw swords, they would have.

"The country club bores you, does it?" he asked, his voice heavy with sarcasm. "You'd rather socialize with Mexicans, an old drunk, a preacher with a scar across his face, and a punk kid."

I wanted to slap him. My pulse was throbbing in my ears, but I willed myself to be calm. "Well, you named them all," I said evenly.

"Your conduct is inappropriate. You have no right to have those people here."

"I did nothing wrong. Two of those people, Louisa and Carlos, were in *this* house before you ever were, and 'that old drunk' as you call him, made his living the same way your wife's father did," I reminded him. I headed for the bathroom to put on my bathing suit. Suddenly I was uncomfortable undressing in front of him.

"Where are you going?"

"For a swim." Briefly a tremor of fear ran through me at the idea of what could happen to me in a swimming pool.

"No, you're not." In an instant he was across the room. He grabbed my arm as I tried to close the bathroom door. I felt a pain shoot through my shoulder as his fingers closed like a vise. "We have to settle some things. You're going to understand what I expect from my wife."

In spite of the pain I looked at his hand then calmly met his eyes. "Those bruises won't be covered up," I said.

With a shocked look on his face he studied his hand then slowly loosened his grip and stepped backward. Suddenly there was a noise in another part of the house. Our gazes shifted to the open door. Malcolm frowned then turned and headed down the hall toward the sound. A few moments later I heard voices in the kitchen.

"Pardon, *Señor* Steele." It was Louisa. I could hear her excitedly explaining that she had forgotten her house key and had to come back to get it. Grateful relief washed over me, I knew she had *not* forgotten her key. Besides, Carlos had keys. I knew she had come back to check on me as surely as I knew that Ben was somewhere praying for my safety. I had nothing to fear from the man who now walked back into the room. I knew beyond any shadow of doubt that I was protected.

"I don't know why you decided to come here," I said, "but I'm sorry that you did. I've found a place to live and I'll be moving next week, but I had already planned this party." Malcolm started to say something but I held up my hand, forcing my palm toward him, stopping him. "If I had any doubts about my decision, I don't have any longer." I walked over and removed the small hardbound journal from the stack of books on the table beside the bed. I handed it to him. "I think you should read this." I opened the page to the 1990 entry.

Malcolm frowned but took the book and walked over to stand near the light. His forehead drew into furrows as he focused on the pages. He looked up at me. "This is Carol's handwriting. Where did you get this?"

"I found it in a drawer when I was looking for clothes for the little girls I told you about."

"You had no right . . ." he began, but my look stopped him.

"Maybe you should read the last few pages," I suggested.

He dropped into the chair and turned to the back of the book, to the last entry Carol had written before she died.

Suddenly the book dropped to the floor between his bare feet and he covered his face with his hands. "Oh, God! Oh, God," he muttered.

I waited for what seemed like forever before he looked up at me. There was a look of genuine anguish on his face. There was also the wary look of a trapped animal. I sat on the bed across from him. When he started to speak it was in a low hesitant voice. He didn't look at me but focused on some unseen image on the floor between us.

"Do you remember when we first met and you called me Mal and I asked you not to?"

I nodded.

"Those were the last words I ever heard Carol say that day when I went out the door. 'Mal! Mal,' she called after me. She tried to apologize for upsetting me. She was always apologizing and that annoyed me. She had been dead for two days before my office located me." His voice became raspy with emotion. "For weeks afterward her voice and those words woke me up at night, 'Mal! Please Mal.' Sometimes they still do."

He stood up and began pacing the floor, his hands jammed into the pockets of his robe. "The children were so angry with me when I finally got here that I don't know how we got through the preparations and the service. You've noticed that I'm not very close to my children."

"Was Valerie with you when they found you?" I asked, shocked at my own question.

Malcolm swung around to stare at me. "How . . . ?" he began then closed his mouth. He nodded. He sat back heavily in the chair, looking every bit his sixty-five years.

Anger rose inside me. I was angry for myself and for Carol. "You created a relationship that didn't exist so that you could live with your conscience," I accused. "You created the role Carol was supposed to play, and you pretended she was content with it, that she was happy with her luncheons and her charitable organizations, that her children and grandchildren were all that she needed to be happy. That certainly removed any responsibility from you.

"Now you want me to fit into that same mold," I continued. "Well, I can't. *I can't be Mrs. Malcolm Steele!* My name is Jessica." I got up and began gathering my nightclothes. "I'll sleep in the guest room," I said.

"Jessica," he called quietly. "Can we talk about this tomorrow?"

I drew in a deep breath and faced him. "Does Miss Chang share your quarters in Beijing?" I asked.

He lowered his head. "Sometimes," he replied.

"Then there's nothing to talk about."

As I crawled into the unfamiliar bed my heart felt as heavy as a log inside me. Tears rolled down my cheeks and into my ears then made damp, cool patches on my pillow. I could not go back. We could not begin again. It was over, so I cried at the loss and the failure. I cried for unfulfilled lives, for Carol's, even for Malcolm's and vowed that mine would not become one of those.

It was ten o'clock when I woke the next morning. Malcolm was nowhere about and when I went into the kitchen I noticed that the small boat was gone from the dock. There was not even a reminder of last night's party except for foiled wrapped packages of leftover food and the piece of birthday cake Louisa had saved for Malcolm. I grabbed a cup of coffee and a glass of juice. I had just time to make it to church. I had to go.

I slipped into a seat near the back just as the service began. Ben scanned the congregation and caught my eye. I saw a look of relief in his. Afterward, as always, he stood on the steps speaking to each member of his flock. When it was my turn to greet him, he placed my hand between his two just as he always did.

"Thank you, Pastor Ben," I said with great propriety. I wanted to throw my arms around him just to feel his strength. "Thank you for your prayers last night."

The corners of his mouth lifted in his crooked smile. "Would you like to talk sometime?"

"Tomorrow," I said.

Malcolm was in the kitchen when I got back to Huntington House. He turned from the table he was setting. He'd shaved and looked relaxed in his casual knit shirt and Dockers, but there were dark circles under his eyes and sallowness to his tan. "I thought you might like something to eat," he said. "I've made a shrimp omelet and a salad."

"That sounds good," I said, surprised that I felt hungry.

"Coffee, tea or lemonade?" he asked.

"Tea, please."

He poured our drinks and sat down across from me. "I read all of Carol's journal last night. I had no idea." He hesitated then began again, "I mean, I was too busy with other things—things I thought were more important. She had the children. I guess I thought she was okay with that." He drew a breath. "That doesn't paint a very pretty picture of me."

"Where do we go from here?" he asked when I didn't say anything.

"I think," I replied, "that we go our separate ways."

"Is there any way we could work this out?"

I looked at him in surprise. "Why would you want to?"

"I do care for you. You're a beautiful, lovely woman and I *have* made a commitment to you."

I shook my head in disbelief. "Commitment, Malcolm? You're going halfway around the world and will be there—for how long? Even if I came to China what would I do? How would I fit in to your life? Would I share you with Miss Chang?" His mouth tightened at my words but I went on. "To reconcile a relationship takes willingness on both parts. Would you be able to accept my friends? Could I be the kind of wife you want? I doubt it. It would require serious counseling on both our parts. Would you be willing to do that? I'm not sure I would."

"I don't think that would be necessary," he countered. He shoved back his chair and went to stand at the sink, his back to me.

I pushed my plate away. The half-eaten omelet had become cold and rubbery. "Then we don't have a chance." I tasted the bitterness of the words in my mouth.

When he turned to face me, Malcolm looked old and defeated. Fleetingly I felt sorry for him, but the man I had come to know, if not understand, I was sure, was not defeated. "You are welcome to stay here in this house," he said. "You don't need to move."

"I don't want to stay here. I've found a charming house. And, as soon as I can, I'll see that my things are out of the New York apartment." I stood up and started toward the door.

"Jessica?" His voice stopped me. "I have to go back to Beijing now—I really do, but why don't you think about this. I'll come back in a month."

No, I thought, Malcolm Steele has not accepted defeat.

CHAPTER SIXTEEN

I loved my new house. It was one I'd passed often on my morning walks. It was pale peach stucco with cream trim and a perfectly manicured yard of Saint Augustine grass, Sabal palms, and hibiscus. I learned from the realtor that the owner was a "snowbird" who spent only the winter months here in the south. Her husband had recently died and she wasn't sure if she'd be coming back here.

The house was only a few years old, bright and airy and completely furnished. There was a master suite that opened out onto the typical, enclosed Florida room, which contained a swimming pool and a Jacuzzi. When the land had been cleared for construction, a large, old live oak tree had been spared. Now, its filigreed shade gracing most of the backyard gave a feeling of permanence to the place. Best of all, the house was only two miles from Jack.

Yesterday, after our painful discussion at lunch, Malcolm phoned his pilot and told him to have the plane ready to leave at six o'clock that evening. Afternoon clouds began to roll in and I heard faint thunder in the distance. I suddenly felt exhausted. I went into the guest room, lay down on the bed and fell instantly asleep. It took me a minute to realize that what I was hearing was not thunder, but someone knocking on the door. I squinted at the clock beside the bed. The hands read four-thirty. "Just a minute," I called. I splashed water on my sleep-puffy eyes.

When I opened the door Malcolm stood there dressed for travel. His luggage was stacked near the entry. I noticed he had several more pieces than when he'd arrived the day before.

"You look beautiful," he said. I ran a hand through my disheveled hair and tugged at my wrinkled blouse. I felt anything but beautiful. He came over and pulled me to him. When I resisted he tugged gently. "I won't hurt you, Jessica," he said in a thick voice as he folded his arms around me.

I felt a lump in my throat. This is going to be harder than I imagined, I thought as I allowed myself to be caressed. The room grew dark as bursts of lightning and cracks of thunder came closer.

As tall as I was, Malcolm was able to rest his chin on top of my head. I felt his throat working. "If this is what you want," he said above the vocalness of nature, "then we'll work out a suitable arrangement, but I want you to think about it for a month." He pushed me back and held me at arm's length. "Will you?" he asked when I finally looked at him. There was nothing to think about but I nodded.

"I'll phone you when I get to Beijing." Then he hesitated. "I won't know how to reach you," he said, his voice breaking. Just then we heard the onslaught of rain. It sounded like a hundred snare drums beating a staccato rhythm on the roof and the windows. It was deafening.

"I'll phone *you*," I said, raising my voice above the elements. We heard a horn honking. The limo was here to take him to the airport. "Safe journey," I whispered and raised my hand in farewell as the driver stowed the bags then held the umbrella as Malcolm made a dash for the car. He lowered the window and blew me a kiss, and then they were gone down the driveway. The taillights, distorted circles of red, disappeared as they turned the corner.

It took me no more than half a day, with Louisa's help to move my belongings to my new home. Tears rolled down her caramel cheeks as we stepped over splintered twigs and plastered leaves that littered the driveway from the storm the night before.

"Louisa, I know endings are always sad, but," I scolded gently as I put my arm around her shoulders, "I'm only going to be a few streets away. You promised you would come help me. And of course, we have to keep Mr. Webster from going back to his old ways. You will help me, won't you?"

"*Si, Señora,*" she smiled. "There will not be anything to do in this house anymore."

For the next two days I euphorically arranged and rearranged my house. I was being allowed to rent it until the terms of the contract were finalized. There had been no problem with the sale when I met the full asking price. I made no effort to get in touch with Ben or Jack and felt a freedom in the isolation I'd never known before. I had gone from my grandparents' ranch to the apartments Mari and I shared. There was my sojourn with Philip, and then of course, there were Malcolm's houses and apartments, but for the first time I owned something truly on my own. It was exciting.

The house was fully furnished and equipped with everything one needed, including a bread machine, as if anyone would ever need one of those. I eyed the contraption perched on the kitchen counter. Even the instructions and recipe book were beside it. I had little to do but shop for groceries and a few personal items. There was one bedroom with lots of windows and good northern light that I decided to make into my studio. I set up my worktable and supplies. When I recognized the queasiness in my stomach as hunger, I stopped and ate—sometimes a shrimp cocktail beside the pool, sometimes a peanut butter and banana sandwich in my new studio. At times, I just sat and licked my wounds. Knowing I had made the only decision I could make didn't help much. I felt loss and a certain embarrassment at having failed.

On Tuesday evening I picked up the telephone and called Christine. It didn't surprise me that she would be the first person I contacted. After all, except for Ben, Jack and Louisa, who even cared? I was every bit alone as my mother had been. Maybe we weren't destined to have close, permanent relationships.

"Oh, Jessica, I'm so sorry," Chris kept repeating when I explained that Malcolm and I would be divorcing and the reasons why.

"It's not your fault," I insisted.

Our conversation shifted to more comfortable topics. I gave her my new phone number. "Come down for a visit," I said. "I'd love for you to."

"Maybe when it gets cooler."

"Jessica," she said as I began my good-bye, "it's not because he's so-oo old is it?"

I burst out laughing. "Now that's the Christine I know!" I exclaimed, remembering her words of three years ago. "No, *that* is not." We were both laughing as we hung up.

When I turned into Jack's driveway Wednesday morning, I was amazed at how much progress had been made in my absence. I hadn't paid much attention when I got back last week. All the dead and dying trees were gone and most of the pruning was done. Grass between even rows of shiny green-leafed trees was neatly trimmed and free of weeds. The bright green fruit of this year's crop of Valencias was already baseball size and the blossoms for next year's crop had dropped to the ground, leaving tiny nubs that were the beginning of other oranges. Only the old house was in its continued state of disrepair. Bits of it barely hung on—a drooping shutter here, a sagging porch there. The rusty drainpipe that had been held only by vines growing around it, had finally fallen to the ground. It must have been the storm Sunday night, I thought.

Jack and Roberto were working over a piece of equipment hooked to the back of the old tractor. None of the other men had arrived. Jack held a garden hose, filling a reservoir while Roberto studied each of the numerous nozzles on the mechanical arms that extended from either side. Jack's expression of pleasure was brief before he resumed his natural scowl, but I could tell that he was happy to see me.

"You're getting ready to spray," I exclaimed.

"And it's time you got back to work," he muttered. Roberto gave me a wink.

"What do you want me to do?" I asked, feeling better than I had in several days.

Jack merely nodded his head in the direction of the large oak tree at the side of the driveway. Underneath it were several dozen budded rootstock trees in short wooden crates, six to a container. Their fragile roots were housed in damp burlap and the entire mass was covered with netting.

"They're here!" I ran over to look.

Jack followed. He was moving well on his newly healed leg,

but he still used his cane to lessen the weight on his arthritic hip. "These are waiting for you," he said.

"For me?"

"You want to be a grower. See what you can do with these."

There they were, the young cultivars Jack had instructed me to order several weeks ago. Most were Valencias but there were a dozen honeybells and a few, early maturing Hamlins. Late August was not the optimum time for planting, but neither of us was inclined to wait.

"Where do I begin?" I asked in an unsure voice.

"Don't you know? I thought you'd been studying." His words, while still sardonic, were spoken with a smile.

"I guess I should get the soil ready." There was an acre that had been cleared of diseased trees, and isolated places in the rows of mature trees where trees had been removed that needed new trees. Of the nearly seven hundred thousand acres of commercial citrus in Florida, my one acre seemed overwhelming.

"The soil *is* ready," he replied. When I raised my eyebrows, he scoffed. "What do you think we've been doing while you've been running around?"

"Well, I think I'll check the pH anyway."

"Good." He nodded his approval. "Roberto and I have to get on with the spraying." He squinted at the hazy, yellow sky. "If it looks like we're gonna get rain this afternoon Roberto will get his men here so we can get started. We have to water by hand."

"By hand!" I exclaimed.

"By hand," he repeated defiantly. "Otherwise it would mean unhooking the sprayer. We'll be through spraying in a couple of days." With that he made his way over to the idling tractor and using the steering wheel to pull himself up, hitched his body into the seat, blatantly refusing Roberto's help.

Roberto pulled on a jumpsuit that covered his entire body, except for his face and hands. He donned goggles and a ventilator. When he offered one to Jack he shook his head and pulled a red bandana from his back pocket, which he tied, bandit style, around his nose and mouth. Old habits die hard, I thought, and some never die at all.

Jack positioned the tractor and the weird contraption behind it between two rows of trees. Roberto adjusted the height and extension of the arms so that the highest nozzle was just at the top of the tallest trees. The lowest one rode just below the bottom branches and leaves. Tiny hoses fed each of the openings with liquid, pumped from the large barrel-like reservoir. While Jack drove ever so slowly, Roberto stood on a platform at the back of the machine and, with rubber-gloved hands regulated each of the openings to just the correct angle to deliver maximum coverage. From time to time they stopped for adjustments. Once everything was working to Jack's satisfaction Roberto left him and came back to work in the shed until it was time to refill the tank.

"For want of a horse, a battle was lost, or some such thing," I muttered to myself as I headed toward my van. I had indeed read about planting new rootstock and plenty of water was a must. "If my little trees need water, they'll have water," I declared. As I opened the door a black streak shot past me with a loud meow. "Soot," I exclaimed, "look how you've grown." I said as I picked up the sleek black kitten from the seat and cuddled him to my chest. His purring machine kicked into high gear.

I decided I should check the house for supplies so that I could shop for them as well. Jack was staying by himself although he had a "life line," which he'd begrudgingly promised to wear at night. I saw it on his bedside table. There was little in the way of food although there was an ample supply of cat food. An empty cereal bowl and a glass were in the sink, no doubt this morning's breakfast. There were no other dirty dishes. I looked through cupboards and out-of-the-way hiding places for any sign of a whiskey bottle. Although it was not my place to monitor him and I was really overstepping my bounds, I even looked in the garbage for empty bottles. I prayed that our efforts—mine, Ben's and Jack's—would not end up like a pile of rubbish at our feet.

My first stop was at my house to pick up a pH meter and a soil-testing kit I'd bought. Then I thumbed through the Yellow

Pages of the phone book until I found the business I was looking for. I'd seen the kind of thing I wanted, a small tractor with a water reservoir on the back. They used them along Palm Beach Boulevard to water trees and plants. They were fitted with hoses and wands that reached difficult places. Eventually we would have to buy one, but right now renting was faster.

I found Cal's Complete Garden and Equipment Center in LaBelle who seemed to have anything and everything a "wannabe" or "needabe" gardener could want. A pleasant young man, proportionally large by all standards, greeted me. He was tall and heavy with hands the size of baseball mitts, shoes the size of boats. He was equally congenial and knowledgeable. The embroidered name on his green and white-striped shirt informed me that his name was Verne. He assured me that the unit I rented had been thoroughly cleaned and would be delivered by noon.

It was past eleven o'clock by the time I began pushing my grocery cart down the frigid aisles of the supermarket. I was grateful that a population on the go demanded easy-to-cook or prepared meals. I picked up a couple of roasted chickens and some shish kebabs, already skewered and marinated and ready for the grill. I got several cold salads from the deli department and bakery desserts and breads. I managed only the simplest of meals. I'd never really learned to cook. Mari wasn't interested in it. We often ate in restaurants or delis or prepared easy meals at the apartment. Since I'd been married to Malcolm there had always been someone else to do it.

When I drove into the driveway just after noon Jack was nowhere about and Roberto's pickup was gone. A truck with the tractor on its flatbed was idling near the shed. As I came to a stop the same mammoth young man scooted down from the driver's seat. "I was wondering if this was the right place," he said, eyeing the woe-be-gone house.

"It is," I said.

Verne engaged some motor inside the truck and the front of the flatbed rose while the rear slowly descended to the ground. He unhooked the chains that had secured the tractor, and climbing on to the seat, started the engine and backed it off. As I shook Verne's hand and thanked him, Jack walked out of the house. He stood rigid, watching. I couldn't believe he hadn't heard us. He'd probably been watching from the window. One thing I'd observed, that although he was arthritic and probably had a liver the size of a football field, at seventy-three, being hard of hearing was not among his ailments.

"Where were you?" I asked. He didn't answer. "Had your lunch?"

"Yes."

"What?"

He pushed his lips together. "Cornflakes."

"What did you have for breakfast?"

The corners of his mouth began to twitch. "Cornflakes," he replied.

I laughed as I went to the van to bring the groceries. "I haven't, so indulge me and join me for a turkey sandwich." In the kitchen the laboring fan circulated only tepid, oppressive air. I suggested that we eat outside. Carlos had found an old picnic table and repaired it for us. Someone, I noted, had painted it. We were only a few days away from September and the promise of cooler weather.

"Where's Roberto?"

"Gone to get his men. They'll be here at three o'clock."

A tingle of excitement ran through me. "I'm going to check the soil," I said as I headed toward the shed to get the four-wheeler. "Want to take a nap?" Jack waved me away, but by the time I'd back out of the shed, his head was nodding on his chest.

"Not bad for a city girl," Jack said after I'd practiced driving the tractor around the yard and up and down a few rows.

"I used to drive a tractor on my grandfather's sheep ranch when I was young," I told him.

He looked at me curiously. "Where was that?"

"Colorado."

His brow folded into a frown as he stared at me. Just then Roberto's truck drove into the yard, followed by a yet older truck, with a small forklift chained to its flatbed. "It's time to move,"

Jack said as he eyed the clouds forming to the north of us. We could smell the freshness of rain in the air. No rain fell on us that afternoon but the clouds gave us cover from the sun, and we benefited from the cooled air of someone else's showers.

I was surprised that Jack left me alone to supervise the men while he and Roberto went back to their spraying. Soon we had a rhythm to our work—a dusty, muddy rhythm. The man with the forklift transported the crated young trees to the cleared land, land that had been worked to perfection. Not a weed or a runner of grass could be seen. The soil had been loosely spaded and the rows were already laid out. We measured distances twenty feet apart where we dug holes two feet deep and three feet across. One small, dark man with muscles that billowed on his strong arms like knotted ropes, expertly sliced through the ball of the roots with a sharp machete-like knife to stimulate the formation of new roots, I was told. Then the tree was placed in the hole we'd made which we filled about one-third full with dirt, watered it generously, then tamped the soil to remove air pockets. We worked two rows at a time, new cultivars on either side, staggering them so that they weren't directly across from one another. We didn't mind the water that splashed on our dusty skin and we sometimes put our hands under the hose to mop our faces.

We made several trips down each row, adding more dirt and more water before the final mound of dirt was shoveled and patted smooth around each little tree. The men worked steadily with little conversation. Occasionally one cast an eye toward the sky. Late-August dusk settled quickly and by the time we finished the last few trees we could hardly see. We still had to form a water basin around each tree, but that could wait until tomorrow. For today our job was done. The new trees were planted.

As I drove the tractor out to the end of the row I was surprised to see Ben standing there with Jack and Roberto. My heart flipped at the sight of Ben. I was surprised that I had not thought of him or about my new situation all day. Jack pulled his customary roll of bills out of his pocket, and as he paid each man, I shook his hand. *"Muchas gracias! Muchas gracias!"* I murmured through tears of fatigue and gratitude. I suddenly realized how tired I was but, oh what a good kind of tired.

After we washed up I served the cold roasted chicken and the salads I'd bought. With the light from a lone street lamp at the entrance of the drive and the soft glow of the light from the kitchen we sat at the picnic table and I told Jack and Ben what had happened with Malcolm and about my new house. When I told them about Louisa coming back on the pretext of looking for her keys Jack shot Ben a knowing look.

"You knew, didn't you?" I whispered. When they didn't say anything I looked at them. "You were there too!" My breath caught in my chest as tears formed in my nose and eyes. Suddenly I felt a hand on mine. I hiccupped a sob as a quiver shot through my arm. It was an old hand—a calloused hand, an arthritic hand. It was Jack's hand.

"You hang in there, girlie," he said in his gritty voice. "Now you'd better get some rest." Quickly he jerked his hand away as though he was as surprised as I by his action.

"Do you want me to take you home?" Ben asked as he helped me carry the dishes into the house.

"No, I'll be fine." I took his hand. "Tomorrow when we're all not so tired you can come see my house? I smiled at him and saw his throat work as he swallowed. He nodded.

CHAPTER SEVENTEEN

By Labor Day weekend all the spraying was finished, water trenches had been dug around each of the cultivars, and each one of the little trees had received their first nutrients at one-half pound per tree. When Friday afternoon arrived Jack informed everybody that we would not begin fertilizing the rest of the grove until the following Tuesday. The men's smiles were broad when Jack handed them their pay and even broader when I added a bonus and my thanks. Ben's crew ended their work at noon as well. Everyone looked forward to the weekend that celebrated the toils of humankind.

We kept our eyes and ears tuned to news of a tropical disturbance brewing in the Caribbean. Jack had been one year old when the most severe hurricane in Florida's history killed eighteen hundred people in floods and accidents in 1928. Countless cows, horses, and wildlife lost their lives as well. His memories of that event were only through stories his parents later told him.

That evening when he, Ben, Ginger, and I sat on the dock at the river, he told those stories to us. He told us how the Caloosahatchee rose above its banks, pushed its way through the groves and forced its way into the house, bringing mud and debris into the first floor of his parents home. He told about the bloated animals and some humans that had been seen floating down the river and about later when bodies had to be recovered from along the banks once the water receded. That was before the south Florida waterway had been developed with its series of locks that controlled water between Lake Okeechobee and the Gulf of Mexico.

In the gathering twilight we saw occasional mullets leap from the water and heard their splash as they reentered. We watched low-flying terns in formation, skimming the water. Jack told us how his parents had nailed boards over the windows and then together, with their baby between them, huddled on the second floor of the Cypress House and waited out the storm. When I shuddered, Ben reached over and took my hand.

Jack had never been so talkative. I wished we could have stayed for more of his stories but with the dampness mosquitoes came, so we made our way back to the house. "I'm going to visit Maggie tomorrow," Ben said. "Will you go with me?" I opened my mouth to protest but he continued, "She's had three weeks of rehab, and I have permission to bring the girls with me."

While I wanted to say "no," I realized I wanted to see Peggy Sue and Allie. Both men waited for my answer. "I'd love to see them," I said.

Weather reports on all the local stations on the eleven o'clock news that evening upgraded the tropical depression in the Caribbean to a tropical storm category. Winds had increased to between forty and sixty miles an hour as the storm became more organized. Traveling at its present rate, in its present direction, it could reach Miami within three days. It was all a big question mark according to the accounts of the excited weathermen. It could increase or decrease in intensity. It could keep its course or change its course. I watched with fascination and some apprehension; as if to emphasize the importance of being prepared, film clips of Hurricane Andrew in 1992 were rerun. In that hurricane damages of more than twenty billion dollars wracked the state, however, thanks to advanced tracking systems, warning systems and evacuation practices, only fifty-four lives were lost compared to the eighteen hundred souls in 1928.

I grabbed a pen and paper and quickly jotted down a list of precautionary procedures as the reporter enumerated them: fill gas tank in car; get flashlights and a battery-operated radio with extra batteries, buy canned goods and bottled water; secure lawn furniture and any outdoor objects that could become projectiles.

Having no experience with any kinds of disasters made me all the more anxious. I vowed I would go to the hardware store and the supermarket the first thing the next morning before Ben picked me up. I fell into a fitful sleep with the weatherman's final words replaying in my mind. "The most important decision you will make is whether to *stay or leave.*"

"What's this?" Ben asked as he stepped over a pile of boards I'd stacked on the patio. He smiled as he surveyed my kitchen where every surface was crowded with bags and boxes. Several jugs of water sat on the floor. I'd even bought a butane hot plate.

"I got carried away," I confessed, ducking my head.

"If you'd waited I could have helped carry this stuff in," he said gently. I was once again reminded of his kindness.

"Why don't we take my van," I said as Ben started toward his truck.

"But I know the way."

"You can drive. I have four seat belts."

As we headed south on Interstate 75, I was aware of the freshly showered soap clean smell of his body. Today he wore a long-sleeved cotton shirt, black jeans and, instead of his heavy work boots, low-topped, pointed toed boots like I'd seen other Mexican men wearing.

"Tell me about Maggie," I said. "How did you meet her?'

"I met her when she was in rehab—actually the place where we visited her." When I turned to him in surprise he gave me a sad grin. "It's not her first time. I was there to visit someone else and that person asked me if I would talk to a woman in her therapy group. Maggie is a beautiful, talented woman," he continued. "I have seen her when she is clean and I know what she is capable of. Maggie Sinclair is a stage name. Well, her first name is Margaret but Sinclair is not her last name. She has a wonderful voice and at one time had a promising musical career. She comes from a prominent family who lives in Virginia. Her father is a retired military officer turned politician. You would recognize his name if I told you"

"You mean those little girls have grandparents, and they have to be put in foster homes?" I exclaimed. I had recently read disturbing news accounts about children who had disappeared from foster homes in Florida.

Ben pushed his lips together. "'Fraid so. Not everybody whose life is controlled by addiction comes from a disadvantaged background. However, in most cases the wealthy and famous come up with money to treat family members—not so with Maggie.

"Maggie trained at Julliard and has a degree in music. Her family pushed her toward an operatic career, but Maggie wanted Broadway and nightclubs. Her voice has the kind of volume and range that she can sing anything and give you goose bumps." I detected admiration in Ben's voice but I'd seen none of the woman about whom he spoke that in the haunted, disheveled person I met in the hospital.

"Maggie was strong willed and rebelled against her father. So, instead of continuing her operatic career she joined a band. There was nothing her father could do to stop her. She was, after all an adult—twenty-two or twenty-three years old. It was during this time that she was introduced to drugs by the owner of the club where she performed. He was young. He was handsome. He was wealthy, and she fell for him so badly she would do anything for him. Some of the things he wanted," Ben was silent for a moment, "some of the things were abusive and degrading and even dangerous. He set her up in a beautiful apartment, but he often went off leaving her locked in the bedroom when she had displeased him."

I shuddered, remembering my days with Philip. "When he found out she was pregnant," Ben continued, "*she* found out he was married. He gave her money to get rid of the baby. Then he didn't have anything else to do with her. Instead of getting an abortion she used the money to come to Fort Myers. A friend got her in rehab. She was clean for a long time. But here," he said sadly, "history repeats itself."

"She seems self-destructive," I said.

As we turned on to a street of modest houses Ben looked at me. "Maybe, but I believe there's hope for everybody," he grinned. "Look at me."

"I'm sorry." I felt chastened. "I shouldn't have said that. And yes, look at you—you are a miracle."

We stopped in front of a low clapboard house that seemed to

sprawl in several directions. The yard, enclosed by a chain-linked fence, was mostly dirt with sparse grass and a few desperately hardy shrubs. There was a tire swing suspended from a sturdy branch of a tree, a sandbox, enclosed by railroad ties, and numerous plastic toys. As we got out of the van, a brown a white dog of doubtful pedigree got up from under a tree, wagging his tail. Under the tree also was a low picnic table, painted red. Four children sat eating sandwiches and drinking from colorful plastic glasses.

"They're here!" I heard a cheery voice exclaim as a woman, perhaps my age, came out of the house. She had a mass of frizzy sand-colored hair, and pale blue eyes that sparkled in a face tanned by the Florida sun and seasoned with freckles. She wore a loose-fitting gauzy white blouse, cut-off blue jeans, and Birkenstocks.

The children turned to look in our direction. Two of them immediately dropped their sandwiches and ran toward us. Allie's round angelic face was a wreath of grins while Peggy Sue's worried frown turned into a look of relief and then, even a smile. They were neat and clean and I recognized the clothes they were wearing as some I had sent with them. Suddenly I had a feeling of being a part of this.

"Are we going to see Mommy?" Allie shouted. Ben dropped to his knee as she threw herself into his arms. At the same time he reached for Peggy Sue and drew her to him.

"We are," he declared. "How's it going, Wanda?" he asked, looking up at the foster mom.

"Jest fine, Reverend."

The Bionic Man, I thought as I watched him encompass everybody with his love. I glanced at the two children still sitting at the table and felt like my heart would break with the look of longing on their jelly-smeared faces. They appeared to be siblings— a boy and a girl of mixed parentage, with blond spring-wired curls, broad African American noses, and green eyes the color of sea foam. I walked toward the table, swallowing the lump that formed in my throat.

"Hi," I said as I sat down on the corner of the bench. "What are you having for lunch?" They cast their eyes down at their plates and clutched their half-eaten sandwiches as though they were going to be snatched from them. "Is that grape jelly I see?" The older one, the girl, nodded without looking at me. "My favorite," I said. "I always wanted grape jelly on my peanut butter sandwiches when I was your age."

The little boy stared at me with wide questioning eyes then slowly held out his sandwich to me.

"Oh no, sweetie," I exclaimed. "I've already had my sandwich, but I'm glad you like the same kind of jelly I do."

"Peggy Sue," I said as we were helping the girls into the van, "why don't we let Allie sit up front with Pastor Ben? She wouldn't be able to see very much from back here." She hesitated only a second before quietly climbing into the back seat. Peggy Sue, it seemed, would do anything for her little sister.

The rehab center was only a few miles away, up a palm-lined driveway off of Six-Mile Cypress. Few people who passed on the main thoroughfare would even know it was here. Peggy Sue marched purposefully up the sidewalk, pulling Allie by the hand.

"She knows her way," I said as she pushed open the double glass doors.

Ben nodded. "She's been here before."

A pleasant reception area belied the single story concrete, barred hospital-like structure behind it. The room had floral carpeting in shades of indigo and peach, comfortable sofas and chairs and in the corner, a perpetual coffee pot on a burner with Styrofoam cups beside it. The room could have passed for any upscale hotel lobby. A blast of cold air greeted us. So did a striking young woman with a shiny ebony face, wide set eyes and hair done in neat cornrows interspersed with multicolored beads.

"Reverend," she beamed.

"How're you doing, Celia?" he asked as he gave her a hug.

"Two years and counting." She gave a thumbs-up. "I'll let them know you all are here." She must have been six feet tall, made even taller with her platform shoes. She wore a white knit midriff and jeans that hugged her lower body. A gold circle pierced her navel in the exposed area where the midriff did not meet the jeans. She walked with the carriage of a model as she disappeared through a door behind her desk.

The girls hung back, their bravado gone. Ben scooped Allie up in his arms and made his way toward a door on the opposite side of the room. I felt a small hand slip into mine. I looked down and smiled at Peggy Sue who suddenly seemed apprehensive. "It's going to be all right," I told her as I squeezed her hand.

This room was even more cheerful, a solarium with lots of windows and plants. It had white wicker furniture with lemon-yellow cushions and bright red-orange hibiscus. A child's play area with a small table and chairs, books and crayons, and an array of inviting toys, occupied one corner. Peggy Sue and Allie made no move toward them. Sliding doors opened on to a walled-in patio where small orange and lemon trees grew in tubs. There was a fountain in the center of the courtyard with a bench beside it. Water made soothing sounds as it trickled over stones. Everything seemed to encourage recovery.

"Mommy! Mommy!" the girls screamed in unison as a door opened and Maggie walked in. She braced herself as they plowed into her, and then slid down to the floor, hugging her children in her arms. Tears ran down her face.

"Oh, my babies," she whispered, "my precious girls."

Ben walked over and pulled the girls away. "Here, let your mom come sit on the sofa." He reached down and helped Maggie to her feet. She wore a faded denim one-piece dress that hung loosely on her slender figure. She looked considerably better than when I'd seen her in the hospital, but she still seemed so fragile. Her thick, rich russet brown hair was piled on her head, and was held in place by a massive clip. She walked unsteadily to the sofa, and her hands trembled when she pulled the girls down beside her.

"Can we go home?" Allie asked.

"Not yet, I told you that," Peggy Sue answered for her mother in her big sister voice.

"No, not yet," Maggie echoed.

"Why not?"

"Because Mommy can't take care of you yet. The people here have to help me get well so that I can."

"I can help," Peggy Sue said hopefully.

"Oh, honey, I'm counting on you. When the doctor tells me I'm well enough to come home, I'll be counting on you." Maggie kept wiping her nose with the back of her hand. I handed her some tissues from a box I saw on the table. She seemed to see me for the first time. When she looked at me, in spite of the ravages of abuse, I saw how beautiful she really was. She had wide-set, startling turquoise blue eyes and the thickest, longest lashes I'd ever seen. And, now that the bruises and swelling were gone I saw that she had a perfect oval face. Her lips were full with the lower lip slightly wider.

"You remember Jessica?" Ben asked.

There was a questioning look in her eyes then she said, "Oh, yes. The hospital."

"I'm glad to see you're better," I smiled.

"Thank you."

"Jessica gave us these," Peggy Sue said, pulling out her shirt for her mother to see.

"Yes, these," Allie repeated.

We were allowed thirty minutes, yet now there seemed to be nothing to say. Maggie stroked her daughters, and they clung to her but she didn't ask how they were or who was taking care of them.

I sat down in one of the wicker chairs across from them. "I have something to ask you," I began. "Actually, I have a favor to ask." Suddenly I had every body's attention, including Ben's. "I wanted to tell you that I'm taking good care of Soot."

"Soot?" Allie came over and leaned on my knee. "Where's Soot?"

"Well, that's what I wanted to talk to you about. We've been taking care of him at Mr. Webster's, but I've just moved into a new house by myself and I was wondering if Soot could come to live with me for now? He could keep me company and," I added hastily, "I would take good care of him until you could take him home with you."

"What a wonderful idea," Maggie said.

"That's a great idea," Ben said, almost at the same time.

As if on cue, the door opened and a pleasant, very pregnant young woman in a pink smock announced, "Visiting time is over, Ms. Sinclair."

When Maggie stood up Allie started to cry, but Peggy Sue bit her lower lip and refused to give her tears release. Maggie buried her face in her hands as the attendant took her arm and led her away. I questioned the wisdom of all this. There was so much pain and sadness here, that I wondered if it had been the right thing to bring them today.

On the way back to Wanda's, Ben bought ice cream for all of us. After we left the girls with Wanda, promising to come back in two weeks for another visit, we rode without speaking. The day had grown gray and was heavily oppressive. Finally Ben reached over and squeezed my arm. "You were great," he said. When I didn't answer he asked, "Why so quiet?"

"I was just wondering if we did the right thing, taking the girls there. It just seems to open up wounded hearts."

"I know," he said, "but if you were a little girl and your mother just left one day and didn't come back, wouldn't you feel better if you could see her for yourself?"

"Yes," I whispered. "I never thought of it that way."

"The saddest thing," Ben said quietly, "would be if the court decides to take them away permanently. They could even place them for adoption."

"They would do that?"

"This is the third time they've been taken away. Maggie will really have to prove herself this time. Pray for her, Jessicacita." I hadn't realized I'd given a long sigh until Ben asked, "What was that about?"

I wasn't used to others noticing or caring about my feelings— my reactions, at least not since Mari died. "It just seems so unfair that these people who struggle so with addictions and other problems, are just pushed out the door and told, 'go be a good parent, get a job, be responsible, and don't do it again.' I can't imagine how difficult that would be. It seems to me that they would have a better chance if there was some safe, in between place, where they would have support and instruction, and protection," I added, "while they were getting their lives back together."

Ben turned to look at me. His amber eyes searched my face with a look of recognition and understanding. "Keep that vision, *querida* Jessica."

Even though it was only four o'clock in the afternoon the day was so dark that everybody had on their headlights. Ben turned on the radio just in time to hear a weather update. The storm, which was not yet strong enough to be named as a hurricane, was continuing on its course toward Miami. Gale warnings had been issued for small craft, and the east coast of Florida was now under "hurricane watch."

"Are you worried?" I asked Ben.

"A little."

"What do we do?"

"I think we better get ready, just in case. But right now," Ben said as he made a quick left turn, "I think we should stop here at Rib City and pick up supper for us and for Jack."

"Great idea," I said and realized that, in spite of the ice cream cone, I was starving.

Jack, as I'd suspected, was not convinced that anything should be done. He did agree that we should put the equipment under cover of the shed, which was at most, a tentative shelter. It had, however, weathered other storms. We shuttered most of the rooms on the first floor, but when I asked about the upstairs he told me, "Forget it, girlie."

The rain bands that preceded the storm reached us by Sunday morning. In spite of the steadily blowing rain, Ben's little church was filled to capacity. I'd refused to listen to Jack's excuses, so he was waiting for me when I fetched him that morning. Along with other parishioners, we splashed our way through puddles, shaking raincoats and umbrellas and depositing them at the door of the church. Conversation was animated and interspersed with nervous laughter as we sat crowded in steamy, odiferous dampness until, on *this* day, two little boys bearing lit wands, came forward to light the candles at the altar.

Ben appropriately chose the fourteenth chapter of Matthew for his sermon. Jesus' disciples were in a storm at sea. The boat was being tossed about and they were afraid. When Jesus came walking toward them on the churning water, Peter, ever the challenger, felt he could do the same. While none of us away believed that we could "walk on water," we believed that we could do what had to be done.

At home I made myself a sandwich and sat brooding in front of the television, tuned to the weather channel. The radar-tracking map showed that the bright green undulating movement of the huge system covered the east coast of Florida as it worked its way toward us. A rain-drenched reporter stood on a seawall, mike in one hand, holding on to his hat with the other. Wind-driven rain blew his yellow slicker sideways. Behind him a barren beach was being pounded by raging surf. The drama, I supposed, was to get his point across. He did—at least to me. The storm, centered over the Andros Islands was still on course. "Hurricane warning," had now been upgraded to "hurricane watch."

Locally, we were under a "flash flood watch" as the Caloosahatchee continued to rise.

I jumped at the sharp sound of the phone ringing. I felt my heart palpate as I hurried to answer it. "*Señora* Jessica?" It was Louisa and her voice sounded anxious.

"Louisa, are you all right?"

"Oh *si, si, Señora*. It's *Señor* Steele—he telephoned me. He saw reports of the storm and wanted to know if you were safe. He said he didn't know how to get in touch with you. I wasn't sure if I should give him your number, so I told him I would check on you."

"Oh, Louisa, I'm so sorry. I intended to phone him, but I just haven't done it. I will. I'll call him, but if he calls you again, it's all right to give him this number. Tell me though," I continued, "are you and Carlos okay? Do you want to come here? This house is secure, I think, and I have provisions."

"*Gracias no, Señora.* We are safe. We and our neighbors have taken precautions."

I had intended to call Malcolm and had thought about it several times during the past week, but I just hadn't done it.

I'd used planting the cultivars as an excuse. I used going to see Maggie as an excuse, but I knew I was just putting it off. Now I watched out the window as heavy drops of rain dotted the surface of the pool, and saw the row of tall palms along the street bend as if they were part of a chorus line. Their fronds looked like umbrellas turned inside out. I took a deep breath and wondering if I could get through in this weather, reached for the phone.

Just as I started to pick it up it rang again. I let out a scream. The storm was making me edgy. It was Ben.

"We have the church boarded up," he said. "Would you like for me to come and close your shutters. You have those new hurricane shutters that just roll down. They should be easy."

"Oh, would you?" I asked with tremendous relief. No doubt I could have done it, but I was glad to know another person would be here. I admitted that I didn't like being alone in this—not one bit.

"Ben," I hesitated, "why don't you bring Ginger and your cat and stay here?" I rushed on, "maybe we could convince Jack to come too. He shouldn't be by himself."

"That's a good idea," he said, "but you'll have to be the one to convince Jack."

After I'd informed Jack that Ben would be coming to pick him up I dialed the number I'd been intending to call all week. There was static on the line and after a series of rings I heard a voice coming from so very far away saying, "Malcolm Steele here."

I assured him that I was all right and told him about my provisions. I promised to check on his property. I didn't tell him *that* Mexican and *that* old man were going to be here with me.

Jack, Ben, and I sat with four nervous animals in the family room of my house. Cat would not leave Jack's lap and Ginger would not leave Ben's side. Soot was somewhere under a bed, and Ben's now-healed-and-mobile but unfriendly cat yowled in her cage.

Conversation seemed of little use as we kept our attention on the television as evacuation routes were announced and addresses of shelters given. While people along the East Coast were being asked to leave their homes, no evacuation had been called for here. Local news coverage showed the few vehicles that were out on the streets, struggling through curb-high water. It showed trees being lashed by the wind and boats banging against slips in marinas. Occasionally we heard a loud noise outside as something broke loose or someone's garbage can went tumbling down the street.

"Wanda will make sure they're safe," Ben assured me when I wished out loud that Peggy Sue and Allie were with us.

At 5 p.m. the electricity went off. We sat in an eerie half light, staring at a blank television screen. *Don't open the refrigerator unless you must,* sprang into my mind as I mentally reviewed the list of "dos and don'ts" I'd made. We lit the two kerosene lamps I bought, and turned on the battery-powered radio.

Jack dozed in the chair. I walked over and looked out the window. I could see no other lights. It felt like we were the only people in the world. "I've never been through anything like this," I whispered when Ben came over to stand beside me. "Thank you for coming here," I continued in a whisper. Speaking out loud seemed too harsh. "I really didn't want to be alone."

"I know," he said. He put his arm around me. I felt the flex of his biceps and the muscles in his forearm as he pulled me close. I felt security. He drew a deep breath, "but you wouldn't have been alone."

"I know," I replied, pulling in my own breath, "I'm trying to learn that."

At six o'clock I decided it was time for us to eat. Jack and Ben laughed when I surreptitiously opened the refrigerator just wide enough to put my hand in and grab a package of hotdogs. I felt guilty for violating one of the rules on "the list." We boiled the frankfurters and heated beans on the burners of the propane stove.

Jack laughed again when Ginger refused to go outside to relieve herself unless Ben went with her. It sounded so good to hear that chuckle. When they came back drenched Ben made Ginger stay on the patio until she shook herself dry. We all laughed when Jack said, "I wonder if the men know we won't be fertilizing tomorrow?"

The evening crept on minute by agonizing minute. The pounding rain had become a muted drum roll and the wind only a whirring of reed instruments as hours of listening, programmed them into our subconscious. "I can' t believe waiting and watching can be so exhausting," I yawned.

"Go to bed, Jessicacita," Ben instructed.

By lamplight we situated Jack in one of the bedrooms with an adjoining bath where we placed a litter box for Cat. Ben's kitty, just this evening had been given the name of Storm. He was released in the garage with yet another "potty box." When we finally found Soot, I took the cat and we retired to my bedroom. Ben chose to sleep on the couch in the den.

There were no Labor Day celebrations on Monday. There was no extra day at the beach for workers who looked forward to this extra day of pleasure. There were no picnics in parks or along the river, for the river continued to creep out of its boundaries. And there was still no electricity. We ate cold cereal and listened to area updates on the radio. About one third of the city was without power and crews were working around the clock. Because it was on the list, I had filled two bathtubs with water for flushing toilets and for washing up. We heated water on the hot plate.

At three in the afternoon the lights flickered on briefly then went off again. At eight o'clock, Ben's supervisor called him on his cell phone to tell him not to come to the work site the next day, but to take care of his own damage. Even though there was another bedroom, for the second night Ben chose to sleep on the couch in the den. "*It was the morning and the evening of the second day*" (*Genesis 1:13*).

It was the quiet that drew me out of sleep. I could hear a gentle patter of rain on the roof but the noise of the wind was gone. The clock on the dresser flashed startling red numbers at me and I knew electricity had been restored. I threw back the sheet and threw on my robe. Ben and Ginger were not in the family room. I saw that the sliding door to the patio was open and stepped outside. It must have been near morning because I could see the wash of pale pink in the east. Ben was standing just under the overhang of the roof looking in that direction. I walked up behind him and slid my arms around him. The cocoon of safety in which we'd wrapped ourselves during the last two days made me bold. I felt him tense then relax beneath my touch. "Is it over?" I asked.

He pulled me around in front of him and encircled me in his arms, tucking my head beneath his chin. I breathed in his warmth and masculinity and felt at peace. "Yes, Jessicacita, it's over. It will probably rain for another day or so, but the danger is over. Why are you smiling?" he asked, looking down at me.

"Jessicacita," I said. "Little Jessica. I'm anything but little, but I like the way it sounds."

He gave me his crooked smile and I felt his body shudder before he put his hands on my shoulders and pushed me away. "We'd better take a look at the damage."

"I'll make coffee."

When I went to get dressed I was pleased to hear the shower running in Jack's bathroom. It would make it easier for me to suggest that he install a shower in his own bathroom.

My property sustained no real damage. There was only cleanup to do. In addition to other debris floating in the pool, we fished out a drowned bird. Ditches along either side of the street in front of the house ferried all sorts of matter. Branches and leaves wound together to form a dam, sending brown churning water into the street. It carried contents of garbage cans, children's toys and occasionally small critters—some dead and some swimming for their lives.

Cars drove slowly, headlights on, their tires splashing sprays of water. I followed Ben down the street in my van. The traffic light at the corner wasn't working. A fireman in a yellow slicker, with ankle-deep water swirling around his boots, directed traffic. Ben's church appeared secure behind its boarded windows, but a huge branch from the tree in his front yard had fallen across his porch, crushing the roof. He would not be able to get into his house until limbs had been chainsawed away.

Jack's place suffered the most damage. At least one-third of the grove stood in water from the Caloosahatchee. His rickety dock had been pulled away from the pilings. His boat was nowhere to be seen. Much of the ripe fruit lay on the ground and leaves had been ripped off the trees, leaving behind the ragged look of tattered clothing. Some strips of tin had blown off the shed. There was little damage to the house itself. I noticed some panes of glass in the etched window on the second floor were gone. What's one more tropical storm to this old house, I thought. It had seen so many.

When I saw what the storm had done to my little cultivars I knelt down beside them and cried. They'd barely had a chance. Gullies had washed through the newly worked ground, leaving trenches of erratic design. While most of the trees were still in place many were bent almost horizontally. All were practically stripped of their tender leaves, as bones picked dry. Despair washed through me. I felt Jack's hand on my shoulder. "It's not as bad as it looks. Those little trees are hardy. They'll come right back, good as new. You'll see. There'll be new leaves on them with a few days' sunshine."

"If you say so."

The last of the rain moved out on Wednesday and when the skies cleared that afternoon the sun shone with brilliance we'd not seen for several days. Roberto and his men weren't coming right away; they had their own cleanup to do. We didn't see much of Ben either, but he did call to let me know that Peggy Sue and Allie were all right.

So, Jack and I began repairing the damage. We started with the new plantings, repeating, in some cases, what we'd done only a week before. There were only a few trees that would need to be replaced. It was hard for me watch the difficulty with which Jack moved and see the grimace of pain on his face. I made sure I did as much of the fetching and carrying as I could. Thankfully, the weather was not as hot. We took our usual breaks during the day but worked evenings until we couldn't see.

Saturday evening when I was getting ready to leave Jack was

nowhere around. I went looking for him and found him in the shed. In the fading light I could barely see him. He was bent over the tractor fender, his hands gripping its edge.

"Jack! What's wrong?" He raised his head and looked at me. His face was distorted and the whites of his eyes shown iridescent in the blue vapor of the streetlight. "What's wrong? Are you having a heart attack?"

He shook his head. "Oh, girlie, you don't have any idea how bad it is. You don't know how bad I want a drink sometimes—specially at times like this—when I'm tired."

"Well, maybe just a beer wouldn't hurt," I offered.

"No," he growled, "a beer *would hurt.*"

I spread my hands helplessly. I didn't know what to do to take away his agony. "What can I do?"

"I'll be all right."

"Why don't you come to my house? You can take a shower and clean up. I'll make us something to eat. We should think about putting a shower in here for you," I continued. "It would be easier." I waited for the protest that didn't come.

"I'll get some clean clothes," he said.

The message light was blinking on my phone, but I ignored it as I opened the fridge to find something for supper. Jack hobbled to the shower. I pulled out frozen waffles and sausage, trying not to look at the bottle of chilled white wine daring me to uncork it and have a glass.

I had a glass of iced tea waiting for Jack came to the table—lots of sugar and lemon—just the way he liked it. I'd heard that people crave alcohol as a quick "sugar fix" when they're hungry, so tonight we would have a sugar fix—waffles with butter and lots of honey.

The phone rang again just as we finished eating. It was Malcolm. No, I'd not gotten his messages; I had just gotten home. Yes, I had checked on his house. There was no real damage—just cleanup like everybody else, and yes I would make sure Carlos took care of it. And yes, I was fine. When he told me he missed me, I simply said, "Thank you."

"What are you going to do, Jess?" Jack asked when I came back to the table.

"Before he left he asked me to think about it for a month. I can't see any future for us. We want different things. I'm not sure what I wanted before, but now I know that I want something different for myself than he wants from me. I guess I should have known him better before I married him," I added with a shrug.

"What do you want for yourself?"

I started to stammer a reply then stopped. "You ask too many questions, old man." He laughed a hearty cackle and, for the moment I felt his need for a drink had been forgotten.

Roberto and his men were already at Jack's when I arrived Monday morning. I heard voices off in the trees, but nobody was around. The place was pretty much back to normal, but I noticed once again the missing panes in the upstairs windows and wondered what other damage had been done there. In the years to come, I often wondered what my life would have been like if I hadn't gone upstairs that day.

CHAPTER EIGHTEEN

I stood in the driveway looking around. Suddenly I was left with nothing to do. My cultivars, as Jack had predicted, were putting out tiny bright green leaves. What I need to do, I thought, is to find an attorney and get on with divorce proceedings. It was something I'd intended to do before the storm. But, I didn't know any lawyers here. The only attorney I knew was the woman in New York who'd handled Mari's estate. Malcolm, with dozens of names at his fingertips, could no doubt recommend one. I smiled at the thought. *Malcolm, could you give me the name of a good lawyer to represent me in my divorce?*

Of course, my dear.

I went into the house and picked up the worn Yellow Pages I had seen on the stairs. "Good through October 1997" on the front cover dated it. I put it on the kitchen table and when I started to leaf through the pages I found that they were damp and swollen and stuck together. Checking the steps I saw a rectangular discoloration of the varnish where the book had been. As I followed the trail of stacked papers, books and boxes up the stairs, I discovered that the bottom of each one was wet. Near the top some were soggy and tiny rivulets of water still dripped from beneath piles of old magazines.

Stepping on to the landing I saw that the entire east side of the house was pretty much water soaked. The runner down the hall was squishy, and water still stood in depressions of the uneven old floors. In other areas the wood was buckled and discolored. The stacks of papers on the window seat beneath the broken window were sodden masses of pulp. I wondered if there was anything of value inside the storage area beneath. I stepped gingerly around some of the piles that had toppled on to the floor.

In the two front rooms, rugs near the windows were wet and smelled musty. There seemed to be no damage toward the back of the house. Even though I knew that the two rooms in the back were locked, I tried the handles anyway.

I walked back to the head of the stairs and stared at the window seat. I peeled away the pages that were stuck to the section where the magazines had slid off and exposed a hinged top that could be lifted up. In a depression near the front was a small round metal ring that was used to lift up the lid. I had seen a window seat like this somewhere—but where? I reached over and tugged on the ring. Swollen wood and years of weight on top had sealed it.

"Couldn't leave it alone, could you, girlie?" a fierce voice boomed behind me.

"Oh my god!" I cried as my hand flew to my throat and adrenalin surged through me. I gasped for breath. I turned to see Jack standing on the next to the top step. "Oh!" I exclaimed again, holding my hand against my heaving chest. I swallowed the acrid taste of fright that rose in my mouth. Humiliation washed over me as I forced myself to meet his stare. His hand gripped the railing so tightly that his knuckles were white.

"This is a mess," I said, extending my open hand in the direction of the heap of wet paper. I stared at the lid that wouldn't bulge. "The pictures got wet."

Suddenly it was if the floor on which I stood was electrified as I felt a shock surge through my body. "Pictures," I gasped. "You kept pictures in there." I threw my hands against my chest and tried to draw in air. I could not get my breath. My eyes did not leave Jack's face.

His expression was as still as stone, but his eyes captured me unwittingly, for these were the same eyes I saw each time I looked in the mirror—the same shape—the same stormy gray.

"Oh no," I whimpered. "*Oh no,*" rose as a scream in my throat. I lunged for the stairs. *I had to get out of here.* I thought that Jack reached for me as I pushed past him but I was never sure. Grabbing the banister, I stumbled, half-sliding down the cluttered stairs. Books tumbled and boxes spilled in my wake. I heard and then felt the handrail give away as I landed on a step and slid the rest of the way down. A sharp pain shot up my spine but I didn't stop. Somewhere from deep within my memory I head a little girl's voice ask, "Mommy hurt?" Tears coursed down my face as I burst out the back door. Vaguely I noticed Roberto in the shed and registered his startled expression. I started toward my car but I was shaking so badly I knew I couldn't drive. Even though my legs were rubbery I kept running. Where? To my house, I thought.

As I rounded the corner to the main road I heard a screech of tires, then a thud. Somewhere in a new fog I felt a moment of pain and heard a scream. I thought the scream was mine.

The sensation was one of refreshing coolness. I struggled through murky haze, lifting my tongue toward the moisture as frosty drops soothed my parched throat. I longed for more of the blessed liquid. Then I felt myself being forced away from it, back into a swirling mist. "Jessicacita," a gentle voice commanded.

Where was I? Part of me felt heavy and weighed down; I couldn't see. The fog in my mind lightened into swirls of pale gray bubbles. I heard muffled running steps and suddenly more hands were retraining me. "Easy. Be still." A rhythmic swishing sound superimposed over a steady rapid beep echoed in my ears. I wrinkled my nose at an unpleasant smell. "She's awake," one of the voices, said.

"Water," I mumbled. "I'm so thirsty."

"Welcome back!" said another bright voice. I tried to open my eyes and I couldn't. When I tried to lift my hand to my face a voice scolded, "No, don't. You'll pull out your IV. You're going to be all right. I'll get you some water."

"Thank you," I whispered.

Gradually the room began to clear but I couldn't see all of it. Something was keeping me from turning my head. I'm in a hospital, I thought. I'm hurt. I heard steps going away, and then another face came into focus. It was a round face with a zillion freckles and lots of red hair. The hands attached to the body were busily adjusting knobs and dials on a machine beside my bed. She beamed a wonderful smile. "You're going to be okay."

"You look like Christine," I giggled and found that it hurt to laugh. "Oh, that hurts," I gasped. Then I saw someone standing looking out the window. "Ben?" I whispered. He turned to look at me. Tears were running down his cheeks. Then I remembered. My jaw trembled, and I pushed my lips together in an effort not to cry but tears leaked out of the corner of my eyes.

"Just a few sips," the other nurse, not Christine, said as she placed a plastic straw between my lips. "We don't want you to get nauseous. Are you in pain?"

"My head hurts. It feels like it's in a vise," I complained.

"It is. You're wearing a halo."

"A what? Why?"

The nurse looked at her watch. "I've put a call in for your doctor to tell him that you're awake. He's on his way. He will explain to you what happened. In the meantime I think you should rest."

"Could I stay with her?" Ben asked.

The nurse looked at her watch again. Nurses, I decided, spend a lot of time looking at their watches. I thought that was funny. I wanted to giggle but remembering, didn't. "Until the doctor gets here," she said.

Ben came and stood by the bed. He slid his hand, palm up, under mine, careful not to disturb the needle that intruded my bruised skin. "How long have I been here?" I asked.

"Five days."

"Five days," I mumbled. "How long have you been here?"

He grinned ruefully. "Five days, more or less, when they would let me."

"Why can't I see better?"

"One of your eyes is bandaged."

"Oh," I replied as though that explained everything. "You've been praying for me."

"Yes, Jessicacita," he smiled.

I gave his fingers a squeeze. "Thank you." I clung to his hand as fragments of events eased into my consciousness. When I tried to speak my lips began to quiver. It felt like something to big and too spiky was lodged in my throat. I locked my eyes on Ben's. "He—he's my father."

Ben nodded.

"Did you know?"

He shook his head. "I was never told, but seeing the two of you together, I somehow knew."

They were two white-haired transplants from Pennsylvania, I was told, heading out for an "early bird dinner." They weren't driving fast, just making a turn when I came sprinting around the corner. Their left fender hit me on my right side. I had slid across the hood of their four-year-old Buick and landed in a ditch on the opposite side of the road.

Fortunately, a young nurse's aid just coming home from her shift at the same hospital where I was now a patient was the first one on the scene. Eager to put in to practice what she'd learned, ordered that no one move me, called 911 on her cell phone, and did her best to calm the old people who were so agitated and unsettled that they too were taken to the emergency room. These were things I learned from Ben over the next several days. The young aide had checked on me frequently, and the senior couple came every day I was in intensive care, having a neighbor bring them, because they were too shaken to drive. I later learned that they were in the waiting room down the hall when I woke up.

It was left up to my doctor, a neurosurgeon, to tell me in professional terms what had happened to me. I had a crushed vertebra at the C2 level, several cracked ribs on my right side, a broken right wrist, a bruised cheek and a cut above my eye that required stitches. I also had a hairline skull fracture that caused cranial leakage, which had been responsible for the coma I was in for five days. The latest X-ray showed that there was no more leakage and the fracture was mending.

Dr. Somers was a brusque man, with not the greatest of bedside manners. I was told that he was the best neurosurgeon in the area, and that I had been fortunate he was on call when I came in. My head was indeed in a vise with screws into the sides, front and back of my skull to keep me immobile. The "halo" was a stainless steel contraption made of rods that encircled my head. It was attached by small screws at the ends of other steel rods to my cranium. Still other rods supported a yokelike affair that fit over my shoulders and was strapped to my chest. Turning my head was something I was not supposed to do.

"My neck is broken?" I asked in disbelief.

Lay language seemed to make him uncomfortable. "Well, y . . . y . . . yes," he stammered. The second cervical vertebra was severed. I cried as the horrible news sunk in. I would have to wear this torture device for two or three months, and would only be allowed to go home after I had been to a special rehabilitation center. A good night's sleep, I was soon to learn, was an elusive yearning that I would not enjoy for months. There was no way I could lie down.

I was lucky, Dr. Somers and others continued to remind me. My arm and ribs would heal normally, and with therapy I should regain most of my mobility. I *was* fortunate, I had to admit, when I wasn't angry. Most of the time I was angry. I was angry with myself for reacting so irrationally. My feelings toward Jack bordered on rage. *I had been deceived. I had been lied to.* The other emotion that crept into my thoughts was disappointment. This old man was not the father I had fantasized about when I was young and dreamed of one day discovering. That father had been handsome and dashing had been searching for me for years. I did admit that later in my life I had wished to know my father— whoever he was.

There were few visitors other than Ben. He came every evening and sometimes during his lunch breaks. One Saturday he brought Scott. One day I looked toward the door to see two snowy-haired people peering into my room. They appeared to be in their late seventies. The woman, tiny and waiflike was almost hidden behind a huge bouquet of flowers, and her husband, leaning on a cane with one hand, hugged an enormous basket of fruit in his other. "We just wanted to see for ourselves that you are all right," they explained. For several minutes they repeatedly told me how sorry they were until a nurse came to take me for some tests. "I'm going to be all right," I assured them.

"She's going to be okay," the nurse repeated as she ushered them down the hall.

Ben always lifted my spirits. He brought smiles and warmth and peace into the room with him. He started calling me Angel, somehow making this unwieldy halo more acceptable. If he was there when it was time for my evening walk, his arm replaced the walker. He related stories from church and from work. He kept me updated on Maggie and Peggy Sue and Allie. He reported regularly on improvements made on the grove. One day he brought me a small limb so that I could see the new growth on the cultivars. I no longer thought of them as mine.

But it was I who first spoke Jack's name. "Have you talked to him?" I asked.

"Yes. He wants to see you."

"No," I stated emphatically.

"He wants to tell you—"

"Tell me what?"

"His story—and your mother's."

"What does he know of my mother's story?" I demanded. Bitter tears unwittingly filled my eyes. "I'm not ready," I said finally.

"Take your time. You'll know when you are ready," Ben said as he helped me back into bed. Our usual parting routine was to position me as comfortably possible for my night's sleep. Then he would fold my hand in his, and with his bowed head touching our hands, pray for my recovery, for guidance and for me to find peace.

"You are my rock," I whispered as he left.

My recovery was a full-time job, and I grew more tired as the days wore on. There were X-rays and CAT scans; there was pulmonary therapy with technicians prodding me to breath deeply. Then the psychologists began dropping by—to chat—to casually ask me to do simple math problems, or discuss with me articles they'd had me read in the paper the day before. I cooperated fully because I too wanted to be assured that my memory was going to be all right. It was only when they asked about the accident that I refused to participate.

"I don't remember," I lied.

One by one, the days of September slid away. There were fewer rainy days and lower temperatures, not that it mattered. The weather outside was only a picture on the other side of my window.

Finally on a Friday morning, the last weekend of the month, I was informed that on Monday I was being transferred to Silver Springs, a rehab center in Port Charlotte. That afternoon as I lay there wondering what that would be like a nurse poked her head around my partially closed door. "Are you awake?" she asked. "Your husband is here to see you."

My husband? No doubt those who saw Ben come on a daily basis would assume he was my husband. But why was he here in the middle of the afternoon? Then Malcolm walked through the door.

"Malcolm! Malcolm?" I questioned in disbelief as I stared at him.

The smile he had plastered on his face froze for an instant before being replaced by a look of utter shock. His mouth dropped open as though its hinge had given away. He actually paled. "Jess?" he questioned as he slowly approached the bed.

I must have looked a sight with the contraption that gave me an outer world appearance. Short stubble of hair covered the part of my head that had been shaved for the cranial tap. My hair was growing in its usual dark color except for one area about the size of a silver dollar that was coming in completely white. The right side of my face was now a brownish yellow, jaundiced color as my bruises faded. When he leaned over to try to kiss me, he found that he couldn't.

"What happened?" he asked. He pulled over a chair and sat down.

"What are you doing here?" I wanted to know. "How did you find out?"

"Louisa called me. She thought I should know."

"Louisa?" I questioned in disbelief. "Louisa?" I couldn't imagine Louisa stepping out of her role as housekeeper to do something like that. I made a mental note to inform my psychologist that my mind was working properly. "When?" I asked.

"When, what?"

"When did she call?"

He didn't answer right away. "When the accident happened."

"So you rushed to my bedside," I said bitterly.

"I . . . I couldn't leave right away. There were some things that had to be taken care of." I had the satisfaction of seeing a look of chagrin on his face before tones of defiance crept into his voice. "You know how busy I am. I made sure Louisa kept me informed," he added defensively.

"Why now?"

"I wanted to make sure you were well taken care of. You are still my responsibility." A conversation we had several months ago crept into my mind. *It's not a good idea for you to be walking out there alone. It's certainly safe here, I had retorted. I've been talking care of myself for a long time.* "The rehab center is the best. I checked out several. You'll have everything you need," he continued.

"You arranged for it?"

"Of course."

"Thank you," I replied. I should have felt grateful but inside I prickled with resentment at his interference.

"How did the accident happen?" he asked again.

I told him about going upstairs in the house to check on damage from the storm and about how seeing the window seat triggered memories. "Did you know that Jack Webster is my father?"

"Impossible," he exploded, jumping to his feet. The chair skittered backward, poising on its two back legs before slamming back to the floor.

I laughed—I actually laughed at the look of shock on his face. "I thought so too," I agreed.

I told him about Jack confronting me. "Then scenes crept into my conscious—memories I didn't even know were there. I had to get away. I ran down the stairs and out of the house. I wasn't looking where I was going. That's how the accident happened," I finished. Then I started to laugh.

"What's so funny?" he demanded.

"That both of your wives were born next door to one another?"

He stood there shaking his head. The composed Malcolm Steele was absent. This man was very unsettled. "I'd better go, Jess." He patted my hand awkwardly. "I'll see you tomorrow. You can reach me at the house if you need anything."

Malcolm came to see me both Saturday and Sunday. Ben noticeably did not. I felt an ache of disappointment each time the door opened. He must have known Malcolm was here. On Sunday Malcolm brought clothes. He said Louisa helped him pick them out.

"You've seen my house then?' I asked.

"Yes, it's nice." He seemed uncomfortable, and I noticed that each time he sat the chair was a little further away from the bed. He rarely touched me. When he did it was with hesitation, as though a broken neck was contagious. There was no way Malcolm could accept a less-than-perfect wife. While he could be passionate and protective, he could not be caring. Care and love was what I needed.

"I think we should go ahead with divorce proceedings," I said.

"Now is not the time," he protested. "Why don't we wait until you're better?"

"Now *is* the time," I replied. "I'd like to go ahead. I would appreciate it if you could give me the names of some lawyers. I don't know anybody here."

For a long time he sat with his elbows on his knees and his head in his hands. When he looked up his eyes were moist. He nodded then got up and left the room.

When I arrived at Silver Springs Monday afternoon, Malcolm was waiting with the administrator who accompanied us as attendants ushered me to my suite. I had a bedroom, bathroom, and sitting room. A small table with two chairs was placed in front of a window looking out onto manicured gardens. I could have my meals here, I was told, although it was stressed that the dining room was preferable so that the residents, as we were called, could interact with one another.

The administrator and the staff gushed over Malcolm, explaining the many amenities they had to offer. "It's just like a country club," they said more than once. The "residents" I had seen, however, did not appear to be the country club crowd. They were in wheelchairs, walkers, and braces. Some could speak. Others could not. The place was totally depressing. I vowed to cooperate so that I could recover as quickly as possible and get out of here.

I was helped out of my wheelchair into a comfortable parlor chair. "What do you think?" Malcolm asked when we were alone.

"It's a lovely place," I lied. "I'm sure my recovery will go quickly."

"I've made sure there are plenty of funds to hire all the help you need. Everything is taken care of."

"You've always been generous," I smiled.

"You'd better get some rest," he said. "I have to leave early in the morning but I'll be in touch." He came over and handed me an envelope. Inside were names of several lawyers. "Are you sure you want to do this now?"

I struggled to my feet, leaning on my walker for support. "It was our mistake," I said. "It's time to move on."

He came over and put a hand on either of my shoulders. "I'm sorry, Jessica."

"For what?"

He swallowed, and I saw the muscles twitch in his jaws. "That it was a mistake." He put two fingers to his lips then placed them on my own lips. He didn't look back as he went out of the door. I fell back into the chair as sobs racked my body.

At five o'clock an attendant came to my door. "There are hors d'oeuvres and wine being served in the solarium if you would like to join us. Dinner will be served at six."

"No, thank you," I replied.

With a look at my puffy face he added, "It only seems bad at first. It's not so awful, really. Tomorrow you'll start your therapy. You'll be so busy that time will pass quickly and you'll be out of here before you know it," he said cheerfully. "Would you like to have dinner in your room tonight?"

"Yes, thank you."

When he left I walked to the window. It's not just my body that has to be put back together I wanted to shout. It's my life, it's my psyche, it's my future. I had found a life that excited me more than anything ever had. I'd found a father I had been searching for all my life, and I didn't know what to do about it. And, I was divorcing a seemingly perfect, wealthy husband. None of it made sense. I felt wretched and alone. I hobbled over and picked up the phone. I heard ringing, then background noises and the static of the cell phone. I knew he was on his way home from work. "Ben, I need to talk to you."

CHAPTER NINETEEN

Monday, October 16 was liberation day from Silver Springs. I walked out the door with the aid of a cane. The cast was off my wrist. Maybe, just maybe I could get rid of the halo in five or six weeks. By now it seemed like an extension of myself. I was learning to live with it whether I liked it or not. The screws that were embedded in my flesh had become a part of me. Among the lessons I had learned was to never bend over to pick up something. I learned that one the hard way as aides rushed to help me up from the floor.

My eyes strained for familiar sights as the medical transport drove me home down Route Forty-One, the old Tamiami Trail, to Palm Beach Boulevard. Most of the debris from the storm had been cleared away but palm trees, with broken yellowing shredded fronds, lined the streets and raw dirt, where angry water had flowed remained as ugly scars. I stared hard when we passed Blossom Lane hoping to see how the young trees were doing, but I couldn't see them from the street.

The sight of my house raised my spirits as nothing had in days. The lawn had been mowed and Elaine, the first of my caregivers, was waiting for me. She was a small, sturdy woman, perhaps a little older than I, with compassionate eyes and a friendly smile. I walked through the house, turning my body from side to side to take in everything. Soot was not here. He had, of necessity, gone back to live with Jack. Poor little guy, I thought, he just gets used to one place then he gets moved again.

"Of course," she said when I asked if she could make dinner for three. I had seen Ben only once since that first night when he came in answer to my desperate call.

"I need to talk to you," I'd cried into the phone.

"I'll be there as soon as I can."

"Do you know where I am?"

"Yes, I know."

"What are your rules about having visitors?" I'd asked the man who delivered my dinner.

"Ah don' know, ma'am, but I can get somebody that can answer your question," he replied.

Visiting hours are daily, from two until five in the afternoon, I was informed. "But, he's my pastor," I protested. "I need to talk to him."

"I'm sorry," the man said. "We have a chaplain on our staff. Perhaps you'd like me to call him."

"No, I don't want you to call your chaplain," I retorted angrily. "I want to talk to my pastor. He's already on his way here."

"I'm sorry," he repeated. His name was Brian. It said so on the nameplate he wore on his shirt. "It's getting late and we have to be considerate of the other residents."

"What's it to the other residents whether it's your chaplain or my preacher who's disturbing them?" I demanded, my voice rising.

"Please, Mrs. Steele."

Mrs. Steele? Mrs. Steele, I thought. It's the kind of thing I never do and don't like people who do it, I was telling myself as I prepared to pull rank. I looked at my watch. "My husband should be home now," I said. "I'll phone *Mr. Steele* and perhaps you can repeat your rules to him." I waited, holding my breath.

"Maybe we can make an exception—just this once. It is your first day here," Brian rushed on, "and I can see that this is quite an adjustment for you."

"Being deformed is an adjustment for me," I shouted.

"You—you're n . . . not deformed," he stuttered as he backed out of the room. I suddenly understood the feeling of power that Malcolm must feel as he commanded people around him.

I was waiting in the reception area when Ben arrived about forty-five minutes later. He was still in his work clothes. His sweaty shirt, his dusty jeans, and his heavy boots never looked better.

"Oh, Ben," I sobbed, as I raced my walker toward him. In spite of the metal I tried to put my arms around him. It didn't work.

"It's all right, Jessica," he soothed. He took my shoulders and held me so that he could look into my eyes. The tee shirt he wore today, although faded, bore the picture of a mother robin with a baby perched on the edge of a nest. One tiny bird was already fluttering in midair. "In God We Trust" was the caption.

The room seemed to be full of people. In addition to the receptionist and Brian several others had materialized. Word must have gotten around, I thought. Ben's eyes traveled from face to face. He rewarded each one with his benevolent, crooked smile. "Thank you for allowing me to come. I appreciate it. God bless you."

It was almost as if he's heard the conversation, I thought. I heard a gasp and looked at the man who'd made the exception. Mesmerized looks were fixed on Ben and if anyone doubted he was other than what I had said, they didn't say it.

"Where would you like us to talk," he said, looking at Brian.

Brian opened his mouth. "Let me show you my room," I interrupted before he could answer.

I settled myself in the chair I'd found to be most comfortable and for the next two hours I sobbed and lashed out. I vented words of rage, long buried, for never having a father. I even targeted Mari as an adversary for denying me this knowledge and experienced new feelings about the mother I had always thought of as near perfect.

I was vaguely aware of staff members passing my door from time to time and at one point, someone pulled it almost shut. I was being inconsiderate of the other residents, no doubt, but I didn't give a damn! There was no way I could stay the torrent of accusations against my lost-found father. I called that old man every despicable name I could dredge from my vocabulary of despicable names. When I was through with him, I turned the flailing whip on my failed marriage and myself.

"Why? Why?" I cried from time to time. I never expected an answer, nor did I get one. Ben sat quietly in the chair across from me. At one point he found a box of tissues and brought it to me. Soggy wads of the soft sheets now lay in my lap and on the floor around me. Sometimes I simply huddled in the chair, trapped in my iron cage.

What a mess I must look, I thought. A forty-something—no, make that almost fifty-year-old-woman with a splotchy red face and swollen eyelids, barely able to breathe through her stuffy nose. I straightened myself, furiously brushed the rest of the wadded tissues on the floor and looked at Ben. I felt as If I had gone through a bout of stomach flu in which I had disgorged all the evil viruses inside me. "What am I going to do?"

But, I wasn't quite through. There was one more dry heave left in my body and I directed it at the man across from me and at God. "You've prayed for me," I accused in hateful tones. "You've prayed for guidance and peace for me. Where is it? Here I am stuck in this place. I don't know what to do and I certainly don't have any peace," I said, heaping the blame on this man who'd been there for me.

Ben came and knelt down in front of me. He reached for my hand but I pulled his head into my lap and just held on for dear life. When I finally let go he shifted his position to sit on the floor beside me. "Yes," he spoke softly, "I've prayed for you and your healing and I trust every word I've spoken. Have you ever prayed for yourself?"

"I tried," I said nodding. My nodding, however, was not "nodding" but a sort of bending back and forth from the waist. From somewhere in my mind came the memory of that cool moisture on my lips that brought me back from the limbo of my coma. It was an ice cubes wrapped in a cloth, Ben had told me that had felt so good. Maybe that is what healing is like, I thought.

"Then try again," Ben said beside me. "Repeat these words after me." When I nodded, again rocking back and forth, he began, "Dear God, no matter how dark and difficult my life may seem . . ." He waited.

"Dear God," I whispered. My voice was tenuous and my words hesitant, "no matter how dark and difficult . . .

"I know that I will make it through to a brighter time, because you are constantly with me and loving me.

"When I feel that I can't go on and I don't know what to do, I will let my faith in you lift me above any obstacle. I can never be lost or alone because you are my loving companion. You take away confusion and fear . . .

"I . . . I invite your light to show me the way. Amen."

Silently Ben rose. I took a deep breath. "Okay," I said. Somewhere there was the muted striking of a clock. "Oh, Ben, it's nine o'clock." I hoisted myself to my feet. "I'm sorry to keep you so late. You haven't even been home. I'm . . . I'm so . . ."

He placed a finger across my lips. "Sh . . . sh, Jessicacita. Sleep well."

My healing had begun, and now I was home. I looked around, delighted by everything I saw. It didn't take long for me to discover an added use for the Jacuzzi. Elaine helped me out of my clothes and into the roiling water. The churning water had whipped the bath gel I'd dribbled into the pool into magnificent foam that oozed over the edges onto the tiled patio. It was by far the best bath I'd had in weeks. There were similar tubs at Silver Springs and with the help of aides I was assisted in and out of them. Shampooing my hair was a challenge but the staff, experienced in cases such as mine, devised a crude, but fairly effective method for washing my hair that didn't disturb my various attachments.

"We'll just have to clean the Jacuzzi more often," I said as Elaine helped me from the pool. She rubbed me briskly with a towel then helped me into clean clothes. Blouses that opened in the front, skirts, shorts or slacks that could be pulled on were the order of the day. She insisted that I take a rest and settled me into the easy chair that Jack had claimed during the storm.

I was refreshed and relaxed when Ben drove into the driveway. Tail wagging, Ginger bounded in. If she'd had her fourth leg she would have stood to greet me, but since she didn't, I lowered myself to my knees. Her tongue didn't have any trouble reaching past the network of tubes to kiss me. "Oh, Ginger, I'm so glad to see you," I said, rubbing her neck.

"Soot!" I exclaimed when I looked up and saw Ben holding the cat. I blinked back tears as I struggled to get up. Elaine, who was never far away, was beside me helping me to my feet. "Oh, Soot, you don't know where you belong, do you? Are you sure this is the right thing to do?" I asked Ben. "Is it fair?"

"Of course," he said.

"How do you know?"

"He told me."

I laughed and held the cat at arm's length. "Did you?" I asked, looking into the animal's green eyes. His thunderous purr sounded like snare drums as it reverberated through the room.

Elaine, with all her wonderful qualifications, had one fault. It was her cooking. It was pure Florida cracker—fried, rich, and delicious. However, it was a difficulty I could live with I thought as I devoured smothered chicken, mashed potatoes with golden gravy, fried summer squash, pole beans with salt pork, and then to top it off, coconut cream pie. Besides, I rationalized, I had lost twenty pounds in the last several months.

After Elaine cleared away the last of the dishes and stacked them in the dishwasher, she retired to the den to her needlepoint and television. "This is so good," I breathed, as Ben and I sat in patio chairs and looked out over the deepening twilight.

He reached over and took my hand. "I could do this for the rest of my life," he said. I felt a catch in my chest.

"How's Jack?" I asked after a while.

"He's okay. He's busy." Ben paused, "He's hurting too."

I drew in a breath. "I need to see him. I think I'm ready—almost. I want to have this thing off though," I said tapping the frame on my head.

"Why? That won't matter to him. You saw him with a broken leg. Did that matter to you?"

"That was different."

"How?"

"I didn't know who he was," I replied. "Besides it will remind him of what happened."

"He knows what happened," Ben said quietly.

While it sounded like a reprimand it was true. I had to be ready to deal with the facts. I had to be ready for the truth. I had to be ready to forgive—or not. "I'll think about it," I said.

The next day the second of my companions appeared in a starched white uniform, her shiny black face a wreath of smiles beneath a crop of springy gray curls. Her LPN pin was proudly displayed on her ample bosom. So we added soul food to our diet— fried catfish, not the farm raised, but ones her husband caught from a lake, collard greens, black-eyed peas and corn bread.

To my great delight, the following day Louisa walked through the door. "Louisa!" I cried.

"Oh, *Señora* Steele." She rushed toward me with her arms open. "I begged Senior Steele to let me help take care of you."

"I'm so glad," I said as I hugged her.

So, every third day the smells of Mexican cooking spices filled the kitchen and in a week's time the scales showed that I gained four pounds.

Three times a week I was driven to the hospital. On Tuesday and Thursday mornings I had physical therapy, and Wednesday afternoons were devoted to mental gymnastics when I spent an hour with a psychiatrist. It was painful at first as I reluctantly probed the sore spots of my feelings, but gradually I began to enjoy saying exactly what I thought and felt.

Ben told me the first crop of Valencias were ready for harvest so each time we passed Jack's grove, I strained to catch a glimpse of activity. I saw stacks of wooden crates at the ends of each row and then one day, there they were—*The Pickers*, just like in Dali's painting. Only this was real and I felt a longing to be a part of it. Try as I would, I could not see the young trees from the street, nor did I ever see Jack.

On November 10, I had an appointment for a CAT scan and X-rays. My goal was to be out of this iron cage by Thanksgiving, but when I was ushered into Dr. Somer's office and saw his expression, my hopes shattered like glass, and fell at my feet on the good doctor's rich green carpeting. "Let's give it a few more weeks," he said, "just to be safe." I sat rigidly, without expression in the chair across from his desk but great teardrops rolled down my cheeks and landed wetly on my clenched hands.

That night Ben's company, Della's good food, Ginger's wagging tail or Soot's soothing purr could not cheer me up.

With a lot of time on my hands I spent some time each day in the pool, just lazily hanging on to the side and kicking my feet in the water. I did some sketching and what emerged were mostly black-and-white drawings of Soot—Soot sleeping on his back, stalking a butterfly on a flower or washing his face. Soon I had a whole collection. He was a good subject because he never paid any attention to what I was doing. I didn't read the paper very much because my arms grew tired holding it in a position where I could see the print. Occasionally, I watched television.

Sometime during this routine, vanity died. I picked up the phone and dialed the office of Tom Thatcher Esquire—the name at the top of the list of attorneys Malcolm had given me. To my surprise I was given an appointment the following Tuesday, only two days before Thanksgiving.

When the supermarkets began running their Thanksgiving specials I devised a plan. Ben told me that Maggie had been released from rehab and had gotten a job in a department store.

Her daughters would remain in foster care until her six-month review. "She's not going back to singing," he told me.

"I would like to have Thanksgiving dinner," I told Ben. "I'll invite you, Maggie and her daughters, and Scott if he has no place to go." I hadn't decided about Jack. I knew I had to talk to him first. But, that was before my meeting with Dr. Somers. That was when I thought I would be free of this stupid thing around my body that would make little girls ask questions. That was when I still thought I was in control of things.

Are you going to let this Thanksgiving pass by? A voice inside my head asked? *Would next year be any better?* "Who knows," I said out loud.

On Friday afternoon, the week before Thanksgiving I made my way to the phone beside my bed. The fact that I didn't think Jack would be in the house this time of the day didn't keep my hand from shaking as I dialed his number. On the fifth ring I was about to slam down the receiver saying, "I tried," when I heard a gruff, "Hello."

My mouth struggled to form words that did not seem to want to leave my throat. I knew if I didn't say something soon he would hang up. "It . . . it's Jessica," I said finally. "I would like to talk to you."

"When?" he asked after a pause.

"Tomorrow. And . . . and I want to bring Ben with me."

There was another pause. "All right," he answered and broke the connection. My body was trembling uncontrollably. It was a few minutes before I was able to punch in Ben's cell phone number. When he didn't answer, I left a message.

"Are you sure you want me to go with you?" he asked when he called back that night. "What you have to say to one another is private. No one else needs to hear it."

"You're my rock, remember? Besides, I told him you were coming with me. You know Jack well enough to know that if he didn't want you there he would say so. And, I want you there," I added.

It had been more than two months since I had seen the place and I wasn't prepared for what I saw. "What is this?" I exclaimed when Ben turned into the driveway. Not only had the overgrowth and debris had been cleared from around the house, but also numerous repairs had taken place. The stairs that had fallen at the back of the house had been removed. The front porch sported new, treated corner posts, making it sturdy and level. Most startling of all was that the old, cat-hair covered, mite-infested chair was gone. In its place a swing invited one to sit. The roof of the shed, damaged by the storm, had been repaired and everything looked neater and tidier.

"What happened?" I asked. Ben smiled an endearing smile, his eyes reflecting my awe. "What happened?" I repeated.

"Hope," he said simply as he helped me out of the truck.

I looked around. Jack was nowhere to be seen, but I had a feeling he was watching, just as he'd been the first time I trespassed on his property. "I don't believe it," I whispered as a quiver shot up my spine. Then I saw Jack walk out of the shed.

I held myself erect, tilting slightly backward, as I'd been taught, to balance myself. He had on clean clothes and looked good except that his face looked gaunter and he seemed to have lost weight. He still supported himself with his cane. As he walked toward me, his eyes covered my body, lingering on the brace that enclosed me. I didn't know what to say, so I didn't say anything.

"You want to sit here?" he asked, indicating the metal chairs where we'd so often sat on a summer's evening, "or go inside?"

"Inside, I think." Although the sun was warm now these November days grew quickly cool. He nodded and led the way into the house. Ben and I followed him through the kitchen and into his room. I was surprised once again to see that the old stained claw-foot tub was gone and in its place gleamed a new glass-fronted shower.

As though he'd prepared for this, two comfortable chairs had been added to his room. He lowered himself into his chair while Ben and I slid into the others. What openings I had rehearsed vanished from my mind. I looked at him and said, "I have your eyes."

A wisp of a smile crossed his face. "And my bone structure."

I looked down at my hands as if to confirm that statement and nodded. Mari had been short and petite, and even though Jack's body was bent he was still a tall man.

I raised my eyes and held his gaze. "Tell me," I whispered.

"What do you want to know?"

"Everything. But first tell me *why* you didn't tell me." I heard the bitterness that crept into my voice.

"I was going to."

"*When?*" I demanded. He looked away. His hands gripped the top of the walking stick that rested between his knees and his eyes focused on some scene beyond the trees—beyond the street—beyond time. When he didn't answer I repeated, "When did you know?"

"I suspected it that day when you brought me home from the hospital and chewed me out." He snorted derisively, "You sounded just like me. I caught a glimpse of me in your face. Then, when you said your grandparents lived on a sheep ranch in Colorado— that and the way you said your mother's name, 'Mari.'

"'Mari,'" he repeated. "You said it just the way she did, with the emphasis on the *y*."

"But she spelled hers with an *i*," I corrected.

He shook his head, "Not at first. She changed it—said it seemed more exciting. I remember when she did it. Then of course, there was your name," he said after a pause. "I helped choose it."

Salty tears prickled my eyelids. I struggled to my feet and walked to the window. "This is going to be harder than I thought," I said when I felt Ben's hand on my shoulder.

CHAPTER TWENTY

"What do you want to know?" Jack asked in a husky voice.

"Everything." I turned from the window and sat down. "I want to know everything." Jack propped his cane against the arm of his chair. There was agony in his eyes as he looked at me. He swallowed and nodded then absently began stroking Cat who'd jumped up in his lap.

"I met your mother in 1951," he began in a hesitant voice. He stopped and cleared his throat. As difficult as it was for me, I could not imagine how hard it must be to share such old, painful memories.

"Every year the city of Fort Myers has a festival in February for Thomas Edison's birthday. I think it was something his wife started back in the forties. The city claims him as one of their famous people since he had his winter home here. The festival's been going on for almost fifty years—still is. It gets bigger and bigger every year—lasts for a whole week. Anyway, there's a big parade on Saturday. High school bands come from all over the country to march in that parade. It's an honor to be invited. There are lots of floats too that people have been working on for weeks. Then on Saturday night there are fireworks.

"I was living at home and working with my dad and not liking it very much. When I wasn't working in the groves I hung around with my friends. That made for some pretty rough days because no matter what time I got home, I was rousted out of bed at dawn and expected to have breakfast and be ready for work in half an hour. 'Course, everybody—even my dad—called a halt to work on Edison Saturday.

"My pals and I had started our partying early in the day, so by the time the parade began, we were feeling pretty good. We had plenty of whistles and catcalls for the pom-pom girls and the twirlers, you know, the ones that twirl those baton things with a rubber ball on either end and throw them up in the air and catch them. Our eyes were glued on the short skirts they wore. When one of the girls dropped a baton or kicked high, we strained to see what was under those skirts. 'It's like being in a candy store,' my buddy Red said. And we howled and carried on as though that was the funniest thing in the world. 'Gimme a candy cane—I want chocolate covered cherries—I'll take a lollipop,' we'd yell and snap our fingers inside our cheeks, making popping sounds."

Jack smiled at the memories, and I could imagine him as a tall good-looking man of twenty-three, slightly drunk, preening like a cock on a walk. I hardly dared to breathe because the voice that had begun hesitantly now became fluent with precious memories. I didn't dare look at Ben.

"All of a sudden," Jack continued, "here came this really spiffy little band. Comparatively, they were small, maybe forty or forty-five in number, but they sounded good and had lots of pep. 'Rangely Colorado' was the name on the banner they carried in front. I'd never heard of the place. Their drum major was tall, tall as me. His plumed hat made him look even taller. He stepped high, his knees up to his chin, never missing a beat.

"Behind him were six twirlers, all strutting and kicking high. They *were* precision. When they kicked, their legs were at exactly the same angle. Their batons were so accurately thrown that it looked like they came out of a machine. And they did something none of the others did. When they threw their batons in the air, they would twirl in a complete circle, changing places with the girl next to them and catching her wand.

"That's when I saw her. She was the one nearest us. She was a tiny girl but she seemed perfect. Her black curls shone like coal in the afternoon sunlight and her smile was radiant. Her face told the world that she was having the best time. As they approached us they kicked, threw their batons and changed places. Just as they were even with us she twirled back into her place, reaching for her baton. I leaped out and grabbed it.

"'Hey, Jack, cut it out,' my friends yelled at me. It was too late. The baton clattered to the pavement and rolled toward us. I reached down to pick it up but she beat me to it. Without breaking a step, she picked it up and, with a jab that few people saw, rammed it right into my groin. I gave a breathless yelp and doubled over with pain. I had never had anything hurt so bad in my life. I couldn't get my breath. My buddies tried to help me up, but I just lay there for several minutes before they were able to get me to my feet. By that time she was half a block away, marching and twirling as though nothing had happened."

Ben and I burst out laughing. "It wasn't funny," Jack scolded, but I saw humor in his face. I also heard something in his tone I'd never heard before—tenderness.

"I don't remember much about the rest of the evening. I used my pain as an excuse to drink more beer. It didn't even matter to me that I'd been humiliated. What mattered was that I couldn't get her out of my mind.

"Staying out late on Saturday night never kept me from having to get up for church on Sunday morning anymore than it kept Dad from rousting me out of bed on workdays. I remember sitting in church that Sunday, sore between my legs, wondering where I could find her.

"That afternoon my friends and I headed out for Fort Myers Beach as we often did. There were four of us who'd been friends since college days; Red and I had been roommates. It was a cool February day and we had no intention of swimming. We did that when the weather was hot. We laughed at the tourists who came to Florida for vacation. They were going to go home with a tan— goose bumps or not. Because there were so many people in town for the festival there were people all over the beach. It was always a good place to pick up a girl who wanted to go home and tell about her exciting vacation and the guy she met. We meant to oblige.

"The first thing we saw were rows of bright orange school buses all lined up in the parking lot. Across the back of one of them was a banner that read, 'Rangely High School Marching Band.' I couldn't believe I'd gotten so lucky. 'Look guys,' I shouted.

'She's here. You've got to help me find her!' Do you have any idea
how hard it is to find somebody when there's a couple hundred
bodies, all undressed more or less the same, lying on beach towels
or romping around? Well, my buddies helped me look for a while,
but they only had my description to go on. They hadn't paid
much attention to her.

"I must have searched for an hour. When I finally saw her, she
was standing in the surf. She was not wearing a bathing suit but
shorts and a blouse she'd tied up just under her breasts. Her hair
was tied in a ponytail with a red ribbon. She was talking to the
drum major.

"Without his high-plumed hat he wasn't quite so tall and
without his splashy uniform I noticed that I had better muscles
than he did. I took off my shoes, rolled up my pant legs, and
waded right out to them. 'Excuse me,' I said as I took her by the
arm, 'I have to discuss the damage to the family jewels with this
lady.' She started to pull away but when she looked at my face her
eyes grew wide and her mouth formed a great big *O*. I lead her
down the beach, leaving the bewildered drum major behind.

"'You *do* recognize me?' I asked.

"'You had no right to do that,' she replied angrily, jerking her
arm away.

"'You're right,' I said. 'I'm sorry.'

"'I'm sorry too,' she said looking at me with those big dark
eyes. Then she giggled. 'I had no idea you were so cute.'

"I felt heat rise from my neck to my hairline and it was not
from the sun. I stuck out my hand. 'John Webster,' I said, 'my
friends call me Jack.'

"'Mary Sanchez,' she replied accepting my hand. It was so
small and warm in mine, my knees just about turned to jelly.

"'Buy you an ice cream,' I said, jerking my thumb in the
direction of the snack bar down the beach. That was it. I was
hooked. She sneaked out to meet me that night. Oh, we didn't do
anything wrong. She wouldn't and I didn't, but we tasted love and
it was wonderful. We exchanged addresses and kisses, and she crept
back into her room before wake-up call. I was watching when the

bus left at nine o'clock for the long drive back to Colorado. Oh, there was hell to pay when I got home but I didn't care. I did my work but all I could think of was her. My friends kidded me and told me I would get over it. I didn't."

Jack was quiet for the longest moment then he looked at me. There were tears in his eyes. "I haven't," he said hoarsely. I felt my own throat close up. This was *my* mother he was talking about— *my Mari*. What had gone wrong with a love like that? I wondered. I waited out the silence.

"We wrote. We got to know each other through our letters. Mary was eighteen years old and she would graduate from high school in May. My twenty-three years seemed too old to her. The biggest thing that had ever happened in her life was the trip to Florida. She wanted more. She had dreams. She didn't want to be one more wife of one more sheep rancher. Her 'old country' parents didn't see it that way. Nor did they see the value in her going to college.

"Come to Florida, I wrote. Get a job here to earn money for college. We could be near each other. No, she wrote back. She wouldn't travel across the country just because some fellow asked her to. There had to be a better reason than that.

"Her parents would never allow it. The guy she was dating was serious and pushing her for a commitment. The guy, of course, was the drum major.

"When I read that I was desperate. I was eaten up with jealousy. I even thought of going to get her, but I phoned her instead. We didn't use phones much back in the fifties, the way people do now. A phone call was pretty important. I waited until my parents were out of the house when I put the call person-to-person through the operator. The operator had trouble making the woman who answered the phone understand that the call was for Mary.

"'Jack, why are you calling me?' she said when she finally came to the phone.

"'I love you, and I want to marry you,' I blurted out. 'Did you hear me, Mary?' I asked when she didn't answer right away.

"'Yes,' she whispered.

"'Do you love me?'

"I strained to hear the soft 'yes.' 'Then will you come down here and marry me? I don't have much to offer you right now, but someday I will. I can send you the money.' I was so nervous waiting for her reply that my knees were shaking and sweat was rolling off me. I had the feeling there were other people there who could hear her end of the conversation.

"'Yes, Jack, I will.'

"Oh, my dad had a 'blue fit' when I told him. He said I wasn't ready to get married, that I barely knew her, that being married was a big responsibility. When he asked me where I was going to live, I exploded. I told him it was my understanding that the reason I worked so hard was that I was the one who would keep the operation going when he wasn't able. I informed him that if I wasn't welcome to bring my wife here I certainly knew enough about the industry to find a job with some other grower who would provide housing. Then I did what had gotten to be a habit—a habit and my downfall. I stormed out and got drunk."

I was mesmerized. It was like a recording had turned on inside him. His voice emphasized his emotions and the drama of events. This was the man inside the man who'd ordered me off his property.

"Well, things calmed down. Mary came, and we got married right over there in the parlor on a Saturday afternoon in June, in 1951. My sister stood up with Mary and Red stood up with me. Mom and Dad and the preacher were the only other ones there.

"I had a 1947 Plymouth coupe that I'd paid for myself. I was awfully proud of it. After the ceremony we drove out to Sanibel Island and rented a beach cottage for two nights. That was our honeymoon. It wouldn't have mattered to me where we were. I was so in love. I loved the way she fit into my arms. I loved her spirit. I loved her desire to learn things and I loved her determination. She could be a 'spitfire.' It excited me when she stood up to me and I was proud of her when she stood up to my dad.

"Oh, she was never disrespectful. She had a way with people but, if she felt somebody was wrong, she let them know it. I remember once when a starving cat hung around for a couple of days, and she wanted to feed it. Dad told her no, if we didn't feed it, it would go away.

"If Mom doesn't feed you, will you go away?" she asked. I thought Dad would be mad, but he burst out laughing.

"She wasn't afraid of work either. She took her turn staying up at night to keep the torches going, or worked late to help get out a shipment of prime fruit. She always had a smile for the workers and even knew all the Mexicans' names."

Jack looked at me. "Like you do," he said. Ben smiled and winked.

"We lived upstairs, in the room that was my bedroom. Sis's room was the front bedroom but by that time she'd already gotten married and moved out. Even though Dad was just in his fifties, his arthritis had gotten pretty bad. He and Mom moved downstairs and made this room into their bedroom. Our paradise was there in that upstairs. When our workday was done and supper was over, we retreated to that paradise. It was the best year of my life.

"One night I stayed downstairs to go over some shipping schedules with Dad. When I came upstairs I saw that the bathroom door was closed. Then I heard sounds of retching. I tried the door and it was locked. We *never* locked the door. 'Mari, what's wrong? Open the door.' When there was no answer, I rattled the knob. 'Open the door,' I demanded. Just when I was ready to put my shoulder to it, she opened it.

"She stood there clutching a towel to her chin. Her eyes were wide, and her face was as pale as the porcelain of the fixtures. 'I think I'm going to have a baby,' she whispered.

"'A baby? A baby?' I stood there stupidly repeating, 'A baby.' Suddenly she started laughing. She dropped the towel and threw her arms around me. 'What's so funny?' I asked.

"'You. How do you feel about being a father?'

"Well, I didn't know how I felt about being a father. We'd talked about the family we wanted, but we'd agreed it would be better if we waited until we had a place of our own. Lots of nights we lay in bed and rehearsed our future—the children we would have, what we would name them, the house we would build.

"And then, six months later—there you were—six pounds, nine ounces of you, all read and screaming with so much black hair. I never knew babies could be born with so much hair."

Jack looked at me and waited. I thought I was going to suffocate from the tightness in my chest. I tried to take deep breaths but the air just didn't seem to reach my lungs. *Just breathe in and out very slowly,* I commanded myself.

"May 25, 1953?" I asked when I could talk. Jack nodded. "There were six baby girls born that day in Lee County Memorial," I said. "I've checked. There were four who hadn't been given names, just Baby Girl this or that. There were two whose mother had the name of Mary. I could have been one of them, but then, I also thought that maybe I wasn't born in this county." Jack looked at me with such sadness it almost broke my heart.

"That's when she changed her name. There were too many Marys. 'Mari' had more of a lilt to it,' she said.

"We made a door between our bedroom and the room next to it and made it into a nursery. She had such fun decorating it. It was ready and waiting when we brought you home from the hospital. It didn't take long for you to win everybody over. We kept you downstairs in a bassinet during the day. Even Dad took a peek at you every time he came in the house. Mari was such a whiz with numbers that Dad soon had her doing much of the bookkeeping. That way she could spend more time with you and be around when you were hungry. The world seemed almost perfect then, but I wouldn't let it stay that way.

"Most of the fights I had with Dad were about doing things a different way. I didn't understand why I couldn't use some of the things I'd learned at school. I accused him of being old fashioned. He told me I just wanted to spend money and if things were working why change them? We made money; the fifties and sixties were good for growers. Florida citrus was becoming known all over the country. Labor was cheap. We outranked California and Texas.

"Dad and I had the same temper. When it flared, we never knew how to put out the flame. Even when our shouting matches were over, the tension stayed with us for days. Mom or Mari never interfered with our arguments but later she would try to reason with me. 'He's made the place. He's put his heart and hands and sweat into making the groves what they are. Let him be proud of that,' she'd say. 'You'll have the chance to do things your way someday.'

"'Then why did he send me to college?' I argued.

"'For the future,' she replied. She seemed so wise. She would even tell me all this shouting and tension wasn't good for the baby or for us. Then I would hold her in my arms and promise.

"Sometimes after an argument I'd just jump in my car and take off, leaving my work unfinished. I'd find the nearest bar. In the beginning I'd call Red and ask him to join me, but he stopped doing that. 'Man,' he'd say. 'Don't you know when you got the world by the tail? Don't make me a party to this.'

"Of course the next day I'd be hungover and sorry and work extra hard. Mari never punished me for it by chewing me out or turning her back on me, but she became more withdrawn.

"Oh, not with you. She was so happy when she was feeding you or bathing you or playing with you, but some of the bubble had gone from her laughter and light out of her eyes.

"One day I went upstairs and found her standing, staring out of the window. I asked her what she was thinking about. 'Oh, just wondering how things were going on the ranch, how many lambs they had this year.' When I asked her if she missed her folks, she said, 'Sometimes.'

"I got worried. God, I didn't want to make her unhappy. I didn't want her to leave. So, I tried to keep my temper in check, do my work, and stay out of Dad's way.

"But that didn't last. After one fight when I went out, I fell asleep in my car and didn't come home until morning. Everybody was already awake. Mom and Dad weren't saying anything and Mari looked exhausted. I could tell she'd been crying. 'I can't go on like this' she said. Again I promised. Oh, I punished myself that day. I didn't take time for breakfast but went straight to work. My head pounded, and being in the sun made it worse. I figured I deserved it and maybe if it were painful enough I wouldn't do it again. I refused to believe I had a problem.

"Shortly before your second birthday Mari discovered she was pregnant again. Dad was the one who suggested that maybe we should have a house of our own for our growing family. He even told us he had a spot picked out."

A shiver ran through my body. I knew. "The clearing?" I asked. He nodded. "I had a dream," I continued, "that night, after you told me about your wife and children. In the dream there were a man and woman and little girl. They were looking at a house that was just a frame. The man was holding the little girl and the little girl was crying because she wanted her mother to take her. 'Mommy can't carry you now,' the woman said. 'Mommy has to carry the baby.' The little girl didn't understand . . ."

"We got busy and cleared the land," Jack continued. "I felt proud that Dad so willingly bulldozed some of his trees. At night we worked on plans. Mari was happier than I'd ever seen her. Being pregnant agreed with her. She was radiant. Red was right, I did have the world by the tail. Dad and I did a lot of the framing ourselves. He was in pain most of the time, but he did what he could. In those days you didn't have joint replacements. You just got crippled and stayed that way."

Jack's voice died away and he sat staring at the floor, clasping and unclasping his hands. When he looked up at me I saw such pain in his eyes that I had to look away. "I don't know if I can tell the rest of it," he said.

"I have to know," I whispered. "I have a right to know."

He nodded and cleared his throat. "I've lived with regret every day of my life since," he said.

"One day we noticed that a whole section of trees that had been fertilized weren't looking too good. Their leaves were pale and beginning to curl up. Then we discovered that instead of fertilizer, pesticides had been used and in concentrations that we usually used for fertilizers.

"Dad blew up. Even though one of the men had done it, he blamed me. I was the one who was supposed to be in charge of them. I was the one supposed to check on those things. He told me I wasn't grown-up enough to run the place. He said he couldn't trust me.

"He was right, of course. I had screwed up. I should have been paying attention. But I didn't accept the blame. I did my usual thing. I jumped in my car and raced to the nearest bar. This time though, the drinks just fueled my anger and hurt. I was going to get Mari and the baby and we were going to get out of there—to hell with the house, to hell with working with my father.

"'Mari! Mari,' I shouted as I jumped out of the car and headed for the house. It was quitting time and the workers were leaving for the day. When they hesitated, Dad told them to go and get out. She met me at the top of the stairs. I told her to get some clothes for her and Jessica, that we were leaving. 'This will never work. I'm not staying here any longer,' I said.

"'What about the house?' she asked.

"'To hell with the house,' I shouted. 'I'll build you a better house than this.' I rushed up the stairs and tried to push past her.

"She grabbed my arm. 'Please, Jack,' she pleaded. I shoved her. Oh God, I only meant to move her out of the way but she lost her balance and tumbled all the way to the bottom of the stairs."

The cry that came from Jack's throat was like that of some primordial animal in deepest distress. It came involuntarily, as though wrenched by some primitive force stronger than the man who'd kept those voices submerged within his soul for so many years. He leaned forward, his forearms resting on his knees and his head buried in his hands. Sobs, deep, wracking sobs, shook his body. Tears and drool fell on the floor at his feet.

I began to shiver and tightened my arms around my chest as the shivering became uncontrollable. I had never heard such horrible sounds in my life. From somewhere Ben produced a wrap and put it around my shoulders. Inside my cage I listened to the anguish of the man who was my father. I wanted to run, but I had run before. I could see the floor at the bottom of the stairs where my mother had landed from where I was sitting. It was so visual that I wondered if I had witnessed that episode so many years ago.

As Jack's sobs gave way to moans and gasps for breath, Ben went to him. Only a man like Ben would have known what to do, I certainly didn't. He pulled a handkerchief from his pocket and put it in Jack's hand. Then he stood there with his hand on his shoulder while the old man mopped his face and blew his nose. "Would you like for us to leave?" Ben asked.

Jack shook his head. "I want to finish," he said. Ben went into the kitchen and brought him a glass of water. Jack took a drink, sat the glass on the table beside him and looked at me. "I am so sorry," he whispered.

I gripped the jacket around me and pressed my lips together. I saw the raw open wound of guilt in his eyes. What it must have cost him to say those words, I thought as tears ran down my face.

"That sobered me up in a hurry. Mom screamed. I ran down the stairs. Mari's eyes were closed and her face was so white. 'Mari,' I shouted. 'Oh God, Mari.'

"When she opened her eyes there was a look of horror in them. 'My baby,' she whimpered as she clutched her abdomen.

"Dad and I got her in the car and rushed her to the hospital. Mom stayed with you. She lost the baby about an hour later. It was a boy. He was alive. The doctors put him in an incubator and hooked him up to oxygen. He never breathed on his own. Two days later he died.

"A nerve in Mari's back had been pinched in the fall and she had no feeling or use of her left leg, but doctor told us it was temporary. When we brought her home a few days later, I carried her upstairs. I told her over and over how sorry I was and she would only say, 'I know you are.'

"Things were as quiet as a morgue around the house. We all were in mourning. I went back to work with Dad but we didn't talk much. I was brutal in punishment of myself. When I wasn't working in the groves I worked on the house. Mari had little interest in it. When I asked her to come see how we were doing she would say, 'Later, I don't feel like it right now.' Although we still shared the same bed, she went to sleep each night with her back to me. I accepted that as my punishment too.

"One day Dad had sent me for some supplies while he was out on the far side of the grove supervising some men. Mom had gone somewhere to run errands. When she got back you and Mari were gone. Mom was standing in the yard waiting for me when I drove in the driveway a little later.

"Upstairs in our room was a note. *Dear Jack,* it read, *you don't have to make any more promises. I can't stay any longer. I have to look after my little girl. I hope things work out for you and your father. I gave you my heart and you will always have it, but I have to do this. Love, Mari.*"

From time to time Jack's voice broke and I sometimes had to strain to hear him, but I didn't interrupt. Now he gave a shudder and was silent. I sat there sobbing. There was such a pain in my chest that I thought maybe I was having a heart attack. Ben came over and offered me his hand. "Let me take you home," he said. I nodded and stood up but my legs were so wobbly he had to grab me.

I walked over and stood in front of Jack. He looked at me with bleary eyes. "I'm sorry too," I said.

"I'll come right back," Ben told him.

CHAPTER TWENTY-ONE

I sat huddled in the seat beside Ben, my arms wrapped around myself, shivering for all I was worth. Somehow it had gotten to be late afternoon. None of us noticed that lunchtime had come and gone, or that the sun had shifted from east to west. The November air was chilly, with the feeling of night already in the air. Ben turned up the heater in the cab of his truck. He reached over and took my hand.

"I don't know how to deal with this," I whispered. He didn't say anything, just squeezed my hand tighter.

Della knew instantly that something was wrong. "Oh, child," she exclaimed when she saw us. Her outstretched arms reached for me.

"I'll see to Jack," Ben said as he relinquished me to her care.

Whether it was the training of a caregiver, or the instinct of a healer, Della sensed need. "I've made some soup," she said. "Would you like to take some to Mr. Webster?" It was only five o'clock in the afternoon, but after she sent Ben off with the soup, she undressed me and helped me into my nightclothes, then settled me into bed. I hadn't realized I was hungry, but I ate everything she put on my tray.

My companions and I had an arrangement so that clean linens didn't have to be put on beds every day. Della and Elaine shared the twin-bedded room across the hall. When it was Louisa's turn, she slept in the single bed in my room. Tonight though, after I'd eaten and she had settled pillows around me to make me comfortable, Della pulled a chair up close to my bed, and lowering her bulk into it, held my hand while I told her my parents' story. When I had exhausted myself, she helped me to the bathroom then as she rubbed my neck, my arms and legs and settled me for sleep she sang softly in her deep contralto voice.

Since I had been wearing this brace I was never able to sleep more than three or four hours at a time. Tonight a thought jerked me awake. The clock read 2 a.m. A memory from my childhood surfaced as I pictured a tall young man who sometimes came to the ranch to visit my mother. He was good looking and nice and brought me presents. When I asked her why he stopped coming she told me she was too busy working to have time for him. Later, when the ranch was sold I remember Aunt Jean telling my mother, "The fellow who used to be interested in you was the one who bought it." *The drum major! Of course it was the drum major.*

I woke Sunday morning to the sound of Della's and Louisa's low voices coming from the kitchen. I felt as if I had the flu. I ached all over. Louisa's shocked face told me that I must look as awful as I felt. *"Oh Dios mio! Dios mio,"* she exclaimed. *"Pobre* Jessicacita. *Pobre* Señor Webster. Poor little Jessica, poor Mr. Webster." Tears ran an obstacle course down the folds of her cheeks but her smile could have lit a thousand candles. We held hands and cried. "I cannot believe it. All this time you didn't know."

Ben stopped by in the afternoon. He had already checked on Jack. "I have so much to think about—and so many questions," I told him. "There's so much more I need to know."

"You will," he said, "but for today—just rest—heal."

By Tuesday when Elaine dropped me off for my appointment with Mr. Tom Thatcher Esquire, I felt better, but I knew I was in no condition mentally or physically to give a dinner party. I did, however, want those people who were special to me to have a Thanksgiving dinner. "We'll cook the meals and deliver them," I told Elaine as I sent her off to the supermarket with a shopping list.

I was ushered promptly into the attorney's office, who I noticed by the notation on his door, was *the* senior partner. Somewhere beneath the demeanor of the mild-mannered man with a very English-sounding name and a Florida twang, I suspected was a competent lawyer. When I told him I was not seeking a settlement he raised his eyebrows in shocked disbelief. "B . . . but, you have a right to a settlement," he stammered. "Mr. Steele is prepared to be very generous."

I stared at him. "I beg your pardon? Are you representing my husband?" When he realized what he'd said, his mouth snapped shut as though he was heading off an approaching fly. "Should I seek another attorney?"

"No, Mrs. Steele. That remark was inappropriate. I apologize," he said quietly.

"But you have spoken with him?" He nodded.

"I don't want his money," I explained. "I have considerable funds from my mother's estate, her insurance policy, and funds from the sale of her business. In addition, I *do* have a profession that pays well. I don't need his money," I added.

"I'm afraid that's too late."

"What do you mean?"

"I have five million dollars in escrow. All you have to do is tell me where and how you would like it invested. We have people in our firm who can assist with that," he added in an effort to regain control of the conversation.

"But no papers have even been filed," I protested.

"Either way, the money is yours. Mr. Steele wants you to be taken care of, especially in light of . . . of y . . . your recent a . . . accident," he stuttered. "Perhaps you will change your mind."

It was times like this when I felt really trapped inside this thing that was around my head holding me immobile when I wanted to bury my face in my hands, beat my head against the wall, or scream. I couldn't even raise my voice without my head throbbing as the metal screws bore into my forehead.

There was no reason to prolong this. I was not going to change my mind. "Malcolm thinks money can always fix everything," I muttered as I filled out the necessary forms. I walked out the door leaving Mr. Thatcher holding his five million in escrow.

Wednesday, Della and I cooked, Della mostly, because my culinary talents were limited to chopping, stirring, rolling, and mixing whatever she told me to. I wore an apron I'd found in a drawer that read, "Martha Stewart Doesn't Live Here."

There was a Thanksgiving Eve service at Ben's church that evening, and although I was self-conscious about being seen with my halo, I knew that I had to go—wanted to go. I asked Della to go with me.

On this dark November evening light streamed from the open door, beckoning us to enter. Cars pulled in one behind the other, lining both sides of the street as people moved alone, or as families toward the church. I had hoped to be able just to slip quietly into a back pew but I saw that they were already filled. It was all I could do to keep from laughing when I saw a familiar orange head. I recognized Scott sitting between two of his friends. They had to be his friends I concluded because one's hair was bright green while the other was purple. I immediately named them Carrot, Celery, and Eggplant. Scott sported two new rings in his lower lip. When he saw me he gave me a thumbs-up and grinned. If they could be comfortable here with their multicolored hair and Della didn't mind being the only Black person present, of what consequence was my halo?

As Della and I made our way to some empty seats halfway down the aisle I heard a high-pitched voice scream, "Jessica," followed by yet another, "Jessica," as Peggy Sue and Allie pounded down the aisle toward me.

"Allie! Peggy Sue," I exclaimed as I grabbed the edge of the pew and knelt down to receive the excited welcome I saw coming. "I didn't know you were going to be here. I'm so glad to see you."

"Pastor Ben brought us," Peggy Sue explained. "We heard you were hurt."

"What does that thing do?" Allie asked, pointing to my brace.

Every pair of eyes seemed to be turned in my direction. "It holds my head still so my bones can heal properly," I explained.

"Is it heavy?" Allie wanted to know as she gingerly reached out to touch it.

"Oh, yes, sometimes it seems very heavy."

"Mommy's here too," Peggy Sue announced as I looked up to see Maggie standing behind them. She looked wonderful. The dark hollows beneath her eyes, and the sickly gray of her skin was gone. Gone too was the nervous tremors of her hands. She wore a simple white blouse and a floor-length full skirt, awash with bright flowers on a turquoise background that brought the color of her magnificent eyes. A sash of the same blue-green color cinched her narrow waist.

"Maggie," I said, rising. "You look great. How are things going?"

"Well, thank you." She offered a tentative hand.

"I'm so glad to see you and the girls. Ben told me Peggy Sue and Allie are going to be with you for Thanksgiving."

"Thank you for dinner tomorrow," she said shyly. "I had to work today so I didn't have time to do anything."

"Will you sit with us?" Peggy Sue asked when the organ music began. Della moved into a pew that had space for all of us. I sat beside her, pressed against the comforting warmth of her body. Peggy Sue and Allie sat between Maggie and me. The church was filled, still people filed in. We pushed together to make more space, while men carried in more folding chairs, truly a fire marshal's nightmare.

As everybody settled into his or her seats, Ben took his place in front. Surrounded by pots of persimmon color chrysanthemums that adorned the altar. His skin looked warmly rich in an open-necked shirt that matched the colors of the flowers. His simple wooden cross hung on a chain around his neck. I felt my heart skip a beat at his beauty. Beauty is the right word, I thought, because his countenance conveyed more than just good looks.

When we rose to sing "Come, Ye Thankful People, Come," I saw him. There was no mistaking the back of Jack's grizzled, gray head, nor the deliberate way in which he got to his feet. I felt a tremor shoot through my body. Della sensed it because she linked her arm through mine and clasped my hand. I felt my knees go wobbly but I grabbed the back of the seat in front and held on for dear life. It was uncomfortable for me to sing, so I let myself get lost in Della's rich alto on one side, and Maggie's perfect tones on the other.

Ben's message invited us to recognize and name the blessings that had been ours during the past year. He said that many of us had received unexpected blows, and the greatest reason to be thankful was being able to allow God to guide us through these times when we were on the floor for the count of ten. Several of us listening had had that knockout punch.

Ben asked us to quietly reflect on those things for which we were thankful. The one that came to my mind was the one that brought me here tonight. My heart was filled with gratitude that the Scotts, the Maggies, the Jessicas, the Dellas and the Jacks could be comfortably pulled together in this place; that we didn't have to fit into some preconceived mold or pass some test to feel this unity of spirit.

As we sat in silence, Maggie quietly got up and left her seat. In a few moments I heard the words of, "Our Father, who art in Heaven . . ." as her voice rose clear and full, without accompaniment, to fill the room with the words of the Lord's Prayer.

When Maggie ended with the "Ah . . . Ah . . . aha . . . men," there was not a sound in the room. It was though we were collectively holding our breath. Ben's quiet benediction simply commanded us to "go with thanksgiving."

I waited as people filed past me as Jack made his way up the aisle. When he was beside me, I stepped out and took his arm. We walked out of the church together.

The next morning Della and I finished the preparations for the Thanksgiving meals. We portioned out turkey and dressing, mashed potatoes and gravy, sweet potatoes, corn pudding, and cranberry sauce. We sliced pecan and pumpkin pies, Della's specialties.

The first Wednesday in December is a day I will always remember. It was the day of my liberation. Louisa drove me to the hospital for that long-awaited moment when my halo was removed. I was sedated while the screws were removed from my skull. My hair covered the other lesions but a red and raw circle, about the size of a dime, marked my forehead; I christened it my beauty mark. There would be weeks yet of physical therapy and I could not yet drive a car but, *I could shampoo my hair. I could lay my head down on a pillow.* I felt like celebrating. "Louisa," I said as we pulled out of the parking lot. "Let's go over to Ortiz for some real food." We headed for the open-air cantina.

Malcolm's phone calls had become less frequent, so after I had a nap with my head really on a pillow, I called him to let him know that I was finally out of the brace, and to thank him for the excellent care he'd arranged. He seemed pleased to hear from me. "Malcolm," I said, "I cannot accept your money."

There was a prolonged silence on the line. "I've been doing a lot of thinking," he said finally. "I underestimated you. You are a remarkable woman—your own woman, and—and," he faltered, "I would not want you to be different. I know that we don't want the same things, but you have brought joy into my life. I want to know that you are taken care of. I want you to have the money. It will remain in Tom's stewardship until you decide what to do with it. I'm sure it will be something worthwhile," he added.

"I'm sorry," he said when it was time to say good-bye. "I'll keep in touch."

I heard a catch in his voice. I didn't ask what he was sorry for. I didn't have to. "I'm sorry too," I whispered as I hung up the phone.

One of the hardest things I had to do was to say good-bye to Elaine and Della. Thankfully, Louisa would still be there. While I had not developed as close a relationship with Elaine, Della had been like a sponge of warmth, soaking up my needs. Perhaps I would not say good-bye, but make her a part of my life, as I seemed to be doing with Maggie and her girls and Ben. There was still unfinished business with Jack—still a lot of questions I wanted to ask. What I need is a good walk, I told myself. I slipped into a windbreaker, pulled a headband over my ears and set out on my first walk in many weeks. Daylight hesitated until seven o'clock as the year counted down to its shortest day. From my new house my route no longer took me past Jack's property but I purposefully set out in than direction.

I greeted the statuary Great Dane, ever the sentinel on his porch. I passed the corner where Ben had fed the cats that no longer came. Nobody knew why; perhaps they'd been trapped. Then I turned down Blossom Lane.

Jack's place looked so much tidier than when I first saw it. There seemed to be activity in the shed, and I wondered what they would be doing this time of the year. I stood across the street watching. "Who am I anyway?" I asked the squirrels and the grazing horses across the street. I would soon no longer be Mrs. Malcolm Steele. Could I return to being Jessica Parker? Could I ever be Jessica Webster? I jammed my hands in my pockets and headed back to the main road. The tears streaming down my cheeks were wet and cold.

At home I stripped off my jacket and headband and poured a cup of coffee to warm me up. I was just giving Soot his breakfast when the phone rang.

"Do you want to talk anymore?" the voice on the other end of the line asked.

For a moment I couldn't say anything. "Yes," I whispered.

"I saw you walk by," he said.

"What were you doing in the shed?"

"Getting the smudge pots ready."

"Do you think the cultivars will be all right?" I asked.

"They will."

"May I come over?" *Red Rover, Red Rover, let me come over,* words of a childhood game played over in my mind as I walked back to his house. It was a game I'd played with children of the ranch hands in those high mountain meadows on summer afternoons. It mattered not to us that we fell, and bumped and scraped ourselves. We just laughed it off. There were two teams, each lined up across from one another, holding hands as tightly as we could. One team called, "Red Rover, Red Rover, let someone come over," as they called a person's name. The one selected ran as hard and as fast as he or she could toward the opposing team. The object was to break through the locked hands. If the opponent broke through he chose a player to bring back to his team. If hands held and he didn't break through, he became a member of that team. Sometimes the game would go on for hours before all the players ended up on one side. *Who on earth was Red Rover anyway?*

There were a number of improvements at Jack's, both outside

and in, but dishes piled up in the sink and garbage that needed emptying were signs that an old man was once again living alone. For the first time in weeks I wondered what he was eating and who brought him groceries. We stood uncomfortably in the kitchen. "Where do we start?" he asked.

"I'd like to see where my mother lived," I said, "and I'd like to see where I slept."

As we started upstairs I gingerly stepped around the spot where my mother had lain. Tight hands gripped my chest as I struggled to breathe. The railing had been repaired. Cartons and bundles were gone. "What happened to the stuff you had here?" I asked.

"Gone," was his only reply. The taciturn man I knew as a neighbor would not be any different as a father, I thought as I climbed the stairs behind him. The window seat too had been cleared, but the stain marks of old newsprint remained. I followed Jack's halting gait down the hall. When we reached the rooms at the end, he stepped back and motioned me forward. "It's not locked."

My hand trembled as I turned the knob. I gasped as the door creaked back on its hinges. Memories, so long repressed, came rushing forward, clamoring to be recognized. It was not that I had memories of details of the room, but a rush of familiarity over took me. I knew that I had been there. There was a double bed with its sturdy cast iron frame, still dressed in floral chintz. White lace peaked, like a petticoat from beneath its hem. I had the urge to grab hold of the cross bar at the foot.

I could hear the little girl say, "Look, Mommy. Look at me," as she lifted her feet off the floor and hung by her hands.

Matching drapes still hung, drooping, dusty, and water stained. There was a rocking chair beside the window from which one could see the groves, the shed, and, from this vantage point, the clearing where once there was to be a home. I saw the Mari that Jack talked about after the loss of her son, sitting, staring out that window.

The yellowed wallpaper had once been one of subtle shades of cabbage roses. There were two other pieces of furniture in the room. One was a dresser which had drawers on either side connected in the middle by a low shelf and a tall mirror above. A few of Mari's clothes still hung in the closet. A great lump filled my throat when I recognized them as maternity dresses. Jack stood aside, his hands resting on his cane, and his faraway look told me he was absorbed with his own memories.

I walked through the door into the nursery. Teddy bears in pastel colors grinned and with upraised paws, waved at me from faded wallpaper. The furniture was painted in shades of soft pinks and greens. On one side of the room were a child's wooden bed, and a crib with one slatted side that raised and lowered. I picked up the quilt that lay folded neatly at the bottom of the bed. It was bound by a pink ruffle and in each square, lovingly made by someone, was a different toy. I wondered why we hadn't taken it with us. *That was my bed. I slept here.* The thought passed through me like a shock.

On the opposite wall there was a bassinet, beautiful with its yellowing eyelet skirt and satin coverlet. This was mostly a girl's room, I thought. Of course then they wouldn't have known if their child was going to be a boy or a girl. A changing table with a stack of diapers, a small glass jar with safety pins and a metal can of Johnson's Baby Powder waited for the little boy who never got there.

In one corner was a chest filled with toys. I knelt down beside it. There were wooden blocks and pull toys that quacked and played music and rattled. I pulled out a doll that I had long forgotten and wrapped her against my chest. I remember having only my teddy bear with me when we first got to Yaya's and my mother telling me, "Just wait until Christmas. If you're a good girl Santa will bring you some new toys."

I was so caught up in my reverie that when I heard a crash from the next room I jumped to my feet. "What's wrong?" I cried. An agonizing cry pierced my ears and my heart. It was the sound of some one in extreme pain. I rushed to the door.

Jack was on his knees beside the bed, his hands stretched out across the faded spread. "God forgive me," he cried. "God forgive me."

My heart broke at the sight of this man in his wretchedness.

The guilt he harbored for so many years had finally erupted. I remembered the first time I saw him, when I picked trash up from under his trees. His bitterness and anger had been so evident. How ironic to think that I was part of that all-consuming self-destruction. I could change that. It was not in me to keep punishing a man who had so punished himself. He loved my mother—really loved her—and I now knew that she had loved him too. She never gave her heart to any other man. This man was special, and he was my father.

He startled at my touch as I knelt down beside him, groping for words. Desperately I wished for Ben. He would know what to do—what to say. He would pray, I thought. That's what Ben would do. "God help us," I said as I drew in a deep breath. Jack shuddered and was silent. "If my forgiveness will help ease your pain," I said, "then you have it. I am so sorry for what happened. No amount of punishment you've given yourself has been able to undo what happened. We must have found each other for a reason. Actually," I went on, "I found you."

"On my property," he muttered as he attempted to lift himself off the floor. "Damned old bones," he swore. I laughed and offered him my hand. His red-rimmed eyes questioned mine.

"We have to begin here," I said.

He hobbled over, pulled the stool away from the dresser and sat down, indicating that I should sit in the rocking chair. "Tell me about her," he said.

How strange it all seemed after so many years of longing to know whom my father was, sitting in this room where I had been conceived, in the chair in which he perhaps had rocked me. "I know that she loved you."

"How do you know that?" I saw a flicker of long-forgotten hope in his eyes. "Because she never gave her heart to any other man," I said. He smiled when I told him about the drum major. "I'm sure it was he. We can find out. There were a few other men she went out with in New York, but when they started to become serious she dropped them. There were a couple of nice ones and I even encouraged her. 'He's not for me,' she'd say."

"Do you have any pictures?" he asked.

"I have a couple here. Most are in New York. I'll bring them when I go to pack up my things."

He wanted to know everything. We sat for hours while I told him *our story—Mari's and mine.* There was no heat up here and the room grew cool as the sun shifted positions, leaving the room in shadows. "Let me open a can of soup for us," I said. "We have all the time we need now."

"I don't know what to call you," I said as we sat across the table from each other eating our soup and grilled cheese sandwiches.

"Jack, I think," he said after a pause. "I'm comfortable with 'Jack.'"

"Okay, Jack," I smiled. "Do I have any other relatives? You talked about your sister—my aunt."

"She's dead. She lived over on the East Coast near Miami. She gave up on me a long time ago. She had one son."

"I have a cousin?" I exclaimed. "I have two cousins in Colorado but they are much younger."

"I haven't seen him for twenty years."

"Well, you never know. He could turn up sometime too," I teased.

For the next two weeks I was happier than I ever remember being. I was like a butterfly that had finally struggled free of its cocoon. I had read somewhere that it's the struggle to free itself that makes the butterfly's wings strong. I felt strong. I felt resurrected, with a complete identity.

My physical therapy was helpful but my neck was still stiff, and maybe would always be that way. I tired easily but when I got tired, I rested and then resumed my projects with renewed energy.

"I want to make Christmas special for Maggie and the girls and for Jack," I told Ben a couple of weeks before the holidays. "And for you too," I added. "Will you help me?"

"With pleasure, Jessicacita," he answered, his eyes dancing. When I'd asked earlier what his plans were he said he would probably just drop off gifts for his daughters and stop by to see his mother Christmas day. "I like to celebrate Christmas for what it is, the birth of Christ."

The holidays were a busy time for him. The previous Sunday after church several men put up a beautiful big fir tree in the front of the sanctuary. In the evening the congregation returned to sing Christmas carols and decorate it with ornaments and angels the children had made. The children's pageant was held on Wednesday evening, and since Christmas Eve fell on Sunday, Ben would have the usual morning worship and then a candlelight service that evening.

I had indeed wanted to make the holiday special for Ben, so the tree that beautifully adorned the front of the church was one I'd had shipped from the north. If there was a flaw, I couldn't find it. Massed on either side of the tree in tiers were dozens and dozens of velvety-red poinsettia plants. There was a beautiful wreath for the front door and boughs of pine and cedar with red bows for each of the windows. It was breathtaking. Christine had been my purchasing agent for the ceramic hand-painted crèche complete with wise men, shepherds, angels, sheep, and a smug-looking donkey. It had been moved center stage after the pageant.

"They're beautiful," I exclaimed when I called to thank her. "I wish you could see the church. It's awesome! I'll take pictures. By the way," I asked, "what are you doing for Christmas?"

"Spending it with my mom and my brother and his family." I heard a tone of despondency in her voice.

"Lucky you—with your mom, I mean."

"I know," she said. "Jessica, you sound so different. Have you got religion or something? Are you in love?"

"Or something," I laughed. "I have so much to tell you but you'll have to wait until I come to New York in January. It would take too long over the phone. Then," I said, "we'll just talk until we run out of words."

"I miss you," she said.

"You are a forever friend."

I felt ethereal, unworldly almost as I walked up the sidewalk, Peggy Sue holding one hand and Allie the other. Jack walked behind us. Maggie had come earlier to practice the song she was singing tonight. There were gasps as people entered the sanctuary and beheld the scene before them. Young people stood on either side of the door handing out white candles.

That morning, Ben had spoken of Mary's discovery that she was going to have a child and how an everyday occurrence can change the future of the world when it is part of God's plan. I never considered before that anything about my life could be part of God's plan. Tonight he read the Bethlehem story from the Gospel of Luke and spoke of the awesome responsibility each participant had in bringing Him into the world, from the mother who gave birth, to the angels who announced it to the world, to the cattle that moved over to make a bed for the Savior.

As Maggie's first notes of "O Holy Night" filled the room, they graced the ears of an audience that was collectively holding its breath. Shivers ran up my arms. Peggy Sue and Allie sat on the edges of their seats, their eyes glued to their mother's face. When her notes died away, two teenage boys lifted lighted tapers from the candelabra in front and, passing down the aisle, lit the candle of the first person in each row who in turn, passed the light to the next person. I was surprised to see that it was Scott and his buddy, Eggplant. Tonight they wore black trousers, white shirts and red vests. One hardly noticed the color of their hair, only their serious expressions and the reflections of the candlelight in their eyes as they concentrated on their jobs.

When all the candles were lit and the lights dimmed, someone began singing "Silent Night." Others joined in. People in the back rows were directed to come down the outside aisles toward the altar. Then in front of the crèche, two by two, members of Ben's flock walked out with someone other than the person with whom they'd come. Their faces wreathed in the soft glow of the amber, flickering light, looked radiant and at peace.

The mood at home was entirely different. Maggie and her daughters had been given permission to spend the night with me. They were both excited and intimidated. I think they had never had a Christmas like this, but then, neither had I. My early Christmases in my grandparents' home were typically old-fashioned, European Catholic—Christmas Eve midnight mass, frugal, practical gifts and a roasted leg of lamb. I was the only one who found extraordinary gifts from Santa under the tree, which I ultimately realized came from Mari's hard-earned wages. After we moved to New York, it was just the two of us who exchanged gifts. Often we were invited to join friends for dinner. Most of our celebratory mood came from browsing the highly decorated Fifth Avenue stores when we weren't busy in our own shop. Malcolm's idea of Christmas was to shower me with expensive gifts.

Allie squealed and Peggy Sue's eyes lit up when they saw the sparkle of the tree's lights through the front window as we turned into the driveway. I had put on tiny white lights and deep red Christmas balls, but left the rest of the decoration for my new family. Ben joined us, but Jack pleaded weariness and went home. I made mugs of hot chocolate and a bowl of popcorn, and when the lower branches were decorated Ben and Maggie held the girls up on their shoulders to add the upper ones. Allie kept jumping up and down, clapping her hands in excitement while Peggy Sue thoughtfully examined each of the ornaments.

Maggie glowed. She looked so beautiful now that the harshness of abuse was absent from her body. I noticed that her eyes often followed Ben as he moved around the room. It didn't seem impossible, I thought—the two of them together, if she got her life on track. Eleven years in their ages was not that great, and her daughters certainly adored him. Why did I feel a catch in my chest when I thought about it?

After Ben left we put the girls to bed. I made some herbal tea, and put on some Christmas music while we waited for them to fall asleep. They were overjoyed to see how big Soot had become and were thrilled that he was allowed to sleep in their room.

"What was Christmas like when you were growing up?" I asked Maggie as we sipped our tea and waited for the giggles and high-pitched voices to quiet down.

She snorted. "Lavish, opulent, disgusting. I hated them. The round of holiday parties began for my parents the first weekend of December and lasted through New Year's Day. My father felt he had to put in an appearance at every party to which they were invited, and my mother felt she had to have a different dress for each one. God forbid that she should be seen twice in the same outfit. Of course they always had a couple of parties to which they invited a couple hundred people. My father was afraid to leave anybody out who might be important.

"When I was little I was excited about all the glitter and dressed-up people. My brother and I would sneak out of our rooms and watch from the upstairs hall. By the time the last guests had gone my parents would have had too much to drink and would be shouting at each other. As a teenager I found it thoroughly disgusting and wanted no part of it. You see," she said sadly, "I knew what drinking could do to someone.

"There was never anything like I experienced tonight" she continued. "I'm so glad my girls could be part of that. I've got to do better," she said through gritted teeth. "I've got to."

"You will," I replied.

"I've said that before."

"Stick with Pastor Ben. He and his god will help you get through it."

"Is he your god too?" she asked, looking at me carefully.

"Yes, yes, I think so."

I thought about that as Maggie and I quietly placed gifts under the tree. There were not many packages. "I didn't get carried away," I told Ben earlier. "I know that's not what this is about anyway," I added quickly.

"But giving because we want to teaches about expressing love," he said kindly.

I brought out my gifts and the ones Ben had left. Among the packages Maggie placed under the tree, there were four oddly wrapped gifts with yards of scotch tape holding the wrappings together. After she went to bed I hauled out a big box I'd hidden in my closet and scooted it behind the tree. It was after midnight when I crawled into bed. The Christ Child has been born, I thought as I slipped into sleep.

Tiny whispers and pattering feet brought me to consciousness much sooner than I wanted. The clock read six-thirty.

"Hey, girls," I said, as I tied the sash of my robe and walked into the living room. "How 'bout some breakfast?" They were sitting, cross-legged, just looking at the bounty under the tree.

"Oh, Jessica!" Allie shouted as she jumped up and grabbed me in a tackle around my knees that downed me on the twenty-yard line, which in this case, was the area rug. "He came! Santa came, just like you said he would. He brought us presents."

I felt a twinge shoot up my shoulder, through my neck and into my cranium, reminding me that I was blessed to be here. I motioned Peggy Sue over and cradled her in my other arm. "Why don't you help me make pancakes," I said, "then we'll wake Mommy and have breakfast before Pastor Ben and Jack get here?"

Peggy Sue didn't move. "Jessica," she said quietly, "could we call him Grandpa Jack?"

"I'm sure he'd like that very much," I whispered as tears stung my eyes.

After breakfast the girls peered eagerly out the window waiting for the sight of Ben's truck. Their joy overflowed when we finally settled in a circle around the tree. Ginger, who could not wait for her gift, dived under the tree, pawing boxes out of her way until she found, or rather smelled, what she was looking for. She ripped through the paper with her teeth and carrying a big rawhide bone over to the corner settled down to enjoy her Christmas.

Allie, not to be out done grabbed the four packages she recognized. "Help me read the names, Peggy Sue," she demanded, more eager to give than to receive. Each of us, including Grandpa Jack got a school picture in a brightly colored ceramic frame. Maggie's photograph was larger and the frame was in the shape of a heart.

I gave the girls clothes, pants, skirts, and tops, in colors I had learned they liked. Their mother gave them new shoes. From Jack they each received a stuffed animal, and Ben chose dolls. Intuitively, he selected for Allie, a soft, cuddly baby that was so real you wanted to hold her. Peggy Sue's doll was much different. She was a Spanish lady in a fiesta costume of vivid colors, one not to be played with but to be admired, which was already happening from the look of awe on Peggy Sue's face.

Tears glistened in Maggie's eyes as she thanked Ben and me for the keyboard we gave her. She was living alone in her mobile home while she waited for the courts of Lee County to decide the fate of her daughters. She had bought a second-hand car, which took her to work, to AA meetings, and to sessions with her drug counselor. The rehab program she was on left her little time to be alone. I for one did not want her to give up her music. She was far too gifted.

My gift from Maggie was a CD of her recordings. "It may become a collector's item," she laughed. She handed Ben an envelope.

"Maggie, this is too much," he exclaimed as he looked at the piece of paper in his hand. It was a gift certificate for a hundred dollars worth of gasoline at the Hess station.

"For all the times you've come to my rescue," she smiled, "and it's not nearly enough."

"What a wonderful idea," I said.

I had made a special trip to Immokalee to buy Ben's gift. It was a hand-made vest of the softest, camel color leather that Dali had helped me choose. The color, I thought, would accent the wooden cross he wore as well as his skin. "Thank you," he mouthed as his eyes held mine. Then he handed me a small, elegantly wrapped box. When I opened it, I drew in my breath at the beauty of a cross on a silver chain. I carefully lifted it from the box. The cross, about an inch and a half long, also was made of silver and was intricately inlaid with irregularly shaped semiprecious stones of turquoise and onyx. I held it out to Ben to fasten around my neck, and felt the warmth of his fingers all the way down to my heart. I had a moment of discomfort when I saw Maggie turn away.

Whether by accident or design, Jack and I exchanged our gifts last. I had enlarged and framed photograph of Mari and me taken in front of the Classy Lady on the day she opened the store. The box Jack handed me was heavy and the musty smell of mold reached my nose before I took off the lid.

"Oh!" I gasped as I clasped my hand to my mouth and tears

filled my eyes. Here were the photographs of my memory. I tried to look at Jack, but his eyes were lowered to the picture he held on to with trembling hands. Maggie sobbed, and I saw a tear make a path down Ben's cheek.

Allie burst into the room wearing her new clothes. "What's wrong? Why is everybody crying?" she asked, eyes wide. It was the relief we needed as we laughed and brushed away our tears.

Christmas dinner was a success, thanks to Della's help. I had wanted to include her and Samuel, but their daughter and her family were visiting for the holidays. By late afternoon I was alone. It was however, the best "alone" I ever felt. I put on some Christmas music, changed into my nightclothes and settled down to revisit my early childhood in the photographs I held in my hands.

CHAPTER TWENTY-TWO

Maggie had to work the day after Christmas. "All hands on board," she'd said. It was a day when customers rushed to department stores to exchange gifts, and to look for after Christmas sales. "I may be late," she added as she went out the door.

Peggy Sue and Allie had the week off from school, and the agency had given permission for them to stay with their mother and me. I looked forward to it. That after-Christmas morning they were content to try on their new clothes. I heard them talking quietly in their room, comparing their dolls, as Louisa and I cleaned up clutter from the day before. We made sandwiches from leftover turkey, and since the day had turned off warm, I took them to a nearby park for a picnic.

Ben had promised to stop by after work so while I set the table, and made the salad to go with the supper Louisa had left for us, the girls leaned over the back of the couch watching out the window for his truck. They adored him. I dreaded when it would be time for them to go back to Wanda's. I was well aware too, of Maggie's feelings for this handsome, caring man.

"When is Mommy coming?" Allie asked as we sat down to supper at six-thirty.

"She said she would probably be late," I reminded her.

After supper I put on a Christmas video for the girls to watch while Ben and I put food away and loaded the dishwasher. I noticed though, that every few minutes Peggy Sue's eyes strayed toward the clock. The hands crept past eight. When Ben joined them in front of the television, they climbed into his lap. There was no sign of Maggie, nor had she called. "Please, dear God," I prayed, "Give Maggie strength. It's her last chance. Please bring her home."

When the movie was over I drew the little girls' bath water and suggested they get ready for bed. Dutifully they climbed down and went into their room. Ben saw my concern and patted the space beside him. Tonight there were not the usual squeals and laughter associated with bath time. A few minutes later the girls appeared in their nightclothes. Allie's cherubic face was contorted in an effort not to cry. Peggy Sue, a picture of concern held a crumpled piece of paper in her hand.

"What's this?" Ben asked when she handed it to him. "It . . . it's a place where she might be," Peggy Sue said. She looked at him expectantly. He had been their savior before. "She . . . she used to go there sometimes."

"I know the place," Ben said as he stood up. "I'll go find her."

I noticed that he said, "find," not "look for." I took his arm and turned him aside. "I want to go with you. I'll call Louisa," I added before he could refuse.

"Oh, Ben, I'm so sorry," I said when we were on Palm Beach Boulevard heading for downtown Fort Myers.

"You have nothing to be sorry for," he replied as he pulled me close beside him.

"She's in love with you. You can see that, can't you?"

He was silent for a moment. When we stopped for a red light he looked at me. "I have never been more than a friend to her. We have to help her understand the difference between gratitude and love. We can help her get through this."

"You are so wise," I told him.

At a downtown street near the river, Ben pulled his truck over to the curb in front of a club called the Lion's Den. "Wait here," he said as he started to get out. "These aren't very nice places."

"No, I said. "I'll go with you. He looked at me. I stared back. "Okay," he smiled

Dozens of people spilled out of open doors of the several clubs along the street. Cigarette, and perhaps other kinds of smoke, created a blue haze, and an acrid smell around them. I felt like I was looking through wavy glass. Loud music blasted into the atmosphere. Ben took my hand as we pushed our way from one crowded place to another. He stopped to shake hands with someone with a shaved head, wearing a nose ring. He gave a "high five" to someone else. Nobody had seen Maggie—not in a long time, we were told.

"Hey, Preacher Man," a voice called as we headed back to the truck. "Who's your woman?"

Ben turned in the direction of the voice. I was able only to identify the speaker when I saw a wide smile of white teeth in a very black face almost hidden by dreadlocks.

"This is Jessica," Ben said. "Jessica, meet Tool." I was not able to see the dark hand in the dark sleeve that reached out and gripped mine. Nor was I about to ask how he got the name "Tool."

"Lucky man," Tool, with the white smile, said. "Are you going to keep her?"

"I hope so," Ben said solemnly.

"We're looking for Maggie Sinclair," Ben said as he herded me toward the car.

"Will you come look for me if I get lost?" Tool called after us.

"God and I are already looking for you, Bro," Ben answered over his shoulder.

The digital clock on the dashboard read ten-fifteen as we headed over the bridge to North Fort Myers, and a place called Wally's. It was the name printed on the paper Peggy Sue had given us. "Maggie's place isn't far from here," Ben said as we pulled into Wally's parking lot. The restaurant, well known for its entertainment, was on a canal where dozens of noisy, laughing people sat at candle lit tables on the water's edge. Nobody here had seen Maggie either.

"That's a good sign," Ben said as we got back into the truck. "We might as well check her trailer while we're close."

As we snaked our way along the narrow road that led to the unit, I recognized the surroundings from the time I'd come to pick up Soot. The truck's headlights illuminated the dark trailer. Her car was not beside it. I breathed a sign of relief.

"There's one more place to look," Ben said, "out on the beach, a place where Maggie used to sing."

As we headed over the bridge to Fort Myers Beach, my throat closed up as I remembered Jack's story of how he searched here for the feisty twirler from Rangeley Colorado. I must have made a sound because Ben squeezed my hand and smiled at me.

We had left Louisa Ben's cell phone number, but we'd not heard from her when we pulled into the parking lot of the Spinnaker. There were only a few cars in the parking lot, and one of them was Maggie's.

Ben ushered me through the doors and toward the bar. "Hey, Rev," the bartender greeted him. "Something to drink?" he asked me after Ben introduced us.

"I'd like a glass of water," I said.

"Coming right up. How 'bout you, Rev?"

"Got any coffee that's not twelve hours old?"

"No, but you can have it anyway." Russ laughed as he shoved a mug of steaming brew in Ben's direction. The coffee smelled every bit as stale as he'd promised.

"Is Maggie here?" Ben asked.

Russ raised his eyebrows and gave a slight nod to his right. "Been here since about five o'clock, drinking coffee and club soda. We gave her a sandwich for supper. Is she okay?"

"She's all right," Ben said as he took my elbow and steered me in the direction Russ indicated. The place was big, not unlike clubs in which the Hurricanes used to play. Groups sat in quiet conversation at several tables near the bar. We passed the raised platform that served as a stage. Tonight it was empty, except for instruments shrouded in black canvas. Piped music came from above us.

When Maggie saw us her eyes grew wide, then she covered her face with her hands. Her shoulders shook with sobs. I slid into the seat beside her and put my hand on her arm. "Your girls are worried about you," I said. "Are you ready to go home?"

She nodded. "I'm so sorry," she whispered. I passed her the handkerchief Ben pulled from his pocket. Maggie wiped her eyes and looked up at Ben with eyes full of apology.

When she started to speak again Ben put his hand over hers. "You made it, Maggie. You were tested and you made it."

I insisted on driving Maggie's car home and that she ride with Ben. "It would be good for you two to talk."

Even though it was well past midnight, the moment our headlights turned into the driveway the little girls shot out the door and into Maggie's arms. My heart was filled with gratitude.

This was the most unusual New Year's Eve I'd ever spent, sitting in my van, with the motor running to keep me warm, minding smudge pots around the periphery of my young citrus trees. In the past few months I had come full circle and again claimed ownership of these sturdy but delicate trees that had recovered from a tropical storm and were now threatened by frost. Temperatures dipped into the upper thirties by midafternoon, and were expected to drop further that night. The mature trees, Jack told me, could tolerate the freezing temperature, but the "babies" would probably not survive. It was a problem, he said, that didn't often occur this far south. We'd spent the afternoon spraying the older trees with a fine mist of water to form a moist coating of droplets on their leaves. After we lit the smudge pots, at my insistence, Jack had finally gone off to bed.

I watched the smudges send out curling black smoke from yellow flame, blown by the wind in the direction of the trees. My radio was turned low as I listened to commentary of New Year's festivities from around the world. There was little to do but light new torches when others burned out and move them if the wind shifted.

Sporadic pops of firecrackers could be heard in the distance, and I saw occasional flashes of color light the sky as fireworks were set off. As frost formed on the windows of my car, I sat counting down the minutes to a year in which this country did not yet know who its president was going to be. Suddenly, I heard a different sound and saw headlights in my rearview mirror. A warm happy feeling rose in my chest as lights were shut off and a door slammed. Moments later the passenger door of my van opened and there was Ben, his breath forming little puffs of white against the inky sky. He slid into the seat beside me holding a thermos of coffee.

"Ben, what are you doing here?" The digital numerals on the dash told us that the new year was only three minutes away.

"I wanted to welcome in the year with you."

"I'm glad," I said quietly. "Thank you."

He poured two mugs of coffee and handed one to me. I took a grateful sip as the fragrant, bitter aroma filled my nostrils. "Thank you. Thank you."

When the announcer on the radio began the countdown of the last seconds of the year 2000 . . . thirty-seven, thirty-six . . . nineteen, eighteen, seventeen . . . Ben set the mugs on the dash and pulled me toward him. "Happy New Year, Jessica," he said and kissed me just as the strains of "Auld Lang Syne" came from the speaker. His lips were full and gentle on my mouth as fireworks went off inside my head. Moments later he pulled away and gave me the most beatific smile I'd ever seen.

I turned off the radio that was now only loud blaring horns and whistles. I punched in the CD button and Maggie's incredible voice filled our space. Ben slid his arm around my shoulder as we sat there in compatible silence, sipping our coffee.

"I don't know how I would have made it through this last year without you," I said against his shoulder.

"I wouldn't have wanted to be anywhere else."

"There's something I want to talk to you about," I said. "I've been thinking about Maggie."

"She's struggling," Ben offered as he poured us more coffee. "She's really struggling. She's determined not to go back to the kind of life she had before, but the job she has now pays so little she really can't support her children."

Suddenly anger welled up in me as I thought of her parents—her affected, politically ambitious father and mother—who'd dismissed their only daughter from their lives. "Doesn't her mother ever wonder about her daughter or her grandchildren?"

"That's what I want to talk to you about. Maggie has too

much talent for it to be wasted. If she got her master's degree she could teach. How long would that take?"

"I don't know," Ben answered thoughtfully. "Maybe she could get some sort of grant or loan and work part time, but it would mean that Peggy Sue and Allie would have to stay in foster care."

I was silent for several seconds. Maggie's tape ended and I switched off the power. "Not if they came to live with me."

I shifted in my seat to look at him. "I have a house big enough for all of us. Do you think Social Services would agree to it? I could find a school nearby. Della or Louisa could be there when Maggie or I couldn't." I drew in a deep breath. "I can make my own decisions now."

"You always could."

"Yes," I said quietly, "but I forgot it for a while."

"You are one remarkable lady," Ben smiled.

"Do you think it will work?"

"We know the One who can make it work if it's meant to be."

"Will you ask Him?"

Ben took my hand. "You ask Him."

I bit my lip, wanting to refuse. I had said, "Oh God and God damn!" enough times in my life, and the past few months I had cried, more than once, "God help me!" But I didn't think I could talk to somebody like God. "I don't know how," I protested.

"What is it you want?" Ben asked. "Tell me what it is you want?"

"I want to be able to help Maggie get well, and to be able to have her children back again. I want to help Maggie toward a future worthy of herself and her talents. I feel so sad seeing her life wasted. I . . . I think I'm in a position to help her. I want to."

Ben tilted my chin so that I looked at him. "Say, 'Amen,'" he said.

"Amen," I whispered.

"There," he said, "You did it. God heard it from your heart. It wasn't so hard, was it?"

"You're sneaky," I laughed. I glanced at the temperature reading on the dash and saw that it was twenty-eight degrees. Then I noticed that two of the smudges had gone dark. We scurried in the headlights to light two others, and then climbed back into the warmth of the car.

"I have to go to New York next week to pack up my things," I said as Ben refilled our coffee mugs. "It hasn't been as difficult as I'd imagined. I'm glad it's over." I wanted to tell him about the money Malcolm gave me, yet I hesitated. I was afraid it would change things between us. *You'll find ways to put it to good use.* I heard Malcolm's words in my ear. Instead, I said, "I can't imagine how difficult it is for people with addictions—for them and their families. Wouldn't it be wonderful if there were a place—a homelike situation—where people could live with their families when they leave rehab, where they have support, and counseling, and instruction on how to live with each other. It's no wonder," I said in frustration, "that they just keep repeating their mistakes, and suffering from them."

Ben faced away from me. I saw the rise and fall of his chest, but there was no sound except for the whirring of the heater fan. "*I* wouldn't be here if I hadn't had a lot of help," he said quietly. He put his cup in the holder then took mine and placed it beside his.

"You are one remarkable lady," he said, turning to me and taking my hands. "Don't you know," he said, his eyes pleading, "that I'm in love with you?"

I've heard the expression "my heart stopped beating" but mine did. It took me a moment to remember to take a breath. I could hear my pulse throbbing in my ears. "Oh Ben," I whispered.

He put a finger across my lips. "Don't say anything," he cautioned. "Don't say anything yet. Remember when you came back from New York last August, and I told you that I wanted to be part of your life, even if it meant only as your friend?"

I nodded.

"After I was given a second chance and discovered how good life could be, I prayed that someday God would give me a companion. The waiting hasn't even been very difficult because I knew that I would know when it happened. Do you think you could love me, Jessica?"

I reached up and stroked his cheek, tracing my finger down

the line of his scar. "You are such a beautiful man. I think I began loving you before I knew you—when I hid behind palmettos and watched a caring man feed stray cats."

"I know this is too soon," he said. "I know I should wait until things are settled, but I want you to be my wife."

I gasped and my hand flew to my chest.

"It's a lot to ask. You're used to so much more. I could never give you the material things that you are used to." He hesitated. "You know my history, and you know my future. I can only offer you my love, devotion, and respect."

"What about Maggie?" I whispered.

"Maggie knows. We talked on the way home the other night. Part of recovery is being able to get through disappointments without reacting. She made it once and that'll make her stronger the next time. She understands that we'll be there for her—together or separately," he added quietly.

"But Ben," I drew in a breath. "I'm forty-eight years old and you are only forty-two. With a younger woman you could have a family, you would be such a wonderful father. At this stage of my life, I don't want children, even if I could have them." I didn't understand why I was arguing against something my pounding heart told me I wanted.

"Oh Jess, Jess, I already know that. Marriage is not only about having children. I *have* children, and I didn't know how to be a father to them. There are enough children already in this world who are desperate for love. I've seen you love these children."

"I could never be the perfect preacher's wife," I said. "My faith is really, really shaky, and you know that I'm headstrong like my— like my father."

He smiled. "I am a patient man. I don't want you to say anything right now. I want you to think about it."

"Yes," I said. "I will think about it. Can you wait until I get back from New York?"

Ben pulled me into the circle of his strong arms. I felt the heat of his large hands and the warmth of his love. He kissed me gently.

"Take your time, Jessicacita," he whispered into my hair. "I will wait."

Just as faint streaks of pink dawn appeared in the east, we saw two dim, bouncing lights coming through the trees as Jack appeared on the four-wheeler.

I jumped out of the van feeling as good as if I'd had a night's sleep. "Happy New Year," I greeted Jack. If he was surprised at Ben's presence, he didn't show it. We lit new smudges.

"It'll warm up after the sun rises," Jack said. "Then we'll be all right until evening." He reached in his pants pocket and lifted a twenty-dollar bill from the roll he carried and handed it to Ben. "Take this girl and buy her a big breakfast, then see that she gets some sleep," he ordered. His gruffness did not mask the affection in his voice.

CHAPTER TWENTY-THREE

"You look wonderful," I exclaimed as I opened the door of the apartment.

"You look wonderful," Christine said in unison as we embraced, then we both stood back and really looked at each other.

When I walked out of the terminal of the Newark Airport the night before into the biting cold, I realized how little I'd thought about New York winters—the slippery sidewalks, the piles of dirty snow, the necessity for coats and boots and hats. I had e-mailed Malcolm the dates I was going to be here. I didn't want any surprises or embarrassments.

Christine rushed into the room bringing with her the feel and smell of winter. The cold made her freckled cheeks look as if she'd used too much blush. Her lips were cool as she touched my face. I took her coat as she slipped off her boots, then we just looked at each other, wondering where to begin. It was Friday afternoon and she'd come straight from work. "Cup of tea or glass of wine?" I asked.

She eyed the several boxes I had already stacked in the entry. "Are we going to work or talk?" she asked.

"Talk," I replied, "just talk. Tomorrow we'll work."

"Then wine, white and cold," Chris said.

"You look wonderful," I said as I carried wine and glasses into the living room. "You've lost weight."

She twirled around. "Thirty-two pounds and counting," she announced, her smile of achievement lighting up her face.

"Who is he?"

Her eyes widened and her mouth fell open. "How did you know?"

"Honey, it shows."

He was, I learned, a book agent she'd met when she was hired to design a jacket cover for one of his clients. He liked her work and recommended her to others.

"When do I meet him?" I asked. Her face fell. He was in Colorado skiing with his son. It was semester break. He was fifty years old, divorced with two children, both in college.

"I have a picture though," Chris announced as she dug into her mammoth shoulder bag and produced a black-and-white photograph of a smiling, bespectacled man, sitting behind a cluttered desk. He was a slender man with an elongated face, but the mass of graying curls that sprang from his head, rivaled Christine's orange ones.

"How serious is it?" I asked.

She shrugged. "I love him. He says he loves me. His kids like me. But," she gave a rueful smile, "he's been hurt by one woman. He's cautious. Meanwhile, it's good. He says I make him laugh."

"You make everybody laugh," I smiled. "You'll win him over."

We drank wine and talked, or at least, I talked. Christine responded in her typical fashion with shrieks and "omygods." She cried when I told her about discovering my past, and her eyes grew wide with horror when I described my accident. At eight o'clock I called down and ordered room service. I won't be doing this anymore, I thought, but not with sadness. It was one of those memories I would simply file away as part of my life with Malcolm.

"You've lived a whole lifetime in a year!" Chris exclaimed. Then sadly, she said, "You won't be coming back to New York to live, will you?"

"No, I don't think so."

"Do you love him?" I shot her a questioning look. "The preacher," she said.

I'd told her about the tall figure under the cloak of dawn who fed stray cats, and about the man who was beside my bed when I woke up after the accident. I told her about the night he pulled into the driveway with two frightened little girls in his car. And yes, I told her about his past. When I got through telling her I knew. Yes, I loved him. Tears ran down my cheeks at the relief of it all. Chris came and sat out the sofa beside me. "You are so lucky," she said.

It didn't take long to pack up my things. They would be shipped, along with things I had in storage that belonged to Mari and me. After the movers hauled out the last of the boxes, I took one last look around the room. It seemed as though I had only been a guest here. I had never been asked if I wanted to redecorate or change anything. Once when I suggested it, Malcolm asked, "What's wrong with it the way it is?"

I took the door keys off my key chain and started to just lay them on the table in the entry. On second thought, I walked into Malcolm's study and slipped them into the very back of one of his desk drawers. I would let him know where they were. At the door I willed away the heaviness in my chest and drew a deep breath. I have places to go and things to do, I told myself as I rang for the elevator.

When I walked into my house Monday afternoon the red light on the answering machine was flashing. The first was from Attorney Thatcher asking me to call him at my earliest convenience. I knew what he wanted. I had to make a decision about the money.

The second message was from Ben telling me that Social Services had given tentative approval concerning Maggie and the girls. They wanted an interview with me, and, they would have to come out and inspect the living arrangement. I wondered how it would be with two little girls in the house. Peggy Sue and Allie had been my total experience with children. I needed to talk to somebody.

I phoned Mr. Thatcher's office and made an appointment for the following day, and then I jumped in my car and drove to Jack's house.

There was no activity in the groves, but a semitrailer was parked at the edge of the driveway. It was time to begin harvesting the honeybells.

"Jack?" I called as I opened the back door.

"In here." His gruff voice came from the dining room.

"What are you doing in here?" I asked, coming into the room. He just shook his head as he sat at the table rolling up a long scroll of paper. "What's that?" I asked as I sat down across from him. He placed the roll of paper on the floor beside him.

"When'd you get back?" he asked, ignoring my question.

"About an hour ago. I saw the trailer. Ready to pick Honeybells?" Jack nodded. "How was it?"

"Not as bad as I thought. It seems like that Jessica was another person." I hesitated. "I came to talk to you. I . . . I need to talk to somebody."

He waited, man of few words that he was. I took a deep breath. "Ben wants to marry me," I said.

"Figured," he said hoarsely.

"How did you know?"

"I ain't—I'm not blind," he corrected himself. "I know love when I see it. What about you?"

I looked around the room caught in a time warp of fifty years ago, sagging floral drapes, heavy furniture and a china cabinet crammed full of dusty dishes and silver, black with tarnish. "I want it too," I answered softly. "I . . . I just don't think I'm good enough to be a preacher's wife."

"You are." Jack's voice was firm and his gaze steady. "Give Ben credit for seeing that."

I couldn't believe it! Here I was doing what I'd dreamed all my life of being able to do—discussing my life with my father—*my father*. "And that's not all," I continued. "I told him about Maggie and Peggy Sue and Allie coming to live with me. I told him about the money Malcolm had given me, and about my vision of creating a place where families could recover and heal together.

Jack's bushy eyebrows rose when I mentioned the amount of money, but he listened without commenting. When I paused he put his elbows on the table and buried his face in his hands. "What's wrong?" Concern crept into my voice as he sat there shaking his head back and forth.

Finally he reached down and picked up the roll of papers he'd put on the floor. Slowly, with arthritic hands he unrolled them, weighting down the corners with books he'd stacked on the corner.

What I saw was an aerial view of his property. I recognized the house and shed, the roads and trees. In the center of the photograph was the empty space where once there was to have been a house. He pointed to the space with his pencil. "I wanted to build you a house there." His voice was coarse with emotion.

I drew in a deep breath. My throat closed and my eyes filled with tears. I didn't know what to say. "But . . . but," I stammered.

"I have the money," he assured me, looking at me with his own moist eyes. "All those acres of groves I sold—I never used any of that money. And," he snorted, "it sure doesn't cost me much to live—that is until you came along." I caught the pull in the corners of his mouth, and I smiled in response.

Then he put that sheet aside which exposed another sheet of paper. It was an architectural drawing of a house—his and Mari's house of course. "I could make any changes you want," he added, almost shyly.

"Oh, Jack," was all I could say as I looked at the drawing of a dream that was almost a half a century old. My tears gave way to sobs as I buried my face in my hands. I heard the chair creak as he got up. A moment later I felt his hand on my shoulder. "I wish Mari were here," I whispered. "She would be so happy."

"I know."

I fished for a tissue in my pocket. The day had grown late. "I wonder what Ben will say about all of this," I said when I could finally talk.

Just then we heard the sound of a truck in the driveway. "There's no time like the present to find out," Jack said.

I wiped my face on the hem of my shirt, ran my hands through my hair, and stood up. We were waiting in the kitchen when Ben came through the door. He was carrying Chinese Take-out and wore a look of concern on his face. My expression must have told him what he wanted to know because he placed the bag on the table and held out his arms to me.

January passed so quickly it seemed like the days were sucked up by some giant vacuum. I still had physical therapy twice a week. My house and my lifestyle were thoroughly investigated as to their suitability for children. I was interviewed—no, grilled, by a caseworker.

Maggie, although hesitant, seemed pleased at my invitation. The girls were ecstatic. With my assurance that her expenses would be taken care of, and with the approval of Family Court, Maggie quit her job and enrolled in the master's program in the music department at the University of South Florida.

Jack asked Ben to be the general contractor for my—our house. He agreed to take time off from his job until the house was finished. "Then I'll go back to just being a carpenter," he said. He had my promise that we would live on what he earned and whatever monthly income I had. Ben, Jack, and I formed a corporation to invest Malcolm's money against the day when my dream could be realized. I had their promise that no one would know about that money, and that it would not be used in our lives.

I had never been happier. Ben and I chose late May for our wedding. We had so many plans. We were suddenly anxious to make the most of what life was offering us.

I convinced Maggie to move in with me when her rent was up in February. So, by the time the girls arrived in March, their room was ready. Maggie and I shopped for furnishings and accessories befitting two special little girls. When we stood back to admire our results great tears formed in the corners of her heavily lashed eyes. They made a serpentine course down her cheeks as she put her arm through mine. "I never had anybody care about me like this," she whispered. Six months of treating her body well was evident in the healthy glow of her skin and the shining luxury of her hair.

The girls thrived on the family environment. It didn't take us long to grow into a routine. In the beginning, depending on our schedules, either Maggie or I took the girls to their new school. Soon, though, they were confidently climbing on the long yellow bus that stopped in front of our driveway each morning. In the afternoons, if I couldn't be home, Louisa was there to greet them and feed them.

They began calling me Aunt Jess. Once in Allie's excitement she called me "Aunt Jessie."

"Allie," Peggy Sue scolded, "She doesn't like to be called Jessie."

"Oops," Allie said, covering her hand with her mouth. Her big blue eyes looked at me with apology. I had forgotten our conversation of almost a year ago, but Peggy Sue obviously had not. She was bright and diligent, and was at her mother's side when she was home. If Maggie studied in her room, her eldest daughter studied there beside her. Allie, on the other hand, was busy with her dolls and her coloring books.

And, in the middle of everything, Jack announced that he'd decided to have his hip replaced. Déjà vu, I thought as I rolled my eyes heavenward.

"I won't be cranky," he assured me as though he'd read my thoughts. "I don't have time for pain."

The following week I drove Jack to the hospital for his surgery. I recruited Della and Elaine to help out when he came home, and Roberto and his crew took over the management of the grove.

Even though there didn't seem to be enough hours in the day for all that had to be done, Ben and I always made some private, quiet time for ourselves. Usually it was in "our house." First, we sat on overturned pails on a newly poured concrete floor, then within the skeletal framework of two by fours, rafters and beams. Finally it was within stuccoed walls. "We cannot hear God speak to us if we don't listen," Ben said.

One evening during the first week of May, Maggie came into the kitchen where I was finalizing supper. Shyly she asked if she could invite a friend to dinner Saturday night.

"Of course," I told her. "We'll invite Jack and Ben as well." We were, after all, her family.

Her colleague, Carlton Webb, turned out to be a composer and a pianist who had recently been accepted as a professor at the university. He was a few years older than she, with long slender fingers, and eyes that rarely left her face.

"Maggie has an incredible voice," he praised during dinner. She blushed beneath his compliments.

Peggy Sue spent the evening silently evaluating this new person in our midst, eyeing him up and down, while Allie spent the evening acting out. She picked a fight with her sister, refused to eat the chicken tacos Louisa had prepared, even though they were her favorite. Finally she crawled into her mother's lap and fell asleep.

I was startled out of sleep at six o'clock the following Monday morning by the ringing of the telephone beside my bed. My heart surged and my pulse quickened. Something's wrong with Jack, I thought as I reached for the phone.

It was Ben. "I have something to show you," he said. He sounded excited. "I'll meet you outside in ten minutes." Although he could now set his own schedule it was his nature to begin the day early. I threw on some clothes, splashed water on my face, ran a brush through my hair, and was waiting for him when he stopped beside my driveway. Before he could get out of the truck, I opened the door and hopped in.

He drove to the corner where I'd first seen him, the place I called the Cat Corner. He pulled to the side of the road and stopped. He came to my side of the truck and helped me out.

Just across the fence from us was a large sign, newly erected by the look of the fresh dirt around the posts. *For Sale*, it read in bold letters. *Twenty Acres. Zoned Commercially.* I threw my hands across my mouth and stared. The cattle that had grazed there for the past year were gone. The little ranch house up the long drive past the closed gates looked dark and lonely.

"Oh Ben," I said as I threw my arms around him. "It's perfect for the family recovery center I've dreamed about." It was a mile from Jack's on one side and a mile from Ben's church on the other. "It's part of God's plan."

CHAPTER TWENTY-FOUR

May 25 dawned bright and clear and less humid, a beautiful gift. Surprisingly, the heat I'd found so oppressive last year, I hardly noticed. I slept well during the few short hours I'd been in bed, and woke feeling refreshed. I put on my shorts, top, and walking shoes. Maggie's door was ajar, the way she left it at night. All I could see above the covers was a mass of rich brown curls. I peeked into the girls' room. Peggy Sue slept neatly but Allie could not be still, even in her sleep. The covers were twisted and her pillow was on the floor, but she slept with a peaceful, untroubled expression.

I let myself out of the house and breathed deeply of the citrus scented air, then set off on my morning walk. Aunt Jean, Christine, and her friend Tyler had arrived Thursday. We'd talked far too long last night before they went off to their hotel rooms.

I paused at the cat corner and thought of the man I'd first seen here, who, in a few hours, would be my husband. A board was tacked across the "For Sale" sign. Bold black letters announced that the property was "Sold." The land, already growing up because there were no longer cattle to crop it, would someday be the site of the place of my dreams—a place where hopeless people could someday find hope through responsibility.

I turned on to Blossom Lane, passed Jack's old house, and my new one. I couldn't see the house—mine and Ben's—Mari's and Jack's, from the road. When I walked back on the other side of the street, on impulse, I turned and walked up the live oak-canopied drive to Huntington House. It stood silent and forlorn. I wondered what would happen to it. I doubted that Malcolm would ever come here again. Surely one of his children would want to keep the house that was their mother's. Before I turned my back on it,

I said a prayer of thanksgiving for what Malcolm had given me, and a petition for his peace within.

After I'd e-mailed Malcolm and told him how I planned to use the money, he telephoned me. He inquired about my health and told me about his work. He didn't ask about "my preacher" or my father. I didn't tell him. "You are one remarkable lady," he said before we hung up. "I wish you well."

On the walk back toward my house, I stopped to salute the Great Dane statue that still sat where I'd first seen it. I stopped to scratch the noses of my horse friends when they trotted to the fence to greet me. This is my community, I thought. This is my place in the world.

The ceremony was set for two o'clock in the afternoon. Maggie and my flower girls left for the church a little after one. I showered and carefully dressed in a creation I designed. My dress was sheer, in an ivory tone-on-tone floral pattern. Loose sleeves ended just below my elbows and, while the skirt was fitted at my hips, it fell away in flowing folds just above my ankles. I slipped the cross with the silver chain Ben had given me over my head. Roberto was driving a car Jack had rented for the occasion. When I saw them turn into the driveway, I retrieved my headpiece from the refrigerator. It was a tiara of fresh orange blossoms that had been delivered by the florist this morning. I picked up the single white rose, with its ivory streamers that was to be my bouquet. It was for Mari.

Jack looked handsome in his dark suit as he waited by the open car door. I swore that he was at least two inches taller with his new hip.

"I don't know if I can do this, girlie, without making a fool of myself," he said, as his eyes began to water.

"Then we'll be fools together," I said, giving him a quick hug.

I hadn't wanted anything elaborate—no limousines, no fancy reception. Oh, the reception would be big enough—more than a hundred people—since Ben's entire congregation was invited. Ella and her staff were providing the meal, trays and trays of her Mexican specialties.

Roberto pulled into the parking space that had been reserved for us. I waved to Christine, Peggy Sue, and Allie who were waiting on the steps of the church. Magnificent music spilled out the door. The organ had never sounded so good as Maggie's talented friend extracted rich tones from the instrument. Christine's summery dress in muted shades of peach was sheer and flowing and looked good on her new slimmer figure. In the sun her hair was halo of fiery of curls.

When the first strains of the wedding march began, Peggy Sue pulled her sister into place. "Pay attention, Allie," she scolded. A cone of sunlight, spilling in through the open door, pointed their way down the aisle. Christine followed.

I took Jack's arm and smiled at him. Then we too stepped into the cone of light. My father walked straight and proud as we slowly made our way to the front of the sanctuary. When I saw Ben I caught my breath and tears blurred my eyes. He was so beautiful. At my request, he did not wear his hair in his customary ponytail. It hung loose and heavy around his shoulders. He wore an ivory satin shirt, and his cross lay on his chest in the open *V* of his shirt. He had on black trousers and stood with his legs slightly apart, his hands clasped in front of him. His eyes met mine.

Scott, who was so proud to be Ben's best man, stood beside him. I saw the tremor of Scott's pant legs and knew that his knees were shaking. He gripped his hands together so tightly that his white knuckles seemed luminous against his beach tan.

Ben and I had carefully planned our ceremony to reflect our feelings and beliefs. The minister was Ben's longtime friend—the prison chaplain who'd helped change his life. He stood just to Ben's right, a stooped man with a weathered face, a shock of steel gray hair and a beatific smile.

When Jack had taken his seat, the congregation sang the hymn, "Love Divine, All Love Excelling." As her gift, Maggie had written a song for us. Her friend Carlton had composed the music. It was called, "I'll Walk with You." Maggie sang it in a clear, unfaltering voice. Christine slipped me a handkerchief to blot the tears that streamed down my cheeks. Ben squeezed my hand.

As part of the ceremony we chose to read passages from the

Song of Solomon, the love poems of the Bible. When the minister handed him the Bible, Ben turned to me and read from the second chapter, *"Come then, my love; my darling, come with me. The winter is over; the rains have stopped; in the countryside the flowers are in bloom. This is the time for singing; the song of doves is heard in the fields. Figs are beginning to ripen; the air is fragrant with blossoming vines. Come then, my love, my darling, come with me."*

The minister then read the first words of the Sixth Song in chapter eight. *"Who is coming from the desert, arm in arm with her lover?"*

I took the Bible from him and seeing the look of love on Ben's face began to read, *"Under the apple tree I woke you, in the place where your were born. Close your heart to every love but mine; hold no one in your arms but me. Love is as powerful as death; passion is as strong as death itself. It bursts into flame and burns like a raging fire. Water cannot put it out; no flood can drown it. But if anyone tried to buy love with his wealth, contempt is all he would get."*

Our vows were sealed with simple gold bands that we placed on each other's fingers. When we turned to the congregation and the minister introduced us as Reverend Ben and Mrs. Jessica Rodriguez, I knew who I was. I no longer wondered what name I would use. *I am Jessica Rodriguez.*

During the afternoon we mingled with our guests and received their congratulations. Other than the congregation, our friends were few. In addition to Christine and Tyler, Aunt Jean, Maggie and her daughters, there were Louisa and Carlos, Della and Samuel, Ella, Dali and Roberto. Ben's daughters came. One of them was now married and pregnant. Shyly they congratulated their father. That sight, of all that was happening this day, made me realize how full my year had been. My goodness! *In two short months I would be a grandmother.*

As the food was cleared away, we said good-bye to the last of the guests. Ella handed us some foil-wrapped packages. "You haven't eaten much today," she said. "Take these for later."

Even though our house was ready and waiting, I wanted to spend this night in Ben's cottage. I wanted our marriage to be consummated in a place that was part of him. Tonight we would be here, and tomorrow, I would walk across the lawn to the church with him as his wife.

We had planned no honeymoon. In the fall we were going to Colorado—to the mountains—when the aspen had turned yellow. Jack was going with us. I wanted both my husband and my father to see where Mari and I grew up. We would visit Mari's grave. In some way my mother and father would be reunited.

Ginger followed us across the lawn, wearing her wedding bandana around her neck, but when Ben opened the door and stood back for me to enter, she lay down on the porch, sensing these moments weren't for her.

Ben took me in his arms and kissed me deeply. "Oh, Jessica," he murmured. I ran my fingers through his thick hair as he pressed himself against me. "I'm through being a patient man."

"Thank goodness," I whispered as I began unfastening the buttons on his satin shirt.